Dear Reader,

I am delighted to partner with publishing imprint dedicated to shining a light on underrepresented literary voices.

I am so excited to share our incredible books with you.

The imprint name is inspired by my own Ashanti heritage and ancestry from the Akan people of West Africa. Drawing on the oral storytelling traditions of this ancient community the colophon of Akan Books depicts Anansi the spider, a master storyteller from African folklore, who revelled in creative resistance and liberation: the perfect character to spin a great story.

With the imprint's identity and ethos firmly rooted in the origins of storytelling, its continued aim will be to remove barriers and make space for storytellers and stories that have been overlooked and yet to be enjoyed by readers at home and around the world.

Wild Moon Rising is a powerful novel about coming of age again post-marriage and post-menopause. The author, Jenny Knight, is a working-class woman who has taught creative writing in prisons and worked with storytellers and actors for the UN and Comic Relief. I found it so refreshing to read Jenny's novel, which not only centres but celebrates women in mid and later life. As women, we are so often told that marriage and motherhood are the peak and the end of our story, but we have so much life left. It's empowering to accept that, and I hope *Wild Moon Rising* will inspire readers to embrace their power.

I'd love to hear from you after you've read our amazing launch list and thank you in advance for all your support.

June Sarpong OBE

AKAN BOOKS

Jenny Knight is a prize-winning writer of short story, fiction and memoir and a contributor to Kit de Waal's celebrated collection *Common People: An Anthology of Working-Class Writers*. Jenny has taught creative writing in prisons, worked with storytellers and actors for the UN and Comic Relief in Somalia and Kenya, chaired and spoken on panels, and held workshops about writing, rejection and resilience. She has a degree in English Lit & Drama and studied Creative Writing at UEA. She has also worked on farms, in pubs, factories, as a roadie, a short-term temp in the 80s music industry in London and renovated a former pigsty.

@jennyaknight

@knightjennyk

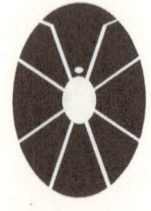

AKAN BOOKS
@akan_books

Wild Moon Rising

Jenny Knight

AKAN BOOKS

This novel is entirely a work of fiction. The names, characters and incidents portrayed in it are the work of the author's imagination. Any resemblance to actual persons, living or dead, events or localities is entirely coincidental.

Akan Books
An imprint of HarperCollins*Publishers* Ltd
1 London Bridge Street
London SE1 9GF

www.harpercollins.co.uk

HarperCollins*Publishers*
Macken House, 39/40 Mayor Street Upper,
Dublin 1, D01 C9W8, Ireland

This edition 2025

1

First published in Great Britain by
Akan Books, an imprint of HarperCollins*Publishers* Ltd 2025

Copyright © Jenny Knight 2025

Jenny Knight asserts the moral right to be identified as the author of this work.
A catalogue record for this book is available from the British Library.

HB ISBN: 9780008650292
TPB ISBN: 9780008650285

This book contains FSC™ certified paper and other controlled sources to ensure responsible forest management.

For more information visit: www.harpercollins.co.uk/green

This book is set in 10.5/15.5 pt. Sabon by Type-it AS, Norway

Printed and Bound in the UK using 100% Renewable Electricity at
CPI Group (UK) Ltd, Croydon, CR0 4YY

All rights reserved. No part of this publication may be reproduced, stored in a retrieval system, or transmitted, in any form or by any means, electronic, mechanical, photocopying, recording or otherwise, without the prior permission of the publishers.

This book is sold subject to the condition that it shall not, by way of trade or otherwise, be lent, re-sold, hired out or otherwise circulated without the publisher's prior consent in any form of binding or cover other than that in which it is published and without a similar condition including this condition being imposed on the subsequent purchaser.

Dedication (to come)

Epigraph (to come)

PROLOGUE

September – Harvest Moon

Something had got right into her today. Perhaps the excitement of signing a contract, making it all official. Or the fear of that. Or perhaps simply as straightforward as a harvest moon, due to sear the earth tonight so intensely it made global news. She never slept well before a full moon. Never had.

Even more of a relief, then, to leave the diesel stifle of city, drive the half-hour through soft waves of field to the isolated pocket of one she'd be living in not long from now. The heat sat lighter out here, as if balanced by the weary tinge of the hedgerows, the trees beginning to blush at autumn, though it pleased her to see gold still prickle a few fields. The artist in her stirred, the same way a child raises a drowsy head to ask: *Are we there yet?*

The last time she lived in Suffolk, she was eighteen – more than old enough now to be that girl's mother, share little but a flash of familial resemblance. Still. At least it made sense of that shock in town, about to apologize to the older woman glaring at her as they narrowly avoided collision.

The jolt of pure horror in understanding she was about to *Sorry!* a mirror.

But whatever. Here she was. *There yet.*

She felt her gut flutter as she got out of the car. Another reminder: this time of leaving all those years ago; how excitement and fear share the same gene pool.

With no keys yet, she could only peer through the dark little windows at the front of the tiny cottage, into rooms that even from outside she could feel echo with emptiness. But everything here was empty. The vast, and unfeasibly clear, sky. The road that was more of a lane. Even the ancient Suffolk house looming and listing to her right seemed vacant; paint peeling at its sills in fat blisters, a few arterial cracks on the pale render over a door devoid, she was surprised to note, of the obligatory chocolate-box roses.

She couldn't help thinking it made that house looked naked somehow. Empty or not, she felt oddly self-conscious, too. She lifted the latch on the dusty wrought-iron gate that led to the back, where at least she could snoop to her heart's content and check out the garden she'd seen only once, and then in the full throes of a late summer storm.

More trees than she remembered; some sort of hedge attempting to selvedge the field behind it, a lot of – what? She didn't do gardens. Plant stuff, then: shrubby stuff, fieldy stuff, garlands of those sticky green balls that draped like cobwebs everywhere and which she remembered picking endlessly off her white ankle socks as a child.

And so, so quiet.

She stood, eyes closed, listening to the gentle shush of

summer-tired leaves. A rich scent drifted past – unmistakeably a rose – and she opened her eyes again, scanning the few leggy blooms. A cabbage of deep red-black, sensual as velvet, caught her eye and she dodged a thistle her height to stick her face into it, only to find what her grandmother would have called 'all mouth and no trousers'. There was another as she straightened; taller, smattered with white-pink petals so thin she thought of the diaphanous dresses of golden age film stars. Smiled at herself for that. She and her easel – as dusted shut as that gate – had spent too long out of one another's company.

What, she wondered with another of those strange, shivering thrills, would come out of her in all this silence, this space, after all these years?

A little disappointing to find most of the rose spindly and peppered to the core with beetles, the whole thing clinging to a tree in such a way that if it, too, were a film star, this one would be wrinkle-sagged and trying to stop mascara clumping in the crinkles of its eyes. Yet it was also this giving out that magnificent, *proper* old-style perfume. There was a honeysuckle, too, she saw now, sprawling on an old wooden pergola near an oil tank further up. A possible wisteria. Blots of red, black, green on a scribble of bramble opposite; a little cluster of small, storybook apple trees. She had a vision of a potential future her: tanned, smiling, head-scarved; brown curls made blonde by sun, clothes paint-splatted by daring creations, perhaps a plaster on a finger, even, where she'd smacked it with a hammer putting up her new (prize-winning) canvas(es). Lighting candles by the juiced apples and homegrown veg. Picking, preserving – *pickling*, even – as she baked, sugared, and harvested her way through the autumn she'd see in her year here, contented, fulfilled, alone. At peace. At last.

Her phone pinged. Her younger son: My scabies is back can u get more cream pls. Her estate agent: A polite reminder to send measurements of bedroom slope heights for buyer, as requested. And finally, Ben: Thought we agreed you to sort twat estate agent?

The moon was already rising in the open blue as she walked back to her car – faint as a faded photograph, but there, nonetheless. She was curious to see how it would look out here. Night would start to come so much sooner now. Days start that little bit sharper. But best not think about winter here, now, in this last shout of summer. She just hoped that when she did finally sleep under tonight's feted moon, she'd be spared the weird dreams of late. Particularly the sex ones.

She didn't know any of the tall spikes of yellow or ground-level blue stars as she walked back towards the house, but she did recognize buddleia – both Rasputin and rabbit of the plant world, as she always thought of it; breeding as it would in the soot of a train station wall, in spite of the lack of light. She'd always admired it for that alone, actually.

The last thing she did before she opened the gate was reach out and touch one heavy bloom, bend to see if its delicate buddleia smell – a little like opening a jar of raw honey – might still be in there.

And it was, for all its cones of pink and purple were as summer-spent now as the dying end of a Bonfire Night sparkler.

January

Wolf Moon – Full

'Held' was the word that came to mind. Someone once held this garden: held it together or held it in their head while someone else did the work of it – whatever. It had been a loved thing, and now it was not.

Claire shivered, pulling her wrap tight against a sharp breath of wind. *Responsibility to maintain garden*, her contract said. She almost laughed, grizzled as it was: grass jazz-scatted with worm casts and molehills, borders a jungle. Like all unloved things it seemed to alternately broaden its shoulders as if for protection, but also to shrivel into shadow – if it could have spoken, she'd have expected a surly face in that teenage way: *What you looking at, huh?*

It made her feel unconscionably sad, and she didn't know why.

She was distracted by a cat crouching at the end of the garden. Gingerish. A bit pitiful. She liked cats – usually. But their old cat died shortly after her younger son left for university and it hadn't seemed right to get another with the situation as it was.

'Go away,' she said. 'I'm sorry, but this is not your home.' She wondered, briefly, who she was talking to.

She went back through the French doors into the dark little kitchen, grabbed a pair of scissors from one of the removal boxes still in a corner, and began to hack at the brambles and branches arcing at the window by the sink as if trying to peer in. She didn't stop until she had a small blister on her thumb and a satisfying pile of dead cluttering her feet.

A pheasant let out a loud *cuk-cuk!* and Claire jumped, hand to chest, half-laughing at herself. It used to be car alarms, but in this silence *any* noise was amplified, even the wind as it shushed at all other sound. But she'd forgotten the way robin and blackbird song could spiral through cold grey like a swirl of colour, a soft counterbalance to the raucous shout of crows.

Wait. Was that a voice?

Was someone talking on the road or – and God forbid – was someone at her front door? Well, friend or stranger, they could fuck immediately off. She didn't want to see anyone or do anything, and she certainly didn't want to have to explain again why not. She swore under her breath. The whole point of starting this new life was to do whatever the fuck she wanted, whenever she wanted. And most of all, to be alone.

'HELP!'

A woman's voice. And not young by the sound of it.

How to ignore the voice of distress? But she didn't want to get involved in anyone else's life, either. The whole point of this was she was Not Available.

'Lord!' said the voice loudly, edged now with irritation. 'Though a fat lot of use *you've* been, I must say. Simply not on. You know perfectly well I will accept anything not involving hospital. And' – this last almost a wail of despair – 'now you'll send me hope, too, no doubt. Oh, drat and damn and – yes – *balls* to you, then!'

But it wasn't just the words. It was the way they were said.

Claire had never heard anyone swear in such an old-fashioned, upper-class voice. It made her snuff out a small, silent laugh.

'Hello?' she said, walking to the six-foot fence panel to her right. 'Are you all right?'

'Hello? Oh, thank heavens! I'm terribly sorry, but I've rather fallen putting my recycling out and it appears I can't get back up. All rather pathetic, I know, but—'

'No, God, no – look, how do I get to you?'

She didn't want to say she thought the old lady – *You'd better call me Tansy* – had broken a hip. The way her left foot stuck out sideways as she lay there, the fact she couldn't move at all, the size and age of her. She was truly tiny – birdlike in the same way some small people seem fairylike, others more Tolkien-like – and her twisted ankle made Claire think of the kindling she'd seen for sale further down the road.

How lucky it wasn't raining. She'd tried to move Tansy – she guessed her at about eighty – but the old woman cried out, face contorted in the way of true pain, and all Claire wanted to do then was calm her, coax out a smile while she located what was needed. A phone – landline fixed to cord in the way only old people liked; at least a handset upstairs – an ambulance, emphasizing the urgency (pain; the fact old ladies dying of hip injuries was practically an occupational hazard), the half-prayed hope A & E was quiet.

All this she did smoothly, calmly, sourcing blankets, pillows, cushions too, in a house she'd never set foot in. *Yes, August 1942. Yes, forty-two. No, not age 42, NINETEEN-forty— If you could, thanks . . .*

The kettle, like the rest of Tansy's kitchen, was almost as antiquated as the house; if not Seventies then a definite throwback. No gas for hobs, either, in this backwater – evidently it would take about a week to boil. She'd been in beamed houses before – impossible to grow up in Suffolk and not – but rarely the sort that counted 'modernization' as half a century ago. She looked at the Post-its stuck to a piggledy blue Formica cupboard – *Lavatory! Pay Bob!* – and wondered what they meant; a half-smile at the word her grandmother used to use.

The old-fashioned strip light blaring between the low beams seemed harsher now and she felt old herself suddenly, though she must be thirty years younger than Tansy. Or maybe only twenty-five. Whatever, she still felt old and tired, and she wanted Ben. To talk to. Be comforted by.

Strange how that happened intermittently, however much freedom was more important. How much comforting had he done, after all? Wasn't it more the other way around?

'My father would say I was being a dreadful attention-seeker,' said Tansy as Claire knelt back beside her on the cold concrete, wrapping blankets so they padded under the tiny woman's thighs; she didn't dare lift her.

She smiled, wondering what Tansy's usual colouring was; shock, she assumed, was stopping her feeling splintering pain, but also painting her as grey as her hair; steely despite the powdery skin. She was remarkably unlined for her age, with prominent cheekbones and dark, shiny button eyes, but it was her voice that fascinated Claire. Once, it would have done little but leave her feeling intimidated: that visceral dread of the chisel-vowelled you only knew if you wanted your regional accent to be equal to theirs. Thankfully, at this age it only felt like listening to old-school BBC footage.

'Which is pretty rich,' Tansy went on, 'when one considers the same man bestowed his *allegedly* beloved daughter with the sort of name one will cringe admitting to when said paramedics arrive. Lord have mercy on us. And them.'

Again, Claire smiled, patient. 'Tansy's a lovely name. Unusual. I think it's pretty. Like the flower – is that what you're named after?'

Tansy snorted. 'Ha! I wish. But I am not, and nor do I think it's pretty. Or that other sappy word: *lovely*.'

Sappy. 'And there's no one you'd like me to call? No relatives, or . . .?'

'Fortunately not. If they're not already dead, they're certainly not in *this* country.' She made a small hmm sound. 'Such are life's blessings. And I can't disturb my cleaner or her family, they're at *work*.'

She subdued her rising irritation. 'Oh. Right.'

A wave of a bony hand. 'And it's not my real name, you see.'

Non sequitur, but at least spoken a little more softly. Perhaps Claire's glance at her watch did it. She was, after all, a complete stranger who also might have a job. Not to mention a history the length of her arm of putting other people's needs before her own.

'No, my name . . .' Tansy closed her eyes – 'Oh, how the gods must be laughing at me today!' – then opened them again. 'My *real* name . . . Oh, must we?'

Despite herself, Claire laughed. 'Not if you don't want to.

I think I gave your initial as T, though. Mrs Tansy Howard? But if you changed it by deed poll?'

'Ah, you see, therein lies the rub. I have not. Not that that's of any particular concern. They'll still have trouble finding me. I haven't been to a doctor since the turn of the century, see. *This* century, I might add, not the last – however much appearances deceive.'

'Wait, you haven't been to a doctor since *2000*?'

'Er. No. Do I sound somewhat sheepish? I rather feel it given the look on your face.'

'Oh, no, I didn't mean— What I mean is, you must have been incredibly lucky or—' Claire was about to say 'have the constitution of an ox', but it seemed inappropriate looking at the tiny bundle of bones huddled under blankets.

'Well, let's just say one prefers not to put one's faith in the institutions. My late husband . . .' But here, again, Tansy stopped, wafting a hand again as if to wave the words away. 'Irrelevant. So late, in fact, one could indeed quip he is *dead*. But you're right. I have, I suppose, been terribly fortunate.'

Lucky didn't seem an appropriate word either, after that. Claire sipped her tea and tried not to grimace. It tasted of the smell of stale Tupperware. 'I'm sorry about your husband. Have you been alone long?'

'Oh, one gets used to it,' said Tansy. 'He died – apologies if you're of the "passed" vocab, but *die* is what he did – a few years ago. I assume you're married? Haven't had a chance to meet you, though I know you moved in some days ago. Your rather enormous removal lorry shook the entire house.'

'I moved here alone,' said Claire. Now *she* was the one who sounded blunt. She added quickly, 'I haven't had a chance to introduce myself, either. My youngest only went back to college recently. And you know how moving is . . .' She could hear her gabble, tucking a blanket around Tansy's hand, clucking at another that wasn't loose and didn't need rearranging. 'I'm sure they won't be much longer. Can I get you anything?'

Tansy looked at her with such sharp, bright eyes Claire had a fleeting image of the snip of scissors. 'What a pair we make,' she said. 'And what a way to meet. Though having said that, my mother would be positively spinning. I should be thanking you rather than sticking my snout in . . . ah, it appears I've forgotten not only my manners but your name?'

'Claire. Claire Bywater.'

'And what a name it is,' said Tansy. 'Makes me think of Debussy's *Clair de Lune*, just about the only thing I liked to play on a piano when forced as a child. One of those grisly teachers that hit one's fingers with a ruler. Thereby ensuring I never went near a piano again as an adult.'

Claire smiled. 'One of my sons did drums at school. He begged us for a kit, but we bought him' – *we*. She still flinched at that – 'an electronic set with headphones. And it still drove me mad. But at least it wasn't a recorder or a violin.'

Tansy laughed for the first time, wincing at whatever it made hurt. 'Children were not to be my lot, as they say. But drum kits and recorders? I can't help thinking that's rather like *choosing* one's instrument of torture.'

'Talking of which,' Claire said. 'Your real name. It can't be that bad?'

Tansy fixed her with a fierce look. 'For an American, perhaps. Or the sort of novel found in airports in the Seventies. Otherwise, must we? *Must* we? I'm in enough pain as it is. They used to say "let it all hang out" when I was your age. Personally, I'm more of a fan of stuffing it all back *in*.'

The unmistakeable squeal of a siren made them both jump; both simultaneously sighing out the relief.

The light was almost completely muted by the time Claire got back; the long stretch of garden barely visible now in a collection of shrouds bringing to mind hospital sheets. She did a small shudder that couldn't place itself between relief at being home again and resentment for being taken out of it in the first place. The shudder had a parent, too, waiting in the wings: the repercussions of nurses assuming she was already part of Tansy's ongoing care package.

She squinted at the garden, distorting it; an old art trick, a visual cue to distract herself from the sense of guilt. Here and there a plant took on its own form – she could just make out the umbrella-shaped leaves of one, the handspan of another, two more that fell somewhere between tree and shrub, and made her think, oddly, of mafia dons. But mostly it looked like a jungle of ghosts.

The cat was still there, too, slinking a little deeper into shadow as it realized she'd seen it. It was probably hungry: it looked thin and rangy, but that could just be age. Or worms. At least the rising moon was lovely, the dank air laden with the sharp scent of winter earth. She inhaled deep; a memory of her country childhood, her sons as boys: *I love you to the moon and back*. How it was never quite far enough for them back then.

Another sigh. Christ. Soon she'd have a sigh to suit every sodding occasion. But – positives! – at least with grown-up kids her own days of dealing with worms were well and truly over.

She stared at the moon again, low and lightly amber; massive. So clear, so full, in fact, she fancied she could see every pock of its craters; feel, even, the cool shadows of its seas, taste the white of their dust. It bleached the black right out of the sky, otherworldly, so even the field beyond the garden rippled lake-like and the frost at her feet glinted on every blade of grass.

Hunter's Moon. The name had struck her at first as twee – the sort of cottage that came with a cutesy 'Gone Fishing' sign at best, or a 'You Be My Honeysuckle and I'll Be Your Honeybee' at nauseating worst. And though it might look cute outside – pink in the colour-of-ham Suffolk way – and though it had a reassuringly fat, eighteenth-century chimney and a couple of drunk windows (albeit twenty-first century plastic), it was a teeny-tiny, and very cold, magnolia box. All she could afford, let alone find in a rental shortage. She was grateful to have been so lucky, however far it felt from the Victorian townhouse she'd spent twenty-five years carving into a family home. She shivered, aware of how cold she'd been and for how long, staring hard at the cat.

'Don't you have a home to go to?'

She got it now, though, that name, unable to see even the faintest leach of streetlights, just as she remembered as a child. A perfect moonlit night for hunting. Seeing.

What must it have been like hundreds of years ago to stare out and up at such a view – how many people had stood, as she did now, wondering about all the loves and losses, the sorrows, happinesses: all those tiny victories and bitter defeats that thread together to colour a life?

January

Wolf Moon – Half Waning

At least Tansy Howard wasn't dead. Or so it seemed – her house had lights on for the first time in a fortnight. Claire exhaled, relieved. She'd seen the lights early, dawn too loud to ignore: breaking as it had with such winter-bruised beauty. She stood at the French doors marvelling at the billow of purple-pink welts splitting the sky; almost biblical. Rightly or wrongly, if that old woman had died in hospital, it would have felt like some kind of omen.

That sky felt like a soothing gift to the cartel of her waking feelings, sifting a little settle into the dreams that constantly ruffled her nights now. Last night Lucian Freud cleaned her stairs and messed up her recycling. Then a tilting Titanic sex dream that started off wriggle-fuzzy and warm but ended with her clinging to railings high above the sea, cold and naked. Then she was sitting on a sofa that was a raft, a boat, a ferry full of people staring at her nightie. Maybe social media had a hand in that, to be fair. Last night 'Naked Swims in Norway' followed her on Instagram – his shots taken only from behind, thankfully, though that didn't stop her laughing out loud at how they still managed to snitch on just how cold that water was.

Who knew, though, what all these strange, new dreams meant. Thoughts. As hard to reckon with at times, to balance, as money, time – or love.

She was caught by a feathery curl of her breath that matched the mist leaking from the wood at the top of the back field; early morning magic she knew wouldn't last long. Before she could think herself out of it, she stepped inside, zipped her coat over her pyjamas, and blew at the cobwebs lacing the snow boots she'd had since the kids were little. A long time since she'd walked fields with no bra, let alone this early: childhood, probably.

Beyond the house, the world had turned silver. Tussocky headland crunched under her boots, the only noise she could hear, not even birds, not yet; the verge so uneven she could feel her footsteps reverberate in the untether of her belly, buttocks, breasts. The jiggle of it all made her smile, think again of the bounce of sex; though the only word that came to mind, watching dawn smoke through trees in a way she hadn't since childhood, was *girl*.

A thousand icy eyes winked from every inch of grass, each prick of desiccated teasel. She was completely alone and lost no longer in thinking but unconsciously mixing, blending, melding one colour into another from her first-ever paintbox. Magenta for that blue, some kind of what? – violet? – to coax that pink away from sickly. A definite raw sienna and yellow ochre for the rusted leaves left from last year that made her think of the mixing hollow under the palette; a tin dent where she'd have battled blacks, greys, whites, to capture the chandeliers frost and cobweb made of cow parsley and hogweed just on the cusp of drip. Impressionist-ish backdrop, yes – with perhaps—

Except what she *should* be doing was work: painting the first proper layer of Ransome McSnooze, the treacherous tittle-tattler dormouse with his sneaky little snout and radar ears: a friend if you needed to know when beaters were walking the fields, or the eggs hadn't been collected; an enemy if you didn't pay for the privilege.

A sudden cacophony of flutter and squawk made her jump, swivel to see the pigeon that caused it; watch as an owl swooped out, low, from the same set of trees, its head a perfect globe between the broad sweep of wingspan. What a painting that would have made.

She watched it fly over the field; a silent ghost melting into the woods beyond.

'No one my age does that shit,' Dan said as he crunched at the vat of Cheerios balanced on his knees, pearls of milk clinging to his beard.

She'd forgotten it was still only breakfast time in California for her older son. At least the weed farm Dan worked on kept normal hours, which made contact a lot easier when he went there after university – the reason he and Ben weren't speaking. She didn't have a problem with the weed thing herself, but if anyone asked, she did as Ben wished and said Danny was travelling in the States. Which he was, of sorts. To and from work. And at weekends.

'Too full of needy twats.'

She adjusted her laptop to see him better. 'Why thanks, Dan.'

'It is, though, Mum.' He waved his spoon at her. 'Social media is designed to be that kind of addictive. All peer pressure and shit – it's seriously as bad as smoking. People only put their fucking shit on there because they're attention-seeking sad bastards. Seriously.'

She watched a black, hatchet-beaked bird slice the twilight, remembering a saying: if it's a rook flying solo, it's a crow. That stupid list. Why had she got sucked in, and worse, told Dan? *It's a new year! Introduce yourself with five things most people who know you don't know.* A Venn of the inane and downright tragic spanning *I can stand on my head and do the splits!* to *I once shared a bag of chips with Bono.* A wormhole of trying not to remember things she knew about herself – and most people didn't – that ended only in wanting to curl up in a cave with the woodlice, the bat droppings and all the other unsettling scurries of the dark. She'd only FaceTimed to see her son's face, spend a few moments warming herself with a little bit of love instead.

'Anyway,' she said now. 'Stop swearing so much. It's not big and it's not funny.'

'I don't. Everyone does. You do. And yeah, it is.'

'And nor is it – what's that word Joe used? – *bussin'*, either.'

'Please don't. And fuck that. Anyone who uses *bussin'* is totally begging to get bitched about.'

She shook her head. 'Well, bitching isn't exactly good practice to get into, either?'

'So is. Use it or lose it, Mother.'

Lists, in fact, full stop. A life lived by them for two and a half (count them) decades. Daily to-do lists. School and work lists. Lists to remember lists. If she put them all together, they'd unroll like a Book of Kells into a manual of working motherhood. She could illustrate it like those old monks did, except instead of tonsured, hessian sorts she'd dangle women in the margins, clinging to a liana of school bags or stitched into robes of name tags, wearing saucepan hats as they nimbly skipped through the countless emotional gargoyles of family. Then, just as freedom hinted at itself like a snatch of sky at a window, those middle-aged women could just fall off the bottom of the page like the world seemed to expect them to.

She frowned. 'What about good karma, then?'

'Still good for the soul.'

'No, it is not.'

'Fucking is. Aw. Mum. Bless. Love you, Ma.'

Kids. You watched their limbs grow long and their minds spread wide, and a part of you wanted nothing more than to punch the air; celebrate this unfurling life, so alive, so vital. But it was hard not to feel the other side of that, too: not to feel each wrinkle in your own face, brain, heart; the ache of scars, of the what-will-never-be now.

She turned her attention back to her brush.

Bernard Bristlé looked up at her with a raised eyebrow. Funny how a head could flit about so easily in your fifties, as butterfly-hard to focus as being at school; back to being told off for doodling. Pronounced Ber-naard Briss-lay (author's insistence), he was chief player in Claire's commission for a revamp of the successful series – and associated merch, if it took off – handled by the small book-packaging company she worked for who did words, artwork, and print-ready copy to supply a far bigger publishing house. Bigger, if not better. It was way below her skillset, but it was guaranteed work.

She liked Bernard, though – she disliked most of her illustrated creatures, any novelty long worn off by now. He had a particular charm that showed itself in the slightly haughty expression and sly eye all good foxes should have. He stood smirking in mustard-coloured breeches, bushy tail bursting out like a firework. She hadn't been able to resist adding the emerald Regency smoking jacket studded with gold buttons, a purple silk cravat, cheeks pure nineteenth-century facial hair. He had one forepaw raised in a caddish manner, as if he'd just made a suave joke or charmed his way into the chicken house only to be outfoxed again by Mother Clucklock (or Fucklock, as Claire called her), or oiled his way out of Farmer Massey's fields and dodged that knife-sharp daughter of his, Fergie.

God, the quiet, though.

Hard to admit she even missed the boys' earbuds, despite the endless repeating herself. The way they'd pull one out like a charging cable, as if gorged on enough voltage from their world to venture briefly into hers. The world where she sat on all the nags, sighs, shrill words – and all the other things her mother did, and she swore she never would. She told her sons she loved them, was proud of them, because these were things her own mother didn't do enough. Talked sex, offered to buy condoms, said she'd happily talk drugs (two comedy-retches and pantomime laughs respectively); said if they wanted to live in a skip eating roadkill she'd even (eventually) support that: *Yeah right, thanks. So you're saying that's what you think I'll become?* She'd also accidentally left her vibrator in the bathroom at Christmas, which was also something her own mother didn't do. But best not dwell on that.

She had never once told them, though, how much she hated

them leaving. How much weight she'd lost because she could not get the taste for cooking for or eating by herself.

How to change the habits of decades?

She shook her head. She hadn't managed to focus all day and now it was almost dark. She caught herself envying the insouciant way Bernard leaned back on a hind paw, all jolly and cheeky, all just *bristling* with life, and picked up a pencil. Anthrax Kit would not draw himself, however fierce his feline ability to face off Bernard; the only animal in Bank (*do not call it Wank*) Farm who could. But she still couldn't settle, wondering whether to focus on Haslet Chubb, the pig, instead. She wanted to get his suit right; strike the balance between porcine-with-standing and the strain of buttons, of greedy pockets big enough for the endless 'troughy' bags of peelings he used as food or bribe – tempted as she was to toss in the odd hidden cadaver just to see if anyone noticed. Christ. And 'wanted' was a strange word. No wonder her friends worried about her working at home alone so much. But she needed this work: money made mantras of its own. As did a lack of pension.

Positives, Claire. Come on!

This vast, dusking sky. The field, trees, all this nature. For all the brown, sodden tapestry of winter that wasn't exactly cheering, she was made here, in Suffolk. She didn't understand why that mattered more than it ever had, just that it did.

She jumped as her phone rang – would she ever get used to this silence? – and saw the familiar icon. Ben.

How did it happen, she asked herself, that she and Ben could still slide into such a familiar pattern.

'You're doing yourself an injustice. You're *good* at what you do, successful. At some point or other you're going to have to deal with this fear of success of yours, Claire.'

'Are you serious? Have you forgotten *Crystal Healing for Hedgehogs*?'

His heavy sigh. Her petulance. Why? She didn't want upset or bad feeling. And she definitely did not want to make him say it again: *You chose this*.

'No, I haven't, and yes, I am. Otherwise you'll end up making it a self-fulfilling prophecy. It's up to you now to make what you want to happen, well, happen. Just do it. Be *confident*.'

'Okay, I get that. I do.' *Don't say it*. 'I feel a bit like that about you and Dan.'

Silence.

She could see the line of Ben's mouth in her mind's eye, thought of the Bucket of Shit theory she coined towards the end of their marriage: how everyone walks through life with a bucket and how, sometimes, people are all too willing to dump a load from theirs into yours. Your job was simply to decide whether to hand it back or carry it. A revelation of the solitude she'd so longed for right there: no one to mess up your mood with theirs, but likewise, no one to blame for your own bad behaviour. Or check it.

She softened; it was hard for him too. 'Ben? You haven't spoken for months now. I'm sure Danny would be—'

His tone was clipped. 'I only really called because I've got some news.'

Typical Ben. How liberating not to feel that if she didn't coax, persuade, or downright pull the difficult conversation out of him, she'd be blamed later for Not Asking the Right Questions, or Not Caring Enough. But still. *News*: such a loaded word at this stage of life.

'Wow. That's – *wow*,' she said a few minutes later, steeling herself to sound positive, talk sensible options for reasonable problems. If only they'd been able to do that at the sunset of their time together. However hard her mind could gallop off with how famously fast men moved on, she knew whatever narrative he wove, how much of Ben simply wanted to run from the end of it himself. All that anger. 'It's brilliant. It really, really is.'

And it *really, really* was: a six-month contract in the States, the chance of moving into consultancy after all his years of management. She was happy for him. She was. So why did she feel somehow – punctured?

'Thanks,' said Ben. 'It means a lot. I wanted to . . .'

A pause, sad, heavy, filling her mind with the high humidity of the autumn morning the house sale was finally agreed; how they'd celebrated with a glass of fizz in the garden, and it was just too summer-hot for so many dying leaves and mouldering apples.

'We did all right, you know, C.'

They knew so many of the matryoshka dolls of one another.

'I suppose what I'm saying is,' he added, 'I wouldn't change a thing. I just wouldn't.'

A punch to the heart. She hadn't expected that.

'And they're happy, aren't they – our boys?'

'Yes,' she said, swallowing the angles of it all. 'They are, Ben. They're happy. And I'm happy for you, too.'

Confidence. It seemed to come so much easier to men than women. She didn't used to think so once: back when to shout

Patriarchy got you dismissed as a feminazi, practically knitting protest banners from all your body hair. There'd been no road map for her generation hitting this age, either. If you couldn't see it, how to be it?

Oh shit. *Shit.*

Absorbent paper. Carefully painted brush strokes. Eyes threatening to bleed water.

Enough. She was done walking around like a woman full of holes, a colander to it all. Enough, too, of twenty-somethings with twenty A-stars who couldn't explain a brief (*Try giving it a sort of Thrones meets Beatrix Potter kind of vibe, yeah?*). Or working for mates' rates and/or for free. She'd try work again tomorrow. When her hand might be able to fill paper without some kind of sketched-out primal scream.

No moon as she leaned against the French doors, soothed by the cheap red she'd promised to save for at least one day; the sky sullen, trees a volley of surprised-sounding creaks and tired-sounding groans in a wind raw as bone. A reminder, at least, of how the past was only ever a shapeshifter dancing to the mind's relentless speaker.

Confidence.

Had she just spent so long fitting her roundness into her life's neatly squared holes that she'd forgotten what curves felt like? Why, perhaps, she hadn't seen Bernard's allegedly 'dicky' eye when Mary-Cate, the design manager, mentioned it? She shook her head. Once upon a time she'd have known instinctively that just questioning whether her work was, well, *working* would have meant it absolutely wasn't. Regardless of anything all the Mary-Cates of this world might say. Perhaps her own vision had skewed so much over the years she couldn't even see herself clearly any more.

She could call Stephen, of course: her brother would happily therapize her free of charge; tried most times they spoke, annoyingly. But she had their mother in her head, for some reason, now. One of her better, non-advice life gems:

'It's like warts, girl,' she'd say. 'You get used to anything eventually.'

She thought of all the fantasies mined over decades – and never more polished than in pandemic – diamonds sparking with the fires of liberation, self-love. A shame Revelling in Nakedness hadn't accounted for a cottage she had to go outside to warm up from, or a bathroom so tiny its shark-toothed door frequently savaged careless hips. That was the trouble with fantasy. Like philosophy, it so often proved one thing in theory and completely another in practice.

She wanted to make this work. She *had* to make it work.

Earlier, hunting old paints, she'd tripped on a box in the garage, surprised to see it disgorge her little blue autograph book from middle school, a total craze back then, and mostly full of either:

If I had a cabbage, I'd split it into two
The leaves I'd give to others, the heart I'd give to you.
or
Roses are red, violets are blue
School stinks like dogshit and so do you.

She'd hated that headmistress: all fuse wire, cat's-arse mouth and bony, slapping hand. But she could still see the swoop and curve of the old woman's beautiful copperplate – red, the only colour pen she used.

Red ink. Yellow paper. Blue book. It never occurred to Claire how primary those colours were. She could see the words now, as if emblazoned, heraldic, right in front of her:

The future lies before you like a sheet of driven snow.
Be careful how you tread it – for every step will show.

January

Wolf Moon – New

The door knocked. *Go away.* It knocked again. Claire swallowed her paracetamol and told it firmly to sod off. It knocked again. She closed her eyes, tightened her dressing-gown, and instructed her face to smile, resisting the urge to cough, side-hustle it with a theatrical sniff. Justify her current state.

'Hai!' A tanned, blonde woman somewhere in her late forties stood on the step, smiling. 'Claire? Sorry to disturb— Oh, have I got you out of bed?'

The South African accent threw her. The smart clothes. The keyboard of teeth. 'No, not at all.' She was still in pyjamas at ten a.m., yes. And a tad stained by hangover, admittedly. But so what? Here was emancipated joy in the guise of jersey cotton after decades of watching a clock like it might detonate if it caught her in her kitchen after eight a.m. Even so, she held the door across her like a shield.

The woman extended a hand: a glint of diamonds, glossy claret nails. 'I'm Hope. Hope Becker. Mrs Howard's niece?'

It took a moment. 'Oh, you mean Tansy? Yes, I'm Claire,

I found her.' She shook the hand, awaiting the thanks, prepping the *Oh, least I could do, blah. Bye, then!*

'And thank God,' said Hope Becker. 'Or her cleaner would have found her like that as a total stiff. Now *that* would have killed her.' She laughed: the clatter of a teaspoon on china.

Claire smiled again. 'Well. The main thing is she's okay. Just lucky I was here, I suppose.' *Bye then!*

One of Hope's eyebrows arched so perfectly it made a circumflex over a pale blue eye. 'Lucky for *her*, sure. The aunt can be quite the handful. I hope she wasn't too much of an ordeal?'

'Not at all. I'm just glad she's all right now.' She closed the door another subtle half-inch. Detached rural cottages, she'd learned, heated up quickly, but cooled even quicker. And that kind of cold knew no muzzle for the biting of bones.

'Oh, very much alive.' Another clatter-laugh. 'And kicking if she could.'

'Well. What are neighbours for if we can't look out for each other, especially somewhere like this?' *So far so bloody Pollyanna. Now read the eyes, love. Read the eyes.*

'Yah, literally the arse end of nowhere, isn't it?'

Claire's whole face, not just her smile, felt rictus now. Evidently not arse-end enough.

'That's why I'm here, actually. I'm leaving for Joburg today.' Hope smiled her dazzling smile. 'And though the aunt is tough, I worry. I keep telling her to sell that house, get proper *professional* care, stop being stubborn about it.' She shrugged. 'You've met her? Hardly Little Red Riding Hood's granny. I'd worry more about the wolf, to be honest.'

Despite herself, Claire laughed. 'I can kind of see that.'

'And it worries me, her in that big old house. A vulnerable

little old lady. It worries me a lot.' She looked earnestly at Claire. 'What I mean is, *people* worry me, Claire.'

No shit. You and me both.

Hope put her hands in a prayer position. 'So, I wondered if I might ask a tiny favour?'

A chill ran through her. *I wondered if . . . You couldn't just . . .*

'As in, perhaps you could just, say, keep an eye out?' Hope fished her phone from her back pocket. 'Let me know if you happen to see her and she says there are things she can't find, or you see people snooping about or doing things to the house? I'd like to know.'

The penny dropped. 'Right.'

Hope wince-shrugged. 'I'm not saying categorically bad stuff *will* happen. I'd just appreciate someone trustworthy looking out for her. But do say if it's too much?'

Claire thought of something Stephen always said: how No is a complete sentence. *Say it, then. Say it.*

She smiled. Easier just to recite her sodding mobile number.

Where did all that – she – go?

Claire looked at the tools of her trade, softly spiky in jam jars and Italian tomato tins on her desk or the floor, punctuation marks to the work folders flanking the walls, and a wave of fatigue rolled over her. She missed her old study, suddenly, fiercely: the absence of magnolia and, more importantly, of a bed – dangerous so near a desk, but outside Joe's bedroom where to put the boxes of books, photos, candles, oil-burners, that once populated her shelves? She particularly, and it was a surprise, this, missed her old, dog-eared paintings, rolled up now in the garage with all the other old-house stuff that didn't fit. They were, if nothing else, viable proof she'd once – yes – been a promising artist who played with media, colour, form. Bold strokes: 'bold strides' as an old tutor said once, adding '*Passion*'.

'I think it's our age,' said Emma on her daily call to check in, reminding Claire she wouldn't always feel 'meh' about everything. 'I didn't feel like this in my forties, I just didn't. And it's not just my body, it's *me*. It's like being a teenager again, as if it wasn't bad enough first time around. Anyway, I've been thinking about that list. Do you want my five?'

Nothing beat a good girlfriend on yet another wet, grey day. 'Please.'

Emma grabbed a cushion, settled, her face expanding and shrinking again on Claire's screen. She wished she could hug her, inhale the woody perfume and freshly washed hair of Emma's signature smell. At least she never got that urge video-calling a son.

'Okay. One, I drink far more than anybody knows, even my husband. In fact, especially my husband. Two, I count crisps and wine as two of my five-a-day – potatoes *and* grapes. Three, I love a bit of porn; classy, mind, no jackhammer-plumbers. Four, I've had Botox. Five, and I lie about it. Oh, six – I hate my husband's sister and call her Little Miss Conniving Cow behind his back. But his brother told me he hates her too, so – seven – I sometimes think I married the wrong brother. Bet no one put that. Feel better yet?'

Claire laughed again and said she did, though despite the blackout blinds, ear plugs, the walking to the toilet with one eye closed and half a hand over the other, 'I'm still wide awake at stupid o'clock. The only thing left to me now is an actual coffin.'

'Listen, I saw something today,' said Emma, 'that really made me think. And I don't know who else I could say this to so it doesn't sound quite so, well, *shit*. You know I've worked for everything I've got – no one's given me a thing, ever. But here I am, lovely new house, both sets of kids finally gone, little bit of cash to spare at last. I should be happy. Except I went to my nearest supermarket today and had a sort of epiphany in the car park.'

'Was it a Waitrose?'

'It's Surrey,' said Emma. 'Of course it was a bloody Waitrose.'

Claire smiled at the standing joke that bonded them back in the Baby Aga-saga world of twenty years ago: a shared working-class background, a consequent view of John Lewis as a middle-class answer to the Damascene Road.

'Anyway, so this brand-new Jag pulls up,' Emma went on, 'which was weird because I thought no one was driving until I saw this weeny old dear puttering about, checking her teeth, patting the fake blonde, all that, before she swung her legs out like you just know "a hip" is involved– don't laugh!'

'I'm not,' said Claire. 'It's hysteria. That's our future. Well, not the Jag, obviously.'

'That's it. That's the whole *point*. Don't get me wrong, I'm grateful to be here – God, after all the people we've lost by now? – and I'm happy for her if a big new Jag makes her happy. The way she looked at it, locked it, so sort of . . . lovingly. But that way, that *way* you could almost feel her thinking *I wish I'd had this when I was younger*. And I just sat there thinking how much I don't want to get old. Or not even old. Just not, you know – bobbing along until the fat lady sings?'

It caught Claire off guard. Emma was a radiographer: she did the practical, the pragmatic . . . rarely, or never, this. She'd never forget Emma once taping a carrier bag to her face to do the school run with norovirus. 'Em, I think you've got a while to wait for that?'

'But that's just it, Claire, I want the things I want *now*. Not stuff – *life*. Not just working, worrying about grown-up kids, coming home to cook, slump, wait for him to watch some crap TV, go to bed. I want to feel love again, to want the man I supposedly love, even if it's ridiculous at my age; party, play loud music, drive with the roof down. Enjoy it all while I'm still young enough.' A pause tight as the moment before elastic snaps. 'Because God knows, at this age it'll be gone in a fucking flash.'

A flash.

The word made Claire think of Hope Becker's hand. She should go and see Tansy; check she had what she needed, at least. The January nights were sinking their sharpest teeth in now and there were almost no other houses beyond Tansy's for half a mile. Wickham Parva boasted all the usual ingredients: a mansion gentry would once have wafted about in when not embroidering or shooting, a few big farmhouses, the sort of obligatory hall she remembered from childhood that morphed from old people's home to happy-hippy commune to rich people's playground. But otherwise the village offered little, the pubs, shops, post offices that characterized the Suffolk she once knew either closed now or dotted among the endless Lego-brick builds and rampant housing estates.

There was, of course, the minor fact she didn't really want to. Her lips twisted at the pressure of that, the words of two other close friends, Jules, Asha, which she also hadn't welcomed: *We all need some fun, at the end of the day – you need to join things, do things, come out with us, get out there again. You can't just rot in that house.* 'Please don't say at the end of the day,' she'd told them. She loved them both, and dearly, but: 'I'm worried you're going to start talking journeys, and I don't want a journey. I want a lie-down in a darkened room for a long, long time. That's what I want.'

But she didn't have time to make a compost of herself, in any case: Ransome McSnooze was waiting. She'd been enjoying concentrating on the curve of him sleeping, curled like a serif quote mark, eyes sealed against the world, the peaceful face of needing nothing until it was warm again. She added a few almost imperceptible black streaks to his fur to reach the right shade of ginger, stippled the base and tip of his tail; a thin layer of yellow-creamed white for the fur just above one leg. After so many grey days, she felt a need, like her slowly evolving dormouse, to turn her face from shadows.

So many shoulds. A life lived by them for so long that, empty of them, like lists, it felt like she had all the jigsaw pieces but no picture on the box.

She looked again at Tansy's house: hard not to, given the sea of tiles peaking steeply into a sizeable portion of sky. It must be three times the size of her rental. And it did seem to change the way you looked at a house when you could picture its rooms; perhaps in the same way you looked at old lovers.

But. *We don't go there, remember?*

'I come bearing no flowers, I'm afraid,' she said, looking into Tansy's little hall, so dark she could only just make out an old-fashioned wooden barometer on a wall, no more than a handful of carpeted steps leading up the steep staircase. 'I just wanted to see how you were; if you needed anything from the shops. I didn't know if you'd have anyone to—'

'Look after me?' said Tansy, leaning hard on a hospital walking frame. It had taken her a while to reach the door and Claire felt bad, apologizing, which Tansy dismissed with a fleeting free hand. 'God forbid! If there's one thing practically guaranteed to kill me, it'd be that. Or *hope*.' She shuddered so ostentatiously Claire couldn't help but smile, albeit the old woman was clearly a bit mad.

'But how kind of you,' Tansy added, though she looked surprised, and her hair seemed more unkempt. Perhaps because Claire had only ever seen her lying down, perhaps just that voice again; its prismed angles and valleys so reminiscent of old-fashioned crystal glasses. Perhaps she'd expected the same sort of hairstyle as the Queen.

'Except I have just made you get up and come to the door? I just thought—'

'Oh, you thought right,' Tansy interrupted again. 'It seems one is expected to run a marathon these days as soon as they've turned the last screw. Just as I was hoping for a few weeks' dossing.'

'Are you in pain?'

Tansy smiled thinly. 'Not too much. Particularly since you are not hope and you haven't bought me flowers.'

O-kaay. 'Oh! Sorry, I didn't think – I haven't been to the shops yet.'

'No, I don't mean it like that. What I mean is *far* worse. More a case of my ingratitude and being so wretchedly particular about flowers.'

'Oh.' She didn't know what to say to that. Didn't everyone like getting flowers?

'I don't particularly like them in a house, you see,' said Tansy. 'And I always want to check how they're tied and with which hand they're offered. And to have a bud or two in there.' She held up a palm as if to stop herself prattling. 'Long story.'

'Ah,' said Claire. *You be as barking as you want. I'm not here to make friends.* 'Well, each to their own.'

'Oh, it isn't that I dislike a bloom, not at all. Give me something big and red and one can be relatively happy. Unless it's a poinsettia, in which case I will unwittingly murder it – as is my wont also, and sadly, with orchids. But give me a carnation, anything frilly, fluffy, spindly or one of those ghastly alstromeria abominations and I will *wittingly* kill it. But I suppose you'd better come in – Claire, isn't it? Tea? Though you'll have to make it yourself, the nurses aren't due for another couple of hours.'

Shit. She smiled. 'Impressive. I can't seem to stop calling people what I think they look like these days.' *And I've become a person who also says 'these days'?* 'But no, thank you. I really should get back.'

'Debussy, see?' Tansy hobbled back from the door. 'Well, don't just stand there, Clair de Lune, I haven't got all day.'

She'd only glimpsed Tansy's living room through its open door – dark enough to leave no impression of the astonishing space it was. If Tansy sounded old-school British, here sat the Miss Marple set to complete the picture. Low-ceilinged, beamed like a ribcage spanning from a central oak so thick it looked as if whoever felled it barely bothered with more than squaring off the trunk: all Claire wanted to do was touch it.

The room held little else; a small chintz sofa with two sagged and scruffed matching armchairs, the ubiquitous sage carpet of that generation (her parents had the same for decades), floral curtains with prolapsing hems, edges furry with spent cotton, a small bookcase and the old-person, indefinable not-wood nest of tables. Otherwise, nothing but the ancient beams that stood sentry or wavered around the walls, and a vast inglenook housing an old, brassy electric fire so unashamed in its plastic coal pretence the dark scratches on the huge fireplace bressummer scowled at the travesty.

Tansy waved a hand around. 'Do forgive the dust. It isn't, as one's nurses evidently think, simply the product of age. It's a cleaner off on a jolly and the welcome fact small windows grant fewer sightings of the carnage caused by one's hatred of all things domestic.'

It wasn't until Claire stepped inside that she'd realized just how tiny Tansy was, even standing: how she had to look down at her, despite being little more than what her grandmother called 'five foot and a fag-end' herself. The windows seemed to reflect that, too, the low ceiling; so surreal she felt a little like Alice in Wonderland.

'What an amazing room!'

'Ah, well, the house was once a forge, it seems.' A *hmph*. 'Ironic when one considers how dratted cold it can be. It would have been part of Wickham Hall's estate in its former life, as indeed would yours. So, Claire, how are you finding it?'

She felt herself tense. A forge. It would be a sodding *forge*. And she did not want to get into talking about her life. Hard enough with people she knew well and trusted – age so good at teaching you that was not always the same thing. What to say?

Concrete floors under a thin skin of lino? Pipes that sobbed to the bathroom floor about how old they were? She settled for: 'Oh, I'm lucky to have it. Do you know it at all?'

Those bright, squirrelly eyes. 'Not really. Jim, who used to live there, was a fine man. We used to swap gardening tips and I remember Ken – my husband – helped him out a few times with cars and suchlike, but when his wife died Jim rather took to keeping to himself. And enviably so. But – how are you settling in?'

A new cooker, the landlord had said, as slickly pleased with himself as his oiled hair. A cooker so mercurial Claire has found herself asking it nicely, or shouting, depending on her mood: six attempts to get it to turn on at all last night. *A lovely fire, too*! A wood burner so decrepit it felt like she was resuscitating it every time she lit it, only to find by morning it had forgotten who it was again.

'I've had some lovely walks in all this morning frost,' she said instead. Tansy was both old and *terribly* British: the weather should do it. 'Beautiful. I even saw an owl a couple of days ago – in daylight.'

'Ah, good. That being a somewhat better omen than at night,' said Tansy. 'Positive transformation as opposed to death. Well, positive for *some*, I suppose. So, tell me, have you made yourself at home?'

Quite piercing those eyes, the more you looked at them. And nowhere near as mad as their owner sounded. 'Well, it's still all a bit, new, compared to—' Claire almost said *home*. Again. ' . . . living somewhere for a long time. You know.'

'One assumes to raise the family. I heard your boys kick about outside at New Year.'

'Oh, God, that's my youngest and a mate. I'm so sorry. The swearing. Sorry.'

Tansy laughed – surprisingly loud. 'Not at all. Rather refreshing, frankly. Allegedly, one should always swear copiously when planting basil or parsley. It helps them grow. But I mean, rather, not just the fruity language, but that *joy* of youth. Isn't it marvellous? I gather your sons are not with you all the time. Do you work?'

She dodged the question. 'Ah, the boys are mostly grown up and gone now.' Like catching a finger cut by a serrated knife. She swallowed, smiled, affected bright. *Think of the poor old dear swearing at her herbs.* 'So hopefully they won't bother you.'

'As I said, not at all. One does wonder, though, never having had children, if it's a curse or a blessing when they leave one behind.'

Claire's smile the image of stretched cling film in her head. 'Oh, probably a bit of both, I think. Love them and all that, but I couldn't eat a whole one, ha *ha*.' The laugh too loud, bouncing off the windowpanes, the dimpled copper triangle of world's ugliest fake fire. Why had she reverted to that sad, tired old expression? 'And I wouldn't be as grey.'

'Well,' said Tansy. 'At least when you're my age you'll have a sensible excuse for looking like either Beethoven or Einstein – rather too long since one last saw shears. So, Claire, do you think you might be . . . settle here?'

She had chosen another word and immediately Claire wanted to know – be what? 'Well, it's all still new and a bit beige as yet, so . . . Not like this room, at all. It's incredible.'

'That's very kind. But it is rather past its best, I fear.'

'I don't think houses like this ever get past their best, do they?'

'Ha! I might agree if I didn't think *everything* gets past its best after a while,' said Tansy. 'And thinking about it, are you a gardener at all? It did once have the most beautiful garden, Hunter's Moon – prodigious gardener, poor old Jim. Such a shame they've let it go. I see it from my bedroom windows – and don't look like that, I shuffle up the stairs on my rear when the nurses aren't about. Must rankle, given you have an even better view?'

'Oh, I'm no gardener,' Claire said too fast. She tried to look relaxed, shrugged. 'A few pots in summer, that kind of thing. I used to help my mum and granny as a kid. Granny gave me her old flower press, actually . . .' Why that age-old need to overexplain herself? *Shut up, Claire!* ' . . . and I'd use it for my collage books. But gardening doesn't really, you know, interest me much.'

How often a mouth opens to give information the brain didn't know it had, either in truth or lie. Both her grandmothers kept beautiful gardens that inspired in her a nascent love of the sensual, of shape, shadow, form, texture. How she would lie, body in sun, head in dappled shade, nose full of the drifts of jasmine, rose, honeysuckle, wisteria, watching the sun flicker red-black on her eyelids as she rolled lavender between her fingers. She'd attempted a garden when Dan was a baby. But baby. Then another. What wasn't already dead from neglect a victim to the force of nature that was small boys. They'd paid another mother to keep it tidy in the end, which Claire had secret guilt about. She didn't come from people who paid staff. Unlike Ben's family, they *were* the paid staff.

'I'm pretty sure I'd be the human equivalent of Roundup now,' she said. 'I'm not exactly good with houseplants, either.'

Tansy looked at her for a second, as if lost in thought. Or about to have a stroke. She looked waxy, resiny, in the way people did when they'd been in hospital or were seriously ill.

I am not available, Claire thought. *This is my mantra. Please do not die on my watch.*

'Claire. Could I ask you to look behind you at the bookshelf? Bottom shelf, yes, large folder. Red. Could you pass it to me? Thank you.'

She forced another smile that transitioned into a closed-eye snatch of irritation as soon as Tansy's head bent. She didn't want to talk gardens – the sacred text of the retired. And nor, come to think of it, did she want Tansy Howard looking out of windows and judging hers.

'Some notes here which may be of use. You really must sort it; the wretched thing is an absolute eyesore. And the drawings are all mine,' she added as Claire handed the folder to her; an old, poppy-red ring binder every bit as utilitarian as the reams of notes it was heavily, if neatly, stuffed with. 'Contrary to popular thinking, we reliquiae did have our uses once upon a time.'

How could she say no now? Was nowhere safe?

She ignored her garden as she walked back with the tatty folder; stubbornly refusing a glance at either. She didn't want some bonkers old bat encouraging her to shout at herbs. Nor would she be bullied (*eyesore!*) into what essentially boiled down to working for someone else's profit. She heard herself sigh 'Home,' as she always had unlocking a door. But.

Maybe it was just being in another house for the first time

in weeks. How, if she closed her eyes, she could still see every board, tile, cove, curve of her old home; known like she knew the body of the man she'd shared it with. Sometimes, lying in dark, she felt safe in a way she didn't in daylight: under the black void of Suffolk sky, she couldn't tell where she was. *Home* was still what she expected to see in the liminal slipway between sleep and waking; the cottage still so unfamiliar she wore a permanent rash of bruises.

A flash of standing in the garden back in September seeing herself in paint-splatted smocks, smiling at solitude, pickling cucumbers. Like an idiot.

She reached for her basket of cleaning stuff. *The devil makes work for idle hands*: her maternal family motto. Old Nick at her shoulder with his smirk. How insane the world didn't want to employ the Gen X empty nester: the women she knew ran rings around men when it came to juggling, delegating, organizing, simultaneously making it all look so *effortlessly* good. She stared at the basket. She could let loose the inner slut that had sat half a lifetime in the shadows of oughts and shoulds, and not a soul would see. Worth celebrating in itself.

She poured a glass of wine. Satisfying. Liberating, even, as she toasted the basket, herself: *Fuck you, cheers me.* She caught herself saying this last to the cat, back on her path again. Was that where it started – the knotty hair and the herb-swearing? Worse still, if the cat wasn't there, she'd likely have said it to the dishwasher she apologized to last night for stopping mid-wash.

She picked up her phone and turned her speaker on, just for the noise.

A small *hmm* at the song almost a soundtrack to her childhood.

I don't want love—

Four letters and just the one solitary syllable. And yet. Such a complicated word. *Do you love him? / Are you in love with him?* Forty years she'd been asked this. And yet the older she got, the more she saw to say you love someone could mean not just the thousand things she'd thought at half her age, but an infinite number. It was like a one-size top. So much depended on the shape of where you started from.

—what good can love do for me?

She snapped the speaker off.

How do you quantify the love for the one you lost your virginity to – a first lover, if not a first true love? And then the actual first, the purest – and perhaps truest as it plucked you from the rising bloom young women are so blind to; broke you, forced you to make a *kintsugi* of your heart. And how to talk of the love you feared for the one who damaged you, or the one you *should* have loved because he was safe and good and would take care of you – and oh, because, because, *because*? Or the illicit one that saw you swear at times *some* sort of love was there, at others curse the corkscrew of your legs that opened up a part of your heart, if not his. Or the one a hundred-seeming summers ago you shifted into wrinkled fruit and sagging branches with; a legacy, if life was lucky, to outlive you both.

She rested her head against the door glass, hoping for the comfort blanket of stars and silvered clouds, disappointed to see the sky mostly black, only the faintest white halo to show where the moon was. She remembered something her grandmother said once about widowhood: *You don't miss the water till the well runs dry.*

It wasn't supposed to be like this. Bare walls she didn't know how to fill. Books and a TV she stared at but couldn't see, her mind the red shoes of the fairy tale, dancing her to dizzied exhaustion. Where was the music so loud it would bounce her to back-back, back before Ben, to the last time she'd lived alone?

Love. Alternately baggy, shrunken, and not always comfortable – who even was she before all that began?

And who was she meant to be now?

February

Snow Moon – Full

Mother of Mary. Where to start? Where to begin unravelling and untangling all of that?

Claire rubbed her lower back. 'Growing,' Stephen said repeatedly when they spoke last night. 'Learning.' But growing how – and learning what, exactly?

She'd slept badly again. A dream of roiling seas, white horses as if ankle-nipped and crazed from chase by wolves: she could almost see terror whip their knees, spines curve, stagger, tumble; waves flaying spume that drenched her. He took her then, the worst of all her lovers. She could still see the filaments of black hair curl at his collar, as if trying to escape him as much as her. Not because she didn't want him, but because she wanted him so much.

She'd sat astride him, levelling knees to ride him, slow at first, held by the glue of their kisses, eye deep into eye, until he shifted, clutched, sank his face to her neck, breast; unable, as she was, to concentrate to kiss, only to fuck, rising, falling, higher, deeper, the swirl of it psychedelic at her eyelids, the feel of his tongue, lips, grazing her nipple. The colour changed then: sea blue-green to paint-water purple, and she was standing on a groyne: a thin, slithery shelf of sodden wood gripped by barnacles and the sometime decoration of bladdery seaweed. She'd worried it wouldn't take her weight, that she'd slip, be subsumed by the simmering fury until all that was left of her was floating scraps; woke in darkness, breathless at the churn of it all. When sleep came again, she dreamed of stillness, though still of water. A lake that grew more bog the closer she got; damp, brackish, the liquid of overgrown ditches. Nothing lived but thick green slime pocked by gas, as if life haunted its edges only in putrid exhalations of decay.

No wonder she felt a need to be outside, moving. The big Suffolk skies always made her feel better. She grew up some miles from here, under skies like this that spread over fields like ink on watercolour paper, changing colour, texture, depending on mood. A constant reminder of the smallness of everything under them.

Hands on hips in that way of women for time immemorial. Staring. Again.

The pile of scrappy stems she'd left on the lawn was slowly being scattered by a wind drifting in with an open-freezer smell of snow. Claire hoped not: gone were the happy days of admiring ice from a radiator so hot it all but dried the liquid of her eyes. She corralled the scraps to an extant pile backing the field that (ugh!) old man probably pissed on. She was convinced it was full of rats and snakes; would burn it if she wasn't so put off by hearing the screams of the immolated, no matter how verminous. A woodlouse scuttled on a log in the wood burner last night and she couldn't stop herself burning a finger to save it. She returned to another. Another. And then the smoke alarm shrieked, and she'd had to open every window and waft the front door to silence it; the only way then to warm her own will to live via the medium of half a bottle of red. Just as well she couldn't afford to drink it all.

She shivered, needing food, comfort. The former niggle in her back felt lumbar-punctured now and Jules and Asha had texted asking if she was all right; she should answer. She had the sensation, too, and again, of someone watching her. Not the cat – who'd stopped staring in favour of an arse-bath – an actual person. She'd only just realised it wasn't just cats or white goods she talked to; apparently, she was pretty good at giving plants some, too. What did it say when you didn't want to see anybody but found yourself sweating at a clump of unwieldy and deceptively prickly grass as you told it to *piss the fuck right off*?

A bacon sandwich. That was what she needed. And not cooked cleanly, either. The dirtier the better: fried so it wore in bronzed grazes the fat-rust from the bottom of the pan. Filthy enough for the sheer sight of it to make a middle-aged artery cry.

Disheartening to see her ripped-out dead barely register: the garden still looming at her like Miss Havisham's table; all dusty seedheads and clotted strings of stalk. Equally disheartening, too, to look at her work with no idea of what to do. So much for those plans to dig out her easel. And why the Havisham thought, as if ex-dreams weren't bad enough?

The only green appeared to be ivy; skeins of it threading through the brownish greige, belligerent in defiant health. Claire wrenched at it, surprised by the force needed, the satisfying give. She could smell the tang of earth raw with winter and spiked with the prong of baby nettles, splats of other weeds she didn't know, as rain began to clap a soft applause on the soil. She couldn't be inside. She couldn't be outside. And everyone she could have faced was either too far away or at work.

She sighed. She was not a woodlouse. No one was coming to save her.

So. Where was there to go?

'Just get rid of the rubbish first and don't think about anything else. Man was not born to take more than one step at a time. Especially man, actually.' Tansy wrinkled her nose. 'Poor things. Women are so much better at doing more than one thing at one time, don't you find?'

Claire laughed. She'd felt odd ringing the bell, though it felt somehow rude to just post her mobile number through the letterbox. And Tansy seemed pleased to see her, which felt gratifying.

'Oh, I'm trying,' she said from one of the chintz chairs in Tansy's living room. Something so calming about all those beams, that old fireplace brick. It was like being in a wood, but a warm, dry one. 'But apart from all the dead stuff, I don't know what most of it is. The only things I know are the obvious. Buddleia. Rose bushes. Ivy. Oh, and sticky willy.'

Tansy looked amused. Before this Claire had asked about the hip ('boring'), the carers ('worse'), the pain ('not as bad as the carers'), the frame Tansy was getting better at walking with: 'Effectively a serial killer for the ego. I am practically a fossil.'

'Sticky willy? Not familiar with, I'm afraid. Describe?'

'That strandy green stuff that sticks to everything and looks a bit like those Christmas lights you get with little groups of balls on. And I know. I *know*. But my mother always called it sticky willy.'

'Ah, *goosegrass*!' said Tansy. 'Or "cleavers", as some prefer. *Galium aparine*. Part of the grass family, and a rather interesting one, too. Said to be the "deer" plant after the does that hide in it to give birth. Allegedly, it also represents a return to one's truly wild nature.'

'Wow,' said Claire, genuinely surprised. 'You really were a keen gardener, then?'

Tansy waved a bony hand. 'Oh, ish. Long time ago now. But if you want more, then I can tell you witches reputedly used it in binding spells for relationships and so forth. But mostly, it was used herbally as a diuretic for urinary infections and bladder issues.' She gave Claire a wry look. 'Not that one would want to be the guest at that particular party.'

Again, Claire laughed. 'But how do you know all that? Did you train?'

'No – perhaps in another life I might've. But for years I loved the look of gardens and loathed the idea of dirt. The *work*. Life took a turn, as it tends to do, and, well, here we are. And you? I asked you before what you did, and you didn't answer me.'

In another life, Claire thought, she'd have asked about that turn. 'I'm an illustrator.'

Tansy nodded, her eyebrows high. 'Gosh.'

'Not really, but it pays the bills. I work on sh— kids' books mostly, nothing special.'

Tansy's brow stayed high. 'Unless you're the child reading them, perhaps. One should never denigrate what one does to earn a crust, Claire. Like you, I did time at art school. Unlike you, I did nothing with it. *That* is' – she made air quotes – '"nothing special".'

Well, that was her told. Claire sipped her tea trying to think how to follow that. It tasted of both stale Tupperware and UHT milk. 'So, can I ask – can you use all plants like sti— goosegrass?'

'A great many, yes. But I'm not about to advise you to start on that yet, just the weeding. If you're still interested, of course, I can talk – oh, for hours, you poor thing! – about what one can put in salads and soups, or what the ancients thought. Let alone the "cunning folk".' She winked at Claire. 'My tribe. Part wartime baby, part haggy old witch, you see.'

And part total nutter? 'But how will I know what's what?'

'With me or the garden?'

Claire smiled. 'Er, can I say both?'

'Well, as far as I'm concerned, I suppose I am more witch these days if one is to go on looks. And proclivities.' She flashed a wicked grin. 'Childhood me would be *thrilled*. But as for the garden, well, you won't at first, and it doesn't matter. To get down to where the actual plants are, the things that *need* nurture and attention, one has to wade through the layers of useless old stuff.' Those sharp, bright eyes. 'As in gardening, so in life, one might say.'

Claire felt her innards sink. Gardening. She had never seen herself saying that word related to her own life. Perhaps all she'd really been wanting was that sense of spiritual cleansing she got – however tragic – sorting out an avalanching cupboard back in her old life.

'Oh,' she said. 'Just— I don't really have any tools apart from some knackered secateurs and a manky trowel.'

'You can use mine, if it helps.'

'Oh, no, that wasn't what I meant! I couldn't. No, I'll have to—'

Tansy fixed her with a stern eye. 'I mean this kindly, but do shut up, Claire. I am too old. Either say yes or no, or I might be dead by the time you've prevaricated and finished with polite. Ken and I began euthanising the garden while he was still alive, before it went to seed – why can't they do that with people, I ask you? – and they're in the shed doing nothing. So, if you ask if I'll need them, well, on your head be it. Which it will. But I do find not saying what one thinks so very tiresome.'

It was so unexpected Claire didn't know how to react. She listened, hands folded in her lap, as Tansy told her where and what the tools were, what she'd need for what, before thanking her again.

'And do stop being profuse! I haven't offered you a kidney. I've simply suggested using tools doing nothing but inviting rust. I do so hate lack of generosity. You know, there are tribes in Africa that have a policy for theft I adore. If one steals a neighbour's animal, one must not just give back that animal, one must give one's *best* animal as well. If not more. Funnily enough there wasn't much cattle rustling.'

How she flipped from one thing to another. Dementia? She seemed too astute for that.

'Oh! That reminds me. I met your niece, from South Africa.'

Tansy's smile dropped. 'Did you indeed?'

'I meant to say before. She called round before she left. To give me her number.'

Tansy's fingers interlocked in front of her chest. 'I see.' Index fingers tapped knuckles. 'And was the niece's illustrious visit a mere recce, or the full Inquisition?'

The niece; *the* aunt. They clearly didn't get on, then. 'Sorry, I don't quite follow?'

Tansy scowled, her gaze fixed to one side. 'Talk about a namesake!'

A lightbulb in Claire's head: *I suppose you'll send me hope now.* She'd just assumed the old woman was having a go at God. But whatever, this was beyond her remit. She did not like that look on Tansy's face. 'Um. Her number was all. In case anything happened?'

Tansy did another of those loud snorts. 'That woman is more stubborn than a blood stain.' She turned a fierce face to Claire. 'Don't be fooled. My niece is merely hoping to continue her badgering *in absentia* – her only saving grace being how far away she lives. It's the house she worries about, not me; nobody really *cares* about you as you get older, unless one has children. In any case, you may inform the niece I manage perfectly well and all I wish for is to be left alone. Now, I'm sure you have plenty to do, so I won't keep you.'

Air so sharp it prickled at the tips of Claire's ears. 'Oh. Of course, I didn't mean to . . .' She stood, Ben's mother in her mind: *If you try and put me in a home, I will give every last penny I have to a donkey sanctuary.* 'And thank you for the advice, I really appreciate it.' She stooped in the hall for her boots, not waiting to do up the zip. All but sang: 'I'll do my best not to kill anything.'

A loud *hmph*. 'Claire. The longer one lives the more one learns how nature, mostly, wants to live. Though it might be an idea to photograph unidentifiables on your phone. One finds Google useful, of course, but it is so blasted full of American whatnot and pernicious grammar.' Another of those raised eyebrows. 'And you are an artist, are you not?'

Claire closed her door; flattening herself against it. Something else her grandmother said: *Love many, trust but a few, and always paddle your own canoe.* Whatever was between Tansy and Hope Becker she wanted no part of it: *fini, finito, el fin.*

She was relieved to be at her desk, remember how meditative her work could be. How it allowed a mind to slow, wander, settle, retrace steps back to almost before memory, this effortless marriage of left hand to eye and, yes, natural talent; she liked being old enough to admit that now without the inevitable twat-attack. So why, then, did she not see what Tansy had? Or Ben always said? Believe what they saw as untruths and what she did held no value, didn't matter. Why did women lie to or about themselves for so much of their lives?

As far as she could see, hunched over blocking out Ransome's two-tone tail, so much of it had to do with the menu of how women – her generation, at least – were conditioned. With an added side of neurological construction. Men, in her experience, mostly looked outward if things didn't go as planned: hunting for hooks to hang blame on. Women tended to drive that hook inward, if anything. Following the tracks of where they went wrong.

Sugar and spice and all things nice.

She was fed that growing up. Not *ladylike* to raise a voice. Or argue. Or leave brows unplucked, refuse a skirt. Swear. Drink pints. Want sex as ardently as men. Wear the 'wrong' clothes or give the 'wrong' impression, too much make-up or hair *if you want to be taken seriously.* Not to mention periods: suffer in silence even if they eviscerated you. She'd still done this at forty-five, crippled by ovulation pains, her father-in-law asking why she couldn't stand upright as he dropped off a forgotten kids' toy. 'Something I've eaten,' she'd said, because otherwise he'd have outwardly struggled while she inwardly died and saddled the shedload of weirdly shaming guilt.

You learned early.

Lie about how vile to have that middle-aged teacher lean over you, fetid breath crawling to your breasts; or your revulsion for the penis pressed at you on a Tube; again with your laugh (as you were instructed) to lie to the flasher, the masturbator, that greying boss-creep you kept sweet. And so many women lied about motherhood. How easy or how hard they found it. To themselves, as much as anyone else.

*

'What is women's desire?'

Him. He asks me this in the days when it's still just friendship, talking: Rego, Frink, Picasso, Velázquez, Freud, Vermeer, Van Gogh; a lot of time on Bernini: the power of art on immutable objects. Blacksmithing came later, he says, art first. Except now he comes out with *this* sort of thing. And men like that annoy the shit out of me, as a rule.

'Do you mean for life, or only about sex?' As if I didn't know. *Ask me about my dreams, what I wanted, what I still want now, old as I am – or as you see me.*

'Men always want to know when it comes to sex. It's all a mystery to us. However it sounds, I think most women just want a man to slam them up against a wall and fuck them.'

Younger, this would throw me. But. All those decades of the deceptive fronts of motherhood. Wifehood. Womanhood.

'Is that so?' I am cool; like the sound of myself. A long time since I've felt anything approaching *cool*. 'How very twenty-first century of you.'

A half-shrug. As if we're just talking about which part of the Arts and Crafts building is leaking now: the knackered art studio I work in, or that castrated-looking forge he does. 'I know how to please a woman.'

'I'm sure you do. More to the point, do they know that, or is it just you?'

He shrugs his shoulders fully now and I watch the skin ripple at the side of his neck in slivers of sweat-coated black. 'I'm confident. What's wrong with that?'

'Nothing. Just that some women might find that a bit – rapey? Or plain infuriating?'

'And which are you?'

I can't fight the upward curve to my lip. He's fifteen years younger, for crying out loud. 'Old enough to see both sides.'

'I notice you're not saying I'm wrong.'

'No. I'm not. I think—' What? When was I last asked my opinion on sex outside HRT, hysterectomy, atrophy, or UTI; other than my (ex) optician sharing his vasectomy issues and his wife's menopausal frigidity before asking if I'd like to go to Amsterdam with him? *Ugh.* I have to think. My own desire does not work like so many women I've talked to.

Voice, hands, steady. 'I think sex is a primal thing. And women are lynchpins in both home and society. So, like birth, death, anything natural beyond the controlled rational, sex can make animals of us all.' *Eat that.*

'Is that why you think people have affairs, then? Because they're basically animals?'

That he could think me so naive, so easy to unbalance.

'I think men have affairs for sex. Men desire, women desire to be desired. Mostly.' I hadn't known I thought that.

'I think you're probably right. But they also have them for sex, in my experience.'

I will not back down. 'Of which I am sure you have plenty.'

'And you don't?'

I smile. 'I am a good girl.' But I can't resist: 'With a past, admittedly.'

It piques; I see it in the way his mouth twitches. 'And you've never been flattered enough then?'

Oh, please. 'Happy people don't have affairs,' I say. 'Why would they?'

*

She'd been a sexual being as long as she can remember.

That disgusted *We don't do that here* as she soothed her small, scared self with a hand in her pants as it dawned on her School meant all day, every day. The shame led her to prayer, though the longing persisted even so. Always interest in a boy: funny Matty first, who wanted her to touch his 'lump of jelly', which she had – with a ruler at first, unsure if it might sting like an actual jellyfish – and who wanted to smell her fingers if she put them in her trousers. The fuzzy feelings on a bike, a bus rumbling bumps, knees pressed together hard in sleep. Something else, too: a climb of sorts with a definite exult at the top. She liked it. A lot. Even though *We don't do that.* So she didn't. She just apologized to God, freak that she was – Eve with a serpent.

How much worse it got as the daughter of Eve paid for the

maternal crime. The first period; the restless, sleepless *Will I be sick, will I be sick* before it arrived at just ten; not red but terrifying rusty-brown; desperate to ask her mother if she was dying. The story of the next forty years of her life cracking open its spine and turning its first page.

Blood. Blood, blood. Blood on sheets and blood on car seats. Blood on the backs of skirts and dripping down legs, down tap-running sinks like watered-down ink; ripping out knots inside her that brought back everything ever read of lances, swords, spikes; of hung, drawn and quartered. Of the birth woman with the purple-blue face whose screaming put the fear of God into the girls watching the wheel-in TV at school. You don't wheel in that kind of blood, it wheels you; blood and pain so synonymous for her she laughed decades later as a midwife declared advanced labour: 'I've had worse periods than this!'

But she didn't know that younger, when life took on two distinct halves: the one that saw a quarter moon turn half and knew itself, and the one that saw the half turn full and took her as its changeling.

She didn't know to call it desire, the nagging maw between her legs that mewled at her from chasms of ache. Once, on a seaside trip at thirteen, the throbbing burn of oestrus came on her as she walked a promenade, played crazy golf with parents, grandparents, brother. Nothing she could think, look at, to stop it intensifying as she walked; her parents mystified by her short black fuse: *If that's the best you can do, young lady, go and sit in the car. You are not spoiling everyone's day!* She was so terrified of climaxing, she had to take herself to the public toilets, do furtively what took mere seconds; despite wanting to drown herself in the calcified bowl with its shit streaks, Izal paper and nasty bin, sanitary towels licking at its lid. She would never forget that; dreamed of being caught out, coming at a supermarket conveyor belt, anywhere else she could be certified as certifiable.

No choice but to handle it as best she could. The sweat-sleep explosions that left her fearful of sleepovers should she noise with painful pleasure; the egg hungry, blood craven for the sweet: stale cake with crisping sides; cooking chocolate that tasted of the smell of carrier bag. The hunger turning to tears, tears to rage, rage to tears and back again: an ocean all its own. The nipples pierced with needling shafts of pain. She learned the mask that hid the smelt of inner steel; cast herself a warrior's weapons as she vomited, or bled into two tampons: fourteen and 'fresh as a daisy' as a man said at her Saturday job till. She bathed daily; partly to cope with the ferocity of lubrication: the sharp-sour musk of armpits, the milky liquid chalking knickers. And partly to cope with the dirt of her.

Women had appetites and lusts, she knew from furtive books at school, but she was raised to be 'a good girl'. To be fucked was to be *fucked* – pregnancy the worst any woman could ever do, and always her own fault. Look What Happened to Her (insert family/friend/apocrypha). Good Girls Don't. Wait for Someone You Love. Don't be a Slut/Tart/Slag. That *Well, you know what men are like.* Ladies' Man. Womanizer. Player (fun for who?). Heartbreaker. Casanova. Don Juan. Romeo. Stud.

But however much it floored her every month, she did feel an empress in another way. This body could make *life*. And this body, with a value she had never known before, bore signs she was realizing she did not have to write for men to read.

How she had wanted that – so proud of it now. To be a woman, not a girl.

Growing. Learning.

The kettle clicked and Claire sighed again – the lead-heavy sigh, this time, of sliding into places she didn't want to go. Like remembering the Jimi Hendrix poster with the torn corner she'd stared at losing her virginity, but not remembering leaving her desk, or ignoring the kettle and reaching for last night's leftover wine instead; that fail-safe fast-forward to help the hours elide, a pause button for the lonely, the sad, the stuck. The mind that wouldn't stop slipping about like wet soap in the hands.

She turned the kitchen halogens off; too much in a room so small, so low. She'd change them to something softer, she thought, remembering with a snap loud as the light switch that it was not her choice now. She'd been spoiled, owning a house for so long. It made the earth under the tiles she stood on, even the scree under those, shift like the clouds that had just exposed the moon.

She stood sipping her wine, looking at it, waxing full again, so bright it seemed even bigger than last month's. She wondered what it would do to the tides, how, once, it would have affected her own, made her period early. More babies born at full moon than at any other time, too; she knew this from working on a midwifery manual. And the more she stared, the more the moon did indeed seem to gleam, swell, shine. *Smile*, like some kind of beatific new mother.

Jesus. It was happening, then. She was a heartbeat away from becoming the living embodiment of the sort of thing she illustrated.

She finished her glass, reached for another, her phone – for the first single she ever bought. She wanted to dance like she had as that teenager, or when she'd hide in her kitchen away from Ben, the boys, waiting for wine to seep into her senses so she could do what she did before any of them, or whenever she was alone, miserable, madified: close her eyes and let the music preach the only religion of joy, love, loss she'd ever found outside art. She could funk it up. Sway it down. Smooth over all her cracks and find balance in a binaural beat she hoped would help her sleep.

She stepped outside, curious to see how loud she could make her music before it leaked; wanting it to fill every cavity in her lungs but with no desire to upset Tansy Howard any more than already, however inadvertently. All she wanted right now was the snowy light of this February moon and the sweet delights of the kitchen disco.

'The best thing to do with the past is put it in a box and bury it,' she heard her mother say as she closed her eyes and started the swaying slide into oblivion.

'And then forget it ever existed.'

February

Snow Moon – Half Waning

The mornings were sticking to a uniform of opaque greige – despite the teasing, blushing sunrises on one side of Hunter's Moon – that sat cantankerous in clouds on the other, fast as a teenager in the fade back to sullen grey. It did not stop Claire slipping a coat over her pyjamas again; wanting to recapture that taste of liberation, breathe in this new life where nature overtook the wondering when *home* would stop feeling like an Airbnb.

    She'd piled her life's collection of books against a wall in the living room last night, ridiculously pleased with herself for making it look a little less bare. Realized too late she'd only ever be able to remove the top few or the whole teetering stack would bury her. Resisted the urge to cry at her stupidity, congratulated herself for that. Then caught her hip on that *bastard* bathroom door again and dissolved into strings of snot.

    Her phone pinged. Asha and Jules – did she want to meet up? No, sorry, and thanks, but she was badly behind with work. Okay said Asha. You know where we are. You won't be miserable for ever, old bean. We won't let you xxx

Another ping. Hi. I hope all is good with you? The aunt tells me you've visited a couple of times, so just wondered how's it all going – everything okay? Thanks! Hope x

A tiny stab of anger at that. She couldn't help thinking how, back in the landline dark ages, and before he told their parents he was gay, she made Stephen laugh during a bad break-up; picking up for him when his ex rang, stating in her best RP voice *The number you have dialled has been changed to f-u-c-k / o-f-f.* Shame she hadn't been able to do the same with her worst ex. She shook her head. The present was quite enough on its own.

She put her phone on silent, tipping her head back to draw in a breath of the cold, sweet air.

Hard to find beauty in it, winter. But she felt better out here, as if she could only be at one in open country, blissfully anonymous and mostly out of reach. Out here it didn't matter if she didn't have the right to feel as she did; trees and fields didn't notice, nothing did, and still less did any of it care. Her footsteps were the only thing she'd found to outpace the rage or slog out the sorrow, slow her to a softer mind.

The number of oaks was striking as she neared the wood; always her favourite, a reminder, too, of a kids' mythology book she worked on while pregnant with Joe. The Norse pages captivated her, not least for the joy of drawing and painting trees: Odin's tree, Yggdrasil, the world tree, the tree of life, not the oak she'd always assumed but a vast and mighty ash. She'd made it tower, branches span in delicate infrastructures and meandering filaments, almost an unconscious rendering, as any winter tree, of a human brain. She remembered the roots she'd twisted deep into the earth, twining around the Nine Worlds where the Old Gods met.

It was then she learned to distinguish oak from ash: oak a fluffy cloud, ash spoked with branches; ash bark smooth, only the oldest bearing vertical wrinkles, oak with its deep ravines. Oak was Thor's tree, disappointingly, she'd far rather it was Freya's instead of lime, which she didn't care for. *The Limes* was the biggest house her mother cleaned; home to Mrs Double-Barrelled, who always smiled and said thank you and gave her mother a poinsettia and a box of Quality Street every Christmas – and also, to Claire, a first awareness of her class. Being told by her parents to put on her 'best voice' if Mrs Double-Barrelled phoned. How it always left her feeling intimidated; somehow *lesser.*

She stared at the oaks guarding the wood's perimeter; her impatient feet and lack of bra arguing with the *Keep Out*. How much freedom, though, she'd enjoyed as that rough, rural, braless girl. Flying kites with Stephen in fields in their underwear to get a tan, or skating shallow marshes and ponds, making dens in woods – his always more decorated than hers, as his homes always were, even student digs. Finding rope swings slung over streams, cycling miles to rivers – the Waveney, Deben, Gissing – to hurl themselves at the mercy of pike. Their pleasures came cheap, as was the way of necessity. Good to be reminded that this shot of joy at gnarly oaks and mists filtering the sunlight between trees cost nothing.

She flung out her arms to celebrate the loose freedom of it all, walking in a circle, head back as she drank in the sharp, earthy scent, exhaling out a *Fuck yeah*! This – this solitude, and in such beauty – was bliss. No one to see her but for half-awake blackbirds and pigeons, a few scratchy crows.

Except the man with two dogs on a leash walking up the middle of the field.

No way to hide in her scarlet Santa-patterned pyjamas; a joke Christmas gift from the boys, a riff on the obese old tree decoration she dragged out every year (*False beard? Grotto? Mum, the guy's so totally a nonce!*) She brighted out a *Hello!* Which the man, roughly her age, returned as they passed.

But the way he looked at her drove so deep even the soles of her feet winced.

'I assume you're here for the tools.' Tansy stood at the door, hunched over her frame. 'Or the niece has been in touch?'

Claire forced herself to smile. 'No, I just wondered if you needed anything from the shops – I'm going later.' In fairness, she was more surprised at herself for the visit than the lie, though she had felt bad for not answering Hope's text. Female guilt. Like bubbles of cloth in water – push one down, another just popped up somewhere else.

The door, almost closed, opened a crack. 'I do not.' A dip of the wire-wool head. 'Though many thanks for both offer and thought. I trust you are well?'

'Yes, thank you.' Claire took the slip of paper from her parka, handing it over with a sense of exoneration. 'My mobile, in case you ever need it. I forgot to give it to you last time' – best just to gloss over the *why* – 'and I do know how hard it is when all you want is to be left alone.'

Tansy's brow lifted. 'Oh. Well. Yes. But since you *are* here, do you want my tools or not?'

The door opened wider.

'What's that saying about weeds?' said Tansy now. 'Emerson, I think.' She scowled. 'Ironic I can't remember for toffee when the great man's motto was *trust thyself*. Not that it's bad advice, *per se*, as one learns by my great age. If, conversely, the great age also leads one not to trust oneself at all.'

Claire nodded, cringed. 'I think I'm getting to know the feeling.'

'You're a mere baby!' said Tansy, though a hint of a twinkle sat in her eye, Claire thought. She could imagine how sharp Tansy might sound were it not. 'Though, in fairness, I do remember that rather odd time around one's late forties, early fifties. And all too well the horror at shoplifting a stalk of garlic, even though the money was in my purse. Whatever was all *that* about?'

Claire laughed. 'Hormones – must be. I did the same in the year after each of my boys were born, though it never happened again, and I still have no idea why. Full disclosure, just for you? I nicked an actual bra from John Lewis once. I think it might have been some kind of pathetic rebellion against all the Chelsea tractors in their car park. As I say, *pathetic*.'

Tansy cackled. 'I had a spell of driving into other people's cars, if one is to *really* spill the beans. Your face! Not as bad as it sounds. Once or twice I merely shunted said cars when they'd parked a tad too tight for one to un-park freely.'

Now Claire raised her own eyebrows. 'Really? And did you do damage?'

'No idea. Certainly not to myself: it all felt rather liberating as I remember. And I was so riled I didn't care by that point, in any case. Dear Ken never said a word if he noticed.' A sharp *hmph!* 'Probably didn't dare. What a terrible wife I must have been at times. Though he did escape ultimately, of course, by dying. So there is that.'

'Oh, I'm sure you weren't,' Claire said, shifting in her chair. She was keen to steer away from more talk of menopause. Too many reminders of adolescence. Her teenage years haunting her weeding efforts was bad enough. 'And I'm sure we can all say that at times. So – this. Is this one a weed?' She leaned so Tansy could squint at her phone. They'd already identified a nascent foxglove and the yellow scruff of feverfew.

'Oh, that's fat hen. Wretched stuff gets everywhere. Takes its name from fattening poultry – eaten by us too, once, like spinach. It's of the quinoa family. And as hessian as you'd imagine, absolutely chock-full of vitamins. And look, the little indigo-blue plant you see there—' She jiggled a finger and Claire noticed, for the first time, she still wore a wedding ring '—is an ajuga. I do so hate "carpet bugle", its soubriquet. I think of it as more a ground-hugging mint beaten into submission'.

'Ah. And the fluffy stuff – here, by the goose grass?'

'You called that cleavers last time, which rather reminded me later of poor old Catherine of Cleavage at boarding school, so called owing to the unfortunate creature having none and her long hair. *Abominable* place.' Tansy studied the photo. 'Do you like it?'

'Oh. Right. And I do, yes, lovely textures. I'd like to draw it if that's what you mean.'

Tansy pointed an index finger straight up. 'Another reminder. Now, where is it?'

'Where's what?' She tried not to let her expression show alarm at all the conversational non sequiturs. Too many reminders of the aftermath of stroke, or the start of dementia.

'I have something for you, printed it off' – Tansy pronounced it 'orf' – 'from the computer. Would you pass my diary, please? Just there.'

Claire reached for the black *Lett's Weekly* beside a copy of the *Radio Times* on the not-wood nest of tables.

'Aha!' Tansy pulled out a folded piece of A4. 'It arrived in my email and I thought of you. A quid pro quo, if you will, for the kind offer of your number. Ordinarily, one would pop it through a letterbox, but at least I remembered and therein lies *some* kind of victory, however small. Here.'

An advert for a scheme offering artists the chance to apply for financial help and do something blah. Claire fought her face. How many times had she seen this sort of thing? And how many times was she the wrong demographic, age, too this, not enough that? But it touched her Tansy had thought of her. Funny how you didn't realize you missed that until someone did. 'That's so kind. Thank you. I'll have a proper look when I've got my glasses.'

Tansy hmm'd and fixed her with those rodent-black eyes. 'Make sure you do.'

Claire licked her lips, caught herself. Tansy didn't know her well enough to read the sign that spoke of rankle; the same as when she saw Jules and Asha's texts asking again where she was, why she wouldn't come out: *Get off my back*.

She took a deep breath – so much anger during menopause: confusing, frightening, at times – nodded. 'Thank you, I will.'

'And that fluffy plant you said you'd like to draw? Yarrow,' said Tansy. '*Achillea*. Mostly white and weed or plant, depending on whether one likes the look. Personally, I dislike yellow flowers unless they have the decency to be daffodils – the symbol, unsurprisingly, of new life and hope. But did you know they also stand for unrequited or broken love, or a cure for heartache and sorrow?' Tansy paused for a moment, a little sadly it seemed to Claire. 'I gave someone a bunch once, not that he ever knew all that. But it made me feel somewhat better.'

She wondered whether – wanted – to ask more, but Tansy looked up then, bright, back. 'Whereas *achillea*s? Healing and love, said the ancient Greeks, but, oddly, divination for the Chinese, given it's said to grow on Confucius's grave. Sadly, they always remind me of gone-off broccoli. Genus *Achillea millefolium*, I believe. From Achilles, who healed his men with it in battle, we're told. Not so sure myself. Medicine mixed with men does so tend towards the cutting of bits off. Surgery, you know, hails from the battlefield.'

What a curious little woman she was. 'I didn't,' said Claire. 'And I thought achillea was fennel. How do you *know* all this stuff?'

Tansy peered over her glasses. 'I was a vegetarian in the Seventies. And a coeliac, to boot. They couldn't even give me a cheese sandwich – and the salads back then were *ghastly*. So one looked to Mother Nature and the wisdom of the Crones. All plants have, or are, stories, dear girl. And yes, yarrow is rather a trickster. Looks like umbellifer but is, disconcertingly, a daisy: a member of the *Asteraceae*, the aster family. Makes one think of the Astors'. She shuddered. 'One's jury is *still* out on Nancy. Beastly woman, I suspect. Like most Yanks.'

'You don't like Americans?'

'Oh, Claire.' Tansy gave her a wry look. 'You'll soon realize, should you be fool enough to visit more, I don't particularly like *anyone*.' She dipped her head forwards a little. 'Present company excepted, of course.'

Claire laughed. 'Thanks. I was getting worried for a minute there; I don't want to—'

'You're not. Unless you start saying *we* like the new carer on my alleged team.' A half-snort. '*How are we? Have we been to the toilet? Have we been eating?* I did say that *we* haven't done anything. *We* are not at primary school, the Queen, or that frightful Thatcher woman.' A full snort. 'So, we're pretty sure she hates us now, and that's us somewhat scuppered if she's not a temp, as it were.' Tansy scowled. 'But I digress. Yarrow, you say?'

'Oh, yes – what's the other one you said, the umbilif-ic–'

'Umbellifer,' said Tansy. 'Feathery. The *Apiaceae* do tend to that leaf shape. Of sorts. Think fennel. Celery. And actually, carrot, parsley, lovage, chervil, and so on.'

Claire sat back, disconsolate. 'I can't even remember my own family's birthdays most of the time, let alone Latin or plant families. How far am I going to get if I can't even take in what's a weed and what's a flower?'

'Ah,' said Tansy. 'See, I wasn't aware you were planning to exhibit at Chelsea.'

It threw her completely. 'Sorry, but *what*?'

'Well, I thought I was merely watching a woman battle a garden back from near – and very ugly – death. Surely anything is better than that? Unless, of course, one is old enough to wake each day surprised to still be here and wondering if it wouldn't solve a few problems.'

She couldn't help but smile at that. 'Don't say that. Your hip will mend and—'

'I'll break the other one?'

'No. Or I hope not. I meant that you'd be able to get around again.'

'And *then* break the other one,' said Tansy. 'Or – ha! – the same one again?'

Now Claire laughed the first proper laugh of her visit. 'No! You'll be pain-free, able to move around again, freely. Surely that would be better than now?'

Tansy smiled gently and raised an eyebrow, fixing her with those searing eyes. 'You tell me, Claire of the Moon.'

She shifted, again a little awkward. She wasn't quite sure what Tansy meant, but her voice and expression were not hard. There was a brief pause – Tansy one of the few people she'd met who evidently felt no need to fill gaps – until the old clock chimed its quarter hour.

'Got it!' Tansy said, suddenly, triumphantly. 'Yes!'

'What – got what?'

'The weed quote. What is a weed? There was that hippy stuff about it *being a flower but without judgement* – what rot! What about genus and cultivation, for heaven's sake! But it was definitely Emerson who said the other one.' Tansy's free hand banged the chair arm. 'Thank heaven for that! The wheel may be rusty, but the hamster hasn't carked quite yet.'

Claire shook her head, confused. This was like dementia on speed. 'What quote?'

'What is a weed, but a plant whose virtues have not yet been discovered?'

God, the mess of this garden, though. Shrouding and clouding everything once clear. It made her think of Tansy's parting words: 'The only way, Claire, like art, is to *start*.'

Armed with weapons of hoe, fork, rake, Tansy's 'ladies' spade' and a scary pair of loppers that looked like bolt cutters – if she could, she'd use them to cut the cords in her brain keeping her unable either to work or just *be* – she decided to see this garden as a blank canvas. Or white space, as she preferred: like white noise, something and nothing at the same time. And – positives, because she did feel better for the laugh – at least this was one thought she hadn't said out loud to an inanimate object or Ransome sodding McSnooze.

Her art, her own particular way of translating what she saw, the split between the explicit of detail and the splashing passion of the abstract; and especially the combination of the two, was the only thing she'd ever excelled at. She'd forgotten that, too, thinking of Mrs Double-Barrelled; how whatever happened as she grew away from her home village, she always had the art that never made her feel less than. How strong it ran in her once.

She put on an old pair of Ben's leather gloves and flipped a thick tea towel over her shoulder. Brambles and nettles: *Voila! The two things any child would recognize after a run-in* as Tansy had pointed out. The cat was back, too, and she found herself almost pleased to see it. It didn't ask anything of her, just stayed a little longer each time, moved perhaps a centimetre closer. Curled its tail around its legs and sat and watched her calmly.

Equally calm, methodical, rhythmic, she began again to pull and rip; as if to coax even just a small square of dishevelled plant life to unwrap itself, show her what it was.

She jumped when her phone beeped. Emma: *I need you! Urgent!*

'Say that again?'

'Rob,' said Emma. 'The love of my life, Rob. The one before I hooked up with Twatface and got pregnant by him. That Rob.'

It took a moment, even so. 'Rob?' Claire blew on her coffee. '*Pisshead* Rob?'

Emma laughed. 'Not these days. Three kids and 10k runs now.' A sigh Claire couldn't decipher; hard to parse without the tics and tells that only came with flesh. 'So, apparently, he's loved me for twenty-five years and even his wife shouts my name when they row. And he wants to tell me this before it's too late.'

Claire frowned. Before she moved, she saw a friend from the kids' old school who told her how it 'Would've been better for you both if you'd left him in your forties. Before it's too late to meet anyone else'. Step one on the ladder of wanting to avoid so many people she'd known during the marriage. 'Too late for what?'

'Well, he kept on about being in our fifties. So, I suppose before either of us dies? I told him I was married again – didn't say to Miserable Git of the Year, mind – and he said he was sorry Twatface turned out to be *such* a twat. How much he regretted it, would've taken better care of me, because he never stopped loving me. Even when he married his—'

The gasp so sharp Claire felt the stab of it in her own chest. 'Oh, Em. I mean, *wow*. I can't take it in. Let alone how you must feel.'

'I feel like he's dropped a bomb on me. And really bloody angry, actually – like how could he do this to me? What am

I meant to do with it? I've just had my last kid graduate, I'm married, I've just moved. I'm meant to be making a new start?'

'All of which is fine,' Claire said, calmer herself at the crescendo of Emma; a legacy of motherhood, that instinct to hold out a hand, becalm the storm. 'Because everything is still the same. And it would weird anyone out. But he might just be fishing? Or a sex addict, or just bored, he could be—'

'Except he lives on the other side of the world, Claire. Not as if he can just arrange a bit of sleaze in a Travelodge on the A10, is it?'

What would happen if he could? 'So how did you leave it?'

'Insanity.' A beat. 'Even if he's not a nutter, I bloody am now. What do I do? Ignore it, tell Misery Guts, tell Rob to piss off? I'm two husbands down already, it's like a joke I can't tell anyone. The worst thing is I can't even work out how I feel, apart from fucking gutted it's come when it has because he was All. I. Ever. Wanted. I loved that man like I never loved anyone before or since.'

'Oh, Em,' she said again. 'Do you need me to come?'

A sniff. A moment of silence. The point at which, if they were in a room, she would wrap an arm around Emma; sit her down in that landscape of long friendship that unrolls like a carpet to comfort blistered feet.

'Just tell me,' Emma said eventually. 'What would you do – if it was you?'

'Oh, God, easy one, that,' said Claire. 'If you look at my history before I got married.'

*

Cherry Boy. The first. Not the first to French kiss, or suck out a love bite, or be fingered by. She wasn't sure she'd have gone out with him at all if he hadn't been so keen and she hadn't felt such a need; never one of those girls the boys marked highly out of ten.

She was fifteen, pub-waitressing over the summer; he two years older and living above the pub kitchen, with the holy grail of a car. He drove her to the coast and made sandcastle cocks in the sand; in autumn and winter to other village pubs to play cards, poker dice, pool. But mostly they hung out in his room, rolling around to records and the smell of stale beer, scampi, second-hand fag smoke. She rarely took him home; her mother insistent her door must stay open; her father, if there, rapping knuckles at ceilings if she played records on anything other than volume 2. A year of heat before they did anything, not for want of his trying such sexy acts as rubbing a condom wrapper at her face whenever she got wet. With him, she learned how incendiary the negatives: how little increased a flame like a *We mustn't, I can't.*

When they finally did, she didn't like it. Not one bit.

It wasn't anything like anything in books or films, this splitting, tearing need to dig nails into his back as she tried not to cry out – or cry. But he loved her, at least: a friend deflowered in a playing field concrete pipe to a boy who dumped her a week later (*slag!*). Nothing in *Jackie* about it being shit. Less still about it being the same the second time, too. Which didn't stop her humblebragging to her friends.

The third time, her parents were out, taking Stephen to uni, staying overnight. Cherry Boy persuaded her to have some wine, and something changed. It didn't hurt – or rather, did, but with a pleasure-pain that left her with a lifelong love of the first penetration of any fuck she'd ever have. She'd had the most intense, beautiful orgasm of her young life then, melting into the swirling, thorn-wrangled roses of her parents' living room carpet, nectar-filled, every muscle in the complex flower of her contracting.

And that was it. Seed sown.

Anywhere, everywhere, and at any time.

On a kitchen work surface while her mother ironed upstairs, outside in snow, straw, fields, riverbanks, meadows; orgasms that electrified her, left her wondering once if she'd had a stroke in the back of a VW van.

She started A levels and adulthood; her creativity as hungry as her body. She began to paint in a way she hadn't since primary school; bold, extravagant, brush dancing with confidence as she explored new media or strode out with lino cutter, tools, metal, clay. On a trip to visit a friend's divorced dad, he took them to the National, the Tate, the Royal Academy; her first time ever, more excited than half the people there drifting listless, blinking at one work before moving on to another. At an exhibition of Old Masters, she had to stop herself reaching to touch silks she couldn't believe were paint – Rubens, Holbein, Caravaggio, Van Eyck. The powerful passion of Turner, the softness of style of Seurat, Monet. And, oh, Cezanne. She wanted to study every brushstroke, feel the breath of the painter settle its tiny hot droplets on the canvas.

She painted her first self-portrait then, but only in blue, enraptured by Cezanne and uncaring whether it fitted A level diktats; she knew it was good. She rendered trees in red, playing with Klimt, fantasized about trips to Amsterdam to see

Van Gogh battle it out with Vermeer; Madrid to see Picasso's *Guernica*, *Weeping Woman*, queen of one of her most beloved postcards. One day she'd visit all the galleries of the globe. Maybe one day even stand by a painting of her own. She was soon to learn to drive. Life had a capital L and curiosity gnawed at her.

Cherry Boy was sweet and kind. He would never have hurt, cheated, or even said a horrible word: the boyfriend any parent wanted. He was kind about her mother, too, the duality that saw her laugh and chat one day, confine herself to waking coma another.

And he loved her. But try to love him as Claire might, he began to bore her. It felt as if he had a lack of ambition, sometimes even of backbone; as if he wore the trace of a welcome mat on his forehead – and all that did, however it made her feel about herself, was make her want to pull on a pair of stilettos. But he loved her. On her seventeenth birthday he gave her a ring studded with miniature sapphires and almost invisible diamond chips; both his sisters were married by nineteen, and he *already knew*, he said. She was never one for jewellery that wasn't silver and more thick than thin. She'd stared at that little gold ring and seen only the bars of its setting; the way they caged in those tiny precious stones.

She broke his heart, but worse, she wasn't kind. Like so many teenagers she'd once scorned for doing the same, she tried to make him hate her – do it for her.

Except he made her tell him, then threatened to kill himself, so all Claire hated was herself.

Cobwebs. Memory. So often made of gossamer threads; strands strung like the spider silk between the low stubs of a harvested field in certain lights and at certain times of day; a darning of animal into mineral. She'd always loved how their patterns seemed so solid: as if they'd take your weight like little string hammocks to bounce between. Only as you trod towards them did they disappear, fading into the float and seamlessness of illusion.

But still that question kept coming back. Two years since she last saw The Blacksmith; the truth of what it made her face. What was women's desire – and more to the point, what was hers?

Sex. The famous topic after twenty minutes with any group of women she'd known – even now, with men 'wielding dicks that don't always work without help', as Jules said. Even Asha, whose sex life Claire had always envied; always the one who stayed quiet when sex got slapped on the table like a fresh bottle of wine. 'I couldn't care less' so many friends of fifty-plus said. 'Give me the dog and a cup of tea and I'm good, thanks.'

'Well, I do still have sex,' Asha had confided to Claire. 'But it's not the same. I mean, we're still *happy*. But there's nothing in it for me any more. Not since menopause.'

She thought of Asha's sad face as she pulled a long strand of dead stuff stuck to the gloves, the old fisherman's jumper of Ben's she used to decorate in, picking off the tiny burrs. She thought of Jules, who used to 'shut up and give in' to her first husband's incessant demands, 'just to keep him quiet, happy, or bloody both'. A woman at Pilates once, who she overheard tell another woman with a grumpy man: 'Just give him a blow job, he'll be so much nicer. Think of it like cleaning out the fridge'. She scorned it then, and always would.

Desire meant so much more to her than sex when she was young. It had been the drive to get her out of the soul-suck of all those mapped-out lives and baby-faced mothers; the dead-end jobs she did herself and wasn't snobbish about but wanted only to escape.

And yet. What to do with a sexual desire that wouldn't just shut the fuck up?

*

'I've brought you up a coffee. Can I join you?'

How she wishes Ben wouldn't do that. Why can't he just get in? It is still *their* bed, if years since they've shared it for a full night. Pregnancy set the seed: she a restless growbag unable to ignore his snoring. Babies. Life. And then, as *coup de grâce*: menopause. A sex dream has left her with a gnawing from groin to torso; a snake working out whether to strike. Of course, she says, as she picks, gently, at the crusty aftermath of sleep. Since when has waking up been a dangerous act? Eyelashes like spent Christmas tree needles; stiffness needing steady care for fear of triggering some agonizing spasm that will last all day – or week. Treacherous dreams.

'Guess how many times I had to get up for a piss?'

She sips her coffee as if inverting a whistle. Her drinks, like most things, are all-or-nothing – cars either big or small (she hates saloons), liquids hot enough to welt a tongue or cold enough to weld it to metal. 'This is a fun game. Two? Nine?'

'Three. *Three.* How can you need to piss three times in eight hours?'

'You're asking the wrong person. I can piss three times in an hour just looking at a car, getting in it, then getting out again half an hour later.'

'Yeah, but. Women are freaks, it is known.' Ben nudges her. 'Joke! I know it's early.'

'Ha ha. You should get your prostate checked. That'll wipe the smile off your face. Maybe you drank too much?'

'I didn't drink anything. *You* were the one drinking.'

She checks a knee-jerk temptation to snipe. 'I meant like coffee or tea or—'

'Nope. Just my age, I think.'

'Yaaay.' She slides back under the duvet. When the kids were small this was a perfect time to sneak sex. Now those kids didn't sleep until practically dawn and she and Ben are perma-jetlagged from ensuring they didn't start life crippled by debt like their middle-aged parents.

His newspaper rustles. 'God, they're such dicks!'

Warm in bed. Warm enough to feel the slippery residue of the dream's truncated ending. She edges her bottom close to Ben's thigh. The newspaper rattles again. 'He's a bloody joke!' She wriggles closer; backside actively pressing his leg.

'Wow. Did you know Jeff Bezos could buy every person without a house in the States a small one, give them a hundred thousand dollars and still have fifty billion left over?'

She *mm's*, hoping he'll ask if she's sleeping, slide down beside her.

'That's if he didn't go into space, of course.'

She wriggles again, presses his leg harder.

'Woah, mind my tea!'

Something in her sinks. Ben must feel it too, because his arm reaches across a second later, drawing her into a spoon. Her breath stills at the press of him through his pyjamas. She hears the shift in his breath to slow, stilted.

A half-snore.

She coughs, yawns ostentatiously. Arches her back and pushes into him again, feels a hand run over her hip, roam to her waist, waits for it to reach her breast. She might make a joke herself now: about that pencil test she and her girlfriends did, younger: what you could hold under a breast to assess pertness; how a flatmate once did a thin Yellow Pages but Claire suspects now she'd manage half of Ikea. Then Ben would laugh, and she'd roll over and—

He pats her bottom, definitively. Pulls back the duvet, stands and yawns noisily. 'Right. I'm getting up. Things to do. You coming or staying here?'

'Oh. I thought—'

'What?'

'You might want to—'

'What?'

'Stay in bed for a little—' But she didn't want to spell it out. *Ask*.

'Nah, I need some breakfast.' A pause. Always a pause. Like a marker of the sometime no-man's land between them now. 'You okay?'

Two things too dangerous to row about: sex and money. Too raw, too much potential for slow-release poison; lead paint coating wood. Money happened a couple of times – how could it not with not enough and scales so far out of kilter? – but they entered marriage determined to be as equal, as *modern* as they could. God. All that trying.

'I'm fine,' she says. 'Just tired.'

She turns her head under the shower's sweet-sharp needles to soothe the stiffness in her neck. She'll have to sort herself out if she is not to be a total witch. They've not had sex for months now. Many months. Too many months. Maybe even a year.

She washes her hair, slathers it in conditioner – never knowingly under multi-tasked – before putting hand to pubis. Why did so many young women get rid of it all? She had a Brazilian once, to avoid spider-legs on holiday, and felt strangely neutered by it: a girl, not a woman. If anything now, she was All Woman: no one told you how your sacred garden rewilds in midlife. For what? To protect itself from cold now it isn't in demand from the gene pool: a blanket for old lady knees? Her hand slides lower, middle finger speaking the lifetime language, the true mother tongue, of cunt. She shuts her eyes, tries to imagine her finger someone else's, but it feels examinatory; ridges and ripples she finds herself checking for lesions, lumps, the coil of desire cooling. She withdraws, hand still on vulva, exhaling into imagination; leaning first head, then other hand against the dripping tiles, breathing in dream-memory from the vault of fucks and sucks The Poet left her with. The way he drove into her, how she bucked, the wrap of his arms, his groan, the thrill of his release inside her. Two more nothing-to-write-home-about orgasms before the sweet spot – the spasm that sweeps her entirety, instantly loosening the jaws at her neck.

God, I needed that. God, I needed that!

She raises her head to rinse her hair. And she is sobbing. So hard she has to hold hand to mouth for fear one will escape, leak from bathroom to landing, trickle into an ear. Her other hand clutches her belly as if to hold herself in, but she cannot stop. She kneels, holds on to the bath tap and chokes out a soundless line of sobs, as helpless as if laughing, water cold rain on her back, snot at her lip, the back of one hand gelatinous at the plughole.

It's okay, she whispers. You're okay. You have a good life, it doesn't matter. Let it go, let it pass, you'll be fine. You will. It'll all be fine.

She allows herself a moment, watches herself as she once watched children calm; sob shifting to hiccup, breath slowing, panic passing. At least now she can face the day, him, without slamming, banging, or whatever shrewism she's capable of – and she knows she is – breath as steady as her hair is squeaky-free of chemicals. She reaches for a towel, bends for cleaning spray. Might as well give it a going over while she's here. Nothing if not pragmatic.

Start as you mean to go on, and all that.

*

Her first thought was it was a scrap of paper, perhaps a faded old fag end. It stalled her, surprised to see that the smudge of pale was a snowdrop; just one, barely out of sleep, tiny and white as a faraway moon.

'Oh,' she said. 'Oh.'

The threat of tears so often came from nowhere. She could be cooking, changing a song on Spotify and then – lightning – fighting the urge to sob into the curry paste. Doing nothing apart from waking, and there it was like a ship woken to the searing splintering of wood and gush of water. How it hit, though, whatever it was the indefatigable cannon of grief shot out. Bullets of anger, balls of grief.

She forced herself – again – to stop. And yet the snowdrop

raised, for some reason, a kind of tenderness she wasn't used to feeling any more; the tears that stung two tracks down her cheeks drying in the gentle February day. So much time trying not to feel the feelings.

She wiped her nose with the back of her glove and bent to touch the snowdrop's head, as if lifting its chin to smile at it, reassure it like a child that she would not hurt it.

March

Worm Moon – Full

It was proving addictive. The sun was throwing razor-sharp shadows at the garden, at *last*, a spotlight on the thousand tiny shoots and clutched baby fingers of furl: a whole new world breathing up through the dank earth. Claire looked at the tiny deep purple violets, the wrapped poke of a crocus, the little blue stars Tansy said were spring anemones. The deeper she got into weeding, the more of what lay under the dead she was beginning to see.

Some things were just thistles, admittedly – 'the inevitable garden junk mail' as Tansy put it – but Claire felt such a surprisingly powerful joy at anything green after so long of winter, she'd scrummaged bare fingers over sticks and spent flower stems to clear space, uncaring her hands were numb, nettle-stung, or that soil was silting up her nail beds, opening a door to any nematode or other cat-shit horror wanting to wriggle its way into her. She could hardly believe she'd rather kill her back than see those bruised-looking ajugas bullied by some fat-leafed bastard she knew instinctively wasn't a weed – too proud, too pretty, too *of itself*; overpainting Mother Fucklock and her new beau (Brian Gosling. *Really?*). Or that she'd waited for this all through the painting-by-numbers as it felt now.

Joe had come back last night, last minute – 'Just for, like, I don't know, a bit, and shit' – though she knew when he rang something was wrong, consequently careful when she picked him up from the station: no mother of a teenage son looks him in the eye if she wants him to talk. Ironic. With Ben she'd always insisted the polar opposite; hating how he refused to look at her if he was angry. Men may be more straightforward – a hill she'd die on – but that did not mean they lacked complexity.

'I'm not *obsessed*, love. I just asked if Asmita is back home, too?'

Joe's head had tipped to the side, his hands wide: a ham act of disbelief. 'You saying you expect her to dump me? Like, you want your son to have no self-confidence?'

Why were men so fucking defensive?

It made her think of Danny: helping him once with art homework when he spun on her, accused her of calling him 'crap' when all she'd said was she thought his stroke suited charcoal better than carbon. Of Ben: how his *sorry* never came without a caveat. Of men she'd worked with when teaching: so many women hiding behind hair when it came to showing work in class; so many men clearing throats ready to explain. And yet she'd always loved men's company, had so many male friends once. It saddened her how hard that got after marriage.

Joe shook his head, reached for his AirPods. 'Any woman would be lucky to get this piece of ass.'

'Is that right? Guessing it's the modesty that wins them over?'

He laughed. 'You're lucky you had me and not another one like the bisexual Jesus you gave birth to first. Seriously.'

She'd laughed too then. 'I'm glad you're home. And sorry if I'm— a bit . . . you know.'

Joe met her eye then, his face soft. Nodded.

'I've been feeling a bit down, is all.'

'Aw, Mum.' His head on one side again. 'Do you want me to pass you a ladder?'

She laughed again – *You are my ladder!* – but all night he'd kept asking if she needed any help, was she all right, and did she want a chunk of his Toblerone?

For all their *bantz, Mum!* they were turning into good men. She reminded herself her sons had been lucky. Stereo parents; the comfortable triptych of that, home, an unpressured focus on being happy: all the ingredients she and Ben hoped would bake a good pie. You wanted to protect them, and that didn't stop when they could peer down a nose at you. It was around then, if anything, you realized nothing you did could ward off the vagaries of love. What she wouldn't give to have a potent cocktail of words to stop her son from sobbing about the girl who'd just smashed his heart.

Joe hadn't said, of course. She'd just stood, morning coffee in hand, about to knock on his door, sensing staggered air and whittled breath behind it. She hugged him, tried to give him some of the heart she had now: old enough to know some pain never really died, it just eventually stopped blistering your feet as you walked your world trying to live with it. She even had a piss outside, not wanting to hassle Joe out of his bath. And not entirely unenjoyable, either: something about the air of it, the quietness of pissing into grass.

You thought parenthood would get easier. And to a point, it did. But even when they'd left it was never truly easy, just *different*. So much nobody told you. Or perhaps they did and you didn't listen, people so very good at hearing only what they wanted to.

'You're only as happy as your unhappiest child,' her grandmother used to say. 'Doesn't matter how old they are. It still kills you every time.'

'He's okay, though?' Ben asked, calling after her message. 'I sent a text, but I didn't know what to say.' She heard the sounds of city streets in the background, could see all the shapes of his face frowning at it. 'And I knew you'd handle it, you'd *know*. You always do.'

When Danny got dumped, Ben had left the room as if about to weep himself seeing Danny cry. She bit back her *Well, I never had much of a choice, did I?* Apart, but together in the lives of their kids, they'd agreed, the four of them still a family. *Just get on with it.*

Claire stared at the dead leaves covering the new snowdrop shoots she'd found, as if coveting them. Some sort of purpled primrose thing lay near those, another tiny trefoil-leafed plant, its scalloped edges so miniscule she marvelled at its form, precision; almost ran for a sketchbook, an urge which surprised her. The last thing she'd sketched outside work was the boys when they were younger. She took a photo to show Tansy.

'Oh, Lord,' said Tansy. 'The poor thing. Hearts will never be practical until God makes them unbreakable. Isn't first love the worst thing? Frightful.'

'Well, yes and no.' Claire handed over the specific – and

eye-bogglingly expensive –yoghurt and peanut butter Tansy had asked for. 'And actually, I feel bad even saying this to you when you lost Ken.'

She moved to help Tansy with the jar, pot, realizing Tansy had no free hands now.

'Don't you dare help me! I do not need help – in fact, if you so much as touch this frame, I shall positively batter you with it!'

Claire backed off, allowed only to hold the yoghurt and follow Tansy to the kitchen.

'And don't say lost, either,' – Tansy pronounced it *lorst* – 'I loathe that expression! It always makes one want to ask if the *losee* retraced their steps. Or, and infinitely worse, ask where they last saw him or her.' She walked through to the living room, sat down heavily in her chair. 'The imp of the perverse, I believe it's called. Or the perverted imp, in my case, I'm sure. And "passed"? *Deplorable*! As if the dead merely drove off in a car. He *died* is what he did. And jolly lucky I think him, too.'

Claire sat a little stiffly. She was growing more used to Tansy's mercurial manner, but she still felt unsure what to say to that.

'And I know how that sounds. I know,' Tansy added. 'I would not espouse it to the carers, constantly checking one for Alzheimer's as they are.' She fanned out a hand, rubbing her thumb joint with her other thumb as if to soften it, or remove something. 'The fact of the matter is one has to address it. I have been asked to consider a nursing home.' She shuddered, looking, Claire thought, a little like a child; something she'd not seen in Tansy before without the cheeky wicked smiles. She looked furious. And frightened.

Claire softened. Her parents were lucky with a quick death. Ben's mother not so. Years of forgetting who her family were in the slow drain of everything she and Ben's father worked for, let alone the worry of her being abused in some way. 'Don't worry, Mum,' Dan and Joe said at the time. 'We'll get *you* a good home, one where you won't get slapped about and that. And if you do, we'll hide a camera and film it. Partly for fun, to be fair.'

'Ah,' she said, thinking of Hope. 'I can imagine how that makes you feel. But after the accident . . . I mean, lucky I was here and everything, but do you think it could be worth—'

'What I think,' said Tansy, sharply, 'is that the relics who don't end up in homes get off lightly. My friend Margaret suffered – oh, grisly term! – *sheltered accommodation*. Having no future is harrowing enough at this age, but she always said the worst thing was no one really *knew* her. That struck me particularly. As we both know, after decades of marriage one is accustomed to someone having respect for one's whole life.'

The pinch of that. Fingernails nipping the soft skin of inner arm.

'Did I tell you she died? Heart attack in her sleep, her daughter said. Enviable, I tell you, though obviously one didn't say as much. I've had a chat with *her* since, mind.' She looked upwards, held out her palms. 'Come on, Madge! Give me a helping hand!'

Claire couldn't help but laugh.

Tansy's eyes brightened. 'It's wicked, I know. I'm a terrible person. I told the carers what I told the niece – to naff off and that I shan't be going anywhere from this house beyond my box.'

'I don't doubt it for a minute. I don't think even God would dare try.'

'I'm ordering one, you know. Online. Wicker.' Tansy raised her brow. 'So, if I go before Beltane you can use me as a wicker woman – I've always loved the smell of bonfires. Now, show me what you have, I have things to do. Like beg – ardently – for death before they shove me kicking and screaming into God's own waiting room.'

'Ah!' she said a second later as Claire showed her the screen. 'Now that's lady's mantle. *Alchemilla mollis*. A dear little plant of the *Rosaceae* family. Very apt.' She passed the phone back, smiling. 'Used for all sorts of women things in the Middle Ages. Takes its name from alchemy – they believed the heavenly little droplets that sit on its leaves were the purest water, and as such might turn base metals into gold. Magical.'

'The belief or the plant?'

'Both. Why shouldn't we believe in the impossible, even just a little? It seems, for example, to your boy impossible he'll ever be happy again. But we both know he will.'

It seems impossible to me, too, Claire thought, nodding but avoiding Tansy's eye.

'Come to think of it, dear girl, if I still had that huge sum of it in my garden, I'd dig it up and give it to you – what it means is rather special, considering your boy. "Comforting love", or "I'm here for you" sort of thing. Hideous Americanization, mind you, but there it is.'

Claire thanked her, preparing to go, when Tansy said: 'No, thank *you*. Lord knows, the only other excitement I shall have today is googling coffins. Which reminds me, have you done anything about that art scheme yet?'

She winced. 'I'm afraid not. I haven't really had the—'

'If you say *time*, I shall clobber you.'

'Ah, so I won't say *time*, then?'

Tansy's hand slapped the side of her armchair, wrinkling up the little white antimacassar that always made Claire think of a nun's wimple. 'The one thing you have and I do not – with any luck – is *time*. I'm not exactly thrilled with anything in life, Claire. Do not make me feel I've wasted the little I have. If you are not going to bother, say so. If you are, then stop shilly-shallying.' Tansy fixed her with a fierce eye. 'Let's not pretend I am not a harbinger of all that youth fears. Old. Regretful not of what one did, perhaps, but of what one didn't. How can that be anything *other* than a good reason to get on with it?'

Art Calling! Maybe you haven't been able to work as an artist because of finances, physical or mental health, parenthood, caring for others, or life just getting in the way. We want to change that for twelve of the most promising applicants . . .

The website went into more detail about the support and 'launchpad' scheme for *struggling artists who want to make a difference*: how it wanted to put a focus on getting people to interact more with nature, particularly post-pandemic – *when nature showed the world how to heal* – and in some sort of *artistic collaboration with the mainstream*. Whatever that meant. How could so many years have slipped by she wasn't even sure any more?

'Fuck it. Just do it, Mum,' Dan said on their fortnightly FaceTime. 'If we do something and it doesn't work out, you've always told us just to try again now we know what *doesn't* work, or do something totally different.'

She congratulated herself silently – had she really said that? Well, she'd sounded good, at least. 'You were young, though, Danny. It's different when you get older.'

He shrugged. 'The harder you pull the arrow back, old woman, the further forward it flies.'

What? 'Where did you get that from?'

'Gaming. Well – and *you*, Mum. Any time me or Joe chatted shit about how hard something was. You'd always say not to worry about other people doing their shit, just focus on what we're doing. So, unless you're telling me you were massively bullshitting us, just do it. Why not? *Do* it.'

The strange punch of life's irony. For a woman whose knees buckled when she pissed on a stick and saw a blue line – so terrified of the responsibility, of monumentally screwing it up – motherhood was the only thing she felt truly proud of. *What do you want your kids to be when they grow up*, people used to ask, accusing her of hippydom when she'd answer: 'Happy and nice'. That, at least, she hadn't failed at.

Claire inhaled, lifting herself taller in her chair. Why not, indeed? Why couldn't she win a place at her age; change her life? Why *not* her?

She stared again at the web page.

Art increases awareness of the fragility of our natural world and our love for it . . . Art, like nature, leaves us feeling refreshed, uplifted, connected to something bigger than just ourselves . . . Understanding nature is the path to a greater understanding of life . . .

She closed her eyes. Tried not to interfere with the inside of her head, just let it be. Open the space. Allow. Daydream. Wander. Let the sensual, beautiful things in.

All she could see was Wank Farm. Not helpful.

She closed her eyes again; tried not to frown.

A level her would have fizzed at those words: taken them home to her little bedroom, slapped on a mix tape, let all the little bubbles rise in her until they popped with ideas that always came in full colour: an orange sky, perhaps, violet grass, maroon trees. Undergraduate her would have sat in a bar full of velour banquettes, sticky carpets and Fleetwood Mac, sharing passionate discussions over Silk Cut and paint-stripper wine about the power and potential of those words; arguing which artist fulfilled them best. Who made you *feel*. Who made you *care*. Both Claires would certainly have been too impatient to sit around thinking. They'd have just picked up a brush and flung themselves in the direction of a canvas.

And still nothing. Not one single idea, image, nothing. Nada. *Rien. Niente.*

'Ow!'

She'd been absently biting a cuticle, a jagged scrap of skin she'd just sheered off, the iron taste of blood in her mouth. It wasn't going to stop, either; needed a plaster. The thought gave her both a sense of relief – something concrete she *could* actually do – and of sad defeat.

Every bead of her blood had felt drowned by the sediment that rose from decanting four lives into boxes for this freedom, creative space: this chance for opportunity, adventure. How could she have forgotten the reality of a thing – like winter, like ageing – so often sat so very far from pretty?

*

The Suffolk of her childhood fell around Claire, so insanely beautiful it almost burst her heart. These fields she'd known forever felt like breath to her, their rise and fall her own chest, the trees and hedges her limbs; ditches and brooks her veins, rivers her arteries. She was made here. She was only just beginning to understand why that mattered more now than it ever had. It also explained why her bones felt the first sense of home, whatever she did to Hunter's Moon, since she'd moved.

The hill she was driving up rose neither steeply nor sharply, but it rose all the same until wandering out of sight, waiting to be caught up with. On one side, tall hedgerows stood blowsy in spring, in summer thick with leaf, in autumn bowing with berry, fields stretching to horizon like so many slices of bread slathered in chocolate, butter, all the colours of salad. Now all was still winter-sharp, stripped to sticks and secret nests; the occasional crown of church, a low-slung belt of poles and pylons.

It struck her how rare it was to see a view unchanged for half a century. She was not far from the little row of council houses she grew up in; theirs the end corner with her beloved tadpole pond, and nice, Silvikrin-smelling Anita next door with the catalogue, always slightly sad and village-whispered about when she called for weekly payments (*They say Derek shoots blanks. Poor cow. She's getting to the point it'll never happen now*). Then Winnie and Stan Clarke with their windowsill china poodles and the sweet, warm strawberries they'd let her pick in summer. Jean Tallis next, of twitching nets and pampas grass, smoking in her padded jacket with her brass perm and pinched mouth. The Jacksons (four, nicknamed five), and last, the Bells, with that garden of broken pushchairs and Alsatian cage; the only neighbours her parents swore about before or after work; Dad in his lorry, Mum cleaning. She'd cycle this hill just to freewheel down it, in spite of the top farm's rabid collies snapping at ankles like busted power cables. Beyond that no houses, for at least two miles.

Even the texture of her lungs felt smoother thinking that. She had not been here since her mother's last months, her death; time that had not been spent admiring her childhood stamping ground, lost in the stress of juggling that time with kids, work, the formal acknowledgments of death, let alone the emotional. How, sometimes, you mourned the loss of the relationship it wasn't as much as the one it was.

But she loved Mid Suffolk's dozing gentleness, its spreading skies and fields, the shish-shushing coast and shonky cottages, the windmills sporadically Dutching the sky, an occasional cauldron on a signpost. She'd grown here, smoked here, snogged here, enjoyed the freedom of just being who she was before all that got confused with the wider world of love, lust, all the heaven and hell of mating. Not far from here, she even had her first semi-chaste threesome – thanks to a new girlfriend she met working at a village pub, who boasted both a bottle of vodka and a sexy, older-teen boyfriend living in an isolated caravan on an uncle's farm. She forgot who suggested strip poker, and all the petting was fun – but. A Catholic, the new friend shared Claire's terror of sex, and especially pregnancy (perhaps more so), but also a sexual curiosity the evening stoked: the desire to find out what the fuss was about. And here, this particular road she'd just turned into, she'd had one of the most erotic experiences of her young life.

She was seventeen, he the super-sexy boyfriend of a then best friend (the friend interested in someone else: a girl's friends know far more than any man about her life). Earlier, he'd handed her tea – *I want you to have this one* – in a mug saying 'Love me Now' and every bone in her ovulating body curved to him. She'd cricked them back. A line you didn't cross, that;

drawn, in thick yellow and black, by the sisterhood. Not even a friend's ex. And so she'd pretended to ignore it and he'd offered to drive her home, asking in the car what she'd *be doing now if she could choose anything*. She'd laughed: listening to a certain album, she said; smooching to it if she wasn't so tragic and still had a boyfriend. Asked him the same.

'Here. Driving.'

He'd fiddled with his stereo – that album – turning to her, a dark eyebrow high, an upward curl to one side of his mouth. She had to stop herself staring. His beard did something to her. Most beards did, just not good things, like nausea and urges to ferret for hidden horrors. This one prickled somewhere around top inner thigh. She shuffled quickly in her seat: hadn't put her belt on, reached for it, unable to coax it into making its sweet seat-belt love.

He slowed, leaned over – 'It sticks. Let me . . .' – and their brief touch bolted through her fierce as the electric fire she stuck a knitting needle into as a kid just to see if it would 'ting'. Had he felt it too? Or was she some girl's mag saddo – *We touched hands, am I pregnant?*

Stars winked at the windscreen, pricked from a sheath of black – *bow and arrow country,* as they joked – the silver shadows of trees, floating thrust of thistle and all the thorny froth of bramble punctuated only by hawthorn berries red as spots of blood. She could probably have walked faster than the speed he was deliberately driving, certainly cycled, but she couldn't even breathe, aware only of her sex, liquid. A sudden, powerful urge to unzip him, take him deep in her mouth, pull up slow, suck, lick, hear his gasp as she took a breath – the sweet, sweet shock of hot-cold-hot – straddle him, soak him with his taste. Feral, wild, a wolf-woman gnashing with sheer need. *Say something! Do something!* She was silently saying it to them both, momentarily hating her friend: You've already got another, I've got none! But it was playground – *this little piggy* – and she knew it. There would be no forgiveness, no second chances.

Do something. Stop the car and fuck me, God I will do anything just fuck me, make me come, let me make you come, please just fucking fuck me!

Still he drove, mechanical-stroke slow. She couldn't look at him. Knew if she turned, he'd kiss her. That she would not be able not to kiss him back. As if that – he – gave her permission to do the Bad Thing: she could not have stopped it, but that didn't mean she could start it. She hated herself for what she felt capable of if her control was even lightly nudged.

The tiniest shift in speed, gear. She could sense the hair on his forearm as if it made the air shiver. One touch and she'd come. No flashing past of these fields, though. He hadn't gathered that much speed, just enough to stop the surreality of it all. Just enough to get her home to walk into her parents' house drenched from the inside out.

What. The. Actual. Fuck.

She was driving to get a haircut. Why all this now – that friend's boyfriend as forgotten as the fire hazard of her rigid Eighties perm; either dead or bald, or both; that friend married with four kids. And *Him*. Why? What a cruel mistress memory was. Remembering this, but not names or dates she needed, or where the fuck she'd put her tax return.

Well. So far, so post-menopause. Except the joke didn't fit;

the day too grey, too drizzly, too clinging-to-February. She parked, noting the kerbsides clotted and sludged with leaves, trees shivering under last year's last-ditch flames. Only a month or two and yet the difference in a past tense: this year, last year; another page turned on all the others. Except every now again it left you with the kind of tired that grabs you by the throat, pricks a knife at your back and husks at you not to make a fuss, just hand over your precious good humour and any other golden bits of your mind.

She shook her head: enough. Car. Bladder. Again.

She'd been so pleased with herself afterwards; before she spoke to Joe. So pleased.

First, she'd kept her promise to get herself to town so she wouldn't be *a total badger by spring* – even managed another joke to the (very young) hairdresser's comment of not being *that* old; did she know her generation were the biggest uptakers of recreational drugs? She didn't, but she'd save the crack pipe, thanks, for when there was nothing to look forward to but a box set and a box of chocolates for the three teeth she'd managed to hold on to. Second, not wanting to wreck hair she couldn't afford and still determined to do Normal, she'd dived into a coffee shop rain had made busy: only one empty table, near a woman swathed in black, dark wig framing a ton of make-up, spiky orange nails flicking it back.

It took Claire a moment. Those two older and two younger men gurning, nudging. How immaculate that make-up, how pristine the shaking finger texting against the smirk-snickers. She felt a rush of rage as she took her tray over, admiring the towering boots (years in, would the woman feel the joy that was a broad toe space and low heel?), likewise the tights (thrush right there). She took off her coat, accidentally whipping the woman with its hem.

'Oh, God, sorry! I didn't mean to smack you one, I'm so sorry!'

'Oh, you're fine!' A voice like the glide of ink on paper. 'You didn't, not really. And anyway, you'll come off worse than me – you've probably got make-up on your coat now.'

'Won't be the first time. I usually manage that all on my own.'

'Preach! I've taken to carrying Kleenex just to swipe my screen after I've been talking.'

The men nudged one another again, staring. Claire glared so hard all but one dropped their eyes. She turned, smiling, to the woman. 'Ah, the joys of the perfect foundation. If I could invent one, I'd have it go on like silk and dry like concrete.'

'I don't know about perfect, but I settle for pretty cheap. Let's face it, there's enough on me to sink a ship.'

Claire laughed. 'You know what, though? I think you look bloody fantastic.'

Her eyes *just lit up*, she told Joe in the kitchen, adding how glad she was she'd said it.

'Oh my God. You are so *embarrassing*, Mum. You probably made them feel like shit by drawing attention to the fact you clearly knew they were trans.'

She felt a little taken aback. 'Well, only because he already had attention drawn – and negative, at that.'

'It's "she". See? That's it right there – you can't even get the pronoun right, you're delineating. Do you know how offensive that is to people of my generation?'

'What? *She* was thrilled. Given other people – *men* – were pointing, pulling faces?'

Joe put his toast down, threw back his head. 'Oh. My. Fucking. God. It's your generation that make this so hard! You don't even see you're denying people their human right to identify and be identified as a woman.'

'I'm not! I have no issue with that. But at six foot two, with stubble under your foundation, isn't it the sort of mistake anyone could make?'

'I can't believe I'm hearing this. From you. I'm so disappointed, Mum.'

It felt like a slap. The d-word. Handed to you by your child? 'Wait, what? I did something to be nice, remember? I thought I was *helping*.'

'I see that, but you're refusing to accept trans people identify as women in the same way as you.'

She could feel her heartbeat increasing. She thought she was doing something kind – because God knew, she understood exactly how it felt when people read a story from your face. The one written on hers at twenty-one changed everything she was. Only older did she see how compassion sets its roots in the darkness of despair.

'Look,' she kept her voice calm, 'I respect anyone's right to identify as whatever they want. I'm happy we live in a world they can when I think about the shit Uncle Stephen had to go through. But how can I say a trans woman has the same experience of being a woman as I do?'

'They *do* though! They just weren't allowed.'

'And I empathize, I do. But being raised as a girl, treated as a girl, especially in the Seventies, Eighties? And don't even on the hell that is periods—'

'So you're saying you can only identify as a woman if you have periods?'

'I'm not. *I* don't have periods any more. But you don't see how much women like me want the same respect, too, for how hard it's been to *be* a woman, that it *is* different?'

'Jesus. Unbelievable. You're a *bigot*, Mum!'

'A bigot?' There was a beat. 'Fuck you! Sorry, darling, but fuck *you*. Half the reason all your not-bigot uni friends have those rights is because *bigots* like me went on endless fucking marches and watched endless friends suffer to have the right to fuck who they wanted, dress how they wanted, have their stories read in schools. You sit there as a man, thirty years younger, telling me about being a woman? How dare you call me a bigot! The shit in my life *because* I've been a woman – low pay, men telling me how to live, thinking they have some God-given right to say, do, send, touch whatever? Being dismissed. Called names. I've wrecked bits of me you can't even imagine from pregnancy, hysterectomy. How can you say it's the same?'

She was still shouting as he left the room. Red-faced, sweating, heat under hair, fast heart, stabbing tears; the feeling, so familiar as kids grew older, of failing by default.

Later still, teary, she called Ben.

'He's young,' Ben said. She heard the ice clink in his drink; he'd just got in from work. 'Let him have his young thoughts.'

'A bigot, though, Ben? *Me?*'

Ben laughed. 'You see, that's where you go wrong. You argue

with them, I don't. You let it get to you. I just let them think they're right. Life will catch them up.'

'But I don't think it's good to do that. You can't go through life thinking everyone agrees with you all the bloody time – how is that any way to grow up? How is it healthy? And anyway, how do you square that with not talking to Dan *at all* right now?'

Even on the phone she could see that face. The one so often she'd just back off from, shut the fuck up. Would he ever just agree with her? Still. *Pick your battles.*

'You know what? I didn't argue with them because I wanted to *enjoy* them, Claire. I don't have a problem with them just being kids, and I still don't. If Daniel needs to sulk at me challenging his life choices, fine – let him prove his independence from me, like I did with my father, except no one had phones then so no one expected everyone to be in touch all the time. Like I say, life will catch him up. Why is it always you doing this – ask yourself that? Why? Why can't you just chill the fuck out for once and stop being the only one in this whole bloody family that causes problems with everybody else?'

She greeted the dark smarting, greedy for the oblivion of its thick velvet cloak. The moon was all but hidden, a thin sliver as if blotted out by a finger, only a tip of nail left showing. It all hurt beyond words, beyond recrimination. And nothing more than the fact Ben was right.

They'd brokered peace, though, she and Joe: she wanted to make it right, she said; understand more, too. Because she did. She hadn't realized how much she missed being in touch with the seismic shifts of the planet of the young. She wondered what happened to all those doorframe felt-tip lines signifying her sons' changing heights; feeling again that realization of them being nose level, head level, taller; of not wanting age to shrink her. After all, hadn't she done this with her own parents: regarded them with disgust as they questioned why she wanted to 'mess up ordinary working people's lives' with 'her' protest marches or get fined for not paying 'her' poll tax; derided them even, and hard, for musing on whether Stephen might 'grow out of' being gay? She'd always been so determinedly the opposite with her boys. And here she was: not knowing how she should feel, what to think, and less still what to say as she watched her sons' world spinning so far from her own.

So much of her life trying to get it right.

Use your best phone voice for posh people. Show everyone how clever you are with your brush and your certificates. *Who do you think you are?*

Forget where you came from. Stand up for yourself. They're no better than you – everyone's shit stinks the same. *You've forgotten where you come from, young lady.*

That feeling of being lesser growing from the start of high school. The rough edge of her accent, the cheap polyester of her skirt – fabric tells tales all its own. The staying quiet as uni students joked about Artex or Anaglypta; the cutlery fanned like a spiky trap at a birthday dinner for a new friend, the well-timed 'cough' to copy everyone else. Again in London, when co-workers talked skiing, foreign trips, books she'd never heard of, let alone read; her only currency for art the passion that drove her to devour free galleries. Years to learn the codes of a world so different to her own; yet more with Ben's family. She hadn't realized being a woman of this age could – would – make her feel the same.

She remembered a work thing of Ben's shortly before the pandemic: one of those charity quizzes where she knew no one – all *Claire! Hi!* And then, for the rest of the evening, *White or red, Chloe? Raffle ticket, Kate?* How old she'd felt; how none of them wrote down her (right) answers until Ben said them. How one of the younger men, obviously wanting her to put in a good word with her husband, insisted on chatting to her.

'And you, Karen. What's your story? What did you do after uni, London?'

How to say she was once art editor at a good magazine? That she'd travelled; worked a summer for a wolf conservation centre, or that Ben asked her to marry him when they were both high on ecstasy at an infamous Nineties rave, and she'd said she never wanted to be married because she worried what it would cost her. That they'd decided how whatever, they'd always be unconventional, share whatever their future held?

'Me?' she heard herself say. 'Oh, you know. I got married and had my kids.'

How she'd wondered if she shouldn't just add: 'The end.'

*

My laugh. In my classroom he has just called me 'wise' and I have pointed out how wisdom often rides on the back of a lot of birthdays. He asks how old I am.

'Okay, let's play a fun game. How old do you *think* I am? Be careful.'

He surveys me, carefully. 'Forty-four. Five. Forty-seven at the most?'

'Excellent. That is the correct answer.'

'Really?'

'No!' I pull a face. *Ridiculous.* 'I'm fifty-two.'

'Wow.'

'Is also the correct answer.'

'You do not look like you're in your fifties. That's really surprised me.'

'Keep going.'

'You don't though.'

My raised eyebrow. 'Oh? And what do we look like, then, older women – Yoda?'

His laugh. 'No, I think it's more to do with how *most* women look in their fifties.'

'Maybe that's because you don't really see them around – or not in the media?'

'I suppose I hadn't really thought about it that way.'

'And all the women they do show live on air and cucumber or have a face full of rat poison?'

'And you don't agree with that?'

'No. Except, when my friend Emma did it, I felt like a bowl of time-lapse fruit next to her.' This statement a surprise: I always loathed that whole toxic system; the need it created in so many women to cling to surgical or chemical intervention. Let alone the Sisyphean acceptance that to walk that path meant endlessly rolling a boulder uphill only to watch it roll down again. Taking your cash with it.

'You'll never be old,' he says. 'And you have such a lovely smile – you smile a lot. I think that's the best kind of facelift, personally.'

Last night, I cracked – an argument? Feeling undervalued? Menopause? – threw a ladleful of pasta sauce and watched it spray the kitchen ceiling like blood. I could have shot someone and made less mess. 'Oh, you're good – I'll give you that!'

His smile; killer eyes on mine. 'You don't take a compliment easily, do you?'

'Not when it comes with a side of cheese, no.'

'I mean it. You've still got it.' His cupped ear, mocking. 'So—?'

My laugh, unbidden – again. 'Fine, I give in. *Thank you.*'

*

The cat was there again, outside the span of the security light it always triggered. It did look thin.

Claire sighed, put her wine down and went in search of tuna, a bowl. Couldn't not.

The clouds had moved when she put the tuna out. She smiled a little as the cat sniffed, tentative but too hungry to refuse. Watched as it drew slowly closer to the French doors, the jaundiced light from her kitchen leaking into the moon's brief glow to shine a sudden line of gold on the cat's spine. The stars were out, too; the sky like the old damask curtain in her bedroom back in her old flat: midnight blue and so moth-eaten that in darkness she could almost see the vast Suffolk sky again, the way it could centre her right where she stood. She turned off the lights and let moonlight fall over them both. Certain, but still soft, that light. Gentle.

All she'd wanted was to help that woman in the café. You learned that, if nothing else, groping through the thickest, blackest darkness life could throw at you. How kindness was everything.

Would she ever feel like she was getting it right, this life?

The clouds crossed the moon again, the light fading. She sipped her wine. Just enough light still to see the spaces she'd carved in the border nearest the kitchen. Small, yes. But it still felt significant. If she could, if it was bright enough, she'd get in there and expend all the energy coursing through her veins, threatening to overwhelm her. Plant or bloody weed. Out. Fuck it. So what if a few flowers went the way of the wrong things?

She was curious to see what would grow in their place.

March

Worm Moon – Half Waning

Strange how such tiny things could make you smile. She felt the need to be outside after so much intense work – Joe stayed the whole week in the end, lulling her back to a feeling of fitting herself, as productive within that as the endless rain. It amazed her how quickly they could swell a branch into bud, bud into flower: cerise bows on a fat shrub Tansy said was *japonica*, baby pink on the dead nettles, bubbles of purple grape hyacinth, the full yell of daffodils, the one small, but violently red, tulip. She'd always assumed the sun did that. How much, how quickly they grew, even without it.

The wild grass tore with the same noise as the sheep munching it further down the road; another smile slipping across Claire's face as she thought of her fingers automatic with the inherited knowledge all animals seem to share of how to get to earth. She could also now, she realized, confidently identify couch, chickweed, creeping buttercup, shepherd's purse – names she loved – among the weeds Tansy suggested she target first: 'It's rather a compare and despair metaphor but think of it like housework. Or life, for that matter. One clears the space of *stuff* before one even attempts to move the heavy.'

Joe had casually dropped in this morning he and Asmita were talking again. She'd asked, tentatively, if he thought this a good idea.

'Why not? She wants me back. And after she's done this to me, it's not like she can do it again. Ever. If she even started, I'd revenge-dump her anyway.'

'Jesus, Joe!'

A shrug: the exact same shrug as a boy – when he couldn't find words to tell her what was wrong or careened into a grunting adolescence and effectively stopped finding them altogether. She couldn't help thinking, sadly, it felt like she'd waited years for him to prise himself open, emerge as her beautiful boy again. When Ben fell out with Danny, then her for defending Danny, Danny upset with her, too, for intervening on his behalf – *You can't 'mummy' Dad out of shit conversation skills* – she'd sat at the big kitchen table in the old house, head on a hand, trying to eat a curry she'd made that tasted then like wet cardboard. A warm sensation seeped into her neck, shoulder, and she'd looked up, surprised to see Joe looking back down at her, softly smiling above the arm around her. She'd reflexively put a palm to her heart then, thanked him with her eyes, strangled to silence by her throat. Shortly after that he'd left for uni.

'Shouldn't have dumped me in the first place, then.'

Claire had been about to say something to that, shocked by how callous he sounded, found herself reminded instead, with a frisson of shock, of how hard she'd found it to leave Cherry Boy; how from pity she'd gone back. How, when she ended it again, realizing her mistake, her mother refused her hug when she came home sobbing: 'You broke his heart once, now you've done it again. Don't come crying to me.'

She thought of Ben. 'You'll work it out, love,' she said. 'And I'm here, son. If you need me.'

He'd looked at her with that smile. 'Cheers, Mum. And there is something actually . . .'

'Oh?' *Oh God, not pregnant, please tell me Asmita isn't bloody pregnant.*

'I really need your amazing laundry rizz? Love you, Mother . . .'

'Leave it by the machine.' Oddly comforting, that.

Scrolling Instagram as the wash chuntered to itself, she came across an artist painting wall-sized canvases of woods and forests where human faces, mostly indigenous and sunk deep into bark, peered out at the viewer. Then another artist's vast close-up of the inside of a scarlet oriental poppy, almost a tribute to Georgia O'Keeffe, only this one like a black umbrella opened for a flood of blood, at first unrecognizable as a flower until she realized the thin black filaments she'd thought were people were actually stamens given female form, dancing, bending, standing. Something inside her had curled towards both paintings like smoke into air.

Back indoors, she allowed herself the luxury of surfing Art Calling again. She'd need a full proposal, prelim sketches, examples, though *passion and purpose is our biggest judging criterion: awards can be made on the basis of <u>one</u> artwork. We want your love of the natural world to propel people to feel the same – help, however small, in the fight to save our beautiful planet.* She thought of Georgia O'Keeffe again, Klimt's *Tree of*

Life, Ai Weiwei's *Roots*, Van Gogh's last painting, *Tree Roots*, the represented struggles between life and death. But what, if she entered, would *she* be trying to say?

She set about clearing old folders, piled on her desk while Joe stayed, surprised to see how adaptive she once was. How her brushes, pencils, caught all the nuances of a crunch of amethyst: the whitish gums, icy purple teeth; how ethereal her charcoal drawings – her 'spirit hedgehog' in grass had the same wafty look as the whole book.

'You know they're full of fleas and ticks and fuck knows what else?' Ben said at the time. 'You can get salmonella from them, you know. And syphilis. Or is that cows?'

She'd never felt the same about hedgehogs after that.

Her phone pinged. Hope Becker. *Shit*. She'd forgotten all about her.

Hi! Hope all okay? Aunt not picking up calls – lines down?! Hear she lent you some tools tho, so maybe hit head again lol?! Be great if you'd drop a word about her moving somewhere better – so good you're on the case, you star! X H

Claire had an image of Tansy snorting at Hope's name on her phone as she told it to *Naff orff*; half smiling, half feeling sorry for Hope and the dark reminder of Ben's mother's demise. The unwanted sense of expectation just as she was sinking her teeth into the fruits of freedom from young children. You thought motherhood alone taught the contradictory emotions of any deal signed in dribble and sealed with shit, but then along came midlife with its scissor of clutch and accelerator: kids growing up and preparing to leave you, parents growing old and doing the same. Still. Tansy was not family. And she should be working on Silo and Tiller, the twin sheepdogs Mary-Cate wanted in 'funky-punky braids' and 'girl-power piercings'; glasses for Baley, the border collie queen training them up now with wisdom over speed: 'Under pressure to tick the older demographic box,' Mary-Cate said. 'And hoo-fucking-ray for that.'

It didn't feel like a hooray. After Joe went, the cottage shouted such emptiness she'd caught herself telling the kitchen to *Stop being so bloody loud*! For so long she'd fantasized about what a place of her own would look like. A life. And yet here she was, constantly driven outside by still being unable to decide on putting up a picture without anyone to ask how it looked – or hold it so she could see. How younger her would scorn her now. All the things she said she'd never be. Do. Ending up the frame and not the picture.

'Too much time ruminating,' Stephen said last night.

She thought of her brother in his taupe psychotherapy practice in Portland, *Oregon*, of his beautiful, tan-blond boyfriend, no kids, the fact he'd see Danny before she did; small world not so small-seeming when a son sat on the other side of it.

Sometimes, she'd snipped to Stephen, whole days were spent just fighting to batten the hole, keep the ship afloat, let alone throw herself into some new sea; *get out there*.

'Well, just be careful of that, Claire,' he said. 'There's a big difference between rumination and reflection.'

She ignored the cracking of her knees as she began to methodically clear around some of the surviving plants: roses, lavenders, rosemary, sage, something spiky-spindly Tansy called a cloud bush, a purple *Cotinus* that would leaf the colour of venous blood with 'clouds' of hazy white flowers; something else called 'choysia. I think Aztec Pearl, but it could be Sundance. No matter – both smell divine and look heavenly.' Claire liked it, whatever it was, with its glossy British racing green leaves. Liked, too, the prospect of a philadelphus Tansy said was 'Belle Étoile' which bore the scent of orange blossoms 'similar to those one inhales in the glorious Med'. All the colours, textures, smells, captured her; impossible to draw but perhaps possible to evoke. Had to be, head sketching as her hands worked. A caterpillar had already made its way into Wank Farm – watching Ransome from an *Alchemilla mollis*. She'd decided to keep it as a subtle visual theme: later it could become a butterfly.

'He says he won't give up,' Emma said when Claire FaceTimed, waiting for the kettle. She'd promised herself she'd work this evening – ridiculous she still felt a need to give herself permission to work whenever it suited, even now.

'On me,' Emma went on. 'On love. Even if it takes twenty years, he says, he'll wait. What the fuck am I supposed to do with that?'

Claire warmed her free hand on her cup. 'Sweetheart. In twenty years you probably won't remember who he is. More to the point, nor will he.'

'Fantastic,' said Emma. 'I mean, that's great and everything, but in the meantime he won't stop about it being the right thing. No matter what I say. So what do I do now?'

Something about Emma's tone. 'You've spoken, then?'

'Had to. I wasn't going to tell anyone because I felt so stupid doing it. But I had to find out if he sounded mad – which he definitely didn't.'

How the idea of love, even now, still stole a show. Claire

blew on her tea, more to get rid of the thought than anything. 'And how do you feel now? You okay?'

'Honestly? Tired more than anything else,' said Emma. 'And sad. Sad we couldn't have had those years together, that I had so much unhappiness and so did he. That he married someone he didn't love, who knew he only ever loved me.'

'Oh, Em. Look, I don't mean to sound . . . but this is *such* a weird time of life. Are you really sure you believe him?'

'Well, that I'll never know, will I?'

'No,' Claire said. 'But you don't know how it would have been with him, either? Good or bad. Look, I love you, you know that, but surely if it was meant to be, it would have – well – *been*?'

'But there was his job,' said Emma. 'He asked me to go with him, but I'd just qualified, got a job, I couldn't just bugger off halfway across the world. He kept saying there was always time, but before I knew it I was pregnant. Then I heard he was drinking a lot, then nothing until I saw him years later at a wedding. Weird – well, the bit I remember between peeling Twatface off a bridesmaid and stopping four kids eating icing off the floor of the bloody marquee.' Another sigh. 'I'm too old, Claire. I can't do this. All I keep thinking about is him, and my stomach just churns the whole time.'

'I get that. And I worry. I mean, I don't want to see you get hurt. He could be spinning you a right line for all you know, Em?'

'Not though, is he?' Emma's voice uncharacteristically sharp. 'His sister and I still do Christmas cards.'

Claire's innards sagged at the defensiveness. She'd sworn since moving never to ignore her intuition again. When your insides shouted at you, and you chose not to listen, there was only ever one reason. You didn't want to hear what it was they had to say.

If it was meant to be it would have – well – been.

And if not, she hadn't added to Emma, then that's what we all tell ourselves, isn't it?

*

She'd always had a bit of a thing about Guitar True-Love. Ever since he ran across a playground early in high school, stooping to scoop up a tennis ball in front of her and she stood shock-staring at the black-black hair and striking green eyes. Trying to work out why her chest felt as if it took not just the strike, but the shape of lightning.

She'd watched him spin on one foot, arm drawn back, shirt lifting – oh! – as he dipped a knee, bent back like a Greek statue, hurling the ball high, arching, long. The way he'd caught her eye, stared back, smiled. He was the son of a surgeon; as far from her council-house league as her touching the top of the netball ring. Yet it became evident, fast, the magnet pulled both ways. If she was walking past where he was playing wall-ball, and he had the ball, he'd always aim for her arse.

'All right, Texas?' he said one time, as she rubbed the welt and flicked him the bird; the nickname bestowed by some other boy, thanks to her breasts (soon to be so covered by her arms she'd have a slight hunch for years), and a TV chocolate bar ad – *Texan: The Big One!*

'All right, Danger Mouse?' Her TV nod now, him shorter than so many of his peers.

She was never not aware of him; felt his presence on her skin, the roots of her hair. They had a sweet, childish relationship that first year – you 'went out' with boys then mostly because they asked – but an attraction that clicked on and off for years. They dated properly once, but it ended because of how he tried to get his hand in her pants on the overnight bus to the school exchange: fierce, relentless; his urgency stunning, repulsing, thrilling. She fought because she knew she should, but she hadn't wanted to. She knew even then she could take his fingers as deep as he wanted to thrust them – and love every single second.

But that was just it, wasn't it?

She smoked, swore, liked a dirty joke, masturbated like a teenage boy. A freak, a nympho, a *dirty bitch*. That was her secret. Her shame. The thing that still at times made her want to pray herself good. His girlfriends were always posh, sweet as brandy snaps stuffed with the creamy pout of them. And yet she saw how he looked at her, barely able to admit how much she wanted to impress him.

'Texas! I see you won that competition. Did you get someone else to paint it?'

'Mousey! I saw you in that band that weren't shit. Did you feel out of place?'

She went out with Splatty Kev instead, because he asked, but also because she liked where he came from. He was son of Artex Tony, the dad of messy overalls and smoke-smelling van, his mum an Avon lady, and she and Kev often went to his at lunchtime, where Claire found all the things familiar to her: smoked glass mugs of tea that steamed on tables with meals, flowery carpets, fake wood Formica, 'naff' china ornaments of 'ladies' or robins on spade handles, Old Spice and Silvikrin – and no en suites.

And then came Cherry Boy.

'See you got a boyfriend with a car now, Tex? Does his guide dog drive it for him?'

'See you're going out with Jayne's ickle baby sister. Buy her an ice cream for me?'

But as they got into A levels, her girlfriends, boy friends, began to blossom, beard: the reader-writers understanding Shakespeare, the maths and sciences revelling in infinity; languages chattering, humanities wanting to hold the planet in one hand. She grew, too: her mother's lurching yucca painted life-size, the Suffolk sea on an old piece of plasterboard Artex Tony was throwing out, her self-portrait now in squares of blue, her Freud-inspired *Woman in Red*, all the tiny illustrations she'd sketch on bar mats, menus, anything; her appetite never sated, merely teased. She used pub work to save for university, but also to stretch herself a canvas, buy a camera to take good photos. Won herself a couple of prizes.

They kept a good friendship, she and Guitar True-Love; in the same school house, always bantering in competitions and assemblies, but always two of the first to shout about one of the better teachers getting sick or losing a loved one, head to the town florist after arranging a whip-round.

'I don't know – which ones do you think they'll like the most, Mouse? What the hell do you buy someone whose husband just died?'

'Any. Because of what they mean. You're the arty one – and actually the one who stood up and said we should, so you choose. And good on you, Tex.'

Two of the first, too, to be reprimanded for never quite adhering to the rules. Him with his cheeky songs – 'The Tie of the Agar', ripping into the music teacher who often turned up skew-whiff, reeking of booze – her with her cartoonish lampoonings. When not worried about treading on her mother's *nerves,* or dealing with the ghost-home of a mother in hospital again 'for a rest' or 'recuperating' in Norfolk for months, she loved nothing more than to laugh. Her dad worked all the hours then, and with Stephen at uni, she had to learn to live with watchful sleep, terrified of the Rippers treading the bills marked *Urgent* as they headed to her room with their knives. School was safe and, in sixth form at least, fun. She didn't want it to end as much as she needed to escape; the desire for city life – *life* – pressing.

When they danced, she and Guitar True-Love, learning a waltz for the leavers' musical, she sweated such animal musk she'd clamped her arms so tight her ribs ached for an hour, just in the hope he wouldn't smell the strength of her want at the ebony hair peeking where throat pooled to clavicle. The night they finally got together at the leavers' party in a barn on someone's farm – *as you do,* she joked – they took off for a walk in search of fags, got lost, walked for hours and ended up in the soft scrub of headland of a stubble field, ghost-lit by a harvest moon as he took her top off and both lost track of time.

She fell. Hard.

You've got a hell of a mind, he told her, and it meant more than any profession of unlikely beauty. The best she was used to was 'more attractive than you think/when you take your glasses off'. Attractive: older actresses, other people's mothers.

With Cherry Boy she had found a way to be a woman, but

she still hadn't felt like the real deal; the girl still playing with the grown-up clothes to find her style. With Guitar True-Love, the woman in her sang like the strings of his guitar.

First love. So beautiful and so brutal at the same time.

'I love the way,' Guitar True-Love said in the hot summer before university, 'you always answer questions with another question.'

'How do you mean?'

'Very droll, Tex. I'm impressed.'

She always laughed when he said that – *impressed* – which he did often; no way around his seeing through any of her guises. They'd known each other too long.

He pulled her close, into the clean, ironed linen smell of him. 'Because it's sexy. I love your confidence, your energy. You've got a way about you and—'

'Don't say it. Big tits? *Yawn.*'

'Not as big as your feet. It's like going out with a duck.'

He wrote her a song called 'Number One' because: 'You are curves and circles and squares at the same time. You're the number one because you're infinite, you'rse perfect.'

'I love your body,' he said, when she, premenstrual, pulled it to pieces, wished she were thin; snake-hipped and small-breasted *like all your other girlfriends*. 'What was it you said – Rubenesque? And no, not just your gorgeous, amazing . . . *those*. I'm even getting used to your massive feet.'

'Built for comfort not for speed,' she said; a quip-shield used about various body parts to many men, many times, in the pubs she worked in.

'I love watching you play,' she said to him one afternoon off from their respective jobs. 'The way you get so lost in your music, that *look* when you can't get the notes, and then you can. I even like this' – she stroked his Eighties stubble – 'ridiculous bumfluff of yours.'

'I love it when you have red lips,' he told her, smooching at the last of their friends' eighteenths, after he'd just sung along to Barry White, parody-style, in her ear. 'I don't care if it's meant to work like a baboon's arse like on *Life on Earth*; I love it all the same.'

'So, what about when I'm not wearing make-up, then; as in, most of the time?'

'Even better. *Ohhh don't go changin' / tryin' to please me . . .*'

There was nothing to change for him. Nothing else to be but entirely herself. He'd say he loved it even when she kissed him and had flecks of cucumber left in her teeth from a sandwich. When she sweated that musk, and he drew her close and inhaled her deep.

I love it when. Neither committing to making that sentence just the three words. Not so little, after all.

She drew him: sideways in charcoal as he drove, the shape of him bent at his guitar; her passion for him, like his for music, big and bold in paint. She took photos to catch that exact black curl, that fork of hair rising from nape of neck; the way he looked at her from the other side of a room; how she loved to catch his eye at a party when they were talking to other people. That thrill that sent a charge to deepest her: her sex, yes, but also her soul.

He watched her paint, something she usually avoided, never happy to be on a stage, on show, like him; though the aphrodisiac of talent only made her want him more. He said the same to her when he kissed her neck from behind as she stabbed, stroked, tickled paper with brush, laughing as he crooned 'Vincent' in his best John Denver. Most times, though, he'd sit strumming the guitar that rarely left his side, to the point other girls complained, he said.

'Play something for me,' she told him then. 'Not something I know, something you've made up. I'll paint whatever it makes me think about. Or feel.'

He played small tributes to Spanish guitar and she painted a patchwork red sky, a

mountain, a hint of the squares and alcoves of Moorish architecture in rusty brown, the swirling white skirt of a woman dancing in the forefront of it all, waist down only, as if witnessed by a child; rudimentary, but free. He did the same with music, he said.

'Give me something. A person, word, image. A feeling, anything.'

'Okay. Sing me a song about summer. No Louis or Ella allowed.'

He fiddled for a few moments, mutter-singing, testing chords. And then broke into a bluesy, rock and roll-rockabilly riff in the same beat as 'Heartbreak Hotel':

We-e-ll in summer my baby wears san-dals / But she don't got painted toes
And I stare at those ten little pig-gies /And that's just the start of my woes
Cos my baby got Suff-olk ham feet/ Yeah, baby got feet like ham
And I can't tell my baby to paint them /Cos baby don't hear no man

She got ind-epen-dent feet, yeah / ind-epen-dent feet
Her feet just so big they don't play by the rules / And
I cannot cope 'less them hams is in shoes . . .

'You're a goddess,' he said later. 'You make me feel like I'm the best version of me.'

For her part, it seemed impossible she'd ever been told to watch for being *too much* – too argumentative, too questioning, too sensitive – by her parents. Too 'full of ideas above your station' by the teachers not her beloved head-of-art Mrs Sanders, 'bearing in mind where you come from'. By boys who hadn't wanted her but said she was 'fucking great. Like a woman who's also a bit of a bloke'. A backhanded compliment – it meant she could hold her own in a conversation and had a mind that evidently matched theirs, so Stephen said – and one she took, but still smarted at. She took comfort her best girlfriend was the same: how many pints and games of pool where they slurred to one another *If you were a bloke, I'd bloody fucking marry you.*

But she was aware now of her talent, her potential, her passions full of this new adult voice of hers. Protests, marches. Free Nelson Mandela and Fuck Off Clause 28.

'I love a woman with a mouth on her,' Guitar True-Love said another time. 'I love how you're not scared to say what you think, care about, how you just get gobby and speak up, speak out. I want to sing you all the time, Claire. I want to fucking *rock* your gypsy soul.'

He hadn't known then it was one of her favourite songs: how it spoke to her of her the agelessness of the sun, sea, her secret woods; the shed skin of forest in her hair when she lay on its crackling floor shortly after their first real date and slid her hand to find herself so slippery her orgasm felt like spinning silk.

Hours just talking, laughing, unearthing thoughts and realizations to catch the light, marvelling at this horde of secret treasure as they stared at skies that turned the world upside down; sheets of summer black littered with crumbs of stars. With him she learned the erotica of kissing; dizzying, sweet intoxication that left her face sore to simple water. The urgency of him left her breathless; passion that matched her own for the whole of him, as yet still caged in the electrified bars of the unconsummated. Despite, or even because of that, her heart opened as the flower of her cervix once had. One late summer dusky evening, a hot day softened to shadow and swoop, they stared into each other's eyes as she sat astride him staring and kissing, kissing and staring, deep in each other below the ombre of a September moon. She would never again feel such unsullied intimacy.

The actual act hadn't been all that at first. Issues. Nerves. Not that it mattered. It seemed there'd be no end to the falling, like the long summer before they all migrated off to uni. She loved him, *loved* him; taught him how to sexually love a woman.

They fitted – body, mind; how he held, kissed, touched her. It was pure. It was beautiful. It was never just about the sex.

Return to sender.

Three of the worst words she would ever read in her life.

She left for uni first, his accommodation problematic, not yet assigned. To this day she'd no idea how she managed to give him the wrong postcode. A world of no mobile phones, then: he thought she hadn't replied to his letter, a storybook mistake rectified on a mid-term trip home, followed by a heady weekend in his Edinburgh halls; so in love she didn't know how to say it for fear he no longer felt the same (*sender has lost heart?*), that he'd say they should make the most of this new life and not chain themselves down like his older sister: 'Talk about "Too Much Too Young" . . .'

The power and the danger of words unsaid.

Three years of (hard, intermittent) friendship later before she'd tell him how much she'd loved him; both drunk, him confessing his terror of her hurting him, too: why, that first Christmas, he ended it. For the rest of her life, if only occasionally, gently prodded by something seen, read, heard, she'd wonder what was in his letter.

The seam of her altered after that – broken and glued, yes. But never the same.

*

The light was beginning to fade, a half-moon low at one side of the sky: a side-on jellyfish in the cloudy sea of blues, blacks, smoky silvers. She wished she could swim out to it.

She used to swim so much, younger. Rivers, lakes, open-air pools, anywhere devoid of chlorine; queen of them all, the sea.

'So good at control, you and me.' Emma's voice ricocheted around her head. 'And look how we ended up.'

How impossible it seemed, after all those years of marriage, motherhood, demises and deaths, that she'd once been the carefree girl whose only control issues had to do with avoiding pregnancy.

She looked at the text from Ben: *just checking in*. Wondered how he was outside the *good days, not so good days, busy. Staying positive.*

Admittedly, at times adult control had looked a lot like fast-tracking herself a Diploma in Drinking Solo. But it felt, at some point, like all she had for company as she'd watch Ben watching TV, envying his ability to lower his antennae, let go, lose himself so easily.

There is no loneliness like married loneliness. At least alone there's no expectation: that lack of another underlined in **big black boldface** every time she entered or left a room. The feeling that it really, really shouldn't be like this.

At least by now she understood so much of life worked like any other theory on the expansion of time: things can only go so far forward before they begin turning back on themselves. Strange, though, how it still felt selfish to focus on herself after all those years of growing boys and goodbyes, rarely reaching out because that's what *flaky people* did.

But how to survive this particular pruning – how to be an individual, how to be a woman?

She looked at the patch of earth around a primrose not yet in flower, a little 'oh' escaping her at the sight of the striated purple and white flower on the spindly crocus she'd cleared around earlier, the soil still so raw she wanted to wrap it up like a baby. She hoped it would survive. It wasn't always true that whatever doesn't kill you makes you stronger.

Or not at first, at least.

April

Pink Moon – Full

It felt thrilling, slightly illicit, to be here on a weekday. She hadn't been to the seaside alone in years. How many times had she fantasized, after all those people online, offline, *everywhere*, about winter water blessing her brain with positive clarity? It made her brave. Or enough to take her shoes off, at least. Middle-aged women went rite-of-passaging in arctic water all the time – it was practically law. One way or another she *would* claim herself back.

The tussocked stretch of Suffolk coast was as ever-changing as its tides, beach and cliffs gnawed by insatiable saline hunger, though swathes of sand were still spiked with the marram Claire remembered as a child. The sea, like the early spring day, lapped gentle, despite the recent storm echoed in shore shingle, black as coal, edging the bay she'd set her sights on. Her morning had started equally gently: a frost sweet-sharp as sugar on a cocktail glass breaking into sun that lit Tansy's catkins to acid yellow, sprayed the white of Claire's cherry blossom halfway over the sky. Small wonder frost was personified as male, just as the sun was an 'unruly' or benevolent him. Women were moon, boat: things governed by water – though if she drew them, they'd be the tiny swords of ice fringing metal. Fragile enough a touch would melt them, but with hidden power to rip skin from a careless finger or tongue.

She held her foot sideways, wiggled her big toe at the tongue-tip of a wave – *Jesus!* –immediately snatching it back as if it burned. This was insanity, surely.

Right. Here was the deal: if she managed to get in, she'd treat herself afterwards. Coffee. Cake. You couldn't move in Suffolk for local butter, eggs, honey; there had to be local cake? Perhaps it would even nudge her to engage with people again. She'd promised Jules and Asha she'd join them for Jules's birthday with the women they wanted her to meet; strangers and solitude still so much easier. No *Do you get lonely/regret leaving Ben? How are you off for money; what will you do about a pension? Do you think you'll ever be able to get a mortgage again?* Yes/no, both, depending on the day. Badly; fuck knows. Ditto. *So, when will you divorce?* We can't afford it, bought ourselves a year to help Joe to finish uni. *When do you think you'll date again? And Ben – what if he falls in love with someone else?*

Christ. That word again. That *idea* again.

A sigh. Not at the sentiment, but for the fact menopause, *age*, granted the unexpected, if nothing else. It wasn't that you didn't have the inconvenient emotion any more, just that you no longer tried to hide it from yourself.

Fuck's sake – woman up, Claire. She would get in, she *would*.

Her swimming costume was old, bobbled, and crackled under her clothes; almost a cackle, it seemed, as she disrobed, briefly mussed by static. She supposed people had wetsuits for weather like this, but – positives – if she did have heart failure at the cold, she'd surely be easier to defibrillate in a knackered old Speedo? She fought the instinct of her breath as goosebumps pimpled her, walked to the water's edge.

An involuntary *fuck!* just at immersing both feet, hands flapping at her sides like a reminder to her lungs of how to work. She waded a little further, breath jagged in her chest, bones squealing in her knees.

'Fuck! *Fuck*!'

Why did people do this? She forced herself to breathe as the water bit her calves, as her whole body screamed, her heart threatening to pump into overload. Another 'FUCK!' as she urged herself an inch deeper, another inch – she could do this, she could. Her thighs were trying to retract: the softer the skin, the harder her body leapt to get away from the teeth.

But she was doing it, she was!

Bold, she strode a little further forward, knowing the real test was yet to come – the groin, belly, navel – trying to draw her shoulders back down from her ears – *breathe!* – think of the monks and (mad) men and women who sat in snow to meditate.

Something brushed her calf then: softly sinuous, sneaky-slimy.

She screamed, kicking the leg, then the other leg, blundering on the ripples of sand and stone under her feet, splashing her hips, waist, body arching with the sheer shock of cold, of fear. She turned, trying to stride, managing only to blunder-fall back to shore: ice at her belly, hands in sand, knees stubbing shingle – *fuck that, fuck this shit, fuck fucking everything!* – in the scrabble to get out, get a towel, clothes, get to the car.

Get away from something else she used to love that she really, really didn't love now.

*

His laugh. The fine line between confidence and arrogance he walks as easily as he steams the incandescent red of hot metal to black with one plunge into water, one loud hiss. Sometimes he reminds me of Guitar True-Love. Sometimes The Poet. Never Ben. Not even when we talk life, art, and yes, my dreams. At others he makes me think of electricity cables arcing in a storm.

'I know it's what you'd like to do.'

The way his sooted forearms flex and his lips part, hair a dagger of fringe at his cheek, head bent to the fireworks of hammer, arms rippled, veined, swelling into the black T-shirt tight around the tattoo. The space between stubble and shoulder glistens where his hair is tied back. The mesmerizing fire; the glow, the heart, the heat.

'Of course I'd *like* to! But there's a difference if you have integrity between what you want to and what you *will* do.' A scroll of me unrolling that isn't a script I feel I've read a hundred times. I can't see the words at all until they land like winged insects right in front of me.

He walks towards me; smiles that confident-arrogant smile. 'What is it about women and control – I'm asking, in your wisdom, why you think it is?'

What is happening to *my* control that is here but not here? I can't believe my shake as I instruct my face to perform its best vanilla. 'Well, we have a lot of practice.'

'And then you can't let go easily?'

'Something like that.' How to explain? I am only just realizing, as he looks at me, eyes intense on mine, something dormant in me is waking. It thrills and terrifies me.

A finger at my chin as he bends to kiss me.

Shock. 'No! No. No. I can't do this, I didn't mean to give—'

'Fuck. Look, I'm sorry.'

'It's me. I didn't mean . . . I shouldn't have . . .'

'No. It's me. I couldn't stop myself. I just want to fuck you, Claire.'

*

Go away. Get out of my head. I don't want you.

The papers peeled apart like pressed leaves, each leaving a faint imprint on the one before as they flipped and curled on the carpet like landed fish. She still couldn't believe she'd shifted all the furniture and boxes in that hell-garage to get to her easel, her rolls of old paintings. But how long since she'd seen her O level artwork, full of its pencil still lives including, bizarrely, hairdressing items: a bristle brush, tongs, a wide-toothed comb, a pintail mafia-stiletto one, even the old hairdryer her mother broke hitting Claire's head in a row during the worst of her illness. She could still make out the tiny paper-pimples of fierce erasing, the cracks snitching on over-painting and under-confidence: a diary, of sorts. Another roll disgorged hidden innards: sketches, postcard illustrations, sentimental memories ripped, jag-toothed, from her notebooks. This wasn't just a diary, she saw now. It was therapy.

Her fingers landed on her tribute to Escher's *Three Worlds* of water, fish, trees; the lithograph so loved in adolescence.

But her rendering was no calm leaf on limpid lake: her trees were white, gnarly, leaves bent black hearts, and her fish had closed eyes, an inverted-rainbow mouth. She'd added a jetty, too, a Perspex box, the shadow-shape of a girl inside. A pinch to the heart. Hiding in plain sight: there hadn't been any other way to say it.

But here, almost as if another artist had taken over, a resurgence. And how.

Those self-portraits. The bravery of her experiments with colour, using only angular shapes in blood reds or indigo blues, her favourites. Here, a poster for the sixth form board: an African woman's head, at once proud and beaten, her chain-patterned headscarf knotted to a locked padlock. She remembered painting it – her own headscarf, her arm full of jangling bangles, 'Sun City' on her stereo. And here – look! – her tribute to Greenham Common, the 'hairy dykes' as her father called them; a bright red sky, a dark green fence, midnight-blue women holding hands, peace signs for faces, white doves filling the shape of their bodies.

*

The sky is the thing that comes first. It has to be red – who wants blue? *Boring.* White clouds? *Dull.* Green grass? *Boring, boring, boring,* she tells herself in Rik's voice from *The Young Ones*. A thrum runs through her. Anything is possible: in art, but also life. Female comedians talking periods, sperm, thrush, anti-discrimination laws hitting the news, she and other girls badgering school for self-defence classes; *equality feminism* buzzwords.

'What's that when it's at home?' says her grandmother. Though later she tells Claire, 'You must make the most of your education. I'd have given me right arm just for the pill.'

It saddens her to think of her matriarchs bound in marriage and not always to one beloved, restrained by pregnancies, money, by washdays and mangles, fierce stoves and forever trying to feed; never enough, and never enough money to change it.

She cleans her brush, mixes blues, greens, black, starts again.

She wants the Greenham women centre stage, thinks of hearts as bodies, but then, isn't it women's hearts that cause the trouble? She has no illusions, for all the mags shouting how to snare a man: both grandmothers spoke of women on beds they were told (sharply) they'd made. She knows, too, of husbands beating wives and some vice versa; has never forgotten the one slamming into a pub after closing, the sting of slaps before they pulled her off the *fucking lying cheating bastard*. So many different colours of love. There are, of course, her parents; united at eighteen by a love of dancing, incomprehensible as it is. 'Oh, I had ambitions,' her mother said, several times. 'Loved English, art. But I had to leave at fifteen to work, and that was that.' That tiny twist of mouth. 'I always thought there'd be a later.'

When divorce breaks like a rash and women get big shoulders and even bigger hair to boldface this new Bigness in the world, she watches that VW chick shuck off a fur, chuck diamonds in a canal, thinks *Yes! Right on!* Fuck marriage. She will not be a How Did I Get Here like the sad-drunk Alice Coopers in the pub. That, that sporadic-sunshine-English-weather marriage, no, she'll never be that. Her bangles tinkle as her mind trammels this and hand works brush. Here no need to dream escape, or riff on staying childless so she never has to hear *I didn't ask to be born!* No hurt in head or heart at broken hairdryers, the spittle in a mother's mouth. Here is pure, wild, free. Empty of all but colour, joy, expression. Love.

'If you don't take risks, you will never grow as an artist,' her tutor tells her in her first university term. He's older than most tutors, slightly arch, has Mrs Double-Barrelled's voice. 'But that is not to say you don't have much to learn about form. *You can't break the rules, you know, until you really understand what they are.* Picasso.'

She didn't know that; feels small, humiliated. A country mouse: a *hedgemumbly*.

Leaving home is both relief and shock. A woman doctor put Claire's mother on HRT in June, and by September's end there is less time in bed, less complaint of pain, more garden pottering with that familiar engrossed frown. Smiles. Still times a whatever-ache takes a day away but talk, too, of going back to work; still relatively young, Claire urging her softly to *get a life, Mum.* And though she enjoys the freedom of city life, the shock comes in seeing not the shrinking size of fish she'd been, but just how small the pond. Everyone is talented. And nearly everyone is public schooled. She struggled to balance a tightrope of feeling she didn't belong – students pretending penury alongside that unconscious cultural capital she can never inherit – and her desire to connect deeper with art. She's the first in her family ever to go. Back home, working in pubs, people from primary school ignore her. She leans back into dialect, calls uni *college*; feels a new loneliness that sometimes sneaks into her art.

'Risks can be ugly,' the same tutor says in summer term,

when she confesses she can't afford to keep wasting materials. 'They can fail; feel pointless. But in art, nothing is wasted. Practised, yes. What you perceive as 'failure' is often the only way to prise the oyster open, find the unique quality of the pearl. One must ask if one wishes to be artist or painter: they are not always the same. Art can be commercial, while painting more Van Gogh.'

'At least I could sell a pearl?' She snuffs a little laugh, pleading with her eyes for understanding.

He peers at her over his half-moons. '*I would rather die of passion than boredom* – also Van Gogh.' He smiles. 'I like you, Claire, and I like your work this year, I admire your energy, your passion. You're talented. You could go far.'

She is excited by that, refuses to listen to the naysayers in her head that *yeah right* her. Why shouldn't she be the one to exhibit herself one day? Why not?

It takes a year just to get used to university. To lose the not-really friends of the first people met, find cheaper rooms, work. To feel her deep desire to challenge, take risks, to come to love a city, this new, wider way of life. To trust herself, artistically. And otherwise.

Risks can be ugly. But so could stagnation. Hadn't she tackled that leaving Ben? And hadn't he, leaving the country? Ben who, before she knew him, left as often as he could, always saving to see this, climb that, a passport so visa stuck-and-stamped its pages clicked like a photo album.

She picked up a brush. She might shrivel and squeal instead of being the sea swimmer of her dreams, but she was still in here somewhere.

In her head: colour that screams louder than fear, shapes that don't always make sense. The black of the clouds crossing the moon, the tobacco smoke of their downlit edges, the gold of that cat's spine. The pokes of green that gave her a hope she couldn't explain as she worked her garden or walked the fattening lanes; all the noise given, perhaps, to the fight against entropy, dormancy. Death. So much of that in the past seven years. Three parents, Ben's sister, his own cancer scare, Danny's viral meningitis. She'd had the grief counselling, but Ben never wanted to, swinging instead from 'You and the kids are everything to me' to:

'Forget it. I don't want an argument.'

'Why are you assuming there'll be an argument?'

'Because whenever I try and say what I . . . Oh, forget it. No, actually. It's just, I cannot *believe* you had the last apple, Claire.'

A flash of when they first lived together: how he'd pull her leggings down if she got annoyed with him. How she'd laugh despite herself. *You're such a dick!*

'It's just I find that quite selfish. You know I'm trying to be healthier, with my cancer risk, and you eating it means I can't. I just think it might've been nice if you'd asked.'

'Right. So, let me get this straight. I'm selfish because I ate the last apple? When I didn't know you wanted it because you never eat them – and you didn't say?'

'See, you're doing it already! Every time I try and say what I think you *dismiss* me. So *typical* of you – always trying to wing it back to me.'

'This is about an apple, Ben. I'll buy more stupid bloody apples.'

'It's not just about that, though, is it? Can't get your head round, can't you *see* it might just be nice to have a wife who'd say, *Darling, is it all right if I have the last apple?*'

She'd thought of all she did during his sister's cancer, then with his mother. The obvious, yes, but all the unseen, too: the anti-heroic of the domestic, the weight of kids and the wider life they'd grown together on her shoulders like the pails of an old-style milkmaid. 'Right. And you don't think you're being *maybe* just a little over-sensitive here?'

'Fine. It's all me. The ball's in your court, okay? I'm not playing any more of your games, Claire. You win, okay? Happy now? Now go and fuck up someone else's day.'

Win. She'd almost laughed out loud. Win *what*, exactly – what was her prize?

She shook her head, reminding herself what was in it. Yes: loose, free shapes. Colour. The tiny gold glints that hinted at the riches of liberation. Almost medieval, or Caravaggio.

She closed her eyes. Opened them again. On the paper in front of her: sludge, mud, silt, nicotine stains and some sort of amorphous mess that reminded her of a failed pie.

She threw down her brush and walked to the window, rubbing her hands, waiting for the Pink Hour to kick in: the heating that would rid her skin of its corned beef tinge for sixty blissful minutes. She hadn't realized how late it was until she saw the moon, a big, blushing circle in a strange, cement-blue sky. She pressed her face to the glass.

How beautiful it hung over the spread of field, so low it felt as if the sky were offering her a pendant. A gift. A forever thing like a precious stone; older than anyone alive, than the oaks it sat above, equalled only by the stars. Equally free, too, from ever being truly possessed. The closest she'd come to that was reading until lunchtime in bed at weekends like her student self; except the tea wasn't made with powdered milk and the sheets were a high thread count heaven. Fantasies made real, like leaving a house and coming home again, or going downstairs from work to find a house exactly as she left it. And equally two-faced: a home that could prod out either a smile – or a lonely, silent scream.

Fuck it.

She walked downstairs, poured her glass half full. Maybe the old adage was true and if she saw it – like the brain recognized the forty-three muscles involved in smiling, even if you felt like jumping off a cliff – perhaps she could actually *be* it? She walked back upstairs. Picked up her brush.

'Well, the old place breathes,' Tansy said, when Claire pointed out how much her ancient house creaked. 'Old places do. And to give a thing air is to give it life, is it not?' It shifted and cracked constantly in the nascent spring sun. Claire was used to gutters as plastic warmed, but The Forge seemed to randomly belch out noise whenever it felt like it.

Perhaps Tansy's mercurial rudeness was as infectious as her sketches. She'd *hmphed* when Claire rang the bell, held the door ajar grumpily: 'You're *early*.'

Claire had checked her watch. 'Only by seven minutes?'

'But, nonetheless, seven minutes earlier than *arranged*.' A pause she hadn't quite known how to deal with, before: 'Well. *Suppose* you'd better come in, then.'

She'd have said not to bother, *actually*, if she hadn't been so thrown.

'Though I do agree,' Tansy continued now after a sip of

water, 'it is funny how a thing can look so old one can't possibly imagine it capable of continuing to *live* – I should know.' She snorted a little laugh. 'Did I tell you Marie Curie emailed, asking if I'd like to join their Jump for Joy campaign – thirty "star" jumps a day and a T-shirt if I raise enough. Ha. But in any case, you don't so much live in an old place like this as marry the blasted thing. One has to learn not just to love it, but *how*. Its language, its peccadilloes – such as what happens when it rains solidly for a month, or winter is arctic, or summer infernal.'

Claire thought of her painting. She didn't actually hate it, but she didn't particularly love it, either. No real composition, physically or in silent words. No certainty of what it was saying. 'I thought you said it was lovely and cool in summer?'

'Oh, it is – or will be,' said Tansy. 'Almost like the air conditioning we had in Kenya growing up.' She pronounced it *Keenya*, and had only intermittently mentioned her childhood – the colonial house, servants, heat, flies, spiders, snakes (the only creature she seemed to fear) – which left Claire with an awed wistfulness for the romanticism of those TV serials she'd so loved when she was younger. It struck her she'd still like to see Africa for herself one day.

'No, it's more if the heat goes on or it's a prolonged dry spell. The wood shrinks and things drop off, out, or simply seize up. So yes, breathe it does,' said Tansy. 'To the point one sometimes wants to stick its head in a bucket of water and wait for the legs to stop kicking.'

She went on to explain how the house shifted every season, year, and Claire couldn't help looking to where ceiling met wall or wall met chimney or wood met lathe: an endless succession of capillaries, veins, arteries; as if the snaking old staircase was its spine, holding the ribcage of beams in place to protect its lungs, the beat of it. So old, yet so much life. She could see what Tansy meant.

'You'll see the difference air makes yourself soon,' Tansy added, 'after all your weeding. No plant can survive being choked to death by invaders. Unless it *is* an invader, of course. I imagine you're starting to get to those now: the ground elder, the bindweed?'

'I'm still unsure what they are. Can't I just spray some old shit and hope for the best?'

Tansy laughed, flinching almost simultaneously – 'Oh, you do make me smile, Claire!' – before she sat back with a sighing grimace. 'Well, of course. If they're of the dandelion variety and the leaves don't interfere with anything. Piss on the *pis-en-lit*, I say. But don't do that with the elder unless it's in isolation, you'll just kill the plant it's invading.'

It was the second time only she'd heard Tansy swear and something inside Claire felt able to breathe better, whatever it said about her. Ironic. She stopped smoking to achieve that, but all that seemed to have happened recently was she'd forgotten how to inhale and exhale properly – and on the positive side of smoking, she'd always managed that pretty efficiently. But Tansy also looked tired; a whiter shade of grey, eyes rimmed red. Claire offered to bring a duvet and pillows down for the sofa, apologized for taking so much time.

'Nap on the *settee*?' Tansy wrinkled her face. 'You'll be asking if I should like a sherry for breakfast next!' She waved a hand. 'As for time, not at all – a delight to see you, as always. And it'll give the plants the best chance before you get to the real stuff: pruning, *planting*. And then you can invite me for tea so we may admire it *ensemble*. I should very much like that when dratted mobility allows.'

'I should get some tansy in there, in that case, if—'

'Good Lord, why on earth would you do that?'

'Er. Your namesake?'

'Well, if you do, I'd ask you to wait until I'm dead' – Tansy looked skywards. 'Oh, happy day!' – 'given that of its meanings, the main include hostility and declarations of war. Other than that, I'm happy to say it could be a hope for good health or a preservative for meat. Which includes corpses.' Another glance up. 'Are you hearing this?'

Claire smiled, despite herself. Ben's mother was obsessed with death for years, long before the dementia that laced her brain after his sister died nullified her. They found notes all over her house: tucked behind mirrors, in drawers; the legacy, perhaps, of a husband who left nothing in place. She remembered the aftermath of her own parents' deaths: her dad's terrible stroke, her mother's heart attack hard on its heels; how glad to have that will, some sense of direction. Perhaps it was the scar of childhood poverty, but her mother was always adamant the i's were dotted, the t's crossed.

'Have you spoken to Hope, by the way?' She tried to sound casual. 'You probably should. Perhaps she's just worried.'

Tansy raised an eyebrow. 'Worried. Ha! No, I intend to let the niece wait until she thinks I'm dead and then surprise her. It'll give me something to look forward to.'

Claire laughed, reminded of a mouse their old cat caught once; how, despite it being only the size of the cat's ear, it reared up on its hind legs and tried to fight back.

'Oh, and if you can bear it,' Tansy added, 'do leave the nettles until the last minute? They're a sign of nitrogen being present.'

'Right,' said Claire. 'Not that that means anything to me, but I can always google it while I'm slapping the dock leaves on the stings.'

'Oh, I know they're thugs and they tend to come at one in gangs replete with flick-knives, but – like most nasty events, one learns – they are very, *very* good for the soil.'

At first she had thought Tansy said 'soul'. Though for all Claire knew, as she stared at patch after patch, nettles might well be good for the soul. Perhaps she'd end up smoking them to find out when she hit the point of covering herself in woad and dancing round her firepit instead of her speaker, drunk in the kitchen. Not an entirely unwelcome thought.

She looked at the dandelions. *Pis-en-lit*. The little green star didn't look capable of harm, unlike the savage spikes, already evident if only embryonic, of the sow thistle next to it. But even she knew the truth behind the old dares: a diuretic that really could make a person piss a bed. Or at least piss more than usual; never good news for a woman her age. Although she was no longer averse to the wild wee, did one, in fact, whenever she could now. At first she'd told herself it was easier than faffing with boots and coats, but now she did it purely for the bizarre, if airy, feeling of freedom. According to Tansy, *pis-en-lit* was also as powerful as many modern drugs: 'Weeds are so often like that. Take the wretched ground elder, the bindweed, both as deceptive as they are pernicious,' she'd warned. 'Rather like anything that's pretty and likes to spread itself about.'

Wasn't that the truth.

'One must always be mindful even a weed holds gifts,' Tansy went on. 'Ground elder, you know, is very high in vitamin C – used in Europe for centuries as edible salad. I believe they still do in green borscht in Ukraine. Here, we used it to clarify beer naturally. Thank the Romans for that, they ate it like spinach. And I can attest it is rather tasty in a quiche.'

'And bindweed?' Claire had asked. 'Surely not. Even I know it's a royal pain in—'

'—the proverbial, yes. But it will protect the soil by *binding* if it's dry and loose, see. The Navajo used it for their digestive issues among other delights – spider bites, even heavy menstruals. You know, I read online the other day it's actually being looked into now for its potential to strangle the blood supply to tumours. Fascinating, don't you think?'

What to say to all that? 'And so now I can't hate it the way I want to?'

Tansy had laughed. 'Of course you can. So damned self-*aggrandizing*, these perennial weeds. But then . . .' she had such a charming, girlish smile at times ' . . . they do look *so* pretty when they're young.'

*

Practically from the first time she encountered The Poet, he irritated her.

Pretty, yes, but also over-opinionated, argumentative, full of himself. It wouldn't have mattered a year before, as she tried to forget her heartbreak via the medium of comfort-shagging – nice, but no dice – but later she'd find herself wondering about the unconscious carbon-copy search for the one who set the type.

The Poet was dark like Guitar True-Love, but different-dark. Brooding in an intense, Mediterranean and slightly menacing way, thick of forearm and hair, given to backcombing, occasional eyeliner (as if that wasn't warning enough?), pretentious fags; a reasonable poet but a less than mediocre actor.

What flutters as a red flag at the start of a relationship rarely shows itself as green later, however much hope a heart holds: what is seed will likely have roots by the end.

She felt annoyed The Poet got a role with the happy group she was helping to paint sets for since she'd cleaned up her own act, and binned the pill that made her fat, nauseous, moody, brutally mugged her breasts. Her cycle was back to a moon-driven tide of nipples pierced by needles, ovulation pains, lubrication that saw her squirrel spare knickers as a fixture in her bag. Of musk-smelling sweat and desperate masturbation. She missed sex so badly she laughed when a stage manager asked how she knew she wasn't gay. She tried that, too, hopeful, but didn't like it enough to see it through.

She was creatively fulfilled, however; despite or because of a nine-month sexual desert. Art and design suited her well; its patchwork curricula matched her desire to sample everything on the art menu. Over-ambitiously, she even attempted a Grecian-triptych twist on an old screen hanging around the studio, kept it smaller then: crafted earrings in geometric shapes from indigo titanium, sculpted a pyramidical vase she kept dried *Stachys* in and which she lugged from room to room alongside her spider plants and prints: Matisse, O'Keeffe, Cezanne's *Bathers*, Van Gogh's *Starry Night*, her postcards from the Belle Epoque and posters of her favourite bands; making herself at home quickly a skill she would never lose.

A one-night stand was not her plan. She wasn't drunk, they merely lived in the same part of town and frequently walked home together for her safety, and sometimes – looking at his arty array of berets and fisherman's hats – his. Plus, she'd been on her period.

I want to be inside you so much.

There was something in the way he didn't recoil, revulsed, by the blood. Though it was still the first time she ever faked orgasm, and the last. She didn't know how, but The Poet knew a woman's body, and he knew when it was lying, despite what she said.

Despite.

Despite his *car crash of a previous relationship.*

Despite the fact she *still deeply loved* her ex.

Despite how, the first time they did it properly, some days later, they came at the same explosive time and couldn't stop staring at one another in disbelief at *the fuck of the century.*

Despite, kissing his cheek later still, his accusation she was *getting kissy and involved.*

She didn't want to hear it. So she didn't.

They fucked and fucked and fucked. Beds, kitchens, bathrooms, hallways, doorways, trains, car parks, parks, riverbanks, woods, a ruined abbey, even; the more the merrier. Whole weekends. During one of her heaviest periods, even – leaving her crippled afterwards, scared she'd done something irrevocable to her innards.

It seemed to her then that sexual appetite and its fulfilment were vital for creativity – or hers, in any case – that without either, her soul felt somehow trapped inside a dusty husk where light fell only in spangled shafts. Art was making sense, all its forms were making sense and her intellect equalled the hunger of her body, as growing things do before they bloom. There was an honesty, too, to that kind of sex: so much of it as unconscious as the birds that twitterfied trees in spring. Chemistry, she'd thought. Though chemistry in its purest form was a study of change – the first fuck the catalyst – so whatever the truths were, whatever he said, she said, he always ended up fucking her. For all she was worth.

Funny turn of phrase, that.

*

Claire threw the largest dandelion on the weed heap, where it sat straggly, toothy leaves snarling, and began on another with a veg knife that had just the right sort of blade to slide beside, under, dig with force. The blade jarred at grit and stones as hair fell across her face, in her eyes, strands drifting into her nostrils until she swiped at them in anger with a muddy glove.

Desire – such a complicated, complex animal. And it was animal. It could frighten with its primeval power, the way it could turn from fun to flex the scimitar of its claws.

For so long a mantra: *The first time he hit me, it was my fault.*

*

'I am not going to have sex with you.'

'I don't mean that badly,' The Poet goes on. 'But lovers and friends are not the same, and I don't want a relationship. But I think you do.'

They're in his student flats; a tatty Victorian row of beige walls, window sashes enemy to frames, staircases that smell of pubs the morning after. The bed she sits on overlooks broken-toothed buildings where students rub shoulders with sex workers, drug dealers, and she wonders briefly who is in the business of sex below.

'Please don't tell me what I think,' she says, turning to him. Above his head, the stark wavy lines of the black-and-white Joy Division poster make her feel crackly inside.

A grimace. 'Look, last week when Seren was here – just don't pretend you weren't checking up on me. I know you don't want me to fuck her, I'm not sure she does, to be honest. But I want to be able to if she does, and I want to stay being your friend, too.'

Smarting, unsure how much of this is true, aware anything she voices is pressing a thumb to peanut brittle, she keeps her voice level. 'No offence. But even if I did, how would there be room for me *and* your ego?'

Well, she sounded good at least; she should go. Her gaze falls to a mug by his bed, stained as an old smoker's teeth, the grey dandruff of his overflowing ashtray. Why is she even here? Notes he wanted from her theatre design day, ostensibly. She had tried to stay away. And yet the more she did, the more he chased her 'friendship', insisting today on coffee, food, wine. Still time for the last bus. She can't afford more taxis this term.

'It's not my ego.' He shrugs. 'I like you, I really do. And – *that* – is really fucking good. And I'm fine as long as you're not too near me in or on a bed.'

'Thank you,' she says, cold, slamming notes into her folder. 'How lovely.'

An arm out to stop her leaving. 'I didn't mean to upset you. I was just being honest.'

Now she glares. 'What's upsetting me is your bloody arrogance, actually. Do you honestly think I'm just *waiting* for you to be my boyfriend? Like I'm too ugly or sad to get anyone else – is that what you think?'

'No – you're making me sound . . . It's just you *make* yourself so—'

'What – I'm easy, too, now? The Bully bonus being I'm also a good shag?'

'I didn't say that. But every time I see you, you do the eyes thing—'

'You mean that thing I do to *see* stuff?'

A hand flourish. 'The whole, I don't know, *come hither* thing.'

She laughs, incredulous. 'Come *hither*! What the—' But her bottom lip is beginning to tremble, innards holding her as if squeezing through a too-tight gap.

His palms up. 'And I'm weak – *mea culpa*.'

Mea culpa. Who in the name of anything said *mea* fucking *culpa*? 'Right. Bye, then.'

'Wait. Please? I don't want to leave it like this.'

She snuffs. 'It? There is no *it*.'

He's a dickhead, a twat, loser, user. A bastard. Not a patch on other men she's had more than just the once. And nothing – *nothing* – on the one she still loves.

His eyes, as he looks at her, half contrite, are huge. Intense. The black-brown of the Quink he fills his pen with. 'Don't be like this. Pissy. You're far too good for that.' She gestures fingers down her throat and he laughs. 'And you make me smile.'

I make you smile, and you make me want to cry. Whoopee-fucking-doo. 'So. I'm off.'

'At least finish your fag,' he says. 'You'll have missed the bus now anyway.'

She smiles, sarcastic, stabs it in his ashtray. He's looking at her like that first time; when she asked why, and he said he was wondering if he could kiss her. Oxygen catches the smoulder in her. But will she fuck be told when and how and *come-hither* eyes. 'I'll walk.'

'You're staying. I've got more shit wine to share. And I want your friendship, Claire.'

Her own shrug now. 'Whatever. But I'll need a nightshirt. For the floor.'

'Help yourself,' he says. 'One caveat – nothing to make you look sexy.'

She riffles through his wardrobe. A black shirt that would show off her breasts, neck, just enough of her arse. *Watch it and weep, dickhead.* 'Even if I did,' she says. 'Not. A. Chance.'

An hour later she stares into those ink-drop eyes as they climax simultaneously.

Fury.

With her stupid self for lacking strength, dignity. For wanting him to want her. Fury he plays her body like a maestro. Fury too now after they've argued about whether friends can be lovers, he's told her she's naive, stupid, made himself a mute mountain of back. 'Y'know, sometimes you disgust me,' he said in the heat of it. 'You lie and you're a time thief. Making me do things I wouldn't ordinarily. You're pathetic.'

It hurt so much it stunned her. If so vile, why sleep with her? And who gave him the right to talk to her that way then say she can't talk now? She speaks his name. Again. Again.

He ignores her still.

She pokes his back, says his name again.

Nothing.

So she pokes it harder.

The fist glances off her eye socket, catching the top of her cheek, the side of her skull. Lucky, she would think later. Strange word to use, she will think much, much later still.

Shock freezes her for short seconds before she shoots into the bathroom, door locked, shaking. Shock like being slapped. Breathless, dizzy. Horror. Disbelief. His voice at the door. *Sorry. Shocked. Horrified at himself. Please, please, please* come out.

She cries, rails. But she pushed to a point of no return, he tells her.

'You stole my sanity,' he says sadly. 'Your . . . *insisting*. Lover-like. Don't you see?'

She sniffs, quieter. She doesn't know. No. It doesn't give him the right. Or *is* it her?

'I was half asleep,' he goes on, urgent, pleading. 'Having a dream I was under attack – it's happened, sort of, once before. In a row with my ex when she was pushing it. I just sort of came to with my hands on her neck, but I didn't know I was doing it. Don't you see?'

She did. She shouldn't have pushed it, like he said. Her mother used to say that, too.

He holds her as she cries, kisses her, apologizes, makes a tender kind of love to her. She watches his hand work her. Stares at it again as he sleeps and rests it on her waist.

If a dog bites a human, she remembers her father saying, you should put it down because something too wolfish, wild, has been unleashed and you can never trust it again.

*

She jabbed the old veg knife at the earth, punishing soil, stone, root. Here was the thing about those men: the bastards, heartbreakers, all the sexy bad boys. A solid, sordid fact.

The undeniable way you watched other women watch him; the sparking reaction he induced, particularly if schooled in the art of seduction. It worked like a pheromone, as if he reeked of it – not the same as beauty, nor dependent on it. Better-looking people existed. So yes, sordid, if you could face yourself to admit it. You the one he'd *Don't go* so something in you sings. *Meaning matters, and you mean*; you the cat with creamy whiskers. So good at sex, too – and, oh, how they knew you knew that. What you refused to accept, whichever palatable picture you chose to paint for yourself, was that he would get bored, eventually. You were not *the others*; he's *different now*. So what point – sensation, row, erotica – was it that set the little sword above your head at every other woman arm touch, dance, mistletoe-kiss; every laugh or pass of a glass?

Bad enough young, let alone in middle age. Hadn't she learned all those years ago just what, when something was opened, and not easily, it cost to shut it off again?

But then it had started with The Poet. Really started. Creeping up like the growing leaves she looked at now. Corkscrewing deeper like the root she couldn't. She felt as if digging into soil had unearthed a coffin, and not one buried in hallowed ground.

Your whistling days are over.

If only you could breathe into yourself the advice you hold after half a century of life. You couldn't have listened in your twenties: your wisdom wasn't wise.

A tear slid down Claire's cheek, dripped off her chin, making her angry, her swipes futile. It was her memory she wanted to wipe, watch wilt with this other pile her knife was winkling out. She'd thought these memories were buried deep as a daffodil bulb – as out of place in this sunshine as finding yourself singing a Christmas carol in July.

No choice but to accept. But with acceptance comes truth, and the truth was she felt she was going backwards, the battles baited as a gin trap on a woodland floor.

She stared at the sag of leaves and roots flopping in front of her like fish starved of air. The pile was high now; her cheeks sore from her swiping; her knees, legs, lower back, her whole right side aching. She was tired. So bloody *tired*. Of gardening. Of herself: the inside of her head, the recurrent wallpaper of her life.

Of all the beautiful and bruised colours of love.

April

Pink Moon – Half Waning

The dead, the diseased, the crossing and the broken. *With a rose, the shape you are looking for is that of a goblet.* This rose looked like a basket woven by a six-year-old on too much sugar. How to make a bloody *goblet* from that?

Still. Dead, diseased, crossing and broken it must be, just as Tansy said when she handed Claire her 'best' secateurs: 'Felco. The ultimate. They're sharp and they'll do the job, but you must watch yourself. Unless you like the sight of blood.'

Tansy had drawn her an arthritic sketch to help: the rosebush stems opening outwards like fingers reaching up from supplicant prayer hands joined at the hands' heels.

She stared at the conflicted straggle in front of her. It felt like a representation of the inside of her head. But pruning, much as it daunted her, was apparently 'imperative'.

'However brutal that may seem,' Tansy had said.

'I can't even cut hair neatly,' she'd replied. '3D art was never really my thing.'

Tansy fixed her with a sharp look. 'Have you applied for that scheme yet?'

Claire avoided her eye. 'I'm on it.'

Her tone was harder than intended and Tansy studied her – or it felt like she did – for a moment. 'I used to baulk at the job of cutting, too,' she said. 'I think one always does. Making the wrong slice and leaving the poor plant like some kind of Frankenbloom.'

She laughed. She'd gone for a walk earlier, up to a little church similar to the one she grew up near; all drunken porch, jeering gargoyle and lurching graveyard scribbled with brambles that in autumn burst out fat little cardinals of berry – it stopped her feeling quite so *Frankenbloom* herself. Back at her desk, however, she still couldn't focus on Lily Webb, the wannabe goose duck (to the annoyance of Honk Waddle), or Billie Skipper, the new little brown goat who felt overlooked by Feta Butt and her crew; distracted by Art Calling, dejected – again – by a lack of ideas. It felt like being let out of an asylum to set her attention on roses instead.

'But, like anything with fear,' Tansy had gone on, 'practice grows one's confidence. My dear, a bit of surgery became my favourite part of gardening! But I am a Scorpio, and we do make excellent surgeons – or detectives.' She winked. 'Make of that what you will.'

Pruning was good for flowering, apparently. Roots, too. 'Though when it comes to roses,' Tansy warned, eyebrows high, 'the beautiful beasts are both bad-tempered and armed. Be prepared. Delete no expletives.'

The mass of thorny branches tangled to almost Claire's own

height, some green, some brown, black, thick, thin, spindly; a thicket of criss-crossed spears studded with shark teeth.

'Assess the damage before all else. Lord knows what the percentage of standing and staring is, but it is without doubt a vastly important part of the task.'

She thought again of the pencil sketch, elaborate, even in its flimsy detail – and infectious, given she found herself sketching on her sofa every evening now; skeletal trees, mostly, fascinated by how they shared the same biological shape as both the human brain and respiratory system. *Smiles.* She conjured in her mind's eye the small diagonal pencil slashes marked where Tansy would, she presumed, have made the cuts.

'Back to an outward facing bud – those pronounced nobbles on the stem. And all the better if one spots growth there. Just don't fall for the smiles.'

'The what?'

'Oh, as in gardening, so in life. The lines where the stem has grown another phalange – like people, you mostly only see one side, you see: *one may smile and smile and yet be a villain* and all that? And don't be seduced by the stems growing inwards, however healthy. They'll cause no end of trouble.' She notched off words with a bony finger. 'Welts, pests, disease, lack of airflow, blocking flowers. The sheer theft of energy.' A huffed-out laugh. 'I've rather described the process of decaying as a human, let alone a dratted plant.'

'But what if,' said Claire – *As in gardening so in life* – 'I accidentally make it worse?'

'In which case, cut the wretched thing back to its base. The plant can only thank you for it – it's rather hard to kill a rose that's been about for a while. Unlike some of us. So, if in doubt, cut it off!'

Perhaps if she mastered these first cuts, she could move on to something even more lovely and likely to die: the wisteria suffocating the tatty pergola, wild tendrils clawing at the sky for help. She liked wisteria. In her favourite part of Norwich, the white or purple blooms flanked a church wall like a sweetly scented banner announcing spring.

'The job is mostly to cut out the unnecessary,' she said out loud, echoing Tansy.

The rose's base was barely visible, thronged with grass, weeds, and furry, bile-coloured lichen. Some branches held a wizened bud, the forlorn shape of a spent flower, a charred rosehip. It all looked damaged, it all looked unnecessary. Where to bloody start?

The diseased, the dead. Well, at least they were usually pretty easy to identify.

She squeezed the secateurs. She could go full butcher and the only comeback would be watching it not-flower or slowly die. *Whoop.* Was it going to help her if it lived: share dinner, ask about her day? Tell her how to live her life?

The first two cuts were easy: two tinder-dead spikes that practically fell off in her hand. She held them carefully as broken glass – they felt as lethal – and stepped back to look. Laughable difference.

She squatted again, ducking the secateurs through the weave of branches, hunting the black, twigged, leprous (as Tansy described it), the nubbly or grey-wooded. Oddly satisfying to hear that neat snip; a momentary slip into a childhood noise of summer as familiar as her grandad's lawnmower. Even better to feel a finger of sun at her neck; a tender touch to the unseasonable chill. With her left hand she cut, with her right, collected; a small pile of dead surprising her with its capacity to still prick through a glove long after it had ceased to be.

*

She did not tell anyone about the first time.

No marks equalled no need? And anyway, she could not admit The Poet might be right. No one told you 'feisty' little girls needed to change: how 'funny', 'cute' or 'spirited' seemed to be what made you a 'handful' as a woman. But after being home at Easter, having fun with old friends, even Guitar True-Love, she went back feeling strong, healthy; herself.

The first thing The Poet says: 'You look so beautiful.'

He's never said that before. They're walking down a steep hill, the whole drizzly industrial city laid out like a quilt she felt she could stamp on or roll in if she chose. She feels unleashed from him, freed by the bolt cutter of breathing in her roots. He asks her for *a drink, a smoke, nothing smutty – you're too good a friend for that.* She'll walk home anyway; she has a love for both cities at night and fresh sheets on her bed.

The sex that night the most mind-blowing of her life. Her climax wave after wave of sweet agony, a firework of stars that blasts thought, feeling, burns the air she breathes; so powerful she thinks her head might explode, her heart stop. Afterwards a calm she's never known; other-worldly. And a nausea she can't place. How – why – was it so good? How did they make this unique, unspoken language: followed, changed, perfect; a mirror image of one fucking other?

154

'Just to reiterate,' he says as they smoke after, 'I'm not in love with you.'

'I know. And *to reiterate*, I'm not, either.' Guitar True-Love had a new girlfriend – with 'electric hands' – who looked like one of The Bangles. No competing with that: an ex four hundred miles away *vs* a goddess in your uni town. With her AC/DC hands.

'Yeah, but.'

'But what?'

'Well, it's just . . . I don't think you always know yourself as well as you think. Or I do.'

'Wow. I'd laugh except I don't think I'd stop – your statement is *that* kind of funny.'

'I'm serious, Claire. You're one of those people who don't see themselves how other people do. I mean, I know everyone thinks you're marvellous – didn't I say so the other day? – but they don't see the part *I* do. *Little* you. Like trying to hide your period pain, being all *brave*. But if you had the energy of, say, Izzy – like, fuck it, here I am! – *well*. You'd go from marvellous to bloody magnificent. And it's a massive turn-on.'

Her gaze falls to the carpet, so worn it looks like burnt hair glued to floorboard. 'Good to know. If a tad, *well*, bullshit – given Ian's asked me to his for dinner on Friday?'

'As in "wet-pastry Ian"? As in "I bore the paint off walls Ian"? *That* Ian? Thanks for flirting with *Ian* when people know we've been sleeping together.'

'I wasn't flirting. I just like him. He's nice. Funny.'

'He's too dull to be unlikeable. Fucking ridiculous hair, too, if you want *funny*.'

'Look. As you just reminded me, we're not lovers, not a *thing*. I can do what I want.'

'Yes, but. I'm not in "in love" with you, but I love you as a friend. A *special* friend. And if your standards are so low, quite honestly I don't think I can have sex with you again.'

'Oh? Shame. Because I'm going.'

'Why? When you could be with me?'

'You said you didn't want—'

'I was actually planning some fun in bed. But fine. I just need to know where I stand.'

She doesn't go to Ian's for dinner. They eat, drink, fuck tied up, blindfolded, play with whatever they find, or imagine, all weekend. Can't even make it to a pub for more Durex without him pulling her into a disused factory where she takes the first unprotected risk of her life. The more they do it, the better it gets – as implausible to both as it is insatiable.

*

Ugh. She snapped the memory off with the wrestle of one thick, defiant branch that bit back at her, telling herself again *Focus, Claire!*, thoughts slipping into the same unconscious as her fingers gently separating every stem, as she would a maze of fairy lights or the cables that colonized corners every time a son came home.

The satisfying slice of the secateurs, the squeak of the little spring, the way the beak of blades stuck at thicker branches, enmeshed in a mash of green; absorbing to be so close to all its tones. She bent – *For fuck's sake, focus!* – to cadmium yellows, ultramarines, cobalts, phthalo, alizarin reds, umbers, her mind a kaleidoscope of palette and paint, hunting outward-facing buds, turning each stem to see, feel, the snout of them. Some poked like nascent nipples, some glowed almost red with the throb of juvenile health.

She yelped: a new scratch; vicious, jaw-sunk with its pike teeth, painfully pulled out. She already had several on her wrist and inner forearm, though more than a *bastard* or a *fuck*, this one was a *cunt*. She said it loud as she squatted, sucking at the blood beading on her skin.

*

'It's a bad split. Your whistling days are over, no. Who did this to you?'

Muffled by a wall of shock, what else is there to say? 'My boyfriend.'

Grimace. 'You are clearly an intelligent young woman – graduate next year, isn't it? But you should think if you want boyfriend in your life that is one who punches women.'

'Yes. I know.'

'And with this kind of force. No one has right to do this to you, you know.'

'I know.'

'Nothing is so black and white, this I know. But this is assault – you will have scar on inside of lip, underside, not top. It is a small blessing, but you will have it for life. And I am certain this boyfriend did not come off worse. If you wanted, you could report it?'

She thinks. Of the clothes she'd hurled out of his window once, the time she said it wasn't her fault he was stupid. Of how he screamed at her to leave and she refused, shortly before he punched her full in the mouth, but after he dragged her across a room by her hair. *If you'd just left*, he'd said when she couldn't leave the sink for the blood that poured from her. Her disbelief it was not paint. 'But it wasn't just him. I didn't . . . if I'd . . . I should have . . .'

A pause. A kindly look in that Indian face with its concerned bush of eyebrow. 'Look. You are young. Smart. Whole life in front of you, isn't it. Surely no one is worth this?'

'No.'

'Take a leaf from your friend here' – a nod at The Poet – 'who was kind enough to bring you here. This is kind of man-friend you want in life. Not one who does this.'

She cannot bring herself to say another word.

*

Her uncut hand unconsciously clutched in her hair now. Fierce. To the point of pain.

She let go and shook her head. Told herself to breathe, do as Tansy suggested – cut hard anything too complicated, scabby, even not-quite dead enough, and especially anything spindly or weak; the pile of her efforts latticing the lawn so if she drew it she'd have in mind the spectacles, testicles, wallet and watch of Catholics making the sign of the cross.

*

Words come when she lies. Sounds that tumble from her as easily as cartoon figures spit snapped teeth: you think fast when a fist writes a story on your face. If she does not go to the cinema as planned with the drama lot, she'll still have to see some of them tomorrow at home, when lies will be harder to find. She's learning. Better to strike soon then keep silent. Less time to think.

Two of his knuckles have left little purple circles on her upper lip, near the horse-mouth of the actual swelling.

She spins her tale, lets it spool with even-shaped holes in all the right places: *messing about, tickling and* – ah, the timing of the slightly coy pause that whispers Sex Game; the group's suspicion shifting. He stands beside her, affectionate, tender – *Can he get her an ice cream, he feels so bad?* – and she feels them soften in her palm, the way they talk of an audience. *Otherwise*, she sees them, silent, ask, *how could she be standing here?*

Cartoon figures fill her thoughts as cut lip cracks in air-con'd air. It wouldn't surprise her if she split in two like they get sawed in half. Rent from the very apex of her skull, sternum, ribs, pelvis, the two sides of her peeling neatly. Because for all the concerned *does it hurt*s and *God, it looks so nasty*, it is nothing – nothing – compared to the split inside her.

*

The tangle of thorns in the stems that cross. The rusted marks left on stems above, below, beside; the chafe of years feasting on wood. All the tiny spindles of stalk, the thrust and poke up and sideways: a crossword of photosynthesis and wild. Nature and a lack of nurture.

Not you, not now. Fuck off. And when you get there, fuck off even further.

Hard, hard, with the pruners. Stems fell, some still soft and whitish-green inside.

*

She stops peeling potatoes. She likes this housemate, despite the being a little too happy to be true; too likely to burst into songs about TOMORROW and SUNSHINE.

'It's not a relationship.'

'Okay, your "thing" or whatever. It's just . . .'

The pause so awkward she knows the girl knows and the knowledge knots her breath.

'It's just we're all worried you're caught up in something . . . out of your depth?'

We're all. Something at her centre withers; blackens. 'How dare you?'

The girl, stricken. 'But surely you can see what you're involved in is—'

'What I *see* is that you need to keep your nose out of my business. Go on – fuck off!'

She watches the girl flee in tears. No container in her that can take the flash flood of self-loathing. She strikes the potato in staccato jerks. *Just. Get. On. With. It.*

Later she apologizes – *people worrying, y'know*. She's *fine*. And *really touched* they care. Just *overreacted a bit, y'know*. Period due, all that. Y'know.

*

The third cut from the third big rose, focus lost again, just as she'd felt pleased to sort of see what Tansy meant about a goblet, just as it took on a tinge of Tansy's sketch.

This rose so much denser than the rest, so much more

complex she wondered if it might be the one to flower the most – and if so, in what colour. She hoped red. Even if it didn't have a scent. She painted an image – big, blood-red cabbagey petals holding their heart tight on a stem – over the unwanted memory; the rising sense of losing her mind to the pointlessness of the past. She would not be locked in without at least a go at kicking the door down. Perhaps she grasped too hard, or perhaps the rose had a mind of its own, after all.

She shouted in pain, instantly knew this tiger claw of a cut needed a serious plaster.

*

Final year and practically pariah now. She understands; told by a woman she can't stand but still respects – at least the witch speaks her truth, if the sort to take a delighted violence in it too: 'He's like a shitter version of Iago. You, you're all right, Clur. Sound lass. But that knob? You were waaay better before him and you'd do waaay better to get rid. He's a dick of the highest order, a fucking parasite on a dog turd, a—'

'Why don't you tell him yourself?' she says. 'He's over there. Knock yourself out.'

Every cell cringes. Still, if nothing else, it shuts that thin-lipped witch up – who did not, Claire noted, say anything to him. Years later, she will snuff a little laugh at her own naivety to that, but she is not yet used enough to shame to know its workings; her fury little more than plastic packaging to stop it leaking out. Shame is a trickle that unless staunched flows to find a level and keeps filling, filling, filling, until it steeps deep as any quarry. For a time you can paddle it, dip the shiver of its shallows, shake it quickly off again. But soon the sand of it swells so full of suck you lose footing, contract the cramps fighting to get back; legs lead, guts full of stones, arms gasping and clawing for land to stamp, pump, warm your frozen bones. Breathe.

This also the term he fucks her best friend. She's worried she's pregnant, her friend sympathetic, albeit 'Fuck it – let's go clubbing!'. But he turns up later, and later still she spies them kissing, storms out, expecting one or both to follow. Neither do. Perhaps it's the sobbing or the twenty Silk Cut, but her period arrives next day, as does he, alone: *If I'm accused, I may as well commit the fucking crime. You're a friend, she's a friend, where's the difference – at least you like her? You're doing it to yourself.* Then the best friend joins them: *Yes, we talked about you; no, not too drunk for that. But either you can handle that platonic shit or not. You left me. And it's only bodies, it's not the same as* love.

Over years she'll learn quite how many friends he impales (and yes, the thin-lipped witch), but now she confides only in her best gay male friend, in lieu perhaps of Stephen. He's kind, but will lose all respect for her, he says, if she goes back to *that man* now.

No fear of that, she says. No. No way. Never.

*

Steaming coffee in good hand, she stared at the rose. She could swear the bastard thing was giving her a V-sign.

'Fuck you,' she said. 'I was trying to be *nice*. Help you, you ungrateful fucker. Why—' and at this point she flung her coffee, cup after it, hands skyward either side of her head. Shouted: 'Why is it all so fucking *hard*?'

*

Is a crumb of kindness the killer? Few people are born with bones made purely of stone – even serial killers can be solicitous to cats.

London. *What do we want? No loans! When do we want it? Now!* But this is not like Section 28, this uneasy stance of horses, shield, baton. The Poet is there, part of an organized bus, and she can't help thinking – in his beret, backcombed hair, and eyes ringed black – he looks like the world's Most Camp Aggressor as he shouts *Education is a right, not a privilege.*

It's taken until final year to understand why her grades, degree, matter so much: she has absolutely nothing else to rely on. No security blankets, networks, contacts. When friends spout 'Stop asking *Why should it be me* and ask instead why it shouldn't?' she swallows a desire to hack into how they hadn't had to fight for anything as she has, or learn to be in this world, behave like they belong here. She feels herself steered by the crowd, noise swelling like the hot breath steaming the horses' nostrils. And she is full herself now, anger, passion, as red-cheeked and sweaty as sex, shouting with all her might, pushing forward in power and solidarity, a human choir, a human song. But hooves are clattering, barriers crashing as police charge and panic sets in, as she shouts: 'Lay the barriers down! Horses won't cross if you lay them down!' But she's in a sea with no familiar buoys, 'friends' all gone, until The Poet grabs her, his city nous her safety.

They fuck that night for the first time since the best friend, and in this elision he is tender, eyes fierce in hers as he fills her with deep, smooth, even pulses. Breath, too, as if each other's air, until intoxication is complete. When sleep comes, it is thick as velvet.

She does her best to stay away: until the day her chequebook and card are stolen on a bus and she finally gets home to find her rotting window kamikaze. He sees her red-eyed in the bar, persuades her back to his, though he goes out, so she sits and cries alone – how does *a nice girl* end up here? – surprised to see him back with pizza, wine, numbers for rented rooms from windows. He undresses her softly, sadly, caresses her in front of a mirror – *Look how beautiful you are, look how beautiful we are together* – wants her to watch him fuck her. To look at him and only him; turns her chin to face him as, again, they come together.

He's always better when she's down, or far away from other people. When she is completely, and internally, alone.

*

The dead, the diseased, the crossing and the broken.

Her cut hand throbbed. She was still so tired. She wanted to get out, get away from herself, yet she didn't; wanted to speak to people, yet didn't – *still*. Couldn't trust herself: what she'd say, how she'd be. Whether she'd get that strange, numb urge she barely dared admit to herself that sometimes dared her to steer her car into a tree.

It was happening, then.

All the times she'd worried, joked about it: the cats and gin and basket-weaving with home-gnawed bark, the woman who puts a dog in a buggy. Something, anything, to stop the pain.

The sheer loneliness that had nothing to do with whether she was with people or not.

*

It felt like a spell, that treacle time of not taking his calls after the high of graduation. London different, too, now: activism neutered by a recession garrotting potential work, rooms amoebic dysentery would reject. But there is hope yet: she sees it dance in slants of morning sun on the jaundiced wall of the squat she sleeps in.

His letter hits her parents' doormat like the first leaves of that autumn weekend.

Sorrow, guilt. Things he *didn't feel or realize before.* She is confused, conflicted, if resolved: goes back to London and gets her hair cut short, throws shapes she desperately wants to fit on dancefloors.

Drunk, she calls, begs him to back off. 'But we have a world,' he says, 'only you and I know. Give me a chance to make it beautiful.'

The 'no' so hard. Everything in her cosmos pulled by the gravity in his words.

Deep breaths. Be strong. Be proud.

'I love you. I never realized it till now.'

No words because there is no breath. No strength. No pride. Only the hurt of the heart, the hurt of the heart, the hurt of the heart, as he says it to her again:

'I love you.'

*

Claire took up the secateurs and snapped all the remaining stalks of the third rose to barely a foot above its base. Fuck it. It would do what it would.

And she would not stop hoping that, if it did survive, it would bloom fierce and strong. Proud and red as blood.

May

Flower Moon – Half Waxing

She had sketched it, painted it; felt herself slowly falling in love with it. She'd even added it to Wank Farm. Once Tansy explained what wisteria symbolized, Claire hadn't wanted to do anything else. Hoping, perhaps, for some sort of magical osmosis. Love. A word that had the power to make or break a night, a day. A life.

'There's all sorts of poetry about wisteria as ephemeral,' Tansy said. 'It's the ultimate symbol of things that don't last. And, one imagines, that pertains especially strongly to beauty.' She nodded at Claire. 'And as one appears to have transmogrified from Abraham Lincoln to Einstein again since my last mop-chop, I really ought to know.'

'You don't look—' she stopped as Tansy's face said not to even bother; she did look a bit like Einstein and they both knew it. Claire respected that. She'd rarely not felt frustrated by the middle-class capacity for never saying it straight. She smiled at Tansy, warm from the honesty. 'So that's what it means, then – wisteria? All things shall pass and all that?'

Tansy raised a brow. 'Well, yes and also no. To Shin Buddhists, it also symbolizes prayer and humility. The drooping of the racemes is the bowing of the head, or kneeling, to honour' – she pressed her hands as if in prayer – 'the divine essence of our understanding.'

'Wow.'

'Yes, *wow*.' Tansy cocked her head back, laughed. 'To the Victorians, it meant something entirely different, naturally – obsession, like the choking vine it is. It is a legume at the end of the day, you see. But Victorians! Gawd love 'em. Jolly old bunch.'

'So, it stood for love? I thought that was roses?'

'Indeed it is – red or yellow – but wisteria is somewhat more subtle. One only needs look at it: that heavenly scent, those dreamy heads, that wonderful word *racemes*. I think it's partly why I love it so – an emblem for nature in a way; as you say, the passing of all things – but also how it can survive ridiculously harsh conditions and mistreatment. In that way, it stands for what the heart can endure.' She smiled, almost shy, and Claire had another glimpse of how whimsically attractive she must have been younger. 'There's something really rather beautiful in that, if you think about it.'

There was. Something very beautiful that, for Claire, hurt as much as it entranced or edified; made her want to weep like the *racemes* vivid in her mind. She knew if Tansy caught her eye she'd see the glisten, and however much the earlier honesty, she didn't know if she could cope with that. She bent her head pretending to fiddle with a cuticle.

Heart. Endure. She didn't want to think about it. Part of her, she recognized, if not most, had thrown itself at the garden simply to maintain a state of busy emptiness. She'd always wanted a life that ticked along like a monitor heartbeat, with just the occasional blip, and yet so much of hers had been like watching a heart attack happen. And at some point in the past few years – *endure* – that monitor flatlined altogether.

'Plus, it needs pruning twice,' added Tansy. 'January first, preferably, though who wants to go outside *then*, and after flowering for a second bloom. So in its current neglected state the best time is probably now. As indeed,' she added, softly, 'it so very often is.'

She'd left Tansy's soon after, scared her feelings would betray her, and followed her advice to the letter; beginning to cut every stem back, twisting the new, flailing antennae into trunk, following its interwoven example: 'You must trust your artistic eye!'

The worst that would happen now? A fall, an injury she'd recover from – with lots of lovely drugs to catch up on the sleep she so rarely got. The best? The beauty of wisteria rambling into her senses in deep summer; too late now to flower earlier, so hopelessly overgrown. But she didn't care. She climbed off the kitchen chair, pruners in hand, impressed at her own fatalism for once. What once would have stopped her even standing on it on grass – images of broken ankles, necks, or, God forbid a left hand, with no sickness cover – she'd said a solid bollocks to, with a bit of a *Bring it!* thrown in.

'God,' she said to Emma at lunchtime, after Emma reassured her gardening was 'all the rage' in therapy these days ('though, personally, booze and a fucking good boogie are underrated') and she'd listened to Emma's missive to Rob, an attempt at goodbye. 'What did we talk about before all this?'

'Hair? How much we drank? Little Miss Conniving Cow? Oh, and why middle-aged men shack up with thirtysomethings who "only want adventures" then saddle them with kids. I actually feel sorry for Twatface now. He'll be sixty when it *starts* school. At least that can't happen to us.' Emma sighed. 'I don't know. Maybe it's because the more you live, the more you get how short it is, how *shit* so much of the time. The more you want to see happiness.'

'Believe it can still happen, you mean?'

'Yes. That. Exactly that.'

Claire looked at the cat. She'd put out some leftover salmon earlier and he purred so hard she heard him several feet away, though he slunk closer all the time – pleased to see her, she liked to think, rather than just an en suite of cleared soil. She couldn't help envying him a life so free of all the insane, wasteful human angst. That pure, wild freedom.

The wisteria, by contrast, looked shorn as a spring sheep; stark, if satisfyingly tidy. It made her think of her boys turning teen, getting the first haircut on their own; the same sort of spike as these truncated branches. Cutting was infinitely more addictive than weeding. A surprising sensation in the heart, though, to see foxgloves and geraniums pinking with flowers, alchemilla's broad scallops now, hostas unfurling their tight cones. It seemed overnight, too, the choysia had burst like a feather pillow, and a dizzying storm at the base of a tree Tansy called 'snow-in-summer'; so pretty, next to the deep cerise of that spiraea.

'You have another,' Tansy had also told her, 'at the end of the garden, "The Bride". I see it from my bedroom. It's the thing that looks like the wild woman of Borneo, but it'll flower soon and take your breath away – a bride walking the aisle, indeed. Jolly good news it is, too. Wealth, fortune and prosperity, allegedly. Who among us couldn't do with that?'

Claire had smiled, though it felt wan; asked after a smaller, woody plant that looked dead but for a few clinging leaves. As she studied the photo, Claire noticed again how smooth Tansy's skin was: wrinkles all but forcing themselves on her face as she squinted.

'Salvia,' Tansy said. 'I imagine you'll have a few in different guises. It'll be like unwrapping gifts when it flowers: could be white, blue, white with a red scallop: "Hot Lips", would you believe! Terribly popular. Ghastly, for me, but there you are.'

'Salvia *Hot Lips*?' She did jazz hands as Tansy nodded, laughing at her.

'And still a *Salvia officinalis*. Not just for stuffing chickens, mind, this is the plant of wisdom, learning, healing, even. Native Americans burn it to cleanse people or spaces, connect with spirits. There's even one called "Love and Wishes". Isn't that wonderful?'

Claire stood, pruners in hand, top teeth over bottom lip, determined to focus with all she had. She was learning. *Cleanse. Heal.* Look for the living, take out the dead. Just don't cut too far back into the dead or the plant will not – cannot – regenerate.

*

The punch in the face and the split lip.

The spitting in her face that time, kneeling on her arms.

The throwing of wine, beer, vodka in her face. The first two in front of people, if at separate parties. Once for holding up a hand when he gestured her to pass the wine because she was still talking: *Wait a sec*. The other for 'humiliating him in front of people we don't know' by 'touting herself to that guy' when she laughed at a joke.

The mashing of said face into worktop, carpet, bed, wall. Mashing a favourite, it seemed. As was face.

The fucked best friend.

The calling her a whore, oh, countless times.

The pulling across a room by her hair.

The torn knickers and 'Is this what you want, is it?'

The telling her, smile scoring face, how he could destroy her.

And now this.

Do you want to press charges?

This.

The knife had sat on the work surface cruelly oblivious, it seemed, in those stark moments. A phrase entered her head she remembered from A level English: *pathetic fallacy*; the art, in other words, of bestowing inanimate objects with the ability to give some kind of a shit. That knife didn't give a shit. He didn't give a shit. It sat there. He sat there. They both just sat there, oblivious. The blissful fucking bliss of oblivion.

She could do it.

She looked at the back of his head, bent as he took notes from a shorthand book – shorthand, for Christ's sake! – in that fuck-awful kitchen in that fuck-awful semi-squat they lived – no – existed in.

How is she here?

How, after all those speeches about being in the *top two percent and blah* and taking *responsibility to use it wisely and well*, is she eating a bin-found orange every morning, a pitta at night with a few chips in if Chippie Guy felt sorry for her, a Happy Meal for a quid; or nothing. Hunger has phases, she's learned. Ignore the first two and mostly you can manage.

Stick it in.

Would it feel like scoring lamb, like plunging into pork, like a skewer in raw chicken? Would it feel like butter, cheese, slicing ham, or d) none of the above?

Twist it. That will make the damage worse.

Would it turn like as if in the flesh of an orange? Would it stick too fast, too hard, too deep? Twist or stick. Vingt-et-un. Twenty-one. Her age.

Who would blame her?

Her hands shake as she tries to wring the cloth, get the water cold – thank God she doesn't need hot, there isn't any, ever – to try and soothe the burning, the burning, the burning. She can only see out of the other eye. What happened again? Isn't it steak she needs? Or alternate hot and cold? Why can't she remember?

'I need— Could you put the kettle on so I can have hot water?'

He ignores her, back still turned. They have not spoken since— Did it really happen?

Or pull it upward. Rip through something that can't be stitched in time.

Judge. Jury. Who would blame her?

A hand is reaching for it, that uncaring knife. Fingers – pale, shaking, shaping, curling, ready for the handle. Black, that handle, two steel screws; not the sort a bunch of homeless graduates have, the sort your mother has, that slices and cuts with ease, with grace. She watches the hand, wonders how cool the handle is, how heavy its heft, how her hand will fit it.

Her hand. It is her hand.

Run.

This is where it happened, where the bed is, where her shitty little suitcase is and his rucksack is, where the bed is, where she is locking the door with those shaking hands and fumbling with that little gold bar, that little gold tunnel, that Yale, leaning against it and trying to breathe and trying not to cry because she cannot cry, not with this, the pain will be so, so much worse she knows, and God, God, *God*, she's scared, so fucking scared, not

of him but her of what she could do cigarettes are here thank God for cigarettes come on girl stop the shaking get it out the packet and get in your fucking mouth just get it in like that come on now get lighter hold it with both hands and stop that shaking sparking only sparking no a flame now smoke exhale. Exhale.

Exhale.

It is not enough. The burning is back and with it something else, some sensation of throb, ache, nausea. What else – there has to be something else to stop this shaking, this terrible rattling of flesh, bone, organ, head, heart, tendon, nerve. Whisky. There is whisky in this room, she remembers now.

Fling. Tear. Find. Smoke, ash, clothes, tapes, no glass, but a bottle. Victory. It will do, it will do, it—

More. Swig again. More.

Exhale.

Exhale.

Her watch broke, she remembers now. She half saw it smash as she hit the wall, mind-blinded by the fist, by the pain in her face, the kind that is white, like the fiercest part of fire. It burns, it burns, *God*, how it burns.

Swig. Exhale. Less shaking. Still shaking. But less. *Come on, girl*. Exhale.

Bad sex. Furious and bad. Of all the fucking nothing like

the fucking before. Sex like life has been all summer. A student room with no cooking facilities she sneaked him into on the last month of her student card. A terrible hotel in Victoria with everything nailed down but the pubic hair and wank mags in that seedy little shower. A roundabout with a few defeated trees to hide-sleep under for a night. Then this – this half-squat with its cold water and concrete floors and its underlying stench of cat piss and desperate lives. Bad sex. Standing up and at some point wrangling over a blanket. Of all things. Push-pulling. A while to work out, watching that watch, it was a punch. No. Can't be real.

Mirror.

But careful, go slowly. Sneak up with hope in your heart, girl – you might be pleasantly surprised.

Jesus.

Fucking.

Christ.

'Do you want to press charges?'

A week later with a family doctor she's known since she was ten. Her cheek is fractured, she's learned; didn't need to be told he'd burst every blood vessel in her eye. But it is a shock to hear, if she'd had her hard contact lenses in, he'd have punched the sight from it completely.

'I don't know.'

'Two counts of GBH now. I know your parents don't know – you said some random drunk hit you in a club? – but this is very serious, Claire. He could do this to someone else.'

'I don't think so. I had enough warnings, I kept going back. I got what I deserved.'

'Listen to me,' he says, and she looks at the face that has

always been so kind about her periods, thrush, tonsillitis, the chunked-out finger snapping pottery for mosaics at school. His hairline has receded now, a low tide for the smooth sand of his forehead, the intent, but gentle, eyes. That gentle feels even worse than the harsh, the judgemental; pricking tears she doesn't have the currency, she feels, to buy. Own. 'Nobody deserves this. Nobody.'

'But it isn't as black and white as that,' she says. 'Sixty-forty. That's what it is.'

'Who said that – him? Do you really believe it? You're an intelligent young woman with a good family behind her and a potentially great life ahead. And you believe *that*?'

One single tear. But the mouth can't open. The mouth is frozen shut, swallowing the icy water of that quarry. Cramps have set in. Limbs too heavy to swim her back to bank.

The chair draws close. A tissue. A sigh. A look of genuine concern.

'Please think about what I've said. Whatever you think about whether he'd do it again, I personally wouldn't take that risk. I don't want to see you back here with a broken jaw.'

The brutality of that image. 'I will.'

'Promise me?'

'Promise.'

*

She stood back, heart tachycardic.

Once, in anger, she'd called his home, but his mother wouldn't fetch him: he was sleeping, had a headache, she said. She'd only met the woman once, pointed out the fact of her face. 'You have to understand,' the mother said then, 'he'd never have done this if you had not been in the room.'

She'd hung up destroyed, a pool of water on a floor trying to remember the *I hate myself* he told her once, the closest to apology. She took a trip to see her best male friend and Guitar True-Love in London, let the pendulum of their anger and love tick her back into believing in men. Two nights, too, in Guitar True-Love's bed, beautifully chaste – he made her feel so *safe* – until the spark took flame again; *still half in love* with her, he said: 'I'll put my life on hold for you. But if you don't want me, there's a woman I'd like to know more.' All she'd wanted for so long, every other a pathetic facsimile; this the fairy tale she dreamed of too snot-swollen to sleep, or when the heart wound opened again in a dream where this is what he said. But she was too broken by then. Too dirty. Too second-hand and unreliable.

Just about the only thing cataclysmic events were good for were showing you who you really are. And once light shone on that it gained energy, a life it did not have lurking in the shadows.

It *was* your shadow.

Fists curled, she turned from the wisteria to the buddleia crowing all over the end of the garden. She wanted to put an end to that smug, supercilious sprawl. Just because it was bigger. Just because it could. She could even see where it had been cut an eternity ago, the spear of branch from stump.

When she finally went at it, she did so like a madwoman, threading shears through its forest of stems, catching the taller she cut so low, with such ferocity, they fell precise as a dynamited chimney stack. She didn't feel the blisters beginning to form, teeth clamped so hard her gums pulsed. But God, it felt good. Sweating, panting, standing back to see both the carnage and regeneration Tansy so banged on about.

A scar was always there. Always would be, until you died or got dementia and forgot it of yourself. Not always obvious, either. Just there in the same way sand at the bottom of a lake was there, undisturbed until something sank deep enough to rouse a cloud of grit, each speck set to shift, drift; some to settle not so far away, some simply carried in a bubble – despair and happiness alike that way – to break the surface.

What you didn't see was quite how deep it went, just how long it lasted. As a body retained a scar, so perhaps a mind. The heart did, of that Claire was sure. Fifty-odd years might see you saggy and uncertain of eye; fearful, even, of a future with the aches borne of so much bending, kneeling, squatting – who knew gardening was so bloody *physical* – but you were more certain of some things than any other point in life. Wisdom that was earned, not given; mere knowing not its twin.

Bittersweet.

You had the hieroglyphs of half a century scrawled all over your face – though she couldn't really see her face without her glasses now – but eyes and brain compensated each other, memory slinking like a black cat in shadow you couldn't always see, stop, before it twined itself around your feet and felled you.

She'd done two things in the long weeks it took to get her face back, work again. She told her parents the truth. And she did not press charges.

If anyone had told her then she'd back within a year, she would have laughed. Or cried – if she'd let herself. Or both.

May

Flower Moon – Full

Say yes to more than you say no to.

They drank, mostly, at first. Laughed. Toasted each other, laughing that they drank more than their kids; got reprimanded by them for that. Laughed more at that: *We did the Eighties; we knew how to party.* Talked about their fortune to be here, on such a sunny day. Then toasted that, too, because at their ages that sentiment had long stopped being just words.

Privately, Claire raised her glass to herself for being there, too: a resounding success, at last, to the equation where x was intention and y actual action. She'd felt a little anxious about Jules's birthday picnic, mentioned her 'biblical plague' of memories, but Jules was having none of it, insistent there would be women there 'it'll be good for you to meet'. She told herself it had been a long time – Christmas – since all that exclamated encouragement on how to live her New Year life: *Get online, you'll never meet a man if not! Join anything, everything, church fucking choir if you have to!* Well-meaning, she knew. Even so, she'd found herself in Asha's toilet halfway through the party, head in hands, wondering if she could kill herself with Toilet Duck.

But then wasn't now, and she felt that reflected in the day: hot for May, the trees a striking array of greens so fresh they filled her with the taste of gooseberries. She followed the curve of lake from the jetty, flanked by reeds, loosestrife, rosebay willowherb, thistle, nettle, the water a mirror to the few clouds mooching about the sky, trees reflecting like a Rorschach test, thought of her sketches: how differently she'd do that Escher take now.

'I want to get in before it cools down,' Jules said. 'Or I get drunk. Anyone else?'

A unanimous 'Fuck that – it's freezing!'.

'No swimming stuff,' said Claire. 'Didn't think.'

Jules shrugged. 'So? There's no one around?'

'I can't go in in my bra and pants!'

'So take them off – I can lend you a towel?' Jules smiled. Waggled her eyebrows.

'No. *No*. And don't waggle me. The last time you waggled me Ben picked me up and I bruised my chin puking out of his car window. Not good, on so many levels.'

'Cha!' said Jules. 'I swear we only hurled because we ended up scoffing those ten-year-old mushrooms I had.'

'I wanted to *microdose*, I said. After . . . well, you know. It would help, *you* said. Knew I shouldn't have listened.'

'Pfft,' said Jules. 'Microdose! Bollocks to that. I want to *macrodose* – just not with manky shrooms. Fuck it – I'm going in!'

She watched Jules dive – dive! – into water so cold on her feet she felt an ice cream headache just watching her dark head surface, shake itself.

'It's beautiful!' she shouted. 'Come on, Claire, fucking *live* a little!'

Fuck it. She started to laugh, peeling off clothes as the others whooped, launching herself from the jetty as Jules had; gasping with shock as she kicked and pushed until the icy grip softened, silky as she swam to Jules who was floating on her back now, dark hair grey at its roots, the rest spreading around her like Millais's famous painting of Ophelia. Except Jules looked so alive. So happy.

'Aren't we lucky?' she said, as Claire drew level. 'Aren't we just so bloody *lucky*?'

The conversation shifted as the sun lowered, spreading a tarnished gold over their chopping, tossing, scattering, the peeling of lids off this, wrapping off that. One woman with a domino run of family cancers, another with dying parents, a brother-in-law's suicide, an anorexic teenage daughter, and a husband she loved but whose coping mechanism was oiled only by variants, and gargantuan quantities, of booze. Jules asked how she coped.

The woman was stately, calm, well-spoken, a former product development exec for a high-street empire. 'I'm not sure I do. I mean, I drink, do a bit of yoga, all that.' She made a face. 'But, um. Honestly? I have also been shagging my dead brother-in-law's best friend. And I do know how bad that sounds.'

A chorus of *Understandable / Who wouldn't, to be fair? / Fuck – don't judge yourself.*

'I read about this all the time,' said Asha. 'It used to be Valium in my mum's time – the Boomers, or whatever they are that we'll be next.'

'Gen dead?'

'Gen Frigid Fanny?'

'That's your OnlyFans sorted.'

'Don't,' said a nurse in her sixties. 'I went to London to see my daughter and we ended up hammered with these drag queens in Soho at a party in a gay sex shop. Fantastic night. But I've nursed for forty years, and I still lost sleep over the logistics of those toys.'

'Wish I could drink with my mother,' said Asha. 'Might stop her telling me the same thing fifty times. She got low-alcohol wine last time and I was like, brilliant – I'll have twelve.'

'At least our daughters will get *us* when they reach our ages,' said the nurse.

It was only once the blur of child-raising cleared and her own menopause kicked in, Claire said, she got quite how all that must have affected her mother – all their mothers.

'Yeah, but. It was different then,' said Jules, and Claire looked at Jules's glowing skin, the stylish jeans, asymmetric poncho. How different they were to women she remembered at this age. Perms. A-line skirts. Bare Tan tights – 'natural' if you were a camel.

'But I don't remember other mothers being as unhappy as mine,' said Claire. 'Or not especially. God, I envied that.' Cherry Boy's family. Guitar True-Love's. How she felt as if she stood, shivering, looking in at them all cheerily gathered by a fire. Back then, she'd have been the one looking out, clamouring to escape. All her life, she saw now, she'd been trying to marry up those two forces: the need for people, but the need to be free of them just as much.

'You didn't expect to be happy, for a start,' said Jules. '*Happy* was the bingo bonus.'

'That's what the women in my family told me,' said a small dark Irishwoman Claire had met before, liked. 'And I wish I'd never listened. After what Bastard Tom did to me.'

A consensus of quite how much of a bastard Bastard Tom had been.

'Anyway,' the Irishwoman added. 'When all that marriage shite was set up you were a spinster by nineteen, you expected to be *dead* by forty, tops.'

'I was thinking the other day,' said the nurse, 'how, when I met the husband I was with for twenty-five years, I wasn't into cricket or rugby. And then there I was, fat, fifty, sat there watching things I didn't give a shit about and wondering where I went.'

'It just leaves you so fucking tired,' said the stately woman. 'All that *carrying*. You know, my older daughter and all her friends don't want to get married, ever.'

'Look at the French, the Italians,' said the Irishwoman. 'They respect the person they've got the kids, the history, with; they just don't look to them to fill their every need. I'm old enough now for that to make sense to me.'

'We all just need a bit of light in the dark sometimes – a bit of *fun*,' said Jules as she poked a cauldron of a firepit. 'And we're good at change, women. We do it all the time.'

They discussed emerging stories of women they knew: the bisexuality or lesbianism after years of 'trad'; the non-monogamy even in couples together for decades, reluctant to split. *Whatever floats your boat.* As long as it didn't hurt anyone. They'd all seen enough of that. It was, thought Claire, sharing her own story – inebriated, yes; but somehow exonerated, too – one of the best nights she'd ever had. With all their respective badges of honour: the child-raising, lost careers, divorces, diseases, deaths, menopauses *ad nauseum* – the sheer bloody *work* of it – these women leaned so beautifully away from all that younger competitiveness into a need for connection, understanding. Tribe. She was surprised how strongly she felt it as she watched sunset flush the lake a golden peach, plum, the rippling *plip* of jumping fish. For a few moments, they all fell under the spell of the moon, transfixed.

'Wow,' said Asha. 'I forgot it was a supermoon tonight.'

'A blood moon, too,' said the stately woman. 'Lunar eclipse. Really rare, apparently.'

How fat that moon seemed, peering down to admire its perfect reflection, pinked as a drop of blood in water as the women began to chat, laugh again. She'd lost a lot of weight, she knew, blaming it on gardening, the slim pickings of appetite as a single person.

She was, she realized, starting to feel herself substantial again.

She had not seen Tansy this fierce. What a difference a day made.

She wished they could be talking – literally – shit again. She'd only gone over to ask if the horse manure she'd seen when out walking that morning would be good for the garden; her back screaming at all the sitting from work or the now-addictive sketching. Which apparently it would, if the straw wasn't too fresh, 'Or it will just blow off all over the shop. And shit does so have a habit of improving soil.' She'd been tempted to say *hashtag lifegoals* to that.

'One does get somewhat tired of the media blaming *everything* on old people!' said Tansy now, clearly irritated by Hope's latest call. 'According to her news-watching, it's my fault there's a housing crisis now. Pah! Not as if I don't remember old people when I was young!'

At times like this, she wasn't sure she liked Tansy – actively felt sorry for Hope. 'No, and I take your point. But there are now more old people than teenagers. Living longer, too.'

'Unfortunately so. And I should know,' scowled Tansy. Behind her, through the listing window, Claire could see Tansy's willow, hazy as if roughly sketched, preparing to paint the real deal. 'But whatever the statistics, there's still such *bias*. That ghastly woman on the news, oh, whatshername? Voice, like a honking goose, same superior attitude. You know. The coloured one.'

Claire sat, stupefied. This she had not expected. 'Tansy, you can't say *coloured*.'

Tansy eyed her, sharp. 'I didn't say black!'

'No. But you can't say coloured, either?'

'But she *is* coloured. And surely if one can say white, one can say coloured?'

'Well, no, you can't. Not now. It's pretty . . . offensive?'

'But I grew up in Kee-nya. And as I recall, they quite often competed about who was darker than whom. I'm afraid I just don't understand it at *all*.'

Claire thought of her clash with Joe, felt a stab of empathy, however hard Tansy's words made her teeth itch. She wasn't a bad person, just from a bygone era that left her tantamount to alien. A reminder. A warning. She spoke gently: 'You say person of colour now, Tansy. Just not coloured, ever.'

'But isn't it the same thing? Why can we not just call things as they *are*?'

Tansy's house felt darker, too, in a way it hadn't in winter. Perhaps because of the day: ridiculously blue, sunshine turning shadows starkly black. She was glad to get outside.

She'd bought several bags of the manure, bearing in mind Tansy's advice to 'mix it merrily with the dead' – sweating, but surprising herself with a lack of groan as she lugged them to the two compost bins emptied of dark matter smelling vaguely of earth and intensely of forest floor; crusted ashy now from sun, worms blindly inching saddles into soil for relief. A memory: the kids believing chopped worms regenerated, Joe's distress realizing it wasn't true; they only did that if the tail end was sliced, not, and never, the head. How Dan laughed. Until she said she caught him eating one as a toddler, no idea which way up it was. She felt the same thinking about Tansy, Joe. What Ben had said.

She drove her fork into the manure, folding it into the compost as she would flour into eggs and fat, or the hundred years ago she and Stephen made mud pies. Each fold released a new smell by turn acrid, ureaic, earthy, the new-leather fragrance of straw.

'Roses must not dry out,' Tansy had insisted. 'Though, ironically,' she added, as if unable to help herself, 'they were a witches' favourite when dried.'

'Love, I suppose?' She'd hoped Tansy's irascibility might soften with talk of flowers.

'As if witches were simply so wishy-washy!' Tansy snorted. 'If you *listened*, you'd remember about attracting wealth, health – very high in vitamin C. Sacred in ancient Egypt. The highest vibrational frequency of any flower.'

She bit back the *Oh, sod off then!* 'Frequency. Right. Anyway, I'll be—'

'Do not dismiss me so lightly, Claire. String theory, quantum physics – we're now agreeing with the mystics of five thousand years ago – praise be – that the entire universe consists of frequencies. Any imbecile knows sound can drill holes in solid objects. But I bet you *didn't* know tomatoes are partial to middle C. Higher tones slow ripening. Unlike the niece, and you today, I like to think of it as everything having a voice. Even me. *Now you may go.*'

She began to bank a crown around a stem in full, pink-tipped rose pregnancy, the muscles in her arm, belly, contracting. Another surprise: they seemed to actively enjoy it. For so long she'd been aware only of internal rebellion quelled by sheer bullying, often out loud; and also as a sort of punishment, she saw now. Just as well, given both Tansy and everything seeming to grow in May like a childhood on speed. God knew what her cursing did to the poor plants, and maybe it was a nascent descent into cheap sherry and all things cat, but she'd once had such a voice. Activism, yes. But also shouting at The Poet when it would have served her better to sod empowerment and shut the fuck up. And yet.

How her throat had felt for so long, in motherhood, marriage, like it would choke on all the unspoken.

*

His breath at my ear. 'I know you'd love me to take control.'

I didn't know he was this close. I hadn't realized he'd walked up behind me; I only feel the clamp of his hand low in my hair.

Heart staccato, a clamour at the walls of me, and yet my chest barely moves – I won't, can't, let it – my hands static, peg in teeth, print on peg, though I can't make peg meet line to dry the work of my adult learners. Belly coils. Crotch floods.

I hear my voice, low, my words a total surprise to me. The lie. 'What makes you think I'm not in control now?'

His lips at my neck. The press of his hard at my lower back. Hard not to tilt my head to the velvet at my neck as he tugs the twist of my hair, pulls my neck back, licks the ledge of my clavicle. The heat again at my ear: 'I want to know the taste of you.'

Oh God. Oh *God*. So. Fucking. Hard. 'No.' I swallow, keep my ground. 'No.'

His face, voice, burns my cheek. 'I love how older women know who they are. So good at control, too.'

'Oh, believe me. You have *no* idea.'

He lets my hair go, laughs. 'I'll leave you alone.'

My breath hard, my face flushed, glowing with heat nothing else can raise; not winter walks, not the sweat of exercise, not a face too close to a fire. The undeniable flush I had forgotten of desire.

*

How Claire loved it as a word – witching. *We are witching tonight*, or, as the case with the apotropaic marks she stared at now: *We are de-witching* or *We are witch-proofing tonight*. How must it have been to believe you could get rid of the things that haunted, scared, or threatened you, with that erstwhile lover and bringer of life and death – fire.

The black mark began halfway up Tansy's huge inglenook bressummer; burned-in vertical, charred-looking, almost a child's drawing of a candle. Her thumb found the indent of its bulb, worn as the pocks in old rock, a slight stipple where the rings of age refused to stay silent. It prodded in her a kind of respect for the oak it once was, harder now than steel. She let her touch slide to the braille of scratches beside it that only showed in certain lights. *A. M.*

'*Ave Maria,*' Tansy had told her. 'A prayer to the fair one for safety from witches.' She'd laughed. 'And still I live!'

She waited for Tansy to finish in the downstairs bathroom. The stand-in carer – *A foetus! I can't ablute with a foetus, Claire!* – had been shooed out early, and Claire, holding the olive branch of checking Tansy wouldn't mind a small bonfire, wasn't happy she'd shower alone. Though the hip had healed well, she still struggled with stairs; the old, high-sided bath upstairs, unthinkable. And might remain that way, the carers told Tansy. Who was having none of it.

'They do keep on about not wanting to shorten one's life expectancy. And yet, when I ask what happens when expectancy meets or exceeds sustainability, they just stare blankly and say *we* don't need to worry. But I do.' She looked, for the first time, Claire thought, truly aware of her frailty, vulnerable. 'I do.'

'Well, at least you're safe from witches – or bad luck,' she said. 'Though if you want my opinion, nothing will save you from that mat in your bathroom.'

Tansy cackled. 'Ha! Hope is a thing with tassels!' A mischievous smile. 'You know, as a girl I'd terrorize other children, pretending to be a witch. But actually, I thought I was – I had these . . . *hunches*, I suppose. Knew things without knowing how and so on. But I was always fascinated by witches. So much more interesting than Pollyanna, especially in my day.'

Claire pulled a face, glad Tansy was 'back'. 'God. In any day, surely?'

'Oh, I was pretty evil, looking back. Pretending I made spells, set hexes – and Lord knows, if not my poor mother, what a good shot I gave that. Almost believed I *could* turn people into frogs or at least make them wet a bed. Always being told off for frightening others.'

'I was more of a witchy tomboy,' said Claire. 'Always happier making fires or dens, or trying to make pipes and pots from the crap clay in the garden.'

She thought of the spells she'd weave as a child. Riding her mother's broom or the zenith of a swing that threatened to sail the bar, the split-second thrill before chains exhaled. Hunting frogs to spice a charm, steeping sugar-water for bees drugged by exhaustion. But the woods were her favourite haunt: only wise old witches lived in those. She'd wait for them, scorning the harsh bark of deer, fox, the flurrying pheasants testing her mettle in the crisping dark of winter. *Nothing there*, as her father said, *that can hurt you as much as people.*

'Ah, the joy and freedom of that!' said Tansy. 'Stuff childhood, I could do that now and be happy. I think I was born an adult. I found children, awful as it sounds, just so – *childish.*' She wrinkled her nose. 'They're all on *a spectrum* now, aren't they? I think I am. In fact, the older I get the more I think it wasn't them, it was me. And I never looked as one was supposed to as a girl, either, though I suspect that's not an uncommon sentiment. Even now.'

'Especially now,' said Claire. 'If anything, I think it's worse for girls.'

'I think you may be right.' Tansy sounded thoughtful.

'I always thought I'd have children and didn't, whereas my sister thought she wouldn't and did. Which explains a lot.' A small *hmm*. 'And the longer I live, the more I see we all have our disappointments in this life.'

She went on to talk about her father, a diplomat equally distant in emotion, her mother: elegant, sharp, social, famed for her entertaining, Tansy and her sister 'sent off' to British boarding school. Almost, Claire thought, the last of her breed.

'I remember, though,' Tansy added, 'watching my beloved papa being beastly to dear Keziah. She looked after me, mostly – she had many children and grandchildren, and I remember her as a tall woman of two halves: love and angles. Her elbows, hands, jaw. I thought her pure Amazon.' She stopped, a soft look Claire wasn't used to seeing in her eyes.

She let the pause hang. So much time spent feeling a need to fill a void, make whoever a speaker was *comfortable*. A revelation to see how time alone had freed her.

'But there was a morning my father summoned her,' said Tansy, 'shouting. In front of the staff, anyone passing, about her not cleaning leaves off his car properly. She never needed to be told to clean *anything* – put a pinafore down and it was being ironed before one blinked. She was seventy when he did that.' She shook her head slowly. 'The point at which I began noticing how differently women were treated in general to men: one noticed at parties and such. And then I grew up altogether. Which rather cemented it.' She stood, wincing. 'One can only hope things improve. Age is hardly for the faint-hearted, as it is. Tea?'

Claire stared at the mark again.

Did they burn it in: drive the heated poker to scar with a force to make the teeth clench? Did any of them *not* believe? And did the women watch that smoulder of ascending flame and hope to avoid tongues of fire, too? Strange to stand five hundred years later and whisk away a carpet, feel pamments straw-strewn underfoot, hear the spit of fire, the skitter of dog claw, cat claw, child. Perhaps a pheasant has its feathers pulled, a loaf gets baked, a pinching finger finds a scold. Perhaps upstairs a heated mating makes new life. Or a woman cries or dies in childbirth. And when they bled, these women, did they stand here praying *Ave Maria* might bless them better, fill a womb, make a life worthwhile? The actual witches, what of them – did they smile at such naivety, curse for all they were worth? How many women had stood as she did now, looking at all the loves, losses, joys and blood, that made or broke a life?

She did know one thing. She'd be witching; on the side of the smilers. Scrolling Twitter earlier, she'd seen all the decades of woman boxed in illustrations for a diet akin to being stranded on Scott's Endeavour. *Eat the fat! Do LESS, lose MORE.* Blah. Bleurgh. She's seen this yelled at women all her life. Either you liked a pie, a pint, pudding, chips, or you suffered to fit fashion with a penchant for the shape of teenage boy. Not much of a hop, skip and dowager's hump to the horror show of those over-50s infographics.

You couldn't help how a woman's body gets twisted into fictions to suit the scribes of judgement any more now than then. How many of those witch-women were just older – God, probably all of thirty then – and had a knowledge menfolk did not like? How to tell a girl to tolerate a husband; set or stall the seed in a womb; heal a sick man with a herb, help a child with summer flu? How much of this an envied or resented power – the hook to hang the blame on when a harvest failed, a wife reviled, a beloved died. The hag, the crone. What were they outside sex or servitude? A woman old and ugly with no use.

*

'Put your sketchpad down.'

'Why?'

He takes my pad with those huge, scarred hands, throws it down and slams me against the wall, pinning my hands above my head. He does not have his apron on, and as my ribs lift I feel the heat of him, face centimetres from mine; belt buckle just above my own; I smell his sweat, the tang of hot metal, smoke, ash. I cannot breathe, have to fight my gasp.

'Imagine,' he whispers at my ear, 'what could happen if we saw where this went.'

My voice a husk. 'It could easily not go anywhere.'

'But it could.'

'Don't say that.'

'I can't help it. I'm bewitched by you – it's like you've put a spell on me.'

'Don't be so ridic—'

That first kiss. My *I can't* strangled, stroked, stopped, by his tongue.

'I know this is a genie in a bottle.' The way his fingers curled into his palm, tight, as if fighting resistance. 'But I want to uncork the bottle.'

The second. The twist of his tongue so the tip twines mine, so I forget myself at the stagger of his inhalation as I reciprocate; find myself biting, gently, at his lip.

*

'I think it began during all my time with dear old Keziah.' Tansy winked as she handed Claire her cup. 'The content of which my mother knew mercifully little.'

Claire blew on her tea. 'Did Keziah actually practise witchcraft, then?'

'Not *per se*. But oh, that knowledge of plant, bark, leaf! Neem, for instance, the Indian lilac – *Azadirachta indica* – was practically her apothecary.' She smiled. 'I asked her once why she scratched her teeth with its bark – I loved to suck on cinnamon then – and she gave me a stick; I *dearly* wanted pearly whites like hers. Grateful to still have one's gnashers, of course, but no dentist – saying something, sadists all – deserves to see them now.'

'We had this raggy old woman just outside the village who my dad knew as a kid,' said Claire. 'She made herbal stuff when no one could afford a doctor. We kids were horrible to her looking back, poor thing, collecting her faggots; scared, probably. What did neem do?'

'Almost anything. Mosquitoes hate it, for one thing, and jolly good, too, but it cures all manner of skin horrors, alongside parasite or gut issues that shall remain nameless – Keziah used it on me more than I care to remember. Leaf, flower, gum, oil, you name it.'

Claire smiled. 'But no spells?'

'Oh, I liked to think so. She'd squat, boiling water in her old *sufuria* – ah, how I love that word! – chanting at her tinctures and I'd believe she *was* a witch. I loved her hand on my forehead in a fever, too. Mother hadn't a clue. If brandy or aspirin didn't cut it, even God couldn't help you as far as she was concerned.'

Claire's head was cinematic with images: a storyboard for each rectangle of white plaster framed by the cronky beams on Tansy's walls. 'Did all Keziah's children survive?'

Tansy sighed. '*Tch.* Sadly not. One died of malaria, one by puff adder. She *loathed* snakes; went at them full pelt with a besom if they got near the house. I remember prodding a tiny red one I found under a jerrycan, I was *that* sort of child. Never saw a woman move as fast for petrol to douse it before boxing my ears – most odd, as she wept as she did so, then suffocated me in her considerable bosom. It was how I learned poisonous snakes are equally lethal juvenile as adult.' She looked down, smoothing a wrinkle in her plaid skirt. 'She was my fairy tale old woman in the forest, like your poor widow: one assumes she *was* a widow? Keziah lived on the periphery, too. I think the most interesting people often do?'

'How do you mean?'

'Being an outsider.' Tansy's fingers made a small spiral in the air. 'Not feeling one conforms to the norm, or desires it – or enjoys it as others appear to. I vividly recall starting boarding school, which I despised. The fact one couldn't climb a tree to draw if the fancy took – *too unbecoming for a lady* – or sit cross-legged as with Keziah. Couldn't even kill a fly by clapping it – approach from the sides, for what it's worth – without some horrid Miss declaring me uncouth. You may laugh, but I'd often stand outside a classroom before break was over, waiting to get back in. Did you have those children at your school?'

Claire did laugh. 'No. If you did that at my school, even the teachers would bully you. She shrugged. 'It was a rough comp – feral. But university and after was worse. Hard work.' She paused at the age-old reflex of silent shame: *well, that's one way of putting it.* 'And then I met Ben.'

'Whereas, don't hate me, I never did a day's graft before London. The closest I got to hard work was helping move Mother's booze stash to her study if Papa was due home.'

'Because he judged her for it?'

Tansy did a loud *ha!* 'No, because she didn't want him to *drink* it. Former captain of a ship, see. Stomach barely able to tell cognac from meths.' She hmm'd. 'I didn't see it then, but life must've been awfully dreary for her. She always said if one is miserable in one's own company, one is bad company and should fix it, and I agree. Though I also think *unbelonging* makes for a great deal of flexibility, a fluid mind. It makes one a good observer of people.'

'But before Ken – didn't you work in publishing?'

'What else to do post art school? I could've asked for money, I suppose. But I was far too proud to admit to Mother I wasn't as terrific as I thought. And I *adored* my bedsit.'

'And living alone in London was a big thing then. Get you and the Swinging Sixties?'

Tansy threw her head back, laughing loud. 'Silly girl! The only part of the Sixties that swung for me was the coin on a string a boyfriend made for my dratted meter.'

'But it passed, right, when you married Ken – the feeling of not fitting in?'

'Well, no.' Tansy shrugged. 'I wasn't like the other London wives – detested dinner parties, for one thing. All that frightful small talk and men off to smoke. I thought things might improve when I got pregnant. But alas, again, sadly not.'

'So, what did you do?'

'Bizarre as this will sound, I joined a church. I was somewhat flat, no real friends, Mother's advice merely to wait for a baby and spend time with' – she gurned – '*those worse off than oneself*. That being *de rigueur* to kill hours outside husbands then. That, or develop a taste for brandy and naps. But here's the *most* bizarre thing. I'd copyedited a book once on ancients and divinations and an ex-colleague asked me to cast an eye over her tome on tarot – pretty radical back then.' Another wink. 'Gosh, how I loved that, with my "knowing" as Keziah called it. Perhaps it was pure hope my *knowing* I'd never be a mother was wrong. But anyhow, no churchgoers knew, so one also felt quietly rebellious. Which I rather liked.'

'And Ken – did he know?'

'The war left Ken with quite the enquiring mind. He had an army friend who'd see skulls on certain chums' faces, chaps who never did return. And, of course, I had the girls.'

'*Girls?*'

Tansy hmm'd, nodded, as if the two of them were merely discussing a hosta. 'Runaways, mostly, who'd "got themselves into trouble". I took them in occasionally, while they waited for help. Most parishioners refused, but I could never stop thinking of Keziah looking after a rich white girl with two daughters dead. Perhaps she was a witch – rather a slow-burning spell if one looks at it like that.' Another hmm. 'Dear Ken. Always so proud, no matter how I pooh-poohed. I only hope I made him as happy as he did me.'

Claire smiled gently. 'How could you not, Tansy? You could so easily have been so different. You should be proud of yourself, like he was.'

'How so? How can one be anything other than what one is?'

'Tansy. You've always been direct with me, yes?'

Tansy nodded, bemused.

'Well, putting it bluntly, you could have just lived in your ivory tower playing the colonial deb/professional wife game instead of helping women no one else would, even their own family. *You* were trying for a family, too, which wasn't happening. You could, if you don't mind me saying, have been a right snotty cow – but you weren't. And for what it's worth, I think Keziah would be proud of you, too.'

Tansy stared at her for a second, eyes huge as a surprised child, before clearing her throat. 'How marvellously people see us from the outside, don't you think? What a wonderful thing to say. How kind of you.'

Claire shook her head. 'Not wonderful, or kind. *Honest.*'

'Do you know,' said Tansy, 'I don't believe in my whole life I've ever been able to be so honest with anyone as to how I really feel about things – a bit sad in over fourscore years. It is so very cathartic – divine – not to be judged, told to cheer up, how lucky I am, and all the other things which one knows. So, thank you. I can only hope you have felt the same.'

She smiled, broad, warm, as Claire smiled back. 'Yes. I have. *Do.*'

And for a second she could have sworn she saw the hint of a glisten in those dark, dark eyes that matched the one in her own.

She was still thinking about witches as she stacked her little bonfire. You couldn't grow up in Suffolk and not know of Matthew Hopkins, the bones that fuelled his bank account.

She'd also grown up with fire, a language she spoke fluently. She hadn't realized how much she'd missed the seduction of its dance, the sibilance of its tongues.

She made a small pyramid from sticks, lay a few dead branches over the tiny lick of flame; there wasn't much wind and she didn't want to smoke out Tansy; the wood not quite dry enough, the fire needing food to whet its appetite. She hunted for bark, wisps of dead, handfuls of twigs snap-dry; tucking and sidling them into holes fire-hunger would find – anything bent on destruction will feed itself – half-fanning, half-stamping it into fiercer life.

Smoke pulsed around her, the velocity of energy cracking her twigs as the fire began to chatter, hiss, spit. Life-giver. Life-taker. The saviour and the danger.

The smoke began to cloud now, rise, spiral, gather, as if drawing a cloak around itself to keep in its precious heat.

Soon, it would be able to incinerate anything.

*

It had a certain inevitability with The Poet, she'd see that so much later. But back then it felt like a grubby secret she carried like any other high-functioning addict: internally aware of its reeds tangling her feet, weaving round her as she swam that quarry. How it felt coming home from London as train shrank skyscraper and all her shiny dreams of Future, eye hidden by an album cover patch the uni best friend made with: *Come on, we're going clubbing.* Which, for a while, worked. Until a wrinkly suit did *Would you like to sleep with my chequebook?* And she'd had to peel it up to dispel him. Something in that, though, solidified all she felt about herself.

She moved to Norwich, close to the countryside she wanted the comfort of, tried all the tested ways to forget. Sob tapes. Stella Artois. Dancing. *Misery loves company*, so many said, she not used to desiring other men by then; knowing their struggle to hit the notes, not just murder, the song her body could sing. An old uni friend, The Poet's polar opposite in every way – except *his* face hovered over her, and sex you have to try at is a backward-facing catapult. All it filled her with was emptiness edged with the guilt of a good man knowing his was not the cock you wanted. She tried scoring with a stranger instead, so drunk she swayed the *wanna come home with me?* Feeling his 'no' from the emotional Venn of his face. Disgust. Pity. Shame. But she rallied; took a job with a friendly design company, joined a pool club workmates went to: *say yes to more than you say no to*. After a while, she could even sit in her solo flat sober of an evening; if not loving, at least not hating herself so much. And then the letter came. *Sorry, sorry, sorry.* Would she – could she – give just one hearing?

The sex stratospheric. Tenderness, now. Love. And yet.

Something in the way his lips curled that made her think of predator drooling at prey. Something, too, in how she couldn't hear what it was she wanted, though he said he loved her every day, moved *just to be near* her. Something, something, something.

When it started again, it was like the fucking: a new intensity fed by the spiral of a firestorm. One time he shoved her so hard a glazed internal door shattered, another mashed hot pasta in her hair, would *hit her all over again, she's mental, wants him to*, so she did not a hear a friend call by and hear it all. When she complained about the harsh bare bulb above his bed, he picked up a baseball bat and shards of glass made tiny baubles in her hair. She did no art but still sketched in notebooks, phone pads at work: heroin needles, fires, intricate walls, mazes of leaves, but mostly, without thinking, needles. She never drew him.

She promised herself when she was paid enough she'd buy some therapy; still not hearing, still unsure, what she wanted to, but of one thing she was certain. Black and white might be the base of grey, but were not the colour itself. If she hadn't left and did not love him, she must have done it all for sex. Which said it all. It was not The Poet who destroyed her. The person who destroyed her was *her*.

How many wonder why someone sticks with a lover whose attraction they cannot see – how many, knowing this, ask it of the self? She'd asked herself so often she was sick of the question, set her sights on simply living life. One summer night at an 'open mike' among a clique peculiar to such places, all gentle heckle, infectious, fun, she found herself chatting to the venue manager, a lean Gaul with an equally striking wife. That morning, she'd stubbed a toe on shelves she stored artwork on, disembowelling The Poet's file by accident. She wouldn't have noticed if the letter weren't so childishly decorated – what adult used felt pens? But she knew before she picked it up; no need to play detective.

The wife left, but there was wine, full, in Claire's glass now, and – suddenly – hot breath beside her ear: 'When was the last time you had a really good orgasm?'

She laughed. 'None of your business.'

'Mine was about three weeks ago.'

'Okay, so was mine.'

'Are you being serious?'

'Are you?'

The letter paper cheap, the sort that let a felt pen leak like the track of an infection – word-blood, she thought later – hearts over i's, stars in margins, coloured clouds over *now that we are special friends*. She hadn't felt as she'd have expected, knew this woman, found her vapid; a *feminist* to other females, but a flick of mane, a stretch of skinny leg and ample cleavage the second she saw a man, with all the pouted power she knew they wielded. A heaviness, weariness, an odd disappointment. *Her? Really? You can't do better than* that?

Breath on her neck hot as the inch above a flame. But it was her who said 'Come on, then', his kiss too self-satisfied; not that it mattered. It wasn't what she wanted. What was?

She'd said nothing about the letter. Before, she'd have shouted, screamed, cut him out of her life and lived the lie of denying the ego stroked by how he always came back.

She was down on the manager before he even got her wet; his twiddle of nipple a temper-twitch, the too-long nails inside her an urge to slap them away. She watched herself, half revulsed, half with something she couldn't nail. She could only rely on what she felt, for whatever it said about her. All she felt – and, holy fuck, she could not work this out at all – is somehow she was free.

Somehow, she was *back*.

The fire had settled into itself as dusk began to fall; its own flaming sunset. She could smell it in her hair, coat. It suited her.

She'd set fire to all The Poet's letters after that night. Gone home, but never back to bed with him in the same way: her fucking desultory, the usual post-climax nausea inflamed to full-on disgust. If you love someone, it's them you have the luxury of hating when things go bad. But if you don't, it's *you* you end up hating. For being with them in the first place.

She didn't want it any more, whatever *it* was. And so, one sultry heatwave night, alone and naked in her flat, she took a bowl, drew up a sash and burnt his letters one by one, collecting the flakes and ashes of his words in a bag she later buried in a bin.

Three decades later, she closed her eyes, picked up a brush, and trawled her mind to fish them out again. She painted herself in her mind, holding them over her fire, here in her 'crazy-lady chazza-shop' duffel, as Asha called it, hair a bonfire-scented bush, face a smudge of charcoal, mud and chlorophyll. She still couldn't answer why the girl who said *if they keep going back then maybe they deserve it; he'd only have to hit me once* went back herself; time and time again. Perhaps she never would. But whatever she'd forgotten, buried, hidden, lied about, it didn't matter any more. It had stopped the black and white of her, shown her a world that spun on poles of grey. Perhaps the people who don't love you teach you the most about love.

Perhaps, too, she'd been a little snippy on the call with Stephen last night: 'I'm your sister, not your bloody client.'

There'd been a small pause. 'Okay. Just don't be a cliché, Claire, that's all. Jung took four years to have his midlife crisis. Abraham Lincoln had one, Michelangelo, too. And it was the start of the best work of their lives.'

Maybe this would – *was* – beginning the best bit of her life. She thought of the women at the lake. How midlife pivoted its prisoners on one foot; the other lagging, digging in a heel to where the roots felt firmest in the sinking soil. She hadn't known if the 'me' with that manager, The Blacksmith, even, was a me she didn't recognize – or a me she actually did.

What only came back to her with so much solitude was how it happened organically, that day with The Poet when she caught herself thinking *I am changing*. Those the words she used that first time with The Blacksmith too: *I am changing. My life is changing*. Maybe her own vibration was changing again. From hurts to hertz, with any luck.

She thought of Tansy. How she'd said ash was 'so terribly good'; a natural source of potassium, magnesium, phosphorus, nitrogen, calcium. How it helped neutralize acidity. How the roses, some flowering now, loved it. How the ash conditioned soil whatever state it found them in.

How it helped them bloom.

June

Strawberry Moon – Full

She stared at the pot of lavender she'd had since marrying Ben. This morning, she'd added it in miniature to Wank Farm, frothing at the front of a border, wanting to capture something of its centrifugal force; the gravity with which it drew in bees, butterflies – the pollinators the planet was losing 'hand over fist' as Tansy sadly said. It seemed appropriate. This wasn't the same lavender – that died years ago – but it was the same huge pot her grandmother gave her as a wedding present; glazed in a striking cerulean blue. It once held a robust plant that leaked scent as soon as you looked at it; always a reminder of her grandmother saying to rub the flowers between her fingers whenever she needed calm.

The sun was threading the first hot strands of itself into the day, sprinkling dust on the tall thistles in the field headland, the brittle beauty of last year's teasel heads, specks of sleep in nature's eye. It comforted her to see the new stalks wind skyward. She'd been too young back then to see the old woman knew she was dying, wanted a piece of her to stay tangible for her only granddaughter. How she wished her grandmother could have talked to her more about her mother. All she'd ever said was: 'People are as people do, Claire' – that generation of making beds and lying on them; all the secrets stored in boxes underneath.

Had her mother had always been that way, or had her depressive fugue-states only kicked in after motherhood? Were they happy, her parents, Mum with her nerves, Dad who dealt with it, as she understood now, by running away with his lorry? Who could know? Marriage was an abstract painting to anyone but the two people in it.

'Thanks. And hey. You know I don't mean this unkindly, sis, but you weren't the only one who felt abandoned,' said Stephen when she FaceTimed at lunch to apologize for her snit last time, also wanting, she told him, his insight, wisdom. Help.

Claire watched him take a sip of water from a plastic bottle the size of a small fridge with a straw attached. He'd finally cut his hair and stopped dying it that weird, charred conker. Must be harder to age in the States, she thought. At least here you expected to look like a dropped quiche as you got older.

'Why else do you think I left home so early, got so far away?'

'You always said you couldn't wait to get to London because you needed to be gay.'

'Which was – is – true. But even London wasn't enough after the exchange year, seeing how I could live, *be*, here. Mum couldn't deal with her own shit, Claire, you know that, let alone mine. And Dad, well. All I can say is I feel sorry for men of that generation. War babies. It's that poem thing: they were fucked up in their time; all that, you know?'

Their paternal grandfather, a coalman, died before either

of them were born, but their mother's father, a gardener, was a prodigious grower of fruit and veg; their grandmother, like their mother, of flowers; often said how gardening saved her in the war. How much old people talked of war back then. She realized she'd likely equated gardening with war and depression ever since; veg-growing with men who never seemed to be around for long.

'But aren't you contradicting what they say – that by this point in life you really should be over blaming the parents?'

'Well, if that was made law, I'd have helluva drop in clients,' he said. 'And I don't think *blame* is the right word. *Understand* lands better with me. Claire, do you honestly think your kids will grow up and never blame *you* for anything, things they might be able to understand later with age? Like they're the only kids in the world with a perfect parent?'

'Like menopause, or leaving their father, you mean? Brilliant. Thanks. Now I'm panicking Danny won't ever come back. I've already started their therapy piggy bank.'

He laughed. 'Oh, come on, you know what I'm saying. You're not Mum, Claire, you broke the pattern. What I see now, *know* now, is that I needed that kind of distance not just to escape and find myself a new life, but to find a way to forgive them.'

She thought of Danny. Ben. Perhaps they shared more than just a little physical similarity and a lot too much of the stubborn gene. 'You never told me that.'

'I didn't know it back then. Listen, sis, sometimes, to find the way, you kind of have to lose yourself first.'

The sun was drying the soil as fast as she could rip out the ground elder. She watched her fingers winkle out tendrils from the root ball, engrossed in the embroidery of eternal knots, the deceptive, and endless, shoots that ran deep, pale, strong, impressed by the persistence and insistence of both; the bedraggled pile of its discarded leaves lame by comparison. Eat it in salads? Fat chance. Her appetite was returning: the only thing she wanted right now a fat, comforting pie. She remembered something else Tansy said of ground elder:

'*Aegopodium podagraria* – another of the Apiaceae. Good for rheumatism, gout, sciatica, piles, and jolly old water retention. No wonder that cartoon rabbit was so lithe.'

How, just as soon as you ripped up one of its rhizome knots, it shot sideways, kept going, kept growing, stronger all the time:

'Unless one gets rid of every last shred fully, it'll be like playing hook-a-duck until the ducks steal the whole wretched show'.

It occurred to Claire in that way it was like love. Falling in it, being in it, losing it. You could spend so long wondering if you loved someone, or what love was and if it was the thing you'd embroiled yourself in, you forgot how love wasn't a tap turned on and off at will.

It seemed to her that love came for you, not the other way around. Whether you wanted it to or not.

*

After The Poet, she had no appetite for relationships.

Still. She was free, if not physically (they moved in the same social circles) at least in her head and heart, preparing to return to London, get a career back now she'd glued herself together again – albeit one misjudged move, one hearty clink, and *smash*. The irony. All the times she'd tried, hated herself for not, and it happened entirely, it seemed, without her.

She'd emerged that morning fresh from a bath – bathing always a magnet to him – and he'd insistently drawn her to him, murmuring into *that* curve of her neck, fingers at her nipples, cock twitching at her, urgent. And yet she felt nothing, none of the usual belly fire, no – *desire*. If anything, she recoiled at the saliva on her bath-sweet skin, the stubble rashing her, tin foil on a mercury filling. The whole day took on a different colour after that.

The walk into town, to the job she'd soon leave, felt effervescent as she passed open windows, inhaling the last warmth of summer, exhaling the last of the season's songs; leaves yellowing into dip-dye tips of red more beautiful than she ever remembered. She noted the flecks of ivy, moss, tiny fronds of fern in the flint front walls, the tousled semi-sleep of their gardens. Even the curved beauty of a dual carriageway bridge she crossed every morning seemed graceful that day as the neck of a swan. Not the norm by any stretch. Much as she loved walking, early morning was usually a pretty safe bet for locating any latent anti-Taoism. Hormones? Wrong part of her cycle for happy. Leaving her job? No – that meant worry and icky dreams of rich old men on beds made up of credit cards, and so she walked on, uncertain. But good feelings don't work like bad. For the first time in three years, she didn't feel the questions needed answers.

She met Ben a couple of weeks later.

An off chance; sprung from a mood for fun before the grind of finding somewhere cheap in London that wouldn't also prove a gateway to rape, murder, burglary or, at best, more mad flatmates. Ben was a friend of a friend's brother; slightly older and not her type, but he made her belly-laugh and she liked him enough for a one-night stand; a little fun. She just had not expected him to be so *nice*.

They laughed in a pub and went back to his; the friend leaving later while she and Ben sat and talked all night. But he hadn't made a move, even as she lolled, provocative, pulling out all the stops. Asked her to lunch instead. The Poet sniffed around her later: sensing something she brushed off, keen not to anger him, keener still to get away and not have him pursue as he always did; always a grubby hand clutching at her.

'He's a perfect gentleman,' she said. 'What else can I tell you?'

Not, and she never would, that meeting Ben had felt like coming home.

*

Lavender. Such a beautiful plant. Everyone knew lavender, and everyone – as far as Claire could make out – loved it. Those soft spikes with all their hues of blue, red, cyan, magenta, white, yellow, grey; the way they glowed backlit by sun, bees buzzing insect ecstasy, the striated lurex of the rosemary beetles that loved them too.

She'd hardly needed be told lavender stood for peace, purity, grace, devotion. Unless, of course, you were Victorian: 'No fun in denying oneself a little light punishment,' as Tansy said. She'd gone on to explain how to them it meant luxury, vanity, indulgence: 'All the interesting things.'

With every plant she learned more about now, she felt she gained a new understanding, and with it, as often the case, a new respect. Something that made her feel protective; wanting to nurture, help them in their fight not just for life, but *Life*.

'But did you also know,' Tansy had added, 'that alongside the ancient Egyptians using the beloved lavs in art and embalming–' she'd paused to wink with *now there's a thought for the Will* – 'legend has it the village of Bucklesbury avoided the Plague entirely, owing to its being the European capital of the lavender industry?'

She did not.

'Fascinating, isn't it? I assume that's how it takes its name – from the Latin *lavare*, "to wash". Which also explains its erstwhile presence in all manner of cleansing ritual. And if you want the spiritual, it supposedly reminds one to aspire to ideals, make effort to be rid of one's own dirty mistakes and failings, if you like.'

Claire looked at the lavender waiting to be washed by the tap, gifting the soft air around her with its undeniable sweet summer scent. She had not known that, either.

*

Sex. It defined her relationship before Ben, held the majority share in all those that preceded it. It was a bank with a ruthless edge for those who couldn't control their spending, and it did a particularly good line in debt recovery.

She hadn't wanted it to matter. By then she'd fallen in love – enough to put London on hold and see what happened. Love and sex were not, she rediscovered, quite the same thing. Love – proper, true love – was not dangerous. She tried telling herself she was living on an unhealthy overdraft from the massive accruing of ill-advised overspend; that this was simply the bank she was used to – however corrupt – and all she needed do was embrace the change. The good. The pure. But it hadn't felt like that.

Sex with Ben felt awkward, clunky, a little bit – somehow – *wrong*.

Nerves, she'd told herself. Intimacy that mattered: that wasn't about six hundred ways to come and nothing feeling like it needed a fitting, tuning, oil change. The discord would settle. Or she would.

After the first few times, however, he still had not brought her to climax, which confused her – had she simply been lucky before, or was it a sign? Did it mean he thought she had, or he didn't a) notice, or b) care? Had his other women always come, so he'd never had to think about it? He only needed touch her in the right place and she'd gape like a baby bird, ready to come in his hand; but he always stopped, or moved, at the crucial time.

Eventually, she'd had to say something, which seemed all the wrong way around. She remembered her mother at a family wedding, uncharacteristically tipsy on Babycham; joking *her* mother's advice had been a discreet rag handed over on her wedding night with the words *a gentleman takes his weight on his elbows*. But, her mother added, 'Don't think it isn't important, girl. It is.' She never spoke of sex again.

She didn't even know how to ask, Claire cried to a new best friend. 'Everything is perfect! I knew this would happen. And it shouldn't matter – he's everything I've ever wanted. What the *fuck* is wrong with me?'

The best friend shrugged. 'You never have the best sex

with good men. You have the best sex with bastards. That's just how it is.'

An older woman, Monica, Claire had worked with in a teenage Saturday job, had said something similar: how you didn't marry Mr Best Sex because he was unlikely to also give you the best parenting experience. It would have been weirder but for Monica's penchant for sherry, fags and all the gossip she ate instead of food; the oldest woman in that supermarket, a younger one recently caught in an affair with the pub landlord. 'You have three men in your life,' Monica growled under her copper bouffant. 'The one you fall in love with first, the one you have your kids with, and the one you get old with. If you've any sense, love, cut out the middle-man and stick with the bastard you know.' And then she'd sighed and slugged the rest of the sweet Amontillado that lived back then in a plastic barrel for customers bearing empty bottles. It was advice that left Claire confused at fifteen. But she'd never forgotten it.

'It'll get better,' the best friend added. 'And if it doesn't, you'll cut loose. Don't sweat it, it's not that big a deal.'

Whatever it said about her, sex was still the only thing that made her forget the now ingrown need to guard; the carefully considered constructions of self to show the outside world, so it wouldn't – and, hopefully, she wouldn't – think she was as mad as The Poet said she was. Sex the only stress relief that ever really worked: a portal to another realm she reached sometimes with other men, mostly on her own, but always with The Poet. Fucking him, she'd cried at times from the sonic boom of barriers breaking in her brain. But. Afterwards. How to forget that terrible, trickling sense of betrayal of herself, the liverish nausea?

Desire, she realized, terrified her. How, if she'd desired Ben like that she'd be in his – its – thrall again. How to trust herself, her choices, decisions, then?

But love, as Ben was reminding her, was about being the best that self could be. She couldn't bear the thought he'd find her out and she'd be cast aside like the dirty baggage inside her she didn't know how to begin to get rid of. Best to give him the option, she told him, out for dinner, when she knew she was getting in deep.

'I understand completely,' she said, 'if you need to head for the door now.' She'd even pointed to it, a sad smile on her face.

'Sounds like a total cunt,' Ben said.

'Me or him?' she'd half-joked. She'd been upfront about how she saw her role.

'Claire,' he said. 'Did it happen before him?'

'No.'

'Did it happen with him before you?'

'I think so. From what he said, yes.'

'Well, here's how it is for me. You could do, say, throw, anything at me you wanted. You could stand in my way. Argue me until the cows came home from an all-night fucking rave. And I'd still never lay a finger on you. Or any woman. Has it ever occurred to you he *was* just a cunt? And' – this so gently, hand on hers, eyes deep – 'you didn't deserve it?'

She couldn't hear those words, whoever said them, without that quicksand sensation in her chest that pulled everything down: mouth, head, heart. 'But what if I'm wrong and he's right – I can't see myself clearly, and, actually, I *am* a total psychobitch and you only find that out too late?'

Ben smiled – how she loved that big, open smile! – 'A risk I'm prepared to take.'

She could remember barely any of the other conversations of their early life because nothing stood out but for the joy in each other's company; the endless landscape of laughter, the river of their conversation. If Ben had said he was off to the ends of the earth, she'd have found a way to fold herself inside his suitcase.

'I was happy before you,' he told her one time. 'But now I'm *really* happy.'

The sex got better, too; the drink and drug-fuelled Nineties spilling into their bed, car, floors, the holidays that saw them fuck in the sands of warmer lands, the underwear that came in silky boxes stuffed with scented tissue paper strewn with pearly beads.

She got another job in another design agency, which didn't pay much but didn't seem to matter too much, either: they had each other *so we are rich, indeed.* Life was full of love, fun, friends who loved the aura of happiness that infused their atmosphere. *Meant for each other, beautiful to be around.* They wanted to play house, and soon. And pretty soon, they married.

Oh, Ben. The One. The soulmate. Beloved other half.

The disbelief you could have it so good; the in-jokes and the our-tunes. The pride in that, the gratitude. The healing of a love that bloomed, blossomed, survived storms and still grew broad and wide, spread roots so deep it grew impossible to separate the threads of them.

Three decades, though. Fifteen hundred weeks. Just shy of eleven thousand days.

A lot can change when you look at it like that.

All that time wondering if I would. The thoughts that scavenged my daily life, my dreams. The head-split of the illicit; the justifying of the unjustifiable.

'You don't have to do this. But God, I want to be inside you.'

The Poet. *I want to be in you so much.* I fight the memory; turn my inner ear from the flutter of red flags. When he kisses me again, I fall into it. Now or never: one last shout-out before the old lady leaves the building. Is it true it's not the things you did you regretted when you got old or took Death's hand, but those you didn't?

I stand. Look at him. Take off my jeans, my top, and walk towards his smile.

The valleys of his neck, the ridge of collarbone, that spreading hill of shoulder, tattoo a thicket on his arm. The heat of him, the liquid wax of me. He is hard as the steel I've watched him heat, hit, master, as he threads fingers into mine. Stares right into me.

Every which way. Upside down, inside out. Hard. Soft. Slow. Fast. Eye still deep in eye. He licks the sewn slice of my Caesarean. I take him so deep in my mouth I feel him in the cavity of my chest. His tongue fits mine as if precision cut and the first time I come it is despite myself.

Memories fade as fucking takes over. As desire is met and matched and all the dreams made flesh.

As axis shifts and light falls on a different path.

*

The roots of every lavender were clean. Every tiny remnant of weed, every filament of alien stem, every cell of foetal plant unentwined from thick masses of root. No excuse not to recover now, fill the holes, let go the dead. Live.

She thought of bees, the soothing summer pulse of them; the flowers that would go on right into autumn.

She noticed the stems of a geranium which had flowered were long and straggly now – Tansy said 'leggy' and Claire liked that, head filling with how she'd render it personified: red and white stripy stockings on skinny legs, arms spiky sideways shoots, flowers for hair, face a smile of sticks. She reached for her pruners, clipping the plant back to baby leaves, a naked crown ready for the next flush, as Tansy had instructed, delighted to see a single fruit on the tiny wild strawberry she'd left alone all spring, a pear drop of scarlet shy as a child at its mother's knee; its taste pure perfume.

She took time to plant the lavenders back. She didn't want to go indoors yet; didn't want to look further than the blinkers of her hair. Somewhere in her, deep in darkness, she felt a stirring, as if an animal were waking from hibernation: shifting, shuffling unsettlement. A promise of something coming.

It amused her to see the soil fill with birds as soon as she walked away – birds at war, at that. A blackbird bullying a robin; a pigeon bullying the blackbird; another pigeon fighting that, or shagging it; she was never sure. They had a cat once that used to yowl in spring and shove its backside high, yet soon as a male came near it hissed and spat, vicious as a viper. It would kill any other cat, too, even if it killed itself, when it had those kittens.

Reassuring even nature found desire confusing.

It was an ambitious plan, a risk. But Claire also knew this feeling wouldn't just go away. Or if it did, in its wake she'd feel as if the universe had offered her a microphone and she'd only looked at it, her words frenzied bees at a window in her head. She couldn't afford for that to happen again. So much more time behind than in front now.

'The aim of art is to represent not the outward appearance of things but their inward significance' – Aristotle. She'd read it last night, stumbling across Thijs Biersteker's prize-winning installation of a real tree that used real-time data via leaf sensors that told people what it 'felt' or needed: the science showing how data delivered in the form of artwork helped people lean away from preconceived ideas.

She hadn't felt like this since she was eighteen, staring at an empty canvas with nothing but a brush, an image, the tiniest of sparks waiting for her bellows. She was as much a blank sheet then, she thought, as the white she looked at now. When she started university, everyone spoke of imposter syndrome. Secretly, she'd thought they meant something overly arty or just overthought; how to be an imposter to what was inside you? By the time she left, she understood it so well it coloured her paper before she picked up a pencil.

As in gardening, so in life. She'd risen shortly after dawn, wide awake, and walked to the church to make the most of the soft sun; stood admiring the full majesty of oaks that sat so incongruently with crumbling headstones. It occurred to her that somewhere around her – all over the planet, in fact – a tree stood that was born at the exact same time as she was.

She knew this was Big. Big to show and more so to pull off without sounding cheesy or wafty. A conversation: between a nine-world mother oak and our world; sketches and studies spanning rural to urban to form a whole – art as the voice nature didn't have. She picked up her brush, silenced the hope she wasn't just having some kind of last-minute twat attack.

Oh, but. The throb of it.

She remembered that too, now. That feeling inside her that split a seed, sent out a shoot, spiralling through the soil to reach sun, pushing, pushing, up, out; a part of her that could not be contained – *too much!* – and which compelled her, for that was the word, to paint. Look at the leaves! She wanted this art to say. Look at the trees, the flowers, fauna, fungi, all the infinitesimal cells part of everything and nothing all at once. Leaves come, leaves go, but isn't the biggest mark of human kindness, *love*, to leave something behind for others to enjoy, make the world leaf and flower again?

She made herself take a long, deep breath. Lifted her left hand.

At some point you learn it for yourself: how you don't ever live in isolation – nothing does. How we are all in it, this ugly, wondrous, unfair, beautiful life, together.

The wine was in her hand, the speaker on.

If she did this for long enough, on enough of an empty stomach, the wine would set loose a bubble, however brief, of absolute and unadulterated happiness. In her old life, this would see her wander her house; tidying, tweaking, sipping the shiny iridescence that reflected back at her all she had achieved. *Look what she'd done, built, grown, created – look! How happy with it all, all as it should be!*

She looked around her. Okay, so it might not be hers, but she'd done it. She'd made herself a home.

She took another sip as she admired her living room: the cheap freestanding shelves that took three hours to unpack, lug against a wall and level, with the help of a few sticks of kindling. The books, the ceramics, some hers (shit) some not hers (and not shit, though she still had her pride), the framed photos of her boys, oil burners, incense, driftwood from the beach, pinecones from her walks. The charity shop frames filled with her own art. The funky plants hung over dents that sat like scars by the bookcase, reminding her how long it was since she rode a DIY bike without Ben as stabilizer. In her old life, they may have chatted to her briefly, Ben, or whichever son was home, before heading off to their lives as she tidied and bounced in her bubble until music seeped in and she could bounce to that instead. Not always easy at first: maybe something cheesy, a rhythm to puppet her feet, lift her arms to lightly punch its beat: *SorrybutIhavetodancetothis!*

But that was then and this was now – nothing in Hunter's Moon that did not speak of her. Over half her years ago, the last time she saw that.

The moon waxed fat again outside the French doors, redder even than last month's; the colour of the inside of her one wild strawberry. She began to sway to the music of her teens, closing her eyes as wine swam into her senses. Except now, the more she sipped, the more uninhibited, the more sexual, her dance became; lost in beat, in rocking, dropping, grinding, giving it out to suggest, impress, actively pulverize a pelvis. Almost as if she were her younger self, being watched – half the point to *be* watched.

*

'What were you like at thirty-five?' He stabs his fire and I catch the smell of his sweat; acrid, sharp, and not sweet. It tugs the feral in me.

'I was like, why don't you fuck off? With less wrinkles.'

He laughs. 'Your spirit, Claire.'

Manipulative. Narcissistic. I'm old enough, and we've learned enough of one another's secrets now, to hear the injured child in him. In this way I am sure I'm not in love. He has a crush, he says; has 'considered' how a relationship with me would be – *a disaster. What burns the brightest burns out the fastest* – but continues to ask about my life as base metal becomes finial, hammer shapes; water hisses steam and red turns orange turns black and back again. He takes me over his anvil then, makes of my body a bridge, licks my sweat.

How to ignore this being taken out of the boxes of age and domesticity; polished, seen by admiring eyes? In these moments I don't just fly, I soar.

But the price. Big diamonds don't come cheap.

*

She forgot she couldn't sing now – sad to open a mouth and find only a cobweb-stiff gate – but kept on anyway, *sotto voce*, until somehow, she was simply here, now. Not thinking, busying, hiding, all the other myriad things this *Claire* could do to fill the void.

She looked again at the moon. It made her feel somehow timeless. Ageless. Honest. As real as she ever could be outside crying, coming, watching birth or death. She saw herself barefoot in a forest she'd sometimes visit in sleepless dark, dancing under moonlight, singing to the mother moon, not just sexy now, but *sex*: the whole of the moon and the whole of herself; her tides once the moon's tides, her belly once its boasting shine. Now, poised twixt that and outright hag, she felt the force of its settling: free of all the bonds, boundaries, sacrifices; the sheer bloody blood of it all. Silently, eyes closed, Claire danced.

When she stopped to refill her glass, she found herself standing, iced to stock-still.

A part of her wanted to laugh, another to rage. Yet another to sink into the whirlpool spinning in the entirety of her torso.

She'd only noticed because Hope Becker had also texted for the first time in a while: Hi. Hope all good? Just to say I'm back in UK after summer hols – like to catch up if you're around, have a chat. H. No kiss. She'd tapped out a beige reply, putting the slightly uncertain feeling down to wine. If gardening taught you nothing else it was the absolute fact that you had no control over anything, only the ability to embrace whatever sun or storm came. At least age had granted her wisdom. Enough to know there was no point responding to the other text in a such heightened state. Better to breathe, let it roil a while, wait for the sea to shift.

The exclamated greeting. The fact he'd been *reading kid a book the other night and saw you were its illustrator – brava! Xx*

Now. Why *now*?

She probably wouldn't answer. It pissed her off, too – unreasonably – that he knew the Italian feminine. She threw the phone on the sofa, strode off to make a strong coffee. Couldn't drink it without it percolating her guts in a very not good way at her age.

Best deal with it, just get it over with.

*

'I'm happy for you.' *Infatuated* with somebody new. 'And now you don't want to see me again – is that why you called?'

He pauses and I imagine him frowning at his fire, running a hand over the smoothness of his knives. 'That's a very direct question.'

A dagger of fury. After all he's said to me – *direct*?

Oh, little man. I spent twenty-plus years raising children – twenty-plus years learning how to self-shadow as I dealt with and decided, found the words to make sure I didn't make anything worse, hide what couldn't be shown of myself. Or life. I've done that in a marriage, trauma, illness, heartache, menopause, death. I have nursed and cared and held the hand of the dying, helped and given myself away and now all I want is to speak my truth, say my fucking words. I want plain words on plain paper. Even if they dip their ink in my blood.

But what point saying anything?

'Isn't it more,' he adds, disconcerted by my silence, 'about not knowing where paths ever lead, or cross, all that?'

Daggered all over again.

I remember a woman I worked with once: in her fifties but still supremely sexy, screaming under streetlights at midnight, shirt open over saggy breasts, swollen half-moons under eyes, veins shouting from crêpy skin – ugly in her desperation, pathetic in her need. I admired her for surviving a shit marriage (a policeman who broke her arm), her beautiful, grown-up children, verve, wisdom. So what could make a woman scream like that outside birth or death? I remember his guilty pity, that younger man blown cold – weren't these women meant to wither like all the other autumn things? – the curious mix of my emotion as other women did the *He's not worth it, you're worth more.* What was that woman but lying to herself about catching feelings, what was that man but believing what was said; dropping his dollar in the slot before moving on to the next neuron lighter?

The cloak and blindfold of lust, I think later, weeping into a bath so my family can't hear: the way it wraps around sex and weaves threads through skin until one cannot separate from other. Sadness – such sadness – I let myself come to this, if without the bells and whistles of that street show. Still. Too many birthdays not to have learned something of cardinal rules and crowning them all: Know When to Shut the Fuck Up.

'Love is sort of a science,' Stephen said once, 'in that, it happens not because things look good on paper, but when two neurological messes come into contact and vibrate.'

Oblivious to me now, where once he felt the thrum of me so strongly he'd message if I thought of him intensely. So much of life wanting to be right; the worst thing of all when you wish only to be wrong.

Insidious. Horrible. Nasty. Step away from the keyboard. Step aw— *One*, then. I'll get my fix, swallow the sick it will press an internal ejector button on, and move on.

Disgust spirals in me like a corkscrew as I flick from screen to screen – however much I know, little is as powerful as the machination of the limerent mind. I feel as dirty doing this as when Guitar True-Love dumped me and I stayed with a mutual friend in his town; sneaking out to go to his street, then his house, hiding in a hedge to *maybe* hear his voice, *maybe* see his face. Right next to all those bastard milk bottles so I had to run, run, run, so he'd never know. Or that time – all those times – I went back to The Poet. And yet I'm feverish till I find my quarry. Beautiful, of course. No more than thirty-five, max.

I catch myself, stand, sway, stuffed to the gills like a Tudor queen gouty from feasting on black blood.

*

She did not feel the wine now. Her fingers shook, even, as she tapped out a reply, which horrified her. But the words she chose should do it: polite, not unfriendly, gracious, well-wishing. Tempting to feel as if she'd just mastered the Noble Eightfold Path, but she'd never been good at leaving things on a discordant note. Which, on the other hand, and ironically, worked to her and Ben's advantage.

She could not believe the text bubbles that started almost instantaneously.

Miss chatting to illustrious illustrators. If famous you is up for catching up with humble anvil monkeys, be great to see you . . .

She told herself to breathe, the scent of lavender still calm on her hand.

As if she'd go back there. As if.

June

Strawberry Moon – Half

The Suffolk sky was an unfeasible azure that morning as she got back into bed. She watched an aeroplane unzip the flawless blue, so high only the tiny glinting arrow of it headed the parallel lines of contrail. She'd already written the day off. A few degrees warmer and she'd take off all her clothes; stand naked to feel that sky, that freedom, pureness, cleanse her. It was that or a bath full of bleach. She'd forgotten what it was to feel this. By your sixth decade you'd think you were at least old enough, if nothing else, to know better.

She watched the vapour drift into two smoky lines. It was different things you missed after so long being with someone. Talking, yes. Strong hands to open things, even; someone bringing you a cup of tea in bed. But skin – touch – ah, that was the one that bared your bones like teeth to ice. How she wished she could be on that plane. She didn't want to think about last night – ever, if only that were possible. Sleep took a long time to find her, and she'd woken with a strange sensation she felt only once before; in a rare, local earth tremor that rumbled into her old home at some unearthly hour, shaking the bed, and as such, her awake. She'd thought then of the *Three Little Pigs*; of huffing, puffing, blowing; the wolf, the wind, the earth. So, wait – what was making her foundation feel so flimsy now?

A moment, a liminal spacebar, to recognize the machinery of man: builders, heavy lugging.

A series of clanking bangs, rapid as gunfire, filled the room with harsh staccato and she jumped, hand to heart, spilling her tea. In her mind's eye the council notice on the fenced-off acre the other side of Tansy's, so tattered she'd barely noticed it. More houses being built. More homes.

She had a sudden, panicked sense of needing solidity. Something to stop the palpitation of gut, heart, the stabbing sensation at her throat. She drew herself into a curl under the duvet, nose to knees, arms hugging shins, a dark cocoon of herself, her breath, her heartbeat. Safe.

*

Something in how he greeted me. Or was it just me? I couldn't grasp the metric of it. Him.

A cursory hug. He was chatty, chopping veg to a linger of seared lamb. I watched his hand make a big knife small: one of his own, a 'blacksmith's' knife whose thin handle looped in one sinuous curve almost back to blade before curling like the tip of a snake's tail. He showed me a line of them once in the tiny forge he rented: the first a rectangular, red-glowing hatchet, the second long-tailed with an almost-blade, the third rudimentary-handled but recognizable, the last a sharp and slightly coppered grey, short only of its finishing polish. His life was *excellent*: parties, women, *fun*.

I watched the scar I'd kissed on his hand widen, bleach, shrink, redden, as it chopped. The scoop of upper arm just above bicep but before shoulder. The hairs at his neck slipped loose of black elastic unfastened my crotch inside my jeans and so I pressed spatula to garlic, onion, pepper, to tame myself. Drank the wine he poured. Jumped at the finger tracing my arm.

'Good to see you again.'

Like the lamb, that; still unexpectedly pink when prodded.

I could only mouse the food, organs pulsing outside me, wine not doing what I wanted it to: defibrillate my brain, sparkle up my words. In my gut a sensation of the hissing, spitting sear of meat as I pushed my glass to him: 'More wine.'

*

The scrape of stone, the squealing beeping, the meaty chomping of engine unearthing earth. Sweat in crevice of thighs, knees, breasts. She felt she might vomit again, realizing, as with any roiling sense of nausea, her body was about to betray her.

Anniversary.

She tried to think of work, but her head only fuzzed. She tried the garden instead: the fern she wanted to transplant to stop its fringes browning in high summer; the catnip suffering under the cherry; a purple sage she thought was dead which lingered in life despite a lack of light. How she admired that sage, all but a bunch of twigs until Tansy begged her to bide her time – *what's not dead is not always obvious. Work your magic and wait.*

Part of her wanted to hurl herself outside, hurt herself digging, shifting, slicing, anything to render her spent. She felt as raw as the silty smell leaking from four hundred yards away. As raw as she had shown herself to be.

She closed the window, curling tighter as the judder kicked off again, drilling into the deep soil of her head. That banging. That beeping. That chugga-chugga-chug; that churn-churn-churn.

*

Let me show you something. A Bernini he'd seen at the V & A; a tomb statue for a noblewoman who gave both riches and life to help Rome's poor and sick, half-reclined in robes that, while juvenile in execution, predicted just how genius would later enchant marble. One of the statue's hands caressed her bare breast, the explanatory words he read so beautiful I was shocked to feel myself flooded by inescapable sadness, reaching for his hug, realizing I was sweating in the humidity, armpit stamping his skin. Sensitive as nerve in tooth – was that a glimmer of recoil?

He asked questions about my life I batted away until they hit my work, talking Art Calling as if I'd already won it, Guitar True-Love in my head then: *I'm* so *impressed, Tex.*

'Wow,' he said. 'Amazing. I'd love to see what you paint. Your talent, Claire. Stunning.'

Last time I was here you called me *that. My sex. Licked my sweat.*

A little more than a little drunk in the bathroom, I felt the haunt of New Year at Asha's: all those questions on my life

– albeit no Toilet Duck here, he's far too organic for that. But I couldn't shake the feeling of being somehow exposed, of the image of that female face caveated by erosion. Why did I come?

I washed my hands, catching sight of my reflection; almost didn't recognize myself. So much here an *almost* the blur was not unwelcome.

Perhaps more wine would help.

*

Make it stop, make it stop, make it stop.

She tried again: a garden alphabet of all she'd learned from Tansy. *A for ajuga* (cheers the heart). *B for buddleia* (rebirth and resurrection). *C for crocus* (hope, new starts). *D for daffodil*; *E for echinacea* which she wanted to grow not just for its beautiful blue flower but its immune-boosting properties, health, wellness. F. *F. F for* – for what? She couldn't think of a single thing except *F for For fuck's sake*. Nor anything for G. *H, then. Come on, Claire, H!* But she could only think of *hedgehog*; that bloody crystal-healing book she'd illustrated so early on in married life with Ben, which jumped her, yet more irrationally, to *L*. *L for lily* – her wedding bouquet – Ben's mother, and her typical comment: 'So clever to use a funeral flower!' before 'Let's hope a smell associated with sorrow doesn't interfere with the food?'

Tansy had cackled at that. 'Ah, the sort of m-in-law of which dear Ken used to say 'Twice around the room and up out of the chimney'. Until I pointed out that's an insult to the witchier among us. And she's wrong, I have great joy in declaring. Commonly, *hyacinth* is the flower of sorrow. Ghastly things, in my humble, but there you are.'

Claire had laughed, too, then. She also hated hyacinths, partly because Ben's mother loved them. 'But they're such a marker of spring? Seems odd they represent sadness – I did think it was lilies, or is that just white lilies, like I had?'

'Only recently. Lilies are the flower of *death*, yes, but also of love. And hope and purity, so there you have it. Oh,' Tansy tapped the side of her forehead in the way, Claire recognized now, of remembering. 'And femininity if you were an ancient Egyptian or Greek, with a bit more purity and chastity thrown in in Japan. Though in China, strangely, seeing as white flowers *do* usually mean death, they symbolize a happy union for a hundred years.'

'So a good symbol for marriage, then?'

'Ha! Only if you'd snared the right victim. And what a dreadful shame you couldn't give the beloved m-in-law that? Or how the Romans – being Romans – stuffed bedding with them for . . . let's just say the sort of thing fitting for one's wedding night?'

Wedding night.

Sobs ripped through Claire like an earthquake splitting concrete.

*

I waited, unbreathing, after the sex, for a touch that didn't come. I was a dog, head hung, as I apologized – *what was all that about?* (Oh, how I wish I knew) – the acuity of realization as nauseating as the slosh of the wine, though I was far from drunk then.

He was kind, which only made it worse. The words the first

flecks of sleet at the back of a neck: *Shit happens. Vulnerable. But maybe take the lesson?*

How I was the one to check his behaviour once. I heard the sound of my laugh-stroke-sob, the words that slithered in its wake: the oily slide of snakes. My snakes for his nettles; I wanted the snakes back. They couldn't sting the way these tiny, well-meant needles did.

'See you again some time,' he said, as I tried to parse each inflection, the P45 of body. 'Take care of yourself, though, yes?'

I want you to care more than you do. I want you to want me again.

As soon as I hit empty road, a whole globe of open sky, a proper sob escaped me. Not just a tear or two swallowed away with my usual Will This Help? – but an actual, hiccupping sob I tried to stave so hard I had to stop, heave onto all the beauty of a verge scarlet with poppies, purple with vetch, pink with rosebay, and yellow with the tiny smiling face of bird's-foot-trefoil. The fading moon above it all still that strawberry red.

*

Here the tumble of a fortress she once believed would stand forever. Even as the first bricks fell she stayed a willing blind, though she'd felt the pelt of them, smelled their dust, heard the gasp of exposed iron. How blindness sharpens other senses. When did it start, this dissolution of those so-proud vows?

Pain. Like that of death, grief – the sludging suck of quicksand. Years were peeling from her, taking with them the pith of skin, the flesh-stuffed stuff of soul. Tears like she had never cried, from a part of her heart she'd never felt.

F. Try again. F for foxgloves, a favourite – witches' gloves, dead man's bells; the plant to raise the dead or kill the living. *G for garlic*, alliums – prosperity, humility, patience; a concept that engendered something between a laugh, a retch and another sob that bent her like a paperclip.

Hosta. Heuchera. Hydrangea.

'Hydrangeas!' she remembered Tansy declaring with an amused look. 'I used to think they were called pandemoniums when I was a child, though I've not the faintest idea why.' She snorted to herself. 'I like myself far more as a child now than I did *then*.'

'They like acid soil,' she'd added, when Claire confessed she'd always liked them too, and was it worth her trying? 'As do rhododendrons and camellias; all the old lady plants. But you don't have the trees – firs, pines – to make soil acid enough, though of course, willows, oaks and beeches are partial to a bit of acid. Perhaps that's why they grow near yours truly. But you, dear Claire, have mostly fruit and that terribly elegant birch.'

I for ivy, the stuff of everywhere, of Christmas, but no – Tansy back with: 'Nature's dratted superglue. It gets everywhere and you can't get rid of it, hence it stands for eternity, vigour and fidelity. The Egyptians dedicated it to Osiris, the god of immortality. The Greeks, small surprise, to Dionysus, and given their *penchant* for priapism, I offer no further words.'

J for Japanese maple, the acer. A new favourite of Claire's after admiring Tansy's.

'Ah, for that you'd probably need a pot,' Tansy said. 'Somewhat beauty and the beast, given it either sulks or gets suicidal without ericaceous soil. As in nature, so in life, as I always say – few things work if they are not where they are meant to be.'

'So, if I move the stuff under my cherry, it'll live? Why put it there in the first place?'

'That cherry is thirty-odd years old, Claire. Once maintained, too. But it's been ignored, so now it simply overshadows anything beneath it.' Tansy had smiled. 'How *tempus fugits*. Takes its toll on us all.'

*

The kitchen a carnage of party shrapnel, the living room strafed by popcorn, crisps, the shiny foils of celebration; they always did throw a good one, equally good to know they still can. She hears Ben pound sofa cushions, the whine of hoover, turns her music up – both boys asleep at last – worth one last New Year fizz: they'll be back to school in less than a week – as hips bump butler sink at a song. By its chorus, a wooden spoon is microphone, spatula a drumstick. Hot suds flush her hands so her wedding rings sparkle, though she doesn't notice this until Ben puts her hand in his, spins her to face him.

'One last dance for Daddio?'

'Christ!' She flicks a sud at him. '*The Sound of the 70s*. And in such a not-good way.'

He pulls her in, does his ridiculously boyish face. 'Put your hand in my pocket. You'll find something else from back then too.'

She laughs. 'So – is that a SodaStream, or are you just pleased to see me?'

'Oh, yeah. And I know how to ride a Chopper, *baby.*' He tickles her neck with kisses as she squirms, then stretches out her arm so she turns a gracious circle under his fingers.

The CD a beloved from their wedding, so neither can stand still for long: fingers streaking sideways V's, tiptoe struts in socks, her shimmy, his lasso, him reeling her in, an old in-joke from the child-free years. But a change of tempo now; an acapella hymn to loneliness, the quiet keening of a broken heart.

They hold each other close, silent, and she wonders how many thousands of times they've held this shape that makes one life *for better or for worse.* For Christmas, he bought her a Royal Academy one-day course for 'those who work in graphics, design, or illustration, to loosen up their artistic skills' because he refuses to believe, however down after the career hits from leaving London, having kids, she won't 'come good with it' in the end.

'But that's just you, Ben,' she'd told him. 'You *have* to say that.'

'Even if that was true, I'd still wish you'd believe in yourself the way I do.'

'Because you're not an artist. You don't see how many there are out there, and free from childcare – and so much better, too.'

'Ah, because I'm not an artist, is it? Except when I said that years ago – when I told you *nothing* would ever get me beyond my Purple Ronnie period – you bent my ear about Van Gogh being thirty before he even picked up a brush, no art school, nothing?'

'And look what happened to him.'

'Well, the miserable sod should've married me, then.'

She'd been unable not to smile at that. 'Sorry I've been such a miserable cow.'

'Yeah. Me too.' But he'd laughed, nudged her. 'Come on, I know it's hard, C.'

She smiles up at him now, knowing he shares the same relief: *We are still here. We are still Us.* A couple of pecks until one kiss sparks and he moves them towards the table.

'I love how the air changes around you when you want me. I do love you, Claire. No one will ever love you like I do.'

She let him lay her down, thread fingers into hers. 'And you, Ben. Total *Demis*.'

Another in-joke – *forever and ever* from the puke-inducing Seventies song. But how she loved the smell, the feel of him, this man she pledged that dreaded troth to, father of her sons. Smug married, indeed. How – if life was lucky – neither would ever know loneliness again.

*

Here the fast-rubbling riddance of an attic: that host of stored-up pasts and might-need-it-for-the-futures; of beloved toys and discarded hobbies, cases, the changing fabric of the rooms below. Here Christmas. Here kids' stuff, first shoes, all *welcome to the world!* And We Never Did Sell That Cot. And look. Oh. Look. Here a wedding album no one will laugh at any more.

She put it back in its box, then shoved the box as far as she could under the bed, as if the dark might dissolve it; rewind the film all the way back to the liquid it once developed in.

The fortress had bared its teeth at the sky. Windows splintered, sills made shapes of prayer, doors sharded as fire-tongued wires hung hungry. Here the ceiling she stared at sleepless, soothed by the breath beside her – where she lost herself in blissful spasm as sperm pierced eager egg, or sheet grew damp with unlived lives. At least if life is love, they got the making of it right? The years with Ben and then the kids had been among the happiest of her life. Until. But then. And so.

'If we met now,' Ben asked towards the end, mid-pandemic, when they'd exhausted and infuriated each other *again*, 'do you think we'd have a relationship?'

Here the elephant in an empty bed, trumpeting what was. Why wasn't love enough?

How to say after all those years where it started? She could volley blame between them; the he-did-this and she-did-that. The rows that grew like roguish plants: weeds grow in the cracks between concrete far more than on it. She understood marriage is not perfect. But a woman who stops speaking her unhappiness is a woman for whom it is too late. She saw it now. How she'd leaned into a world of waiting, if unsure what she was waiting for. Kids going? Love returning? She'd even thought if he had someone else she wouldn't mind (he'd be less grumpy?), these thoughts as slow, subtle, as the encroach of myopia. 'Don't ever tell me,' she said, so many times, 'I never tried to tell you what was wrong.'

But they never seemed to agree on anything any more. How he accused her in those last years of moods she swore she hadn't had, only now could see how much her hormones stole. You cannot trust your mind, emotions, psyche, in perimenopause, and so she'd clung to Jules, Asha, Emma, limpet-like, to share stories, soften shells, get a grip as they let slip all those secret thoughts to feel less scared, and less alone. After the deaths, a seam of Ben had formed, too, unfathomable, unreachable; a fact she felt ashamed to talk of. How she gave up asking for attention because of how it made her feel; hoping, too, before she gave up even wanting. Easier that way. No more feeling half a version of herself, a cut-out to pin the clothes onto.

She looked again at his text. *Happy anniversary, if you know what I mean.* Sad emoji.

They had it all for such a long time – yes, they did. But outside the past, both knew neither could answer that question of Ben's. They met at the age Danny was now. How much easier if she could say he was a bad man, or she a bad woman: some monochrome hook to hang it on that sat so much easier than the bleaching fade of love? She still loved Ben, but she knew now one genus holds a hundred different shapes of leaf.

Was it love, sex, friendship, trust, respect, humour, shared interests or shared progeny? Looking in the same direction or simple lack of imagination; an opportunity to stray not showing, or one of you not getting round to leaving; laziness, fear – how did they do it, the ones who made it last forever?

By the time the machinery stopped, Claire couldn't tell how long she'd lain there. It seemed every tear she hadn't shed, every sob she'd stoppered with sheer will, like leaves blocking the spout of a watering can, could not be halted now.

She could raise a child to decent man, run a house, three calendars and a self-employed career; switch roles quicker than any actor, negotiate for the sodding UN. She had a hundred different ways of hugging for a hundred different needs: a thousand words for different kinds of pain. She could judge a person's mood with no words needed, know what needed to be done.

Cope. She'd said so many hard goodbyes; watched death enter, and leave, far too many rooms, found words to tell its children. She could split inside with the shots of life served strong and smile so no one saw; however hard the roughest diamond to scratch her soul, it was still her own, never not soothed by the sight of the moon, a stare at the stars.

And yet, and yet, and yet.

Four letters. One syllable. Everything. How to remember that once you lived a life without it, and may well live the rest that way, too, now. Had she said goodbye to all and any of her last chances for love? She felt as if she stood looking around her at a crumbling kingdom, the submerged ruins and dissolved churches, and she didn't want it; God knew how hard she didn't.

But I do give in – I surrender. Because here is where I am. My past doesn't need me any more. But my future does.

She blew her nose, staring out to the sky, still that azure, nudging in her the urge to blend rose madder, cadmium lemon, ultramarine, emerald, cobalt turquoise, a quinacridone violet, perhaps, titanium white, black, on and on until she captured and contained it.

Shadows danced on the wall as the sun rose higher, thrown by the leaves on Tansy's ash it felt in winter as if she'd never see. She watched them, thinking how the trunk, branches, were still the same, however hard to see now.

Not clinging to leaves leaving.

Not looking to any of the other trees it shared its world with – the ancient, ivy-covered oak, the beech, birch, hawthorn, willow – to complete it.

June

◯

Strawberry Moon – New

If only she had a crowbar.

The dead tree stump sat there, just sat there, smack in the middle of the main border like a carbuncle. All around it, June flowered in fat leaves, in roses and wild poppies, the lilac starburst of allium, the wheat turning silver-green in the field. She was struck by a clump of Asiatic lilies under the honeysuckle, knelt to touch the dark, veinous branches on their yellow tongues. Funny how such a tiny thing could make you smile despite yourself.

She would not give in.

Smug, that dead stump seemed to her, crazy as that was: it hadn't bothered her before. But she didn't have a saw and trying to lever it out with Tansy's 'lady's' spade was akin to using tweezers: twice she'd tripped over it (single *fucks*), the third time (double *fucks* with added *shit-bastard*), and now she'd both tripped, lost her reading glasses, then trodden on them turning to find them. It wasn't even *her* dead tree.

Tansy would know what to do. That's all that stump was; a different kind of branch, a different kind of family.

'My women friends,' she said to Emma over FaceTime coffee, with an almost Catholic relief at having confessed *everything*, 'feel more like family than my family do, if that makes sense? I missed you – sorry it wasn't the best holiday.'

'It does, and you too.' Emma glanced behind her, checking her office door. 'Listen, I did a lot of thinking on holiday. How the older you get, the more you see it, especially after menopause – men are men and women are women. That's how it's always been, and I think probably always will be.'

'Even now? You don't think it's just us, or age?'

'I've got two daughters, remember? No, we're more emotional, for one thing; we can't compartmentalize like they do, we're just not as good at it. Weird as it sounds, though, I actually think they're scared of us a lot of the time.'

Claire thought of something her younger son said. 'A lot of Joe's friends won't date, scared of being *too porny*, rapey, or not *porny* enough – he thinks porn is as toxic for men as women.'

'My boy's the same. But I think us being too strong or successful does it, too. They know we can do the domestic shit *and* hold down a good job – we don't need them like our mothers did.' Emma laughed. 'I still think their biggest fear is us laughing at them; especially ratting on their cocks. And we don't bend over for just anyone, either. Not unless we're denying the damage we're doing ourselves – and I'm old enough to admit that now.'

'Oh, Em. I feel so small.'

'Oh, mate.' Emma shook her head. 'Big, small, you're still the same size, my love?'

'Maybe. And still such an idiot. Hardly as if I've got the excuse of youth any more.'

'Listen,' said Emma, 'we all have needs. We want to be seen, wanted, and we don't want that taken away. Like we want the emotionally intelligent man, but we also want him to make us bite a bloody headboard. Let's face it, confidence is sexy. Most of us can't come unless he knows what he's doing, and the hotter he is, the more of a mess, the more we can't seem to get enough.' She smiled. 'I had a super sexy husband and look what happened there – women falling over themselves, women I knew would shit on me given half a chance, telling me how lucky I was – and he was an absolute bastard. You saw that.'

And how. She'd still never told Emma about Twatface squeezing her knee under a dinner table; the stories his fingers told.

'That's why beautiful sexy people marry each other. If one's hotter, it's a difficult dynamic. You know, I realized on holiday I married Misery Guts mostly because I just wanted to be married, and for it to work this time. I ignored signs that were practically fucking neon. You have to think about why you were there, Claire. That's the truth of it.'

Why you were there. 'I'm just so— How could I be so stupid, Em?'

Emma smiled. 'Is it stupid, love? Or are you angry at yourself for just being *human*?'

She closed her eyes, breathed slowly, listening to birds sing the unseen symphony of a thousand feathers, a hundred beaks. How she wished she knew which song was what.

'Mum,' Dan said when they'd spoken at lunchtime. 'You know what'll happen. You'll get the mental one that'll lose its shit over a shiny bowl and eat all your laundry. Just don't. It won't end well.'

Once upon a time she'd say her middle name was Queen of the Universe, or walnuts were where squirrels kept their brains in winter, and they'd believe her. The dichotomies of motherhood. 'Well, to be fair, Dan, a dog wouldn't piss in the bath like our old cat did.'

'Mum. You'll just get one that'll never stop howling into the void. Even silently.'

'I won't! It could be good for me.'

'How?'

'Because it would be happy to see me. Because I miss having people around.' *Because I'm frightened to tell you just how lonely I am because then I'll have to admit it to myself and I don't know how to make friends any more and a dog might just help with that.*

'See, that's what I'm saying. It's not about pets, Mum, you just want *love*. You want something to love you.'

Something had sliced inside her.

But her son could see her face and so she'd tinkled out a laugh. 'Honestly, Dan, you've been in America too long. All that' – she adopted a nasally Californian accent – '*I hear you hearing me that I hear you hearing my need for love and healing my inner child?*'

He laughed then: that infectious chuckle of the boy who'd wind her hair in his fingers, insisting he'd never love anyone else. How hard it felt accepting the fact that your kid was now the one who was right. Thank God for summer. And peak dawn chorus month, as she'd read, which surprised her: she always thought that was spring; remembered instead Tansy saying how spring was the most popular time to kill yourself.

'Surprising, isn't it? But then, if one can't feel happy with sunshine and birdsong after the dirge of winter, one must be *really* mentally challenged, as I believe the saying goes?'

It hadn't been a titbit Claire felt inclined to thank her for; she'd just held on to the fact *numb* was not the same as mentally fucked.

She opened her eyes. Geraniums. Ferns. The scraggy, fat-leaved heuchera, purple as a bruise. She'd even attempt a hosta. She would fill those spaces. Doing things at the 'wrong' time didn't faze her anymore: *something* would grow anyway.

'You'll have to go in hard, though,' Tansy had warned. 'Hostas take no prisoners. Wear stout shoes and jump, if you must, on that shovel.' A now customary wink. 'I think you're going to enjoy this.'

She hoped so. Because despite summer being so late, and their alleged ability to survive if she cared for them well, it felt as if this division business would still be brutal.

She drove her spade into the crown of a geranium, half mesmerized, half horrified by the splitting sound, the severed pink flowers. Remembered Tansy describing how leaf shape dictated colour: 'The smaller, pink geraniums are thalo- and emerald-leaved; blue more viridian, matt, far rarer. Pink meant folly and stupidity to the Victorians – and rather a good metaphor for an overpopulated planet, I say – but Johnson's Blue thankfully positive: friendship, health, kindness, etcetera. But make as many babies as you want. They'll grow practically from a leaf.'

When your children came, it felt like being sawn in half. She'd thought she already knew what it was to feel divided: they came with blood by stopping blood – *veni, vidi, vici,* the only Latin she ever learned at school – until the ultimate division forged by the severing of that cord. Had her mother ever felt like that? Back when parents taught you only what they knew: how not to show unhappiness. *Pull yourself together. No point crying over spilt milk. Be a Big Girl Now* and on and on, all the way back to dead centuries when no one said anything in favour of quiet madness within four walls.

Two plants from one. Another from one more.

She planted them, turning to the Johnson's Blue not yet flowering. She loved blue flowers; they reminded her of holidays, hot places, voluptuous blooms the size of her face. Strange to think of herself standing here in harsh winter winds and dreaming of bees, birds, colour, wondering how it would feel; too afraid of her feelings to let herself feel them.

The fern now. Overgrown and a little unruly, curling its fronds coquettishly – if she'd illustrated it, it would have Rubenesque curves, huge eyelashes, Betty Boop hair.

'Magic.' Tansy again. 'Or witches, as I prefer. Not that you'll be surprised by that.'

'Why, though? Ferns always look so sort of *natural*. Harmless. Like in forests.'

'They thrive in shade. So yes, the dark arts, I suppose, though used to ward off evil in the Middle Ages, strangely. Sincerity and dreaming of someone to our Victorian friends – how delightful! Mind you, when *I* split a fern after moving here, I found a cat skull under it. One rather hopes Mother Nature's doing, though one accepts in a pile of this age, *anything* could be buried, frankly.'

Fronds of the severed fern were falling off as she gently lifted it, fine strands like hairs from a head, each with its own base, its own seeming root.

You can't uncarve the carved. Years of subtle erosion went into sculpting a woman as a mother. She'd wanted to do it 'properly': be with her boys, know them, have them know her; atone, she saw now, for that intangible distance, the difficulty she'd refused to acknowledge most of her life. That her mother – or, rather, her mother's problems – were an installation casting shadows which eclipsed the boundary between parent and child, needy and needed.

'It's her nerves,' they said of her mother: Granny, the doctor, Dad. Not Stephen because back then he never really spoke about it (physician heal thyself?), and absolutely never Mum. She just went to bed for a day. Or weekend.

She wished, as suddenly as she had to know bird by song, she'd asked more questions before her mother died. Had she felt lonely? Was it motherhood? A job she never spoke of liking – *You just get on with it* – a husband half a country away half the time? Why she always kept her distance: did what mothers were supposed to do: look after them, care, school things, all of that. How despite it all, Claire never felt – really felt – her engagement.

She planted the fern, looked at a hosta spearing up to the sky. For however fragile it looked, it had the heft of a parsnip. And one of the best names, according to Tansy: 'Funkia, after the botanist Funck. And pretty funky, too, after rain. An Asian perennial of the lily family. The Japanese call it *Giboshi*, after the metal finials on their wooden bridge spindles – resembles an onion, allegedly. I liked to think of my spade as the wooden post.' She'd smiled. 'I like to think of you using the same spade, especially on a hosta. It means friendship. Legend has it if you give to someone, they'll feel your devotion.'

Perhaps all anyone was ever looking for was the echo of that first devotion, if they were lucky enough to get it.

She raised the spade high, hoping the blade would sever without the need for any jumping. But it only left a horrible dent – as if the suppurating leaves should squeal like the baby rabbit Ben once rescued from the cat but couldn't bring himself to kill, driving it to a field instead (*Yes, I'm sure you could Beatrix Potter it up, but it's fucked, Claire!*). As she let the spade fall again, her mind dredged up only guillotines.

'And they won't grow in sun either, like ferns?' she'd asked Tansy.

'Not often. Or not well, in any case. They're made for shadow. But I suppose it's like anything, isn't it – if it must, it'll make the most of wherever it is. Sink or swim, dear Claire!'

Her phone pinged. Hope. A surprise: she hadn't expected to hear anything after that last terse message until summer's end. She took off her gloves. Another row, probably. Another case of one six and two threes – God, it was like having children again.

All okay? Called and got cleaner – some kind of flood?!! Aunt impossible, just hung up! Could we do speaker call on mobile I gave her? Worried. She likes you – nothing else to try!! Thx, H.

She didn't know Tansy had a mobile, let alone a flood. Though it explained the car beside Tansy's cleaner's this morning. But – a flood?

Tansy's face the same shade as that ubiquitous front door Farrow and Ball: grim, gunmetal grey. 'I don't want to.'

Claire clicked on Hope's number. 'Well, she's your niece, she's worried, and I said I would, so I'm here.' *Just meet me halfway?* 'You're lucky the cleaner's husband is a plumber. How did he know it was mice?'

'Wretched vermin nibbled the only plastic' – she pronounced it *plarstic* – 'pipe in the house. Apparently, my header tank – whatever *that* is – is full of them. If dead, praise be.'

'Hai!'

Tansy pursed her lips, huffing, as Claire spoke. 'Hope, hi. Are you okay?'

'Fine, thanks, but what's happened? Are you, the house, okay – Aunt T, you there?'

Tansy gurned and Claire resisted an urge to kick her. 'Yes, I'm here,' she yelled.

'Why did you hang up on me?'

'I was *busy*,' shouted Tansy.

'You don't need to yell, Aunt. I can hear you. What's happened?'

'I told you. A mere mouse and a subsequent damp carpet. Don't hold the front page.'

'At your age, that's quite enough, though, eh? And is the house okay?'

Tansy scowled. 'Perfectly. Insurance, etcetera. So. No need to worry, and I'm sure you've masses to do.'

'But the cleaner said a flood, the boiler's affected – Claire, is that true?'

Tansy threw daggers but Claire ignored her, affirming it was.

'Why aren't you using the mobile I got you, Aunt T? I told you it's cheaper than a landline – you could've called me.'

Tansy snorted. 'As I'm not mobile, I don't require one. Where, exactly, do I go?'

'Outside? Upstairs? What if you fell, like last time?'

'I'll stay inside then. Break my neck and not just a hip on the stairs. With any luck.'

Christ. Claire couldn't help her slight snap. 'And what if I'm not here? Or I find you with your broken neck?'

'See, Aunt! You can't maintain this: you, or the house. It's not *tenable*. Is it, Claire?'

Ben's mother in her mind; easy to forget how old Tansy was. She inhaled, choosing words carefully. 'I think it's a good time to consider possible . . . future events, perhaps.'

Tansy's eyes widened, part disbelief, Claire thought. And part utter fury.

'Exactly,' said Hope. 'Like Claire says, you can't have floods and boiler crap when it comes to winter, not at your age. Listen. I've been talking to this *amazing* place you could easily afford if you sold The Forge. Not far away, you could still—'

Tansy stuck her tongue out at the phone nastily, thumbs either side of head, and Claire watched, amazed, as she turned and hobbled angrily into the kitchen.

'Aunt? Aunt T – you still there?'

'You should have spoken to her,' Claire said, watching Tansy nip out the tips of a flowering cactus on her windowsill as if they were lice.

Tansy did not turn round.

Claire sighed. 'Oh, Tansy. Don't be like this. I understand it's—'

'A long time since I had a mother,' said Tansy's back. 'Hardly as if I need a niece and a neighbour ganging up on me now.' A pointed pause. 'At *my age.*'

Claire rubbed her forehead. 'Look, I understand how you

feel. I do. And I'm sorry – I'm not your enemy, I'm really not. But nor will I be here forever, so whether you like it or not, Hope has a point—'

'Oh, a point about the *house*. Did you hear? Three times she asked. Three. Times.'

'I did – I'm not going to stand here and lie to you: I respect you too much for that.' How had she ever got caught up in all this *again*? 'But I worry, too. I don't want to see you even more incapacitated, Tansy – or to suffer, either. I've watched that with people I love, and I don't wish it on you.'

Tansy turned then, facing her. 'I may be old, but I'm far from stupid, Claire. I know the future has – difficulties – I can and can't foresee. But this is my *home*.'

'I know. And I know what it is to leave a home you love, too.'

A silence, then. Through the open window, the high mew of a buzzard.

Tansy let her head fall back, sighing a long *ohhh*. She looked at Claire. 'I know I have to think – I know. But I don't want to.'

A pause.

Dark eyes almost pleading now. 'I just don't *want* to, Claire.'

'I know,' she said. Because there was nothing else to say. 'I know.'

The six-month deadline was practically up.

She read the instructions again: *A piece or series of pieces that may be finished or not – for unfinished work, we ask that you submit any details you'd like us to be aware of when the work is complete (see: Other Information). You may also supply details of any work planned for addition in the event you are selected.*

Now or never, then. No excuses, either.

Why you, why this work.

Her heart pounded at the sketches, prelims, paintings, spread on the study floor to best capture the light. She looked again at her words – words she'd sweated over, edited, sweated more, edited more, to the point they began to fly off the screen.

She poured a glass of rosé and wandered outside to a dizzying storm of butterflies on a buddleia: peacocks, small coppers, painted ladies, red admirals, white ones with black-tipped wings that brought to mind the Seventies Pierrot craze, or spots that reminded her of those beloved Dalmatian children's books. A sudden squadron of wasps dive-bombed them: at best biting to get better dibs at the nectar, at worst going in for the kill, she didn't know. So arbitrary, the whole of life.

Why not her, then? Why not this work?

'Hope and rebirth to the native Americans,' Tansy told her once. 'But I much prefer how our friends the Chinese saw butterflies – earthly beauty, love, freedom, the soul. Isn't that the perfect fit? I challenge you from now on *never* to think of that every time you see one. One landed me on me not long after Ken died, with a broken wing, and I took immeasurable – almost obscene, if I'm honest – comfort from that.'

She walked straight up to her study to fill that box succinctly, plainly – no try-hard wannabe words this time.

A tree of life – because every religion ever invented has a tree. Hers an oak, its nine worlds our nine worlds: rural, urban, suburban, coastal, forested, fungal, animal, bacterial, chemical. Her inspiration the roots alive under all our worlds – example: the California Jurupa Oak, a clonal colony thirteen thousand years old that would have squarely faced sabre-toothed tigers, now under threat from housing developments; the four-thousand-year-old North Wales yew; 'Old Tjikko' in Sweden ten thousand. The interconnectedness of nature and human; the macro acts needed to help nature, but also the micro – 'acorn acts', she called them – she aimed to show in almost advent calendar format within a larger work. How, for example, even one pot of lavender by an urban door supported so much life. How she would intersperse the larger, rougher, with the fine detail her illustrating career had honed. Her planned use of natural earth tones and materials to deepen the symbiosis.

And then she settled herself on the floor and began to organize her work for its photo session. Slowly, carefully, methodically. Professionally.

She wasn't going to be a mother. She was going to have a career. A big, fuck-off career full of her being brilliant and free of the limitations forced on the women in her family: a world of difference between *job* and *career*. She'd do it for them; be lauded, too, for busting the balls of men who thought she wasn't their equal – even after years of Thatcher – talked over her, pulled at her with boozy breath, said she'd 'come to bed' eyes and so, really, whatever they did was her own fault? There had been other (lovely) men, and equally difficult women, too. Never overlook women; territorial as cats and versed in psychological fuckery. *Women would rule the world if they didn't hate each other quite so much*, as Stephen often joked.

'I need to speak to someone about work and shit,' Danny said, after leaving uni. 'Like, stuff you need to know – how tax works and my rights and shit. Like, if I get a job how it affects something that was there before the job.'

If. 'I can tell you that. They—'

'Yeah, but, like . . . It's more Dad's sort of thing.'

'Work is work, love.'

'Not really, though, is it. I mean, you work from home. And you're part-time.'

'I'm freelance, Dan. There's a big difference.'

'Yeah, but. Don't take this the wrong way, but Dad's job is sort of more – proper? It's Dad's we live on.'

That was just it, wasn't it? Whatever was said by whomever. Her. Ben. Anything medical, school (who never phoned Ben). No guilt like that of stapling a door with a foot while a child cried behind it and you laughingly lied about that deadline. No work stress like that of a swanky hotel suite full of whiteboard and middle-aged suits talking Hats on Monkeys and Myers-Briggs as your lizard eye watched a clock for the school run.

She thought again of hostas, Tansy's words. *Few prisoners.*

Sometimes she wondered how many other mothers, however fierce the love, stifled a scream at times that if they dared give voice would never stop. You grew your kids: watched them twine to the sun supported by the pole of you, the strengthening of their stem. You watched their petals unfold, take hits from disease, insects, all the whips and burns of weather. You tended. Waited. Loved with a love you learned you didn't know. How quickly seasons changed. Because it still seemed to loom up out of nowhere, the sly sideswipe that swung its blade right through the motherfucking heart of you.

'Why are you looking at me? Stop looking at me.'

'Just enjoying seeing you while I still can, Joe.'

'Ugh. You're being weird. I'm going to uni, Mum. Not *dying.*'

But something is, she wanted to say. The fat lady was deafening, frankly.

Driving home, back seat empty, her throat had ached as she tried to focus on his room, tiny en suite (she'd waited her whole life and never managed that), his boxes of nice stuff.

'He'll be fine. You haven't known if he's in or out all summer, anyway,' said Ben.

'But I know he's coming back. And roughly where he is.'

'Or you think you do.'

'Not helpful.'

'Nor is being negative. He'll be home again.'

'I'm not being *negative*, I'm being realistic.' She'd resented Ben then for driving, the distraction of it, though she couldn't have coped with the stamped reflex-braking; the drama of his not driving. 'Now, he'll have two homes. Home – and home-home.'

'Right.' *That* sigh. 'Why do you always have to complicate things so much?'

'I don't.' A prickle. *Don't say it.* 'Any more than you do when you ignore the satnav and then moan about being stuck on the M1 for an hour.' Why did she just do that?

'Can you ever let anything go? Fine. You are *welcome* to do the driving—'

'Except I'm not, am I?'

'Right. Everything is my fault. Happy now?'

'Why do you have to be so . . . *God!*'

His face a series of lines. Hers a series of wobbles. A tut here. A tilt of the head there. The tiny tell of the infinite ways she could, after decades, decipher even breath exiting a nostril: she'd grown so porous to them, she knew from the back of his head precisely Ben's mood. At least the engine purred on smooth road now; easy to forget how jarring the bumps.

Mummy I wanna marry you when I grow up. She remembered rummaging in Joe's drawers when he started sixth form, hunting a belt after hers broke: weeding widowed socks when one clunked. Frowning, she dove in a hand, a gasp escaping her. Lube. And not just *any* old lube. Lube to 'electrify'. Lube to 'stimulate waves of intense pleasure'. Lube boasting 'over 20 earth-shattering experiences'. Still, no parabens, it added, quieter, so there was that. Her son was at least planet-conscious as he stoked his seventeen-year-old girlfriend's fire. But – her baby. Her baby having sex. It winded her. She hadn't wanted to cry; she wanted to be cool, liberal, European, fit the image projected onto her sons, herself, unwilling to play this round in the motherhood game of dice loaded against you. *Rationalize it. You were shagging at seventeen? And there's a condom there, too – you should be happy he's sensible. Sensitive. The mother would want that; a boy not hellbent on recreating porn. You raised him right.* 'It does not mean I'm losing him,' she'd said out loud. Did men have this; daughters skewered by spotty boys with electrifying lube? *I want him to stay mine. I want him back. I want him.* Words like you'd say, like you'd think of, for a lover.

Ben's sigh, edged with sadness. 'Let's just get home.'

It had carved visceral pain in her all over again. She hadn't wanted to go home at all.

'If I had a dollar,' Stephen told her, 'for every time a client sits in my office and tells me when her kids left all she wanted to do was run with them . . .'

She watered the divided plants again. Stared at that tree stump again.

How, when your kids were small, you could feel such a Nothing at 'only' being a mother. How, when they were grown, you felt a Nothing all over again because motherhood *was* the most important job you'd ever do, but now you were 'nothing else' – plus, in her generation, wondering where your career might be and trying not to shit yourself about your pension.

Perhaps it was all just part of nature's design as you got older – to force you to get out your reading glasses and study what you could make of it still, the same way that stump looked dead, but its buried roots would still give *something* life: everything on the planet had a use somewhere. Even decay fed underground life, as uprooting made space for the new, like these severed baby plants: a chance to grow better than before.

Perhaps Stephen was right, despite all those times she'd told him to get over himself and bury the past in that box their mother so loved.

'You have a mother-wound, Claire. It's classic. Unmet needs from childhood, in this case stemming from Mum's depression because she didn't, or couldn't, deal with whatever her shit was. You should read up on attachment theory.'

'And you should stop saying *should*,' she said. 'Isn't that what most therapists say?'

That smile – Mum's eyes but Dad's 11 at his brow. 'Look. Mum did the best she could with what she had available to her at the time, but it *did* have an impact on us. A big one. Which I seem to have dealt with and you have not.'

'Because she worked hard. And I refuse to blame my mother for everything because I am an *adult* and I take responsibility for my choices?'

'Sure,' he said. 'But forgiving isn't about them anywhere near as much as it is *you*.'

'I'm listening,' she said. 'Keep talking.'

'Fabulous. So. *You can't really love anyone until you learn to love yourself – discuss.* Shall I put my timer on?'

'Don't push it. *Bro*.'

She looked up to the still clear sky, the new moon she couldn't yet see. Stargazing would be spectacular tonight. And one way or another, she'd find a way to clear all this dead away.

This age felt so like being a teenager again: damned then by being fertile, damned now by not. And yet. That same feeling of new-found freedom; exhilarating, terrifying. Of a whole new chapter about to unfold. But she had forgotten this – this want, this desire; like trying to contain an ocean in a homemade garden pond. The need for love, yes, but not just romantic. The need, too, to do the creative work that had hurt so much to give up; to focus on her own life, her own love of – need for – art.

Jules's house-and-pet-sitting business was taking off. Asha applying to retrain as a wellness therapist. Emma desperate to know if a once-in-a-lifetime love could live again. She thought of her favourite boss: her decision to spend her sixtieth and the start of retirement horse-trekking in a desert because she'd always wanted to ride and sleep under stars. How happy Claire was she had; the poor woman died suddenly a year later.

She waited for the soil to settle, sink; watered again, watching the muddy pools, that sink or swim of life. Nothing more to do but see how well they flourished.

A long, slow sigh – the sigh of recognizing some changes cannot come without the need to accept help. How clever we think we are when we forget we're never not learning in this life.

Half a century is a good teacher. But half of learning, the garden has shown her, is always being willing to be a green shoot. When Tansy had softened, she'd ask about the stump – the landlord, under his oily hair, had the wit to write *responsibility for garden* into her contract, after all. He might own the land, but no one owned the wild heart of nature.

It had helped her, and now she would help it.

July

Buck Moon – Half Waxing

Bernard Bristlé looked up at her – again. Mary-Cate wanted something done with that eye for the dust jacket: 'The way the pupil just doesn't *look* at you,' she said in her soft American drawl. 'Like one eye on Britain, the other on Fraaance.' But Claire still couldn't quite see what she meant; couldn't seem to just *do* this any more. Maybe that was why the coast was all she could think of: she felt as restless, as shifting, as the sea itself.

The morning call from Emma was not helping.

'You don't have to justify anything to me,' Claire said. 'Anyone. It's your life.'

'What would you do? Would you go?'

Her first thought was the one she'd had all along: an absolute no.

When she'd sobbed to her mother after Guitar True-Love dumped her, her mother echoed her father – all the *plenty more fish,* however hard Claire wept about not wanting *any old halibut.* And when she'd finally confessed the truth about The

Poet, both parents had been visibly upset, her father more – she knew by the way he declared a strangled-sounding need to 'check his leeks', and her mother had turned to her.

'Listen,' she'd said, her oceanic eyes full of a sort of sad ferocity. 'We all have our skeletons. A bad thing happened to me, too, when I was young – before I met your dad – but I've never told anyone else, or ever will.'

Desperate as she was to know, half-hoping it might make some sense of all the 'nerves', Claire's head had filled with the image of inches-thick concrete. Once her mother's mind was set, if her grandmother or father hadn't found a jackhammer to break it, she had as much chance as one of her mother's beloved birds pecking it open.

Her mother sighed then, as if reading Claire's thoughts. 'What good does it do, girl? You're best to bury it all in a box and move on as best you can. At the end of the day, you have two choices: you stop, or you carry on. What else is there?'

Claire had buried that box as deep as she could dig. In the flood of midlife, though, with its power to turn solid soil to water, the skeletons rose up, fled their coffins; came creeping and clanking back into life.

So her words to Emma surprised her.

'Yes,' she said. She thought of The Blacksmith. 'I would – whatever the risks. To connect, have intimacy again? Have love, give love, *be* loved? Whatever my fuck-ups, and all the potential pain of it, I'd have to know if I had the chance of it again. So absolutely yes, Em. If I were you, I would.'

'I love you,' Emma said. 'I really do.'

After the call, Claire stared out of her study window at the sheer Monet of philadelphus, the dot-to-dot bees made of vinca, lavender, geranium, chives, melissa; even the tiny clover in the grass. So much *life* unwrapped now all around her.

She turned her gaze back to Bernard. His stand-off with McSnooze. Looked at Fucklock. Bernard again. That eye. What was it? What?

Her pencil, brushes, felt as if they actively pulled against her, to the way light illuminated the saucer of a blackthorn flower instead, the allure of its pin-cushion stamens; to sketching all the bud, the bloom, the petalling of summer. Her desk, the walls, felt stifling: she needed air.

If only *buried* meant the same as *dealt with*.

'Have you *seen* your philadelphus!' Tansy exclaimed, opening her door. 'Bridal! Like a white cherry, except deceit rather than the feminine and sexual. Which I thought— Oh, my dear! What on earth has happened?'

Well, this wasn't meant to. If I'd thought for one minute I'd cry as soon as I tried to open my mouth, I'd have stayed at home and tanked the gin.

'I'm sorry,' said, Claire choked by her vocal cords, horror at her tears. 'I'm— I just . . .'

'Come in. Come on. You can't stand on the doorstep like this. Has something dreadful happened? I mean, one wouldn't want to pry. But I'd like to help, if I can.'

The stumble of feet that wanted to run but fumbled the threadbare green carpet. 'No. Not really. I'm sorry, I'll be fine.' She wiped snot from her top lip. 'Sorry.'

'Please. We British are the only people who apologize even for someone else's mistake. I thought, rather dreadfully, someone may have died? Though at least death is somewhat of a *specialty*, as those murderers of English, the Yanks, say. Rather useful, too, if one wants rid of visitors one didn't particularly want in the first place. Do sit, dear.'

Claire sank into chintz; only then aware Tansy had been steering her by the elbow. 'Honestly, I'm – *will* be fine. Sorry for making you think . . .' She accepted a tissue but declined the tea, unable to face stale Tupperware. 'You're very kind. It's just a phone call I had.' She filled Tansy in on Emma, watching as the steel eyebrows lifted, lowered; as Tansy's mouth turned up, down, made a line as if resigned.

'Well,' said Tansy. 'Cheering to hear love still exists above and beyond all realms of what one might term *sense*. Of course your friend must go. And let us hope it is marvellous for them.' She peered over her glasses. 'But for you, I can imagine. You're in rather a different situation in life. Just don't try and apply logic, my dear Claire. Logic and emotion do not a happy marriage make— Oh, now *I'm* sorry. That was clumsy of me.'

'No. Please. Don't apologize. I mean, if you're going to find yourself howling at a friend, it should at least be something *proper.*'

Tansy sat back. 'Proper? Good Lord. I wasn't aware tears came in categories. Should one mark them out of ten to assess weep-worthiness, then? If so, I'm doomed. *Doomed.*'

'What do you mean?'

'I'm not a crier by nature, Claire – or owing to my ancient age. All that never letting one's stiff upper lip get even the tiniest bit flaccid. However. One *can* cry over an advertisement on TV for dogs, if in the correct mode. To my horror, if not shame.'

'Shame?' There was a word. 'Why shame?'

'Because I've never even owned a dog. All that hair and stink and ghastly ablution business. And yet, my dear friend Tilly died – heart attack two days ago – and not a single tear. No, what made me cry was that proverbial friend – man's best, and so on. And if that's not pathetic for someone who doesn't even really *like* dogs, I don't know what is.'

'Oh, Tansy, I'm so sorry about your friend. And now me here.'

Tansy waved a hand. 'Acceptable at our ages, I fear – though I fear living longer more. I did, I confess, ask her for a helping hand, too.' She winked.

'Well, if it helps, after I had Danny I cried at the fireman rescuing the Andrex puppy. And ads with dogs or kids normally make me want to puke.' She smiled at Tansy. 'Cold heart, clearly.'

'Ha!' snorted Tansy. 'At least you've *got* one.'

She couldn't help but laugh. How she loved Tansy when she did that wicked face that revealed the girl running around and scaring other kids with her 'witchcraft'.

How did other people do it? How did they just go on treading the days?

The problem *is* my heart, she wanted to say. And I accept my choices, I do. I do my gratitude list every night, even if all it says is *new teabag was nice*, though other days it's so, so much more than that. And I know time will pass, and all the things to look for, like the joy in just a leaf – and I do. But I still don't know how to help my heart on days like this.

'I'm not so sure about that,' she said instead, averting her eyes from Tansy's gaze. 'Unless mine is a stupid one, to be fair.'

'Well. Affairs of the heart are never easy, my dear girl. That much I do know.'

Claire looked at her hands, busy twisting the tissue on her lap. It occurred to her how little they'd spoken of emotional issues, outside Tansy's teaching the love-lore of how to hold a bouquet to send a message to an admirer. Or how many roses to include (one for love at first sight; six for wanting the recipient to be yours; twelve for 'be mine'; fifteen for sorry).

Tansy's voice as soft, as quiet, as her eyes were piercing. 'I've watched you, Claire. Since you came. I've watched you walk around that garden so – well – *haunted*. As if your ghosts were hunting you even somewhere as cut off from the world as Wickham Parva. That poor girl, I'd think. Because I know that what face feels like.'

Claire sniffed. 'My brother, Stephen, I think I've said is a psychotherapist—'

'—as if that in itself isn't enough to make *anyone* cry.'

'——and he always says it's to do with our mother's depression. That we have some kind of abandonment or deep-seated needs issue that makes us look for the wrong people to love, then cling to them. Or *I* do, he means. And not even wrong – Ben wasn't *wrong* – but . . .' She sighed. 'Anyway. Don't feel sorry for me, I'm not the victim here, Tansy.'

Tansy's head slightly to one side. 'We've all done things we're not proud of. There's a reason why white peonies were so popular in art – from Paeon, the Greek physician to the Gods, who Asclepius tried to kill from jealousy and Zeus saved by turning him into the flower. It's one of the few to represent shame and sorrow. There is no judgement here,' she added, as Claire fought her face. Lost. 'My dear. Let me tell you something.'

Tansy sat back, took off her glasses. 'I had a friend once, shall we say. For two years in my forties. A very ill-advised friend.

A bounder, we used to call them. A cad. He was the dashing tutor on the Art MA I wanted so badly, or so I thought – looking back one wonders if it wasn't just a way to assuage the urge to work, have something of my own life. But there I found myself, seduced to silliness by all the silver a cad can carry on a tongue. Not an affair, as such, not torrid or sordid, and I had no desire to leave Ken. It was my work, really – his passion, his belief in it. For two years, I saw myself through that man's eyes. What I wore. Anywhere I went. Every painting I tried to do, each picture I hung.'

Claire had stopped crying, fixed on Tansy, though the old woman kept her own eyes on the pattern of her skirt, stroking it as if to blend the brown checks into one another.

'You may well hate me – I certainly did – if you'd known dear old Ken, and given the life we could have without children. Principles are everything until they turn into people. And perhaps I was guilty of wanting too much. Or, as I think now, something I didn't have.' She paused, sighed. 'Because the real void was so much bigger.'

Claire couldn't stop herself asking. 'You didn't love Ken?'

Tansy smiled. 'Oh, I loved him. But I was angry with him. And for a long time. For throwing himself into a career I could never have while he allowed *no* investigation into why we couldn't do what everyone else on the planet took for granted. Wouldn't even speak of adoption. If it wasn't of me, he didn't want it, he said. I felt I was giving myself a gift.' She snuffed a small laugh. 'Talk about a poisoned chalice. And you must think dreadfully of me.'

Claire shook her head as they held each other's eye. 'I know what you're saying.'

'I know you do. Witchy hunches, see. It's why I'm telling you.'

A pause. But this time Claire did not drop her eye. 'But what happened? How did—'

'It end? Oh, as they often do.' She waved a hand again. 'The part other people play in your life, my dear Claire, is not always the same as the part you play in theirs. And if one plays with fire and silver when one has no form with either, one ends up with little more than a melted mess. He took up with a pretty French sculptress, and that was that.'

All the parts we play, thought Claire. So rarely aware of the bloody script. She saw now how she'd seen herself unfold with The Blacksmith: a new version of herself, if still patterned with all her roses and thorns. How much she'd liked the new mirror she looked in.

'It was the garden that saved me,' Tansy continued. 'Well. Not so much a garden *then* – I cared little for anything domestic, but it was one of the few things I didn't see the cad in. It was then I planted the willow you so admire. I knew a wise woman who shared its name – dead now, as they all are – who told me one can confess one's deepest, darkest secrets to a willow; it being one of the few trees to live in water, the element of the emotions. And, moreover, that capacity to bend outrageously without breaking, like the strongest of women. Whatever the weather or the world throws at a willow, as one sees, that twisting – *resilience*, I suppose it is – only makes them more magnificent. I adored that. And it did. It did help.'

'And Ken? He never knew?'

Tansy made her *tch* sound, exhaled. 'I didn't want to hurt him. Which was less about guilt than *truth*. That one had lost it – love, respect, decency, whatever *it* was; whatever allowed one to do what one did. The hard thing was accepting one will cause pain, whichever way one turns.'

'What do you mean – how?'

'Because being truthful so often means effecting pain.' A sad smile. 'Sometimes truth needs lies, Claire. It wasn't about passing my guilt onto him. That particular truth didn't need to hurt him because the *actual* truth was far bigger. Far more painful for him, for us both – that I didn't love him, not then. That's what I had to face. Wasn't that enough for him to have to face, too? He effectively lost me for two years. But not forever. My mother instilled in me to always ask oneself, before one opened one's cakehole, whether one's words were kind, honest, and if they'd help. It could never have been kind. And I could not have been entirely honest. So. Would it have helped Ken to *know*?'

Claire closed her eyes to the slick blade of the words. She had made the same decisions with Ben, wanting the marriage to work. But love is not always enough.

There was a harder pill, too, to swallow yet from forgiving The Poet in order to find some kind of closure; of recognizing *sorry* was not the word she wanted, but how she had not, whatever, and however, deserved what he did. There was the one of forgiving herself. Tears dripped from her and she did not try to stop them, her breath still even; the quiet air of acceptance.

A hand on her hand. The slightness of it, the silky feel of the frail skin. 'There was a point, though, when I noticed you did stop telling everything in your garden to eff off?'

Claire cringed, and Tansy wrapped her fingers tighter.

'Take heart, dear girl. You are a *gardener* now. How can you look at any garden, thriving or no, and not see at least *some* of what it needs? Doesn't so much simply depend on what kind of plant it is? Those pines, for example, the ones that only release seeds after a forest fire?'

She snotted a laugh. 'But they don't do that deliberately, that's just nature!'

Tansy took her hand away, laughing a little as she turned back towards her chair. 'Oh, you can want to be a rose if you've been born a wretched hydrangea, of course you can. So many of us do! But since when do you get to choose how you're made? All one can ever do is work with what one has, can't one?'

*

She was alone but for sky, sand, sea: a storm front forecast. People avoided the coast when it was rough enough to send a screwdriver into the cavern of an ear. But she welcomed this shotblast of sand, the waves that spat their excess in her face, sick of the stains of sadness under her eyes. Something in the wildness spoke to her.

She faced the sea and studied the sky. To her left the curl of storm billowing; water whipped to frenzy under it, a stampede of waves to reach the shore. It often struck her as callous, the sea. Nature did not need to be liked or particularly want you to like it: you could marvel at its majesty or despise it for its ugly dealings with death – nature didn't care. It could soothe and settle you, but it could suck you up and eat you alive and very much kicking, too. The sea told you to know your place, just as the stars and moon imparted how utterly unimportant you were, and as such she respected it more than any living thing. What were we but water and stardust?

Rain pricked needlepoint patterns on her face, colder as the sky glowered, the wind gathered breath. At the first crack of thunder, she had the urge to throw herself at its heart, feel its beat on her skin, remembering how it felt to be young, pummelled in waves like this, laugh-falling into the swill of froth and foam. Youth is foolish. But it is also enviably footloose. After everything, could she let herself go again? Wouldn't she fight to keep her feet, worry about water in her ears, a twist, sprain, break, to take payment for the pleasure?

It wasn't careful or considered, the way she took her clothes off, wearing their discard like the left for dead; the shirt feebly waving as if for help, the broken legs of jeans. In the same way, she entered the water: driven by a need for the deafness of under – a duvet, wine, a man; none of which she could have.

She kicked at a slick of seaweed at her calves, water willing her away so she had to brace as it beat the brow of her; barely aware of the cold, only the burn as waves began to slap her stomach, sluice her face, claw at her throat. It infuriated her.

'Fuck you,' she said, fighting harder.

Waves curled watery mouths into grins, baring teeth as they hit her with their weight. The scream came out wild as the wind, unexpected as the stubbing of her toe on a blunt rock.

'Fuck you! Come on, then – do it! Break me! Come ON! Give me all you've fucking got!'

Happiness, heartache, blood, love, lust. Death. And yes – oh, God, yes – *shame*. Body clenching, stomach contracting now. Too late to swim for shore.

And then it came: crashing, snagging her in its jaws, legs not able to hold her, arms not able to swim her, breath not able to breathe in her, no knowing what was up, down, forward, back; umbilical in a world of water, shingle stones stinging as solidified moments frozen in the lava flow of life. The heart punch of hitting seabed. The terrible tumble of it all, flailing, falling, the fear of the abyss.

And so she let go. Powerless; little choice but to acquiesce to power. She was full to the fucking brim of being frightened of herself.

She dived the next wave, shooting under its smile straight into its guts, the smooth skin of its roll, floating in the outbreath of its rage. The next she surfed, dancing to it with her back, jumping as it came, carried laughing on its crest, high above the shore and spat out into shallows, sand in knickers, grit lining cups of bra. She sat, laughing to herself. Good job this beach was empty; but if not, how much would she have cared?

She was light, panting, exhilarated; skin on fire as she dressed, dragging layers to her damp; jeans hating her wet legs, shirt stuck to breasts as when, so long ago, she was full of milk, a baby still asleep. She walked the beach back, watching the waves that would maybe only last this hour, this day. Tomorrow she could come again and find a sheet of rippled steel. Nothing stayed the same.

Terns whistled out their call, gulls shrieked, keening, wheeling slights against the sky.

Hope is not a thing with feathers, she thought. The sky did not have tides and nor did trees. Hope had to be a thing with scales or gills to survive the biggest power on the planet. If love was the thing that mattered – the thing to make matter *matter* – then hope must be its sister; hope must lie in water to ride the ever-changing tide and all the furies of the flood. We were not made to fly.

But almost everything can swim.

July

Buck Moon – Full

Was it London that had changed, or her? It was still the same schizophrenic city: still buzzing and beautiful, still ugly and alienating. It struck her, leaving Liverpool Street, changing Tubes – surprised at the muscle memory of that – her awareness of anonymity was as strong here as it ever had been. And yet that felt somehow schizophrenic, too, now.

In two weeks, Ben would be back; in the country, at least. And she didn't know how that made her feel. She was glad to be ostensibly as anonymous as in the countryside: surrounded by people yet more alone than in any lane or field where sky kissed wheat and nothing else for miles; places she could weep, shout, scream, laugh, drop dead, for that matter – carrion for a hundred different digestive systems – without a single human being noticing. The silent armies of the dispossessed lining so many streets now made her gasp.

Perhaps she hadn't had the twat attack she'd so fretted over on the train, pondering her words for the *Why me, why this* box. And she had been shortlisted. Even if it didn't come to anything, she still had that.

'Because of my age,' she'd said to Asha last night.

'Because of your talent,' Asha said back.

'Or because I tick the granny box.'

'Yeah, damn right.' Asha had raised her glass. 'Because you have the experience and polish to tick that bitch with a big *fuck yeah*.'

Because it was in her now, a green heart, as much a part of her as people wanted the beat of nature in this sprawling urban jungle. She'd seen more vividly than ever the colourful lather of hanging baskets, the shrubs flanking al fresco tables, the window boxes, balconies, gardens, her mind made unconscious inventories of – parrot plant, box, tree fern, acer, iris, cosmos, astilbe – as if clinging to something more friendly to the senses. She'd noticed recently, driving, her gaze drawn to blocked-off roads, the way grass, brambles, weeds, made a map of themselves, not suddenly but over time until the only human thing remaining was the barrier blocking it off. In nature you were alone, but not necessarily lonely; always part of something eternal, bigger; something – yes, mad as it sounded – *loving*.

She tried to ignore the sweaty palms that greased the massive door of the equally imposing building and made her pray no one tried to shake her hand. Which they wouldn't because they'd all be embryonic, or so cool she'd be intimidated just by their aura as she stood hoping she'd got all the hairs out of her chin or whether she'd go full catfish by a window. She ran a finger surreptitiously, relieved to find she had.

The reception area milled with people. Not all so young,

she was pleased to note; some older than her and everybody, regardless, looking as awkward as each other.

'Bit of a first day at school vibe, isn't it?' she said to a tall blonde man, the first person to catch her eye. 'Or is it just me? Claire, by the way.' She didn't offer her hand.

He smiled broadly, seemingly relieved. 'Adam. And definitely not just you. I walked in just before you and had flashbacks to being Billy No-Mates eating my lunch in the loo.'

'You laugh,' she said, 'but I have actually done that before now.'

'I do laugh,' he said. 'Because so have I.'

They moved quickly on – how refreshing not to be asked if you had kids or be expected to talk mostly about them – to the ideas that got them there. He spoke of waterways, passionate about the fight for clean rivers, chalk streams, the life water supported, the oceans, the slowly desiccating planet. An Asian woman with a warm Northern accent joined them then; the same age, Claire guessed, as her; stylish in an orange dress that hit a retina like a shot of tequila, a silver wave of quiff.

She held out a hand. 'Sonya. And before you ask, self-trained former journalist turned media tart after my kids, partly because my feet are too ugly for OnlyFans. I only entered because my daughter made me. So, shall I get my coat, or wait until everyone finds out?'

She was, it turned out from her photos, an astonishing wildlife artist with a gift for capturing expression, a sense of personality – 'It all started with the bloody dog' – who wanted to focus on the relationship between animals and humans; how people regarded them, interacted with them. Or, more specifically, reared and ate them.

'I worked with a big supermarket,' Sonya told them, 'who took us to these factories. Couldn't eat chicken for two years, let alone look at a cow. I do still eat meat, but only if it's had a good life now. But do you think art can really help the planet, seeing how fucked it is?'

A fervent discussion took them into coffee, pastries. It was only when Claire went to the toilet she realized she wasn't sinking her head in her hands wishing she'd been somehow *better*. If anything, she was still smiling. Couldn't seem to stop.

A wall of windows framed a striking view of the Eye, the full glitter of central London in sunshine, as they listened to the scheme's aim, the well-known artists who'd mentor the chosen; how each shortlistee would today briefly talk about their aims, but also how they'd work in collaboration over the year: expected to help publicize, attend development events, schools, festivals, colleges, critique and support each other's work. *A lot of media excitement.* Claire wondered if anyone else felt the same at that: her stomach skittish as a kid on Christmas Eve.

'Think I might be too menopausal for collaboration,' whispered Sonya. 'My GP had a go about me smoking recently and I was like, listen, pal, it's that or kill my children.'

Claire stifled a laugh.

'Not sure I can either,' whispered Daisy, at Claire's other side. She'd unconsciously written her off: all of twenty-five at most. What could they possibly have in common?

'I like working alone?' Daisy added, as applause filled the room like a cloudburst. 'I get too freaked with other people because I can't stop comparing myself?'

It caught Claire off guard, the words settling in her like the dust motes in the sunlight on their table. But it was lunch before she saw her again, smoking on the balcony as Claire wandered out, noticed the bitten nails holding Daisy's phone.

'Hi,' said Daisy. 'How's it going?'

'Good. I can't believe how much I want to be part of it now. It's almost as if I haven't let myself think that, in case I don't get in.' She hadn't even told Tansy yet. 'You?'

'Yeah, I think so. I mean, it's a lot to take in and stuff? Be up against?'

She could feel the girl's conflict, leant against the low wall to face her. 'You'll be fine. You wouldn't be here if they thought you weren't good enough.'

Daisy faced her, huge blue eyes under a messy bun alive with loose strands, a fringe that made Claire think of Astroturf; know instantly she'd home-bleached it from a darker colour. She'd done exactly the same in her twenties, emerged with hair the colour of a food-poisoned face. 'Do you think? My mum said to just be positive . . .' She twisted her mouth. 'But everyone is so much more *experienced* than me?'

Claire smiled at her. 'Well, if it helps, I'm at the opposite end of the spectrum – all the experience, but not so sure I can still be *relevant* like they said.'

'But you spoke so well? I was listening like whoa, man, she's cool, that's cool – like I love that thing you said about micro influencing macro, the way you talked about colour highlighting the changing planet, like how when Earth was born the sky was totally orange and the sea ran red for centuries. Fucking loved that?'

An undeniable glow. 'Well, so did you. *So* good to see someone young talk on how social media makes us lonelier; how we could be using it to come together for the planet – I loved your ideas for schools.'

Daisy lit up. 'Oh wow, really? My mum always says everything was better before SM and she feels sorry for my generation, and I'm like yeah, Mum, but what am I gonna do about it? But actually, that *is* what I wanna do about it?' It was, she told Claire, the desire to do something that mattered that drove her to 'big stuff, like, with non-recyclables, wall art, installations. Like, I wanna make people really *think*?'

Claire held up open palms. 'There you go. You're here because you belong here?' That inflection was like someone else yawning: no wonder Daisy's generation did it.

'I just keep looking at people thinking what do I know? I live in my parents' attic, haven't got a boyfriend, a career – like, all the things you're *meant* to have at my age?'

Claire laughed. 'Says who? I'm twice your age – I should be settling into my so-called golden years. But here I am, alone again after thirty years, skint, and wondering if I fell down my stairs whether anyone would actually find me before a cat started eating my face.'

Daisy laughed, then gurned. 'Your marriage broke up?'

'It did.'

'I'm sorry.'

'Don't be – it wasn't your fault.'

Daisy laughed again, her fret lines softening. 'My folks, too. Except this is London so they're staying in the house because they can't afford to live here now any other way.' She fumbled in a sparkly denim bumbag for rolling tobacco. 'But seriously, I mean, I almost daren't even enjoy today because what if I don't get picked? Or I do and I, like, totally fail?'

She was, Claire thought, the sort of girl she'd have hated, envied, or both, at Daisy's age. How she could still feel it: the seductive crack of that vowelly voice, the ease of a life where Mum and Dad can afford to keep you and had space for artwork the size of a small car. How life, time, changed everything. All she wanted to do now was help the girl if she could.

She remembered a forgotten YouTube video she watched shortly after her mother's death: a blackboard in central New York inviting people to chalk up their biggest regret. The common theme by a country mile was the word *not*: not chasing dreams, taking risks, pursuing love, words not spoken. Some were clearly gutted by those lost chances. But then they were handed an eraser – *A clean slate*, as one wrote – began to smile again. 'It's not my regret any more.' 'It's hopeful,' said another. 'It means there's possibility.'

She smiled again at Daisy. 'Then you wipe your board and start again. You've got years yet. I'm only just starting what I want to do with the rest of my life. The older I get, for what it's worth, the more I think it's about choices, if you're lucky. And it pretty much comes down to two: you either stop, or you carry on. What else is there, really?'

'Oh, man, I *love* that?' said Daisy. 'But like, about age – I don't really see age?' A flash of sun hit her huge eyes, making them briefly limpid. 'I see people? Souls. Hearts. Energy. And I think yours are fucking cool. Hey, so, can we, like, hang out if we do actually get on this mofo scheme?'

'I'd love that, Daisy, I really would.'

She hadn't realized, until Sonya joined them, that since Daisy said that she'd inadvertently put a hand to her chest at the exact place she'd have illustrated as the heart.

It occurred to Claire, now the weather felt as if it was making even the walls of the cottage sweat, she could finally wander her home naked all day if she wanted. She'd even shifted her sofa and chair around, nude, as sun threw whispering shadows of leaves on the walls: an art all its own. The heat liberated other things in her, too.

'Jesus!' she exclaimed, not too many minutes later, as her free hand slapped the shower tiles. 'Fuck!'

Poor Woody: so old now she had to hold the battery door closed if the Sellotape fell off. In that way, but absolutely no other, did he remind her of a man. But *ah*, the sugared joy of it all. Making as much noise as she wanted. As long as she wanted. As many times as she wanted. Until she was spent, pant-smiling, sweet-throbbing; the crick in her neck cracked open, the bones of her shoulders soft, for once.

She dried, feeling lighter, loving the feeling of clean inside and out. So light her step, so humming her heart, she snapped the speaker on and started to sing into Woody as if it were a microphone. Softly at first:

Oh your mummy don't mind / Oh your daddy don't-a mind

Then, as song turned to chorus, chords to crescendo, loud; fist higher than face:

So come on and sta-ay-ay with-a me

She laughed at herself hard, dancing, smiling – the absolute state of her! – as she whirled the hallway, living room, bathroom, kitchen, Egyptian-style, Woody leading the way.

And that was when their eyes met.

Oh, God. Oh, *God*. Perhaps the glare of the sun made mirrors of the kitchen window. Perhaps he'd not seen anything as much as she tortured herself with now. Perhaps he'd seen it all before. Perhaps he'd seen nothing at all apart from her eyes – *please God*. And yet, the other half of her couldn't stop a smile. A laugh, even.

Because how to face him now, that postman?

When Jules stopped laughing, she asked if Claire fancied 'a bit of wild swimming? You know, what we hedgemumblies just called *swimming* back in the day?'

Claire had said nothing to anyone about her sea swim, couldn't have done it justice without her friends fearing for not just her safety but her mental health. How that roiling sea had flashed her guts to light like the silver bellies of the tiny fish she and the boys found washed up on beaches when they were still small enough to be stunned by the wonders of the world. How it had washed her, too, somehow; stunned her just the same.

'I'd love it,' she said, handing Jules her coffee.

'Good,' said Jules. 'Because I'm up for anything right now. Maybe it's menopause, but I've been thinking since Easter how I've always had this fantasy about sex with a woman. Even weirder, when I told Al, he said he'd be fine with it.'

Claire laughed. 'Of course he did.' Men. Put *I fantasize about another woman involved* in the slot and watch the *How Do We Get There, Sex Queen* door swing wide open.

'It's another man he'd have a problem with.'

'You don't say?' Then swap it for *I fantasized about another man*. Enjoy that as you stare at the mountain range of cold shoulder in bed.

If men knew how women talked about them. The things they said.

I can't even bend to put something in the bin without him

grabbing me like it's in a sale on New Year's Day. And then it's the full porn routine, fuck's sake.

I am going to scream if he keeps doing that mozzarella thing with my nipples?

I just let him think he's great – so much bloody easier that way.

You wanna try dating. Have I told you about the one who never knew if he was going to have a fit when he orgasmed? And 'forgot' to mention that to me?

'But actually,' said Jules, 'right now I want the carpenter doing our kitchen.'

Claire pulled a face. 'The ponytail one you said looked like a crackhead Elrond?'

'No, that's the boss guy – ugh, *God*, I'm not having a total *breakdown*. No, the Idris Elba one, remember? Anyhow, we started chatting veganism because he didn't want milk in his tea, and I'm thinking of going vegan, and—'

Now she laughed. 'Jules. You dribble just *talking* about dirty burgers. You're about as bloody vegan as your cat.'

Jules shrugged, Gallic-style. 'People change.'

'Not that fast they don't. Not without a stroke.'

'He puts a very good case! But listen. The other day I came home from a run and Elrond had to go, so it was just me and Idris, and I was all like, 'tea?' and he was like, 'Please' – and yes, I *did* keep my running gear on because he'd said I looked hot – until he said: *Tell you what. I'll take my tea down here and then I'll stop staring* and I just stood there thinking did he just say that? He's forty, Claire. I'm fifty-fucking-three!'

Desire unlocked a door to primeval human clay, thought Claire: the hands of the mind unable to stop their shaping, making, carving; defying the part of you that didn't expect your body to play to your head; not this old, this wise. And certainly not your heart.

It wasn't a woman you needed to be at this age, after everything you'd already lived, she wanted to warn Jules – it was some sort of emotional Boudicca. But Jules wouldn't have listened any more than she had to Emma, herself. People voted with their feet.

'So, what are you going to do?'

Jules laughed. 'Oh, I haven't lived this long just to get groomed until he gets bored. I might be old, but I'm not insane. It's probably all menopause – so I'll just enjoy a bit of a flirt. What harm is there in that?'

After she left, Claire sat outside and let the sun fall on her. All around her fullness of nature shone out, from the feathery, fresh-blood leaves on the smiles of rose stems she'd cut back to flower more, to the swishing gleam of the wheat waiting for a blade as bees buzzed and butterflies flitted, dizzy with desire.

What harm is there in that?

'When we first met you said you didn't like receiving flowers. So, I thought maybe if they were from the garden, you might like them better. Am I holding them the right way?'

Tansy stood in her dark hallway, wire-wool hair haloed by the little window, with a bemused look. 'Oh, I'm such an old fuddy-duddy, I am, really. Though, mercifully, you may like this. It's a Victorian thing. Somewhat like me. Ooh!' She twirled a finger at the spray of small pink roses, the last of Claire's hellebores, the strands of fern and fennel, a stick of pussy willow she'd dried earlier in the year, kept in a vase with others.

'And you're holding them at heart level, so thankfully for me you like what you see. See, if you hold them upside down, it means the opposite of whatever was intended to be silently said. If the ribbon is tied to the left, any symbolism applies only to the giver; to the right, recipient. But as you're not trying to court me, I think we'll be okay.'

Claire wiggled her eyebrows. 'Never say never.'

Tansy laughed – her proper laugh, more of a cackle. 'And one should always have a bud. It represents the continuous journey of life, according to the Chinese. One assumes no need to explain about the wilted. In which case, at my age you may as well have turned up cloaked and waving a sickle.' A beat. 'Please?'

Claire laughed. 'I haven't a clue about pussy willow, to be honest. Or hellebores.'

'They mean have you heard anything from that b-word scheme yet. You did send off, didn't you? *Didn't* you?'

'Tansy, I told you – I'm on it.' She mentally crossed fingers, still scared words would jinx the outcome.

Tansy swatted angrily at a fly. 'Flies shall inherit the earth, I tell you. Oh, they drive me to madness – madness!' She did one of her grumpy humphs, taking the bunch from Claire's hand and gesturing for her to follow into the kitchen. 'We'll start with pussy willow – a Chinese favourite for New Year. Could you fetch that vase please? Apparently, the blossoms resemble silk, the new shoots the colour of jade – lucky.'

And she's off! Claire smiled to herself as she filled the vase, watched Tansy thoughtfully arrange the flowers.

'Native Americans,' Tansy said, tweaking in tiny pinches, 'saw these as inner wisdom – of age, experience, isn't that quite something? They had a saying I adore; how "at menarche a woman meets her power, during her menstruating years she practises her power, but at menopause she *becomes* her power".' She inhaled, smiling to herself, as if content. 'Here, mind, willow was witches' wands. In Scotland, they even thought harvesting it on a waning moon meant the wood wouldn't be as good, willow being associated with the moon, and as you know, water and birth. Rebirth, if one is into that – they'll grow like billy-o from a mere stick. And as for hellebores,' she looked up with a characteristic wink, 'spring or summer, what can I say? Poison. Up there with the mandrakes and the belladonnas.'

'Belladonna was my witch-name as a kid.' She'd have felt stupid saying that to anyone else, but Tansy looked delighted.

'Oh, wonderful! Mine was Willow, would you believe? But hellebores come to us from *Helleborus,* from the ancient Greeks – and hell indeed. Used once, legend has it, to poison an entire city, and therefore a reminder of mortality.' She made a wry face. 'One wonders if I shouldn't make a little luncheon soup with those?'

Claire laughed again. 'Stop – you could have years yet!'

A grimace. 'And if you carry on like that, you most certainly will not.'

'Tansy, listen. Can I ask you something? Seriously?'

The beetle-black eyes sharpened. 'Oh, I do not like the sound of that. But go ahead, if you must. As long as it's not too beastly?'

'Do you joke so much about death because you're frightened of it?' Seeing Tansy's alarmed face, she added quickly: 'You don't have to answer, of course. It's just– you always talk so much about *life*. Or like now, rebirth, all that. Like that owl

I saw when I first came here – I remember you saying it was about "positive transformation"?'

Tansy's eyebrows raised, but she stayed quiet.

'So, I suppose what I'm saying is – well, I'm here. If you ever want to talk or . . . What I mean is, the worst thing is suffering in silence. And I think women are really good at it.'

Tansy dropped her eyes, made a small *hmm* sound. 'Funny you should mention owls, I saw one the other night when I got up for the lav.' She sighed. 'Shall we sit?'

The air changed, it felt to Claire, as they sat in the living room in their respective chairs. Something about it seemed softer, as if just the mention of death brought the ancient beams back to quiet watchfulness. She remembered Tansy telling her death-watch beetle would announce April to her even if she woke blind.

'It's just,' she said, as Tansy fussed at her cushions, 'you've been so kind to me—'

'Oh, Lord.' Tansy sat heavily, facing her. 'Please don't. I'm far too British. One shan't know what to do with one's face if you start throwing compliments at it. But to answer your question – no, Claire. I am not frightened of dying. Pain, incarceration, yes. But death?' She opened her palms, smiled. 'Oh, death is just another part of the journey! And curiosity did kill the proverbial, if not me. I will admit I'm rather curious about it all.'

Claire frowned. 'I can't remember who said life was a sexually transmitted infection with only one outcome. Isn't it enough just to know it will happen?'

Tansy's brow still high. 'Well, for one thing, so much is known by my age, and so little one can do about other curiosities.' She fixed Claire with soft, almost liquid eyes. 'My dear girl, if a garden shows you one thing, isn't it that everything has its time, its season, the end of one thing only ever the beginning of another? And I've had mine. Is it possible, do you think, to be *merrily* dead? If I hold fear it is this: I have no desire to cling on, hapless in some elderly holding pen praying for the blessing of insanity.'

She couldn't bear it. 'Oh, Tansy, don't say—'

Tansy held up a hand. 'And, if I'm honest, I should dearly love to see my Ken again. Share a bit of death with him' – she swallowed, taut for a second before smiling again – 'as I did life. How lucky I was. How lucky *any* of us are to have love in this life. Why else would we be given the gift of it, how else to say we truly lived?'

Claire nodded: if she opened her mouth her voice, eyes, would betray her.

They looked at one another for a moment in comfortable silence.

'Though mark me,' Tansy said, brisk, brushing at something on the antimacassar, 'I shall be back to haunt this ancient pile, evil old witch that I am. I shall *burn* to see who has it after me and what they do, however – and doubtless – grotesque that may be.' She shuddered. 'A conservatory, that's my hunch. Some frightful abomination of glass and finial that conserves nought but bad taste.'

Claire smiled. 'Okay, hellebores then. Shall I make the soup – my eyes are better?'

Tansy cackled. 'Well, the wretched thing does flower in shadow, so supposedly draws one into darkness, but,' she said, thoughtful, 'also, again supposedly, cures madness.' Her voice gathered volume now, speed, until it reached the usual rattling enthusiasm. 'The pink one so beloved of gardeners, like these' – she pointed to the vase on the not-wood nest of tables – 'is the most poisonous. They used to say witches used it to make flying ointments and curses; you name it, the darker the better. Though it is hallucinogenic, so the poor things probably just *thought* they were flying, being somewhat off their heads, Gawd bless 'em. Lucky they weren't dead from it. Someone was. The dementia stops me remembering who.'

'But you remember so much! I think I do, or I google, and it still doesn't work.'

'What do you mean, you silly girl?'

'The honeysuckle. It just flails. That rose up the fence at the back, the same.'

'So tie them in! All we're ever doing with climbers, things that need staking—'

'Staking? I'm not Van Helsing, Tansy!'

'Oh, do stop making such a fuss! You raised children, didn't you? All you're doing is giving the growing thing some guidance, it'll make its own decisions after that. If children haven't taught you that, *being* a child should have, at least?'

'What about my sage, then? I did everything you said, and it just isn't growing. I'll have to bin it, I think.'

Tansy downturned her mouth, shrugged. 'If so, then so. It will offer up a vacancy for something else to thrive. But sometimes one must use one's instinctive witch. Get in there with the skin, the self. Touch it, see if it gives.'

'Sorry, I can do *some* hippy – I am from Suffolk – but . . .'

A smile. 'It's about something less tangible than how it looks, or what some page says. It's as simple as this: when it's ready, or dead, it will give. Nature lets go only when she is ready, unlike us lesser beings.'

'Say again?'

Now Tansy tapped her fingers on the chair arm, impatient. 'Try it with your sage. Get your hands in and see what snaps off easily, and what bends or just *doesn't*. Not complicated – like most things in life, if you think. Those dear little dik-diks in the bush I so loved to watch as a girl, perhaps that's what did it for me. Beauty and utter, well, *shit*. One minute dancing, the next dinner.' She made a face like a bad taste. 'Wish I were a b-word dik-dik.'

'Well, I don't,' said Claire. 'I could listen to you talk about plants, Kenya, life, all day. I really could.' She nodded at the flowers. 'I want to get you round at some point, Tansy. Show you the garden.'

'I'd like that,' Tansy said. 'Very much. One hasn't done much to write home about, as such. But I'm thrilled if my wittering has at least helped you in some way.'

Claire smiled. 'You've no idea how much you've helped. Not least by saving my garden from some form of Impressionistic murder.'

Tansy gave her a shy look. 'Thank you, dear Claire. That means a great deal to an old woman whining about not being a lion's lunch.' A brief pause. 'It's been a privilege for me, too, you know. To become your garden go-to. Your, dare I say it, *friend*.'

The admiration she already felt, sharpened by the added shot of joy, caught Claire by surprise. By this point, you were all too often losing more than you made. Easy to forget, by and in midlife, how wonderful it felt – how b-word fucking brilliant white it felt – to have made a brand-new friend.

Underneath the rising full moon, sipping her wine, her garden shone a silvery gold. Bright enough to read by, to see the barren stems of eaten flowers – muntjac probably – the mouseholes tunnelled near the roses. The mice were negligible, but the roses would not be safe with deer about, Tansy had warned: 'Dank, ruinous beasts! It's as if they're having their own little happy hour should they get hold of them.'

She thought of how Tansy had added that the July moon was named for this being the time of year bucks shed their antlers, soft with the velvet of the new.

She bent, absently pulling at a fluff of dead forget-me-not, a few arrowheads of fat hen and the ground elder that just never gave up trying; a smile escaping her at the sheer tenacity of every cell of this garden. The strength of will of seeds not planted by her but by nature and the alchemy of bird shit; the spindly trunks of baby trees she pulled – surprisingly hard – daily now. That desire always, every leaf, every flower, to stretch to sky, regardless of, and still with, any other plant.

The pushing, pushing, pushing, never stopping the fight to reach the sun.

August

Sturgeon Moon – Full

She didn't know how she knew but she did. She just did. Perhaps that was another thing about getting older, learning to trust her intuition completely: that witchy 'knowing' as Tansy would say. Ben was back, too. Things were changing, would continue to change. Life, like it or not, was moving on all around her.

Claire didn't say as much, but she knew Emma would move to the other side of the planet with Rob. She kept thinking of what her grandmother always said in the event of death: *One out, one in;* how in families it so often heralded pregnancy somewhere else. How Claire once asked her if losses got any easier with age and the old woman smiled and said not necessarily, 'But however your knocks come, you do get more used to dealing with them – and somewhere in the world, a million other poor buggers will be going through the same'.

'Time to get my big girl pants on again,' she said to Emma. 'Wow. A *week*.'

'It's only for two weeks, I still have to come *back*. And it might all come to nothing.' Emma leaned into the screen. 'So don't write me off just yet?'

It wasn't just that. Joe called earlier to announce he wouldn't be home until autumn; back now from a fortnight with friends in Ibiza but wanting to stay in the city, work to fund another two with his new girlfriend, her family. Someone else's home. Claire's heart had sunk. She forced herself to remember the pandemic that stole two of the best years of his life, her pride at how he dealt with that; the freedom, life, she wanted for him now. She'd given her sons roots, yes. But she had also wanted to give them wings.

So, this was what an empty nest looked like. And Dan was right: while she might not know the exact shape of what it led to, it wasn't waiting to be filled by the needs of a dog.

'And while you've got the big girl pants on,' Emma added. 'You could have a think about dating? Seriously. Some of my workmates have had some luck with that lately.'

Claire gave her a disbelieving face. 'You've always said it's a shitshow unless you're a forty-year-old bloke?'

Emma laughed. 'Well, yeah. It's made for them, to be fair. Free sex. Though reliable sources tell me there's a lot of call for younger men wanting older women now.'

'Christ. Isn't that a bit pass the tissues to the boys with issues? And yeah, great. Now I can be some acne king's fantasy from *The Graduate*? Yay.'

'Could be worse. I mean, I'd still take that over looking at being some bloke's carer a few years down the line?'

How life came back round again: free from domestic entanglement to something approaching young-woman you – only faded and creased now from overuse. And while men might barely hold their hard, sprout ear hair, nose hair, moobs, and have testicles like old socks, no one accepted it as a reason to shuck them off like some old oyster.

It was the apple all over again: were you ever really free of serpents?

Claire could think of better ways to destroy her ego, she told Emma: a spot of Compare and Despair, perhaps. She'd gone back on social media to discover other women artists she knew doing exhibitions. Open studios. Commissions.

And she wanted that, too. A lot. Far more than she wanted any man.

The look on his face didn't surprise her. Jake was – what? Late twenties? She hadn't expected someone so young after Tansy gave her the number for 'a funny little old tree man.' Apparently, Jake worked with his uncle, the old being more prevalent now than the funny. Claire looked at the stiff smile that told her he'd probably tried to get out of this, failed, then hoped like hell there'd at least be some old git there to chat football with.

She showed Jake the stump, watched his unlined face crease, unable to read whether it decided the job was paltry or underpaid. Or both.

'It won't be too much of a problem,' he said. Which hardly helped.

She told him she was grateful; that plumbers were the worst of any trade, what with that tendency always to say – she backward-whistled – 'Tricky. Those parts are rare as rocking horse shit'.

Jake's grin still rictus. So – had it taken him long to get here?

The drive had, he said, all those twisting Suffolk roads that didn't allow for speed or overtaking. But compensated for by being, she suggested, 'ridiculously beautiful'.

'I'm not a countryside lover,' said Jake. 'Lest there's a good pub in it.'

So she told him about the Suffolk pubs she'd gone to when she was younger – how some had no actual bar, just an alcove with a shelf, from which you could see the beer barrels with their umbilical pipes and puddles of peaty ale. Most were houses now, she said – the Pot of Flowers, the White Rose, the Low House – born as she was, she added, all solemnity, 'in 1862.' Finally, Jake laughed.

It broke the ice enough that when she returned with tea, he'd fetched his tools, and after she commented on his tattoo sleeve, said his mother cried when he started it; laughing as he confessed her moniker on his phone was Mona. Claire laughed too, then; said in that case her sons would certainly have gone for the full-body sleeve.

He worried, though, Jake said then, he'd upset his mum not going to university: however much school said he was 'bright', he just hadn't wanted to. Wondered now if he'd sold himself short. He had the chance to go to New York, though, stay with a cousin there, work – he'd always wanted to live in a big city: London, New York: 'suff'n like that'. But. *Girlfriend.* A sigh. A turning to the job at hand.

Claire left him to it, went up to her desk, peering out sporadically to see what he was doing. Digging. Hacking roots with an axe. Snapping a long lopper. Dig. Axe. Lopper. And so it went on. A crowbar now, to lever.

She watched as he stopped to wipe sweat, swig from his water bottle, reminding her momentarily and weirdly, his black curls falling over one eye, of Guitar True-Love.

When she took out more tea, she asked him to show her what he was doing and how, and the conversation – as often the case with the focus fixed on an external – turned to the personal. Her life and career. And yes, she said to his question: she was married, though not any more. 'And no, I don't know how you make those things work. Does anyone?'

'I think my girlfriend thinks she does,' Jake said. His mouth twisted to one side. 'And she really, *really* wants to get married.'

Claire smiled. 'And you don't?'

The mouth not smiling now. He didn't answer, asking instead if she'd known when she was younger. No, she said: she hadn't felt like all those *bride-brides* before she got married. Even though she'd really loved Ben. Scared, half hating the idea of the wife thing, half determined to do it her own way.

He got that, Jake said. 'Wow. Weird, though, to hear it said from a woman. With me and my mates it's more the other way around.'

They moved as the sun climbed higher, a couple of feet to the left, under the shade of Tansy's massive ash.

It was funny, Jake went on to say: he didn't feel he was betraying his girlfriend, talking like this. The strangest thing was he felt like he could exhale just *by* talking like this. Did she think men and women could be friends, really – without, well, you know?

Was she imagining that look in his eye? If not outright, as it might have been when she was younger, then at least of interest.

Ridiculous. Of course she was – he was half her age. *Get a grip, grandma.*

Yes, she said, she did, though it was tricky because – *because*. But it didn't mean never. Ben hadn't always liked her male friendships, but he trusted her. In her experience, if anything, the women were worse: that's what usually put paid to her old male friendships.

'My girlfriend gets jealous,' Jake said then. 'It's part of my problem about marriage – marrying her. To be honest, I'm not sure this isn't just a relationshit, at the end of the day.'

Claire laughed and said love was complicated; maybe he just wasn't ready? He certainly didn't feel it, he said. And he agreed love was a *bastard*, but that *you know when you know*. It was the one before he'd felt like that with.

Jake looked at his feet, then, as if hanging his head. 'Maybe I just run scared.'

She felt a warm rush of compassion for him. 'Sometimes,' she said, 'we all do.'

She told him how she felt she ran, too, after what happened in her past – relationshit was such a good word! – once to escape herself with sex, which only proved how bad and unlovable she was, and much later, to find herself with it again. And no, for what it was worth, she didn't think she was sometimes as brave as she could be. But she was trying.

Jake looked at her and smiled a sad sort of smile. 'I should probably end it.'

'And I should probably stop hiding and start the rest of my life.'

A moment's pause as the impact of what each said hit home.

Claire stared at Tansy's willow; at the way it arced, writhed, almost as if instructed to act out twisted tree. She traced the gnarl of its limbs, the trunk, budding out like antlers, the dancing grace of the leaves.

Beauty and ugliness. Joy and pain.

Reality couldn't always be trusted. It could be bent to the will like that willow, like a green stick, until you made of it a basket to hide the truth. *Did you do it to protect him*, people asked after The Poet – later, years later, when she was able to talk about it; explain she lied as she did to protect herself, not him, from the reality of her shame. What happened with The Poet shone light on the full force of her sexuality as a woman: what it was to command, enjoy, delight and revel in all the aspects of female sexuality – he had shown her how to feast on the full menu of herself. But not without showing her the equal power of her shadows. She'd thought she was different from the army of women she despised who sought validation from men – even if all they got were the crumbs from his plate. So easily distracted by the search for a mate. For love to fill the void of self.

So much she was beginning to remember of herself. So much she had forgotten.

With The Poet, The Blacksmith, she'd heard herself say she was *changing*. But a part of her was over: the part that craved a man, always assessing potential, the 'agenda' taken out of the equation now. Now, she recognized, something in her was *forging*.

'How bizarre,' said Jake eventually, 'we're having this conversation. So strange you know more about me now than most of my mates. And we're, like, such different ages – and we'll never meet again, most like.'

'Sometimes that's the best way,' she said.

'It's good just to chat like this, though,' Jake added. 'Like you know, like when you've made a mate. Like if we'd— I don't mean like—'

No, she interrupted, she knew what he meant. In another life. He could shelve that look of abject horror. Jake smiled, she smiled; both of them recognizing the time to move back into the sunlight, for him to finish his job.

Two seconds later a branch crashed down from Tansy's ash at the exact spot they'd just been standing. Both turned, for the first time, to fully face one another.

In *another life*, this would be the point they kissed, possibly, probably. She felt the connection for certain, then – a moment in which if she made a move . . . She may not be after another soulmate, but she still wanted sex in her future, however it forged itself. For far too long she'd believed her desire, that deep, raw part of her nature, to be some kind of fatal flaw.

Jake cocked his head slightly to one side, as if studying her. A gentle gust of warm air caught his fringe, flopping it into his eyes; he tossed his head lightly to the other side to rid them of dark curls. In exactly the same way Danny did.

Oh, fuck. Oh, no. No. No. No.

Whether he caught her expression, she didn't know – and it didn't matter. The moment had passed, and instead they laughed, looking again to the fallen branch, furrowing faces in disbelief at the whole surreal nature of the afternoon.

'Now I'm no wafty wanker,' Jake said. 'But that fucking tree is trying to tell us something. If we hadn't moved when we had . . .'

In another life, they said again, simultaneously this time, it would have been interesting to have met, explore this connection

– plugged straight into socket from all the random wires of chance.

How many times would she say that again?

It seemed to her so rare. And yet, for the first time, that thought did not frighten her, or sling out roots of lonely worry and frowning hope as long and twisting as the dead piles of them furrowing her lawn. It made her think, if anything, of snakes. Of shedding skin.

She turned to Jake. 'You have to go to New York,' she said. 'But you already know that, don't you?'

He held her eye and smiled. Nodded slowly.

And Claire knew right then, too, that soon she would be leaving Hunter's Moon.

August

Sturgeon Moon – Half Waning

Later she would think how the absolute of the unexpected always makes the time just before, the time just after, sharp as the blade of a brand-new knife.

The oaks mesmerized her. She'd taken to walking the crisscross of village lanes mid-morning to admire others that sat beyond the wood, also in their full majesty; enjoying the rising perfumes of unseasonably high summer heat. The fields reeked deliciously of cut straw, the hedges of pungent damp, and a thick scent rose from the tar bubbling on the tarmac, glossy and luminescent as smoked glass. Claire could not resist tapping a fat bubble with her sandal, gratified by its pop; half-filled with the same urges her child-self had on mornings such as this. In fact, the more she thought about it, the more she wanted to do it.

Why not? Who would see her – and who cared? The desire tickled. Irrepressible. She tried a half hop, snuffed a little laugh at herself. *Fuck it. Skip!*

Wind whistled through the hoops in her ears, her feet light as the leaves shading her; her rhythm easy – the unconscious beat of nature forgotten beyond sex, children, walking, dancing drunk. She laughed: just as she once did at Tansy saying you could feel 'the energy of the earth rising to meet you' barefoot. But she felt it now, muscles coming to life, falling into the familiar pulse of herself. Here was who she was. Here she could do what she liked, be who she was – big, small and everything in between; wild with the power of being alive.

'Ow – fuck!'

Her knee – pain either side of the joint; the horrible sensation of bone clunking bone.

'Fuck! *Shit*!'

She stopped, resisting the urge to hobble, gave herself a moment to draw up her thighs, turning her attention back to the line of oaks flanking both sides of the lane. Several were young, thin of trunk but rotund of crown, and still close to bigger trees, if only an extended finger. It had informed her Art Calling submission, Tansy telling her trees spoke to one another, roots a superhighway all their own. How they grew to accommodate each other's leaf spread, nurtured their children with sugar, sent silent pheromonal messages to warn kinfolk of danger – disease, drought, death – or chemicals to attract insects to ward off another's attack. How the young were reckless with their drinking, the speed to shed their leaves. How, even in death, mother trees still sent out all they could to help the living.

How much more powerful they were once you knew that. How much more beautiful.

She stood still for moment under the largest, staring at the brain-like web of branches, the jags of scars and wind-snapped wood, grey where once a bone-bleached gash would have marked the severed limb. It would have sent its wound sap to heal, taken succour from neighbours, grown out in other ways, stronger all the time – not resisting the gnarls that made some fingers bony, or caused older limbs to creak.

She felt a flood of sudden emotion towards this big old mother tree, flinging her arms at its trunk; fingers finding grooves to hold. The sense of comfort surprised her – more solid than the arms of any man. Not cold, not warm, not anything but nature being what it was.

She did not move until she heard the inexorable sound of car, stepping back as if to take a photo, smiling. The things we do to show strangers we're normal, and not some old-hippy tree hugger who stayed there for some, if not many moments, eyes closed, mind empty, heart slow, as she felt the life and love of it infuse her.

The slightly acrid, fetid smell of the air. Musty as an old hymn book in a church.

The spangled dust of a shaft of light from the four-paned window by the stairs.

The insane tick of the living room clock.

The sensation of sudden cool after the warmth of sunshine on her skin.

The equally sudden scent rising from the roses she was holding. One a deep magenta tinged with cyan that smelled somehow lacy; the rose itself a symbol of appreciation, gratitude, recognition. The paler pink, full of fresh linen and speaking of grace, gentleness, joy. The white, with its traces of fragrant ice. The veinous red that had no smell at all but held itself voluptuously, as if dressed in sumptuous burgundy velvet. For love, obviously.

The way the bunch dropped from her hand.
Dark green leaves on pale green carpet.
Thorns red as blood.

'Oh,' she said. Finishing that word, eventually, and running right into it again.

'Oh.'

Before the walk, she'd risen early, sun already fierce at her curtains, wanting to pick the roses before the heat escalated, drunk on her high-summer world; the rambling wisteria a proscenium arch now for a blowsy outdoor ballroom where sunflowers played saxophone and poppies blew the bugle – she'd always felt that was the sound of that particular shade of red. She ignored the beetles trawling the roses, dodged the bees thronging the white lavender, the contusion of heuchera between them giving her little shivers of colourgasm. All around her colour pricked the solid blues and greens of the planet of her garden; the need to touch acute. Soon she'd be able to pick blackberries, mushrooms too; fry a puffball in butter and black pepper as her mother did.

She hadn't wanted to go back indoors, lose the magic of the moment. Something about this day felt different, and it didn't matter what. You didn't always need to know. Sometimes you just needed to be.

The cat had emerged from under the viburnum as she snipped roses; blinking, dozy, loosening limbs as he tried to shake off a back-leg limp: a hip, she assumed, given his evident age. But he looked healthy as he strolled towards her, arching his back and rubbing at her leg.

'I feel you, brother,' she said, smiling both at him and the words her sons would cringe at the theft of. Her own hip gave a tiny *pop!* as she pulled her leg back from its lunge. 'You and me both.'

How soft his fur felt. How happy his purr. How glad she was she hadn't just shooed him off into the endless depths of that hard, cold winter.

How long ago that seemed after a droughtish summer full of heat. Full of the flies that came with it, and that had driven Tansy to distraction.

It was the hand that gave it away. It would occur to her later other signs were there, too; she just hadn't seen them, so eager to show Tansy the roses.

Tansy was in her chair, head resting against the right side wing, hair steel wire against the chintz. Dozing, she assumed.

'A granny nap,' she'd once told Tansy she and her friends called them.

To which Tansy laughed and said, '*a disco nap*, I think the young call it, so I'll have that instead, thank you all the same.'

But the first thing she wanted to say now was 'hello Beethoven'. Tansy hadn't had a haircut for a while again; the curly steel wild around her head, a threatening raincloud to the chintzy flowers.

She got as far as 'hell—'

Which actually, Tansy would have loved.

The day she found out Tansy's real name had possibly been the hottest of that summer: the sun busy firing earth to clay rocks and deep cracks, a combine chomping the field like a slow locust; air so heavy with humidity and wheat dust that, much as she loved the smell, it felt like it sat on her as she walked to Tansy's. Yet Tansy's living room had been cool as a cave.

'I've brought you something.' She'd even wrapped it.

Tansy had regarded her with a slight frown. 'For me? Again?'

'Yes, and why not again? Don't get over-excited, it's not all that. It just made me smile and think of you.'

'Me?'

Claire smiled. 'Yes. You. Aren't you going to take it?'

Tansy was still frowning, though her mouth lifted at the corners, and as she looked up taking the parcel Claire couldn't help thinking of a delighted little girl. 'What is it?'

'I think the idea is you find that out.'

Tansy opened the paper slowly, carefully.

'Just rip it, Tansy. I'm not bloody saving it, so go on. Get in!'

Tansy laughed, tearing the paper. '*Get in*. Silly girl! What sort of expression is that?'

'A good one. So. Do you like it?'

'I might if I knew what it *was*.' Tansy lifted her gift, turning it in her hand. 'Some sort of tennis racquet for the infirm? Is this because I watched one – singular – Wimbledon match? I told you I detest all forms of sport that aren't watching it.'

'Only if you want to play fly tennis.'

'What are you talking about? Have you gone stark raving mad?'

'It's a fly swatter, Tansy. An electronic one – you don't even have to leave your chair or try and get them with your tea towel. You just swat and it fries them.'

'Oh!' She twisted the yellow plastic racquet again. '*Fries*, you say?'

'Yup. Proper sizzles the little bastards. Insanely satisfying.'

'A colourful riposte indeed. But don't said fried pests smell?'

'Sometimes, I suppose. Not that—'

'Oh, jolly good!' Tansy swished the racquet again. 'I shall feel like a swashbuckler, a murderer, and a dragon all at once. Utterly marvellous. Thank you, dear Claire, very much.'

'You're welcome.'

Still gently swashbuckling, Tansy turned to her. 'No one buys me gifts, or not beyond the cursory – the cleaner and such. Not since Ken died, when one had more flowers and chocolates than one could shake a stick at. Oh, there's a book from Hope at Christmas, I suppose, sent online, but nothing *wrapped*. I feel like a child, only better. I didn't really have friends as such back then. They were simply people one *knew*.'

'Aren't so many, though?' asked Claire. 'I've realized how many of the friends I thought I had while I was married were only acquaintances, really. And now I'm losing an actual one.' She looked out of the window, momentarily surprised by the sheer spread of Tansy's willow. 'Talking of which, that reminds me. You never did tell me your real name. I keep forgetting, meaning to ask – despite how often you dodge the question.'

Tansy scowled and pursed her lips. '*Lord*. Can't you ask me something else? The heat is bad enough and now you persecute me further with your wretched question.'

Claire smiled. 'Well, you can't say that and not deliver. So. Constance – that would make a Tansy? Or Tanya? Pansy?'

'Dear God. Help us. I have a feeling you are not going to stop?'

'I am not. Something exotic, like Anastasia?'

'Heavens, no! That poor little princess. And my father would never have allowed *anything* from Russia.'

'Antonia, then.'

'Ugh.'

'Okay, so – Africa. Tanzania?'

'Tch.' Tansy shook her head. 'All right. You win.' She looked a little sheepish. 'It's Athanasia.'

'Athanasia? I've never even heard of it – where's it from?'

'Greek, originally, though Papa would have despised the fact some attribute it to German. Ha! No, he loved anything to do with Greek myths and stories, and mercifully, the word means "eternal life" or "immortal". Derived, would you believe, from *thánatos* – the Greek word for death.' She gurned. 'The irony!'

'You don't mean that.' But Claire laughed all the same.

'I jolly well do. I remembered a great-aunt the other day. Hilda. How I'd wished her a joyous festive season one Christmas and she barked back, *Oh, joy! How I wish I could find a bit of joy in life!* and I thought, Oh dear, poor old thing, I hope I never end up like that.' Tansy raised her hands as if in supplication. 'Oh, Hilda, hear my prayer!'

'Stop it!' said Claire, still laughing. 'Tell me more about that myth.'

'Well, apparently, in ancient times Athanasia was the daughter of Christian nobles. According to Pa, she was innocently weaving at her loom one day when a star came down and merged with her heart, leading to some sort of transcendental, spiritual union.' She raised her brow. 'Quite how he likened *that* to infant me, I'll never know. It seems the poor creature never wished for marriage but ended up betrothed to a soldier – who did at least have the decency to die. Then married a man who wanted to be a monk and buggered off – with her blessing, it seems – leaving her to do as she wished. She became an abbess famed for miraculous healing powers, a saint, no less, St Athanasia of Aegina.' She sat back and glared. 'Well? Aren't you going to say anything?'

Claire had been too rapt by the story to do anything other than stare. 'Why didn't you want to tell me this before? It's beautiful.'

Tansy gave her a sharp look. 'Is it? When one has to go through all of that, every time, and one just wanted to be a Penelope or a Harriet, or even a Mary?'

'But don't you like it even a tiny bit? That story!'

'Perhaps. As I grow ever older. But Lord – who in their right mind would wish for immortality? I can't think of anything *worse*. There are days in the dark months – or were,' she added, nodding at Claire, 'when one wakes and thinks *Oh, Gawd, here I go again*. But yes, I suppose it has rather grown on me.'

'So how did you get Tansy from that?'

That wide smile. It still held so much beauty, even in old age. 'Dear Keziah. When she first nannied me, the poor thing couldn't pronounce it, kept confusing it with Anansi, the African spider god. My mother never liked the name particularly, so decided to stick with Tansy. I think it reminded her of Blighty. Mother never did care for the heat.'

'I still can't believe you never used it,' said Claire. 'I just had boring old Claire. Or Clur, as I was so much of the time at university.'

'But *Claire* is a beautiful name. You'll appreciate it when you're older. Simplicity. Ease. Especially with the b-word computer. With age comes wisdom, as they rightly say.'

'God, I hope so.'

Tansy put her head on one side. 'Life is short, but it is also long, dear *Clur*.'

'I just don't want to make any more mess of it, I suppose.' A surprise to hear herself say this. And a relief. 'I just wish I knew what to do *now*.'

A *hmm*. 'Oh, I suspect you already know. We usually do.'

She hadn't realized her gaze was cast at her lap; looked up as Tansy spoke again.

'Etiolation.'

'Sorry?'

Tansy smiled. 'Don't you love it as a word? It's when a plant or flower gets leggy from lack of light. Like anything, I think. As soon as one starts to show something light, it grows; good or bad. But not knowing where one is? Well. For what it's worth, I think sometimes that's the best place.'

'You do? Why?'

'I do. Sometimes *right* isn't always applicable. Most of us, most of the time, don't really have a clue what we're doing. Sometimes all you ever are is perhaps less *wrong* – as Mother always said: if a cake fails it becomes a pudding. My dear girl, you have just made a garden from next to nothing. Emphasis on the word *made*. One digs things up, prunes with fingers crossed one hasn't just performed terminal surgery; transplants, too, with no idea if said plant will survive post sulk.' Tansy smiled warmly. 'Cold comfort, I know. But nothing is not a bad basis. One sees it most in summer, I think, as a gardener. All too often it means what survives is strong. And, Clur, *true*.'

She knelt before she said anything beyond that *hell*—, looking at Tansy, at the undeniable stains of death – the pallor of skin with that strange softening of lines that so resembled sleep; the slight pooling of blood in one side of her neck and that hand.

She stayed like that, just staring at her friend.

'Oh, Athanasia-Tansy,' she said after a little while. 'You got there after all.'

She picked up Tansy's hand, slipped as it was over the side of the chair. Tissue-paper thin, cold, and mottled as a bruise, though she hadn't shuddered as she would – did – younger. She'd seen enough of death now to feel no fear of it in front of her, and for perhaps the first time was grateful for that. Her mother had laid her own mother out. *It was what you did*, she said. *The last respect you paid.* All the women of her family had done that before her. At the time, whatever she said, Claire thought it macabre, but when her mother died, she too had wanted to comb her hair in the hospital, at least. And she wanted to do the right thing now; give Tansy the last marker of her respect.

She had never felt any of this as strongly as with birth and death, it occurred to her; since something in her found itself, regardless of cognisance, guided by the primal knowledge deep in her, bestowed by her grandmothers, theirs before them, on and on, back and back. Hags, crones, witch-women – who else would do the right thing for the dead? Who else completed the circle of life in quite the same way?

For this she would be the daughter Tansy never had.

She placed the hand carefully in Tansy's lap, so it met its other half in dignity, and walked to the hall, carefully collecting the dropped blooms from the carpet and resting them in those hands. She had a feeling Tansy would have liked that.

'She passed quickly,' they said. Either some sort of stroke, or her heart – they'd know more later – but the one thing they were sure of: Tansy had not suffered. This meant more to Claire than anything. Part of her wouldn't put it past the old woman to have willed it into being – witched it, somehow, if she could.

Did you know her well?

Had she been ill at all?

When was the hip?

Had she complained of any chest pains, jaw or arm pain, indigestion?

And last, they asked, the paramedics she called, unsure what else she ought to do, *Is there anyone we could contact – to let them know she's passed?*

'Died,' Claire said.

And the two women smiled and one said, Well, they couldn't confirm that, they'd have to wait for a doctor; the corpse still subject to the life of law.

'But died is what she did,' she said. Loud. Clear. The words to say how these were not her words – and just how much that mattered – would not leave her lips.

And then the other paramedic woman smiled and said Why don't we have a nice cup of tea.

And at the word, 'we', a single tear tripped and fell down Claire's left cheek.

She was not sure what to do with the roses. All she could think, wanted to think, was which flower would mark the occasion. And which Tansy would have liked.

Even the air seemed startled as she sat on one of the old vinyl stools in Tansy's tiny blue kitchen, staring at the flowers sweaty-stemmed in her palm; edges fringed already with brown, the serration of their leaves less stark for lack of water. She wanted to tell Tansy of her shock. She wanted to tell her how the paramedics wouldn't let her leave the roses with 'the body'.

Steam rose in spirals from the ancient kettle. Tea. The only thing Claire seemed to know to do. The panacea of the nation; coping in a cup. Yet still she had to boil the kettle twice before the tea got made. And still it tasted of stale sodding Tupperware.

She wandered about the house, sipping, almost as much the steam as the liquid, though it did little to warm the chill in her. That question from the paramedics had foxed her; left its musk inside her head.

She'd no idea what would happen to the house – doubtless, Hope would instruct a lawyer soon as. Claire wanted, before she left, to stand in Tansy's living room again, run her fingers over those apotropaic marks in her beams: trace the ascending flame, the scratched Roman numerals that once told builders how to turn a tree into the skeleton of a home. So many people born between the walls of that ancient house, or meeting death below its beams.

She shouldn't be here, in any case, she thought, wandering Tansy's garden. But it was the only place the roses belonged. She couldn't take them home, stick them in a vase and stare at them, and nor could she bring herself to throw them. They were picked for Tansy and they would stay if not with her, then with the things that formed the bridge between where she'd lived and wherever she was now.

Beneath Claire's feet bees harried the white clover in the lawn. She'd forgotten until now, still for a few moments, how

Tansy told her clover served as a reminder others are always thinking of you.

Once she stood in front of it, the willow was indisputably right. Perhaps all that wood in the house; perhaps the fact she could still hear Tansy talk about her reasons for planting it; filled with the urge to stroke its bark, work fingernails into its cracks and valleys, see if she couldn't winkle out some solace, some wisdom, some *way*. As if she wanted it to creak its branches and fold its rigid fingers to the shape of holding her.

The willow whispered: a soft susurration in the gentle breeze.

And there was Tansy. Telling her how it was the goddess tree, bound to a full moon just as it bound a witch's broomstick or made a wizard's wand; the tree of the female Celts, *those most empowered of women* – the way its branches could be severed by brutal winds but grow again from simply resting on the ground.

Back at home she googled. She loved how she could do this now – pick not just the colour and texture of a flower but know (at least sometimes) what it meant. Bestowing things with *meaning* – wasn't Stephen always banging on about Jung: how the first half of life was all about 'proving yourself and acquisition', but the second 'authenticity and meaning'?

She found herself a little shocked, reading about the roses she'd chosen, wondering the exact time of Tansy's death. Somewhere deep down, Claire knew it couldn't possibly be while she was outside choosing and picking them. How, whichever site she scrolled, however many times she read, white roses meant all the bridal stuff, yes, but also stood for gratitude, loyalty, friendship, hope, respect, affection. Love.

And yet Tansy would have known. How the Victorians would never, ever, advocate the giving of both white and red roses together. To them, with all their superstition, it meant a death was coming, and soon.

How she wished she could have Tansy laugh at her as she related this: the ultimate Tansy gift. How Claire would have countered it by saying, Yeah but, she gave them the way she wanted to start living.

Because she did, she really did. She wanted to *live*.

September

Harvest Moon – Half Waxing

Even when trees stopped putting out carbon dioxide they still grew; roots talking through the 'wood-wide web': lattices of fungi that kept new life thriving from the dead. Mycorrhizal networks, a grapevine in nature she'd have known nothing of without Tansy. Funny the things you forgot – like Tansy telling her how ancient shamans surprised the modern world by knowing, somehow, to sit under a willow with a headache. The same properties in its bark – salicin – as aspirin. The same lessons of life, birth, death, pain, joy.

Ben listened to all this, an initial slight frown deepening. 'It's all fascinating and lovely, Claire. But I'm worried about you. Are you really okay?'

'Yes and no. Or I wouldn't have told you.'

How much more brutal sorrow seemed in summer sun. But trees grow, she reminded herself, over, around and through any obstacle.

'It's good to see you. It seems like it's been—' She nearly said forever, quickly reminded that sooner or later, Ben's life would slip further from hers.

'You, too.'

A pause. No words needed. How to define what it was to have spent so long with somebody that drawing the division between where they started and you ended became almost impossible? He was still Ben, though, undeniably.

'I'm so sorry you found the stiff,' he said. 'No, wait – that came out—'

She laughed. He'd never been good at naming the things he felt uncomfortable with, though she accepted that now.

'You know what I mean,' he added, smiling. 'I'm sorry – that's the salient bit.'

So many times she'd listened to him and thought how cold and prosaic he could sound, as if a dictionary had wedged itself between his teeth. 'And are you okay? Really?'

Ben inhaled deeply. 'Yes. I think so. I've had a lot of time to think while I've been away. It's been good. I mean, don't get me wrong, it hasn't been easy . . .'

That was probably as much as she was going to get, and she didn't want to push for more. It wasn't her job to do that work for him, for anyone outside her kids, any more than it was the job of rosemary to taste like thyme.

'Anyway, I brought you something,' he added, non sequitur. Another thing that used to drive her nuts. 'Where did I put it?' And another.

These things now, though, if anything, raised a smile as Claire watched him rummage his pockets, frown lifting as he found what he sought in an inside one. Her eyes widened at the fat – and very neatly rolled – spliff. 'Ben! What the fuck?'

'Okay. Just hear me out, okay?' He spread his hands on the table and looked at her. 'In the past few months I've taken this up again. Please don't start – it's made me feel *so* different.'

'Er, stoned? That kind of different?'

He gave her a hangdog look. 'No. Well. *Yes*, but that's not what I mean.' He smiled, though not with his eyes, she noted. 'I mean about me. Us. Danny. All that.'

'Ah.' She said nothing else, waiting, curious. She'd long ago assumed Ben incapable of surprising her – outside the stuff of the kinky or the dark – though she felt a heart flinch at that smile; a tiny, sad, shiver at *us*.

'Like I said, I've had a lot of time to think. Too much, sometimes. For me.' He shrugged. 'Weed helped me calm down. Drink just made me depressed and so fucking angry I can't—' A sigh. 'Anyway. I suppose what I'm saying is you can't just rage or logic it all away, can you? Like men, I—' She could feel how difficult it was for him, touched the back of his hand. 'It didn't work, C. I've had times where I really had to fight myself. Times I can't. Anyway.' The threat of a tear filled the space between his eye and the side of his nose.

'You want to say long story short, don't you?' She smiled.

Ben nodded, looking momentarily weary and grateful. 'I do.'

'And it's fine. It's fine. I get it.' For a moment their hands tucked into one another. 'It was never just you. It was me, too. The two of us. Life. But I can't say sorry any more than—'

'You don't have to. I get it, I do. You always said women get lost in marriage, motherhood, and I see that. But I think men do, too. Or *me*, the things I never say – Mr fuck-my-eyes-I've-been-blind Generalization. I see the changes in you. And they're good. You're more you than I remember in a long, long time.'

'Amazing how a spliff changes the old view?'

He smiled. 'I forgot how good it was to get away from your thoughts enough to actually look at the fuckers. Work out where you are.' He side-eyed her. 'Here's a thing. I saw an old uni friend the other day and he was saying about his daughter, some hotshot astrophysicist who's got this job with NASA. So I said wow and all that, given I'd just been telling him about Dan and how I'd give my right arm to see him do something with his life—'

Claire raised a hand, opened her mouth,

'No, hear me out, please? And he said, "Well, he is in a way?" So I said yeah, it's the *way* I'm worried about – waiting for him to tell me he's in a Californian jail being rogered by the Daddy. You must be really proud, I said. And you know what he said? "I am," he said, "I just wish I had some idea of what it is she does – not a clue, mate; not a fucking clue. She tells me and I just nod like those dogs in cars. I hoped we'd bond over a pint in the local, like my mates with their kids, except now I feel like I'm sat there with a professor waiting for me to start pissing myself and talking prostates."' Ben paused for a second. 'Can you believe it?'

She couldn't stop her laugh. 'And you've told Danny this? After all your lectures about his choices? Your punishment?'

He sucked in his lips. 'I'm not proud, Claire. I've hated the shit between me and Dan, the way I've been a reminder of my dad, a fucking bully who didn't support me, and probably helped make my mum how she was. I just didn't want him to fuck his life up.'

'But when you're young, Ben—'

'That's what I'm *saying*.'

Still that lightning flash of impatience; the familiar knot forming in her belly from its tentacles.

'Like *I* would have done,' he went on, calmer, 'if I'd had the chance at his age. Meeting you stopped all that, all the country-hopping, the escaping, I suppose. And I think after my sister I just lost the plot again a bit.' He looked down at their hands. 'Or a lot. I don't want to end up like Mum – criticizing everyone all the time. Nothing ever her fault. It's like she took over from him, and I don't want to do that.'

'So, what are you going to do? Are you going to talk to him?'

'No.' He shook his head side to side, slowly. 'We're blokes, Claire. I'll send him a text. And don't give me that face. It'll be a long one. Ish.'

'That's good, Ben. It is. It really, really is.'

'We can still be a family, can't we, C?'

'Yes, we can. *Are*, Ben.'

They held each other's soft gaze, caught in the moment of sad-happy gratitude.

When she lifted her brush to face the blankness of white, she had no idea what would emerge from the tips of its fibres. Only that she'd let her own fibres dictate what did; without herself, as such, getting in the way.

She didn't want to smoke Ben's joint, but she hadn't made him take it either: something in it felt symbolic, full circled. She'd even agreed not to get involved in his way of dealing with Danny; let the two of them sort it, as adults. Not be *Mum*. The talk had been good for both of them; Ben lighter leaving than when he arrived, herself, too. If exhausted. She closed her eyes.

Inhaled.

Exhaled.

She summoned her garden in the inky skies of her eyelids:

a collection of colours, textures, shapes, scents – of everything she'd worked on since she started. The sweet pinks. The breath-stealing scent of those roses. The dead men's fingers, witches' gloves – all the insincerity, pride, creativity, energy; whatever you wanted to call the life and death cocktail of foxgloves. The splash of self-sown poppies and the sheer front of the buddleia she once hated with the same passion bees and butterflies loved it now, bringing it on in rebirth and resurrection. The art unseen she had applied with imagination only, no brief.

You are an artist, are you not?

She began with the pink geraniums that dominated the base layers with their *folly*; tempered by their blue cousin with kindness and friendship. The heuchera that spoke of offering up your talents, being open even when exposed to the core.

She tapped her brush against the bottom of the easel, reached for another.

The ferns full of mystery and all that was buried; half-painted, half-stabbed, jabbing in a little black here, feathering in cadmiums, Prussian blue, chromium oxide, there. Then hostas, blending emeralds into cream for the sweet talk of devotion, her brush broad and sweeping, dabbing into green to get that perfect shade of white, as if her body still held the knowledge – as if she could close her eyes and her brush would simply carry on, borne by the power of the feeling.

Another tap, another switch of brush.

The Asiatic iris now, wisdom and respect in violet-blues. She smiled thinking of Tansy, made mental notes to sharpen up its spotted tongue. The Persicaria, the soft pink voice of restoration to the heartache and sorrow of yarrow. She stopped for moment, her other hand briefly touching her heart; its speed reflected by the light burn at her cheeks.

She rinsed the brush, clattered it against the easel without thinking, watching watery spots of paint bleed into the carpet. *Fuck it.* No time to do more than whip the sheet off Joe's bed and shove it roughly around the easel's legs.

She moved as if with music – dancing her painting, lost in the beat of sliding one colour into another, making shapes as naturally as breathing. The aquilegias tipping bonnets to self-seeding endurance, salvation; the blending of blue, red, grey, yellow, black, to capture the healing wisdom of purple sage; a little more black for the heart-cheer of ajuga, a touch more white for the campanula's peals of gratitude. Back down again for the viridian and olive of chives, alchemilla their canopy of comforting love. Grey, black, white, a smidge of blue for the silvery *Stachys* tall with self-appreciation and love; deep phthalo and cobalt for the artifice and fine arts of acanthus. She smiled for the buddleia, arcing her brush in towering sweeps up and out and – tap, clatter – dot-dot-dotting the regal purples, pinks; a slight sway of hips as she captured next the blackening of viburnum, that bouquet of philadelphus, the hollyhocks' brazen fecundity.

Oh, so many.

The herbs, too. Rosemary, thyme, all the bustle of mint. The basil that would live only a summer before starvation. And that was all right. That was what happened with plants that found themselves in the wrong part of their world.

Her beloved lavenders now. Peace. Serenity. Healing. The only thing she came here with any intent to grow.

She had, of course, stood back at some point – usually the

dreaded point of sighing at the shonky translation of what spoke so beautifully to her mind. Only now, she saw the extravagance of what happened when she was out of the way. Or, rather, completely in it.

The painting was exuberant. Passionate, bold, colourful. Full of the life of her garden without the tiny detail, but nonetheless it made the shape, held the textures, smiled, shouted, whispered and seduced in all the same ways as when she stood staring, drunk on the joy of its beauty; of creating it. She loved it instantly.

It took a few moments to really feel that: unused to the sensation of pride.

She put her hand to her chest again, almost wanting to cry. It brought to mind the wild garden of Emil Nolde she'd once seen at the Royal Academy – or Bonnard, Kandinsky, Liebermann, even Monet; Impressionists, expressionists. It didn't matter.

What did matter was the fact that *she* had painted it. It was only when she embraced her own intensity, completely and without fear, she felt whole.

She could have sat and watched the paint dry. Of course she could. She'd cut herself off from life until she could have watched papyrus dehumidify into a sodding scroll. But look what she had made. This growth from nothing but mess and neglect.

A world of difference between alone and on one's own.

She walked her borders, snapping off spent heads, blooms crusted dry or petals that fell almost at breath; likewise, anything twiggy, mottled, bound too tight to flower by heavy dew. She was conscious of what she was picking, though the action itself was not.

Rosemary for remembrance.

You come into this world alone, and leave it that way, too – perhaps you never learned that more than in the worst of times: how it's you you're left with when your eyes close at night. But plants held stories, too. Who taught you how or gave you what: each sight and smell of flower. The tales they told of people, healing, love.

Sage to cleanse and ground.

Every cell of every plant wanted only to survive and thrive, reach the sun; unafraid to let itself be seen, known, share itself. Desire was nothing if not a creative act: a garden would be dead without it. Still so much to give, do, learn, find, help with.

Thyme to heal wounds and represent the passing of time itself.

The last of the honeysuckles stared at her, belligerent with beauty, fists unfolding fingers to sun, stamens to the probe of bees. She stuck her face in so deep pollen practically tickled her brain. Insurmountable, this lacy fragrance: memories of her mother's garden, her grandmothers', the Suffolk hedgerows where it touted for business, wild and wanton, as she grew from girl to woman. She drew in the familiar tones of peach, honey, the almost-cloy just shy of sickly. Sweet, yes. But not, and never now, without a tinge of sadness – a fading bloom beside a knot of sticky berries – of what had been and what was gone.

Sometimes these were all you had, these moments. You had to take from them what you could. Choose. In a way you didn't younger, enviably free of the tyrannies of memory and time. So little left now. She wanted to a career. Full-on fun again. To dance, sing, run with wolves, to feel passion like she used to: feel her blood a torrent in her veins, her heartbeat thunder at her ribs; the same electric pulse she felt in the throes of a powerful storm. To paint and create and express.

She remembered a thing Tansy once said she'd never paid much attention to, it being back when everything was less ice and fire, more a miserable hymn to mud and flood.

'Nature teaches one staying alive is not natural,' she said, 'and that we've got rather good at defying it. Gardening shows what a human being needs to thrive: the right conditions, the right nurture. But nature, raw, untouched, shows us what we fundamentally *are*.'

The little bonfire whistled and whined before it took, though almost as soon as it had, Claire let it die down to an ashen glow; the wood crocodile-backed, then snake-skinned, and finally flaking crumble. The herbs sparked, smoking in thin wisps as she lifted each to wave it around herself, offer it back to the sky, before dropping it back on the ashy bed: Ben, the life she'd known as wife and mother, all the men she'd known before or since. Her mother.

Rosemary, to remember.
Sage, to forgive.
Thyme, to let go.

She wondered how many women before her had burned their herbs to small and silent prayers for love – and loss – in all its guises. She closed her eyes, hearing Tansy tell her not to waste the fire debris, *dear girl* – how good the ash would be for the roses.

After the fire she ate wearily and headed straight to bed. Talk about old fiddles and good tunes. She'd certainly found a way to sing 'To Infinity and Beyond'! She hadn't had a hobby this good since teenage years – and among the many, beautiful spells it cast, sleep was surely one of the best.

She had a new toy to play with. Buzz. A very welcome friend for Woody.

September

Harvest Moon – Half Waning

An email sandwich greeted her at breakfast. One just above the one from Tansy's solicitors, both of which Claire opened, and one below from Art Calling, which she did not.

Enough to make anyone think. A new rental agreement would be enough on its own – this one back in Norfolk, closer to a city; travel links, the art classes she hoped to, no, *would*, one day be teaching herself again. She thought of Daisy, Jake. She could renew her certificates. Or take a course, even, whatever happened with the scheme now.

She looked at the solicitor's email again.

. . . as executors of the last will and testament of MRS ATHANASIA HOWARD . . . the sum of . . .

No one had ever left her anything beyond a few hundred quid from her grandmother when the boys were small (and which she'd spent on a new stereo 'for the family', mainly so they could play their beloved *Pop Party 987!* or whatever it was that long after 1986).

But as for Art Calling, she still couldn't open it. *Two out of three ain't bad*, Meatloaf wasn't wrong. But it also made three out of three a lot less likely.

The door knocked.

A while since she sighed at that as she did now. *Go away.* She wanted just to sit, savour the last shout-outs of beauty in this garden she'd made, full of fairy tale red apples and gorging, drowsy wasps; find a way, if anything, of somehow thanking Tansy. Maybe she could try a shamanic ceremony, or some goddess offering – except even thinking that, and not having her to ask, made her miss Tansy with a visceral pang.

The door didn't just knock this time, it didn't stop.

'Claire!' said Hope Becker, looking only marginally more contained than her pounding. 'At last.' She gestured with her face to the bundle of plastic folders she was carrying. 'Here. For you.'

Claire had to take a step back as Hope thrust them at her: several bigger folders, some smaller, all incontrovertibly for art. 'Oh! Sorry, I was in the garden – what are these?'

That circumflex eyebrow again. 'Exactly what they look like – the aunt's art.'

She stacked the pile against the banister. 'Wow, I had no idea— I didn't know you were back either or I'd have popped over, sorry. But why are you giving them to me?'

The other eyebrow, too, now. 'Oh, just something else she wanted you to have.'

Something about her tone. Up until that point, Claire assumed Hope's manner the result of that ocean of admin that follows death, the jetlag of that and a long flight.

She smiled, uncertain. 'Something else? I'm sorry I don't quite—'

'Yah.' Hope cut her short. 'So. *Lekker.* Let me ask – how much influence, exactly, did you have on my aunt?'

Ah. So here it was; she might have known from experience. The pissed-off relative. That way they always seemed to show up after the event – you think it's apocrypha until it happens – to chastise you for not doing enough; or doing too much. But death is never easy; Claire determined to be kind. 'Hope, it wasn't like that. Why don't you come in, have some tea, a glass of wine?'

'No, thank you. I would like you to answer my question, if you could.'

Claire inhaled. 'Okay, we'll do this here. In that case, you knew your aunt. How much influence do you think *anybody* had on her?'

'Well, *I* certainly didn't. And I kind of thought you'd help me with that, seeing as you two *neighbours* got on like the proverbial—'

God, she sounded like Tansy when she said that.

'—house on *fiar,* so thank you for that. And are you seriously telling me she left you money just because you were,' here, she made exaggerated air quotes, and again Claire was reminded of Tansy, '*friends* for the tiny time you've lived here? For real?'

Wow. 'Okay. Are you sure you won't come in? I do know how hard dealing with a death is, and I understand your concerns. But Tansy *was* my friend, simple as. I never asked for or expected anything. Let's talk about it over a nice glass of—'

'I don't think that's a good idea,' Hope cut in. 'And obviously it's not *so* much I can contest it. The solicitors won't even hear of it under ten k, apparently. Ridiculous.'

So, she'd asked, then.

The door began to close in the breeze tunnelling through the cottage with both doors open. Claire pushed it wide again; a fleeting glimpse of herself in winter, in her dressing gown, Hope so smart, as she tried not to open this same door beyond her left ear.

'Hope, I didn't make your aunt make any decisions she hadn't already made herself. I couldn't have *told* her to go into a home, it wasn't what she wanted. That was for *your* family – not my call to make. I did what you asked and kept an eye on her. And I assume she left you the house? So, I'll help if I can, but I'm really not sure what you want from me.'

How she wished she'd known how to say all this younger without needing the touchpaper of rage.

Hope let out a savage laugh. 'The house. The *house*? Half of it! The rest of it she's gone and . . . Jesus Christ, I can hardly *say* it . . . left to a nature sanctuary for abused single mothers and a bloody scheme that helps artists. What – the *fuck* – is all that about?'

Claire had to fight the smile desperate to split her face. 'She has?'

Hope's pale blue eyes furious pools. 'And you told me she was lucid.'

'Look, I see how unhappy you are about all this, but the truth is yes, she was, right up to the end. And I am sorry it hasn't turned out the way you wanted.'

A bitter nod. 'Yah. Well, I want you to know how let down I feel on behalf of myself, my family, my – *rest-her-soul* – mother. My kids. So, thank you for your help, *Claire*.'

Claire looked at Hope. It occurred to her she'd only ever seen the woman use the word 'my' in relation to Tansy when talking about the house. Younger her might have spat that in Hope's face. Somewhere-in-the-middle her would have apologized again and often, anything to avoid the conflict and/or *be the bigger person*. But now all she had to say to that was: 'Thank you for sharing that with me. I wish you well, Hope. Goodbye.'

She closed the door, not waiting to hear what else Hope Becker might have to say.

Back in the garden, with a cool glass of prosecco she hoped would slaughter two birds with one stone – the aftermath of Hope and the beforemath of Art Calling's email – Claire wondered what sort of autumn this would make.

The summer – weeks now without rain – refused to be cowed, as if making up for the outrage of such a late spring. The ferocity of all that unfettered sun meant everything had gone 'all over behind', as her mother used to say, an expression that only entered Claire's head because though some flowers had long since surrendered – even the chamomile looked like a crochet for the dead – others kept on.

The world's weather was changing and from where Claire stood, staring across a field where not even a telegraph pole punctuated her view, it felt as if the planet was taking stock. As if it could no longer afford the luxury of time, trees letting go of the no-longer needed; 'switching to survival mode', the journalists said. But not even weathermen, perplexed by a promise of rain that came, but only where it wanted, could predict this particular autumn. Nature did what it had to do, no more, no less. Not everything could be foretold, no matter how good the knowledge; just as not everything could survive, however much the love.

All this she had said in her application, and in her intent to use that first folder Tansy gave her, add to it the meanings of animals: the crows mediating life and death, the ducks speaking of the conscious mind, but also intuition; the owl, symbol of Athena and ancient knowledge, the witches' beloved hare and its creative unblocking. That resurrection of spirit that came with deer and natural power not easily subdued. She'd opted for total honesty. And if that included passionate woo-woo, so be it. Authenticity was everything.

Autumn would be beautiful, of course – how to find one that was not? Even the most determined clouds couldn't sour the mellow of a September mist. No fog that could obscure the warming light of fire, no night so cold it could obliterate the simple beauty of a star. And no way she could look up at that moon now and not smile, say hello to Tansy. Wonder if she wasn't somehow swooshing herself around the dark of the house next door.

'She requested not to have a funeral,' the solicitor's email said. Claire hadn't realized until then how much difference it made to mark a death, say goodbye, with ritual.

She remembered something that did two things: spread the biggest smile across her face, and also helped her understand why.

'I can't behave myself at funerals,' Tansy told her once.

'What do you mean? You're not going to tell me you get too emotional?'

That cackle. 'Oh, but I do. Just in the wrong way – entirely.'

Claire had laughed. 'You start telling them they've picked the wrong flowers? What?'

'Well, of course I do *that*. Old habits and so forth. No, what I mean is that one can't stop oneself laughing. Poor dear Ken used to live in fear of my mortally offending the bereaved.' She grimaced. 'I even laughed at *his*. Whatever must people have thought?'

'Isn't it a shock reaction or sort of hysteria, though?' said Claire. 'I do it, I think most of us do?'

Tansy raised an eyebrow. 'I think it rather depends on what one is laughing *about*.'

'So, what kicks you off, then? The fact the coffin might be dropped – that almost happened at my granny's funeral and nearly everyone laughed. She hated heights. Her idea of hell was being near anything over a foot high.'

'Oh, I wish!' said Tansy. 'One wouldn't feel quite such a savage if that were the case. No – it's all that having to be so terribly po-faced, I suppose; the curse of we Britons, especially we archaics and our cursed stiff uppers. All it takes is the tiniest of things. When my mother was alive she was even worse. We were late for dear old Dad's funeral because the hearse battery died and Mother announced this by pointing at his coffin and telling the congregation not to worry, it wasn't "catching".'

'And Ken's?' asked Claire.

Tansy screwed up her face. 'I laughed at Ken's because of the line in 'All Things Bright and Beautiful', the second verse, where one sings *The purple-headed mountain*. Didn't I tell you I didn't have a heart? Well, now you can add shameless, to boot.'

Claire's laugh reached her belly. 'Of all the things I thought you might have said, *that* was not among them, to be fair.'

Tansy put fingers to forehead, thumbs on her cheeks. 'Oh, believe me, one is so very, *very* far from happy about it.' She looked up and laughed a little, despite herself. 'And you. Claire of the Moon, must never speak of it to another living soul.'

'Even if I change your name?'

'Imperative you *do* change my name. At all times and without need of anecdote. You see, it isn't that one doesn't feel sadness

– I was so overwhelmed when Ken died, I wanted little more than to join him.' She'd sighed then. 'We're such creatures of nature, are we not? Constant transformation, constant survival. The need for light, warmth, love, whatever that is for: people, life itself, nature, art – it's who we *are*.' She'd smiled. 'And you are what you are what you are, my dear Claire.'

The early evening glowed an other-worldly gold, spreading light the colour of harvested corn over the field, echoed by the mechanical trudge of tractor, blade; the air wheat-sweet still but edged now with the raw of unearthed soil. Claire knew now, too, that unlike other full moons, this Harvest Moon, a supermoon, would rise at sunset for several days. She thought of something Tansy told her; about the Chinese mid-autumn festival of Wild Moon Rising to celebrate the lunar cycles of planting and harvest. It seemed apt. The stars were not yet out, the whole sky a tequila sunset, as if to toast the dying summer.

Pouring her second glass, Claire heard a noise in the hall. She took her wine with her, wondering if Hope was knocking again, or just stuffing something through the letter box – arsenic or hemlock, perhaps – relieved to see Tansy's folders slumped, if in such a way it meant she wouldn't be able to reach the stairs unless she moved them.

She squatted, wincing at the rifle rapport of her knees, and began to gather the folders, unable to resist a quick flick. Most were seemingly full of the still lives and landscapes likely for Tansy's MA; but others with botanical sketches, paintings, notes on genus, meaning, ideal conditions, folklore, and it was these that captured Claire, caused her to sit, cross-legged, and let out a murmur at how each plant, flower, weed, branch – either painted or pencil-sketched – was graced with a delicacy, an acuity of detail, not seen in Tansy's larger works. Here a moss rose, ribbony in bloom, furred all along its stem with tiny, hairy thorns. Now a raceme of wisteria half in flower, half still shut, in twenty shades of purple, violet, lilac, blue; a daffodil at every stage of opening; each rendering as precise as Tansy's use of words. She smiled at some of the pencilled annotations – *Beware the dog (rose): bite worse than bark; utter thug. Ragwort: hand-shredder (and – or because? – a sign of moral turpitude!)*. One folder, though, had a piece of paper, taped on all four sides, to its plastic back – *For Claire* in Tansy's fountain pen italics.

She ran a finger over it, but it didn't feel like the paper from the set Tansy bemoaned not being able to use after her friend Margaret died – 'Oh, I'm *such* a fossil, I know. But how I miss missives!'– it felt like one of the envelopes. Hope obviously hadn't seen it. She peeled the tape gently, careful not to tear as she winkled at the seal.

The letter was folded the old-fashioned way, a concertina of thirds, the watermark of Tansy's beloved Basildon Bond apparent.

Dear Claire,

No doubt you will be impressed at my visitation from the afterlife. Believe me, if I could do so in person – and bearing in mind one doesn't yet know one can't? – I should be there, if only to see this make you smile in the way you have me these past months.

Whilst I have no desire to adopt the nauseating tone of American missives such as this, I must also declare (get it?) I have only rarely made connections such as this.

It has brought with it a great joy I shan't even attempt to convey. Let it be enough to know I will be raving all about it to dear old Ken (poor man can't even die to escape me this time).

It isn't much, I know. But I chose eight as a number because to our dear friends, the Chinese, it <u>is</u> auspicious. Do with it what you will, but it is sent from beyond the grave as an aid to growing an art career, regardless of your winning a place on the scheme. I shall, of course, also accept the purchase of plants when you finally 'win' a garden of your own. Plant one for me – and God be with you if you don't choose something suitable, you silly girl!

I do so hope this will help, however the rest of your days on this beautiful planet bloom. Life is nothing if not a garden of possibilities, Clair de Lune. Manure it well.

<u>Much</u> love,
Tansy

If anyone saw her, they'd think her leaning on the lady-petrol perhaps a little too heavily.

It was so bright – swelling, intensifying, as it rose so she couldn't ignore the pull of it. An owl swooped past, a powerful ghost floating on amber-tipped trees that loomed out of the darkening sky. A moment of susurrated flurry, and then it was gone.

Stillness came again, sharper than before.

The wood was pungent with the scent of decay; a crumbling earth fragrance that reminded her of the forgotten taste of truffles from forgotten foreign holidays. Soon, sooner than anyone wanted to think, another six months of winter waited. How Tansy reprimanded her for saying she hated winter; her favourite season, even the blackest, bleakest days 'because you see the bones of it all, the utter rawness of life. Oh, there's beauty in *everything*, Claire of the Moon! You just have to be brave enough to hunt for it'.

Enough light still to see the remnants of a recently gobbled pheasant. Beauty, yes, but a lot of death in the countryside, too. It lay in pools of feathers studded with solitary claw, in dusty mats of spine and clotted fur. You were never far from it, but she'd never realized that as she did now. Winter would never be the same: she'd fight to find the beauty in the shoots on the broken bones of spliced hedges; to see the loves who came and went like leaves, the friends as sun that shone on silvery frost.

'Thank you,' she said to the moon. '*Madre.*' This the word that found her – forever the way she would greet it now.

It was the biggest moon she'd ever seen. She lifted her face, arms wide, to breathe it in, all that was woman-life and woman-wisdom. Four hundred full moons had seen the sea of her blood – maiden, mother, menopause – lived by its tides.

Who knew, at this point, how many more she'd see?

And yet she'd never felt so free, so safe, so perfectly alone, so much a part of all that lived in this world of seen and unseen, rustle and skitter, tall and fallen trees alike. There was no more hiding, no gardening, no man – and no wine – that could take her away from herself now.

'I did it, Tansy,' she said. 'I only went and got myself a bloody *place*.'

October

Hunter's Moon – Full

The hotel Art Calling paid for was a surprise.

    The last time she stayed in a hotel for work it boasted a bed like a ribcage and walls with such suspect streaks they brought to mind illicit sex at best, forensic ultraviolets at worst. Outside it was any other uninspiring generic city hotel not porticoed or stuccoed or full of fat barrels of flowers and bushy box. Grey concrete. City-dirted windows. A taxi rank. But inside – surprise! – sparkle, marble, voluptuous flowers, cucumber-water decanters, smooth receptionists schooled in facilitation. Instantly her best coat felt tatty, her boots scuffed, her washed hair unkempt; the bungee on her case shouting about its fucked zip. She wanted to kick it under the cliff of reception that made her feel like a child herself, tiptoeing to sign the form.

    Thick carpets, a bed full of feather puff, curtains the weight of men: she'd couldn't resist a snow angel on the duvet before she unpacked and rekempted, excited to explore, find the arts venue where she, Daisy, Sonya, Adam and the others would spend the whole weekend.

At sunset she sipped a beer from the venue's bar by a gentrified canal – determined to prove she could sit, drink, enjoy herself alone. She hadn't yet celebrated the sweet joy of telling Mary-Cate yesterday she was leaving Wank Farm (and Bernard's wandering eye) either. *Renewing*, she'd said, *but not this contract.*

She would be brave, she decided, and financially sensible; not eat in her hotel. No need when she could be this mature and independent woman her younger self would have looked at and perhaps – if she could get over the wrinkles, sags, bags – admired. Aspired to.

She decided to dress for dinner. The hotel was warm; she could do the short-sleeved dress packed last minute *just in case.* Had she known then she'd be cheated by the confidence of beer? That when she got back in, bathed, got warm again and heard Friday night outside – all the shrieks of city youth she'd forgotten – she'd find her courage confused, dreading just the thought of stepping into a noisy night full of hormones to find somewhere to eat alone?

Outside the window, the sky was sealskin, the moon full, fierce, even here. Something Tansy said – how the Hunter's Moon always seemed to shine brighter because the leaves had gone.

She stared at it for a moment and let the curtain slip silently back, turned, catching sight of her nakedness in the full-length mirror; scowled, sighed, turned away.

Stopped.

Turned back. Stood still and stared at herself, hard.

This, the body, the face, that postman saw. This the girl, maiden, woman, the 'vintage model' now. And something else. Something that spoke the tongue of crone.

I am old, it said. Over halfway through – and you know

what? That's absolutely fucking fine. I am wrinkly, crinkly, my skin is thin and the wells of me are drying. I am war-wounded, battle-hardened, I know how short the show of flowers, and I know the cost of love. But I know it is still, perhaps only ever, love that saves you. People. Nature – a majestic oak, the peculiar, coal-scented silence of snow, the kiss of summer sun on skin. Art, in all its forms. Yourself – and all your shadows. I am old, but I am alive. And I wear my scars with pride.

She'd been too ashamed to admit it for far too long. But here it was, the truth.

When her mother went to bed for hours upon hours, when her brother abandoned her – because yes, that was how it felt, however much she knew he needed to go, when her father chose his lorry – yes, however entrenched in her that was his only emotional toolkit; and for all those yesses, and all those years she drowned another voice in men, hope, marriage, family, fantasy, even, to fill the void, all she'd ever really wanted was to be loved, and to give love in return.

Four little letters and one stupid syllable. How much she still had to give. How much to take, too.

'I love you,' she said to the mirror.

And smiled.

Fuck it. She was on a high, determined to show herself as the professional she was, eat in her hotel. And order the cheapest thing on its menu, judging by the plink of that white grand piano.

She ordered the burger.

'Chef make his own brioche bun,' said the young waiter. He kissed thumb and fingers. 'But if you are hungry, then maybe fish'n'chip is bigger?'

And a couple of quid more. Anything not burger or fish double both. 'No, I'm fine.'

'You like some sides?'

Bread and chips: she'd be both full and bloating (and farting all night) after that. Still. Sod it. In for a penny. She ordered a full-fat salad, a glass of good red – large.

He was back with the bottle so fast – 'You like to try?' – eagerness draped on his face like the white linen at his arm. 'Water, too? Sparkling? Still?'

'No, I'm fine, thanks.'

'And you like your seat?'

She did, she said. She felt bemused by him. On one hand beautifully served; on the other as if he felt sorry for her.

'You like this view?'

Oh, *God*. He did. He felt sorry for her. All dressed up for a single place setting – had he made a narrative based on the discarded, traded-in, left to dine alone? Did she elicit compassion where once there might have been intrigue, the underlying subtext of sex?

She did, she said. Very much. Her table overlooked the river, all the lights of the bars opposite reflected in rainbows of ripple, the occasional surge-wave from a boat.

'It's beautiful,' she added. *But I don't need you to ask. I'd happily sit and stare at it alone.* There was a freedom she could feel rising in just sitting there. Safe and alone, not just from danger, but attention. Good or bad, women were so rarely free of it younger. And however she might hate, at times, the lack of it, now she felt its soft, quiet power.

'Oh, you should see in rain! The rain on the water is . . .' – another chef's kiss – 'It make me think of my home.'

You had to ask a heavily accented person where that was after a statement like that. Portugal, it transpired: Porto, home of water, light, and which he missed; this his first job away. Maybe she reminded him of his mother. She'd been wondering if he thought she was lonely; now she found herself wondering if he was. Perhaps we all were, in a way. She reminded herself Danny would be home in a couple of months.

'You sure you're all right about the old lady?' he'd asked, from Stephen's. 'You are okay, Mum?'

'Oh, your *mom* is stronger than she looks,' her brother said. 'Though it's good to see you putting on some weight, piglet.'

She'd sniped right back, of course. Be almost rude not to, though things had changed since she'd told him she was sorry for always dismissing his work.

Joe had been more taciturn on the FaceTime last night with her and his brother.

'You still look like Jesus, Dan, you fucktard. I'm kinda low on food though, so if you could just do something with some tuna and a baguette – actually no, wait. That's an insult to Jesus. You look like a homeless person.'

'We can't all look like the poster-boy for footballer skin products, bitch.'

'Better than looking like a homeless Mexican.'

'Is it though?'

'Fuck off, Dan.'

'You actually started growing hair on both sides of your face yet,' said Dan, peering at the screen, 'or is it still *ickle bitch* patches?'

'Yeah, well, at least I don't look like a 1970s paedo.'

'Yet.'

'Fuck off back to your tent, loser.'
'Dickhead.'
'Twat.'
'Virgin.'

She remembered how she sat and drank a glass of wine, alone under the moon, when Danny was a year; amazed, proud, she'd got that far. Christ. Talk about a journey.

She smiled, warmly, at the waiter. 'Well, if this is your first job, then let me tell you your mother would be very proud.'

The waiter's face split in two. 'I hope so. I like that very much that she is proud.'

She touched his arm as if he were her son; as if to comfort, underline her words. 'She will be,' she said. 'I *know* so.'

Outside, the wind skirting the water whipped at hair, made lashes of scarves, pushed people closer into themselves. The steps Claire chose were cold concrete, warmed only by the fart she let slip simply because no one sat beside her – no one in their right mind would sit and smoke in this. But she wanted a good night's sleep and to this end had brought Ben's spliff with her. Something in her felt rebellious doing that – as if a teen again, parents out dancing, she and her best friend topping up the dusty 'Christmas' vodka from the kitchen tap.

The stair's alcove had five wide steps leading to a barred door that looked like a side entrance to a club. A piss- and vomitorium, perhaps. But it was deep enough for shelter and safe from prying eyes, though she could not have done this younger; would not have had the courage. Something about that spurred her on. She cupped her hand to her face to light it.

Inhaled. Exhaled. Sighed at its smooth relief.

On her next draw, the door opened and three European voices emerged among a gust of kitchen sounds that faded fast as they came. Fag break. She could tell they were young without turning to look; hoped the smell of spliff wouldn't carry, its smoke thick and slightly bluish.

Another second and their conversation changed.

She couldn't see their faces, but she knew they'd clocked her. The pause announced their surprise, the ensuing tone, the way the conversation halted, hushed: she didn't need to be conversant to interpret *Is that what I think it is? Is it really coming from her? She's old enough to be my mother!*

She shut her eyes, inwardly grimaced. **Unseemly** the word that came to mind, each bone in her body tensing to stand, walk; smoke at least hidden in a cosmopolitan street, let people mistake her before the double-take, the narrative: people made stories all the time.

Wait.

So what? So what if they thought her a tragic granny with tragic granny issues? She won this place fair and square; her passion infectious, inspiring, they said. And yes, they saw absolute validity in what she wanted to do. Nature mattered more now than ever, they said – just as she'd stated – a planet needing nurture, people needing nature; the symbiotic relationship of sharing, and of love.

She'd been surprised Tansy left her anything; hated the part of her that had felt a tiny hope it might be money; however much cash didn't fit a creative life. She knew people who inherited whole houses, like Asha and Nish, simply because someone else had no one in the world to leave them to. But money couldn't have bought her Tansy's work: all those tiny paintings and searingly detailed sketches. Even weeds. The notes and lists of every plant she'd ever known, grown, encountered – as if she'd kept the loving record mothers do of children.

So that was it. She would be proving herself a year from now. What it was to learn from nature. How it helps us heal, feeds us, gives us the stories to connect to something bigger – the history of us, of nature, that life-death sense of the eternal.

She got out her phone and wrote herself a note.

Style it out

And then she did what she'd told herself to do. Sat and smoked as if an old-school movie star, minus the wand of cigarette holder she'd have loved, exhaling in great feathery plumes to send her smoke into the sky. She was fifty-four. Slightly drunk. Sitting in an *unseemly* fashion on steps that had probably been pissed on a thousand times, smoking something she shouldn't.

Let them look. Let them comment. Let anyone think or say whatever they wanted.

There was no aggression thinking this, no knowing deep down, either, that it just wasn't true. No judgment on herself, or them.

She just didn't give a fuck. Simple as.

She was surprised to find herself smiling the biggest smile she could remember in a long, long time.

Acknowledgements

p1

Acknowledgements

p2